LORE
GOLDBERG

BEYOND THE
BUKUBUK
TREE

Beyond the Bukubuk Tree

A World War II Novel of Love and Loss

Copyright © 2024 Loretta Goldberg
ISBN-13: 978-84-122325-8-5

M
MadeGlobal Publishing

For more information on
MadeGlobal Publishing, visit our website
www.madeglobal.com

Cover Photo: Mary Adam
Cover Soldiers: Tainah Lago
Cover Planes: Dmitry Yakhovski
Cover Copyright 2024 © MadeGlobal Publishing

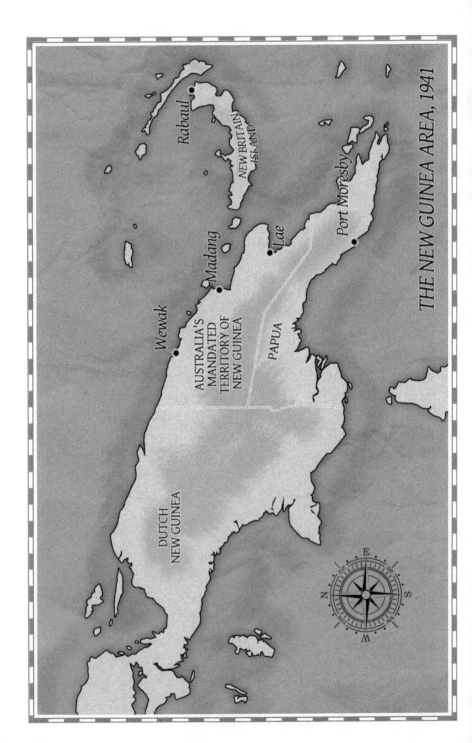

THE NEW GUINEA AREA, 1941

Rabaul

NEW BRITAIN ISLAND

Port Moresby

Madang

Lae

Wewak

AUSTRALIA'S MANDATED TERRITORY OF NEW GUINEA

PAPUA

DUTCH NEW GUINEA

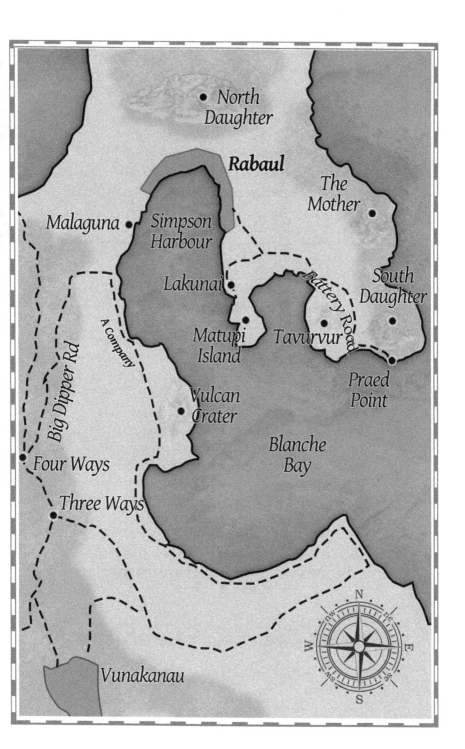

"The bukubuk tree grows and stands alone, unlike any other fruit tree. An adult tree stands over 20 meters tall, its branches stretching out like mango trees. The fruit is just amazingly sweet, with a starchy texture. Since bukubuk trees can reach full height in five years, we often plant the seed, which is hard and shaped like a small brown rugby ball, to mark a place or event with spiritual significance. Tolai myth held that a bukubuk tree could be inhabited by a Tambaran spirit because the bark is rough at the bottom. Putting the bark on boils and lumps could heal them naturally. Now, people sometimes plant the tree to mark the anniversary of the bringing of the Gospel of Jesus Christ to East New Britain Province."

Albert Konie, curator of the Rabaul Histoical Society archives and initiate into the secret Tubuan Society.

BOOK ONE
IMPROBABLE SOLDIER,
FEBRUARY – APRIL 1941

CHAPTER 1

. . . .

Friday 14 February 1941:
A Flat in York St, St Kilda West,
Melbourne, Australia.

D OCTOR JAKE FRIEDMAN had that dream again, his balm-of-Gilead creation:

On-call doctor at Colac District Hospital. He's driving three nurses to pristine Apollo Bay. It's an urgent care call late Saturday night.

"The children! Is it polio?" Scared parents rasp over a crackling telephone line.

Jake and the nurses are halfway along Otway Range's seventy-mile road. The car reeks of anxiety, petrol fumes and disinfectant.

"Why are you slowing, Doctor?" asks Vivien.

She's beside him, kneading her hands as she wills on the car. Her foot grinds a book on the floor: "Treatment of Infantile Paralysis in the Acute Stage".

"Careful. My bible," Jake snaps.

Her foot jerks up, a sucked-in breath her apology.

Sister Elizabeth Kenney's protocols of hot compresses aren't officially approved for acute-stage polio, but Jake has seen them work at her clinics. There's no other treatment.

Grace and Ellen are in the open dickie seat behind, clutching their starched caps against gusts of broiling wind. It's a hot summer. Somehow, he sees around the next bend. Grunting, "Broken glass!" he swerves, swerving back to the right side of the road ahead of an oncoming car. On Saturday night, the maddest of the mad take to their cars.

"No worries," he soothes Vivien.

Masked and gloved, they enter a modest red brick house, a closed universe of terror and wails. His examination rules out polio—gastric flu. Ecstatic parents shower him with praise, which he modestly demurs. Jake and the nurses take a tension-lifting sip of the offered whisky and return to Colac.

Jake's alarm clock jangled him upright. Rolling over, he shut it off, tasting the memory of the celebratory whisky on his tongue. He bent over, head in his hands, as his satisfaction drained away.

Because that's not what happened. He hadn't seen around the curve in the road. He hadn't seen the spilt gravel or broken beer bottles, nor had he felt the tyre flattening. The car had skidded and overturned. He and Vivien had gashed their faces against the windscreen, and he had got a concussion. Ellen had been thrown clear of the car, relatively unhurt, but Grace had been crushed by the vehicle.

They had never reached Apollo Bay. Ellen, the only sentient passenger, had hailed a driver who had taken them back to Colac. At the crash site, no one had realised how badly Grace was hurt. She had died in the hospital of internal bleeding. Compounding Jake's shame, when he had returned to his room from the hospital, Kenny's book had mocked him from his desk; he'd left it in their hurry to get on the road. *Failure,* he'd curse himself after these nocturnal re-writes. The crash had been three months ago, but his dreams invented details as more time passed.

When the police had established that he hadn't been drunk, they'd cleared him of all responsibility. Blame had belonged to the gravel spillers and glass breakers. Still, he couldn't clear himself. He'd learnt that the children he was rushing to treat *did* have paralysis polio and were immobilised long-term in the standard protocol. He went about his duties—lancing abscesses, setting bones, delivering babies, referring tuberculosis cases to the TB clinics—feeling like an impostor with a neon-green "F" for failure on his white coat—green, so that it wouldn't be confused with blood. His creativity while asleep only sharpened his daytime grief.

He glanced at the clock. 5.30 a.m. He shuffled into bathers, shorts, a singlet and runners. Had he woken his sister and her husband? He was living in the spare room of Talia and Simon's flat. Since graduation four years ago in Melbourne, he'd worked as a substitute doctor, a locum, in Brisbane, the capital of the northern state of Queensland; Julia's Creek, an outback hospital in western Queensland; Sydney; and Colac, a rural town one hundred miles from Melbourne. Talia insisted he live with them between contracts, and he was grateful for the convenience. Today, he wanted to swim in nearby St Kilda Beach before he saw them. He needed solitude to get comfortable with his decision and let his future roll around his insides from fingertips to toes. He was going to volunteer for the Army. His family would hate it; not only would he be far away, he'd be in danger.

He hadn't woken the family. A blessing of being a heavy snorer like Simon was that you knew where things stood in terms of consciousness. Snores now rumbled from two rooms away. *Is Tal superhuman to share that bed without appearing sleep-deprived?* he wondered as he tiptoed to the kitchen. Summer's heat warmed the wood and infused the curtains with a tired mustiness.

In the kitchen, he opened the refrigerator. 'You're a bit under-tall for your weight,' is what he'd tell a patient of his age of 30, he thought, rubbing his stomach ruefully. 'Lose a half-stone, or you'll be sorry, and your family will be sorrier.' He was surprised that his hard work and sprawling travel hadn't kept him trim; he wasn't a glutton. *Heredity,* he assumed.

He drank cold tea and ate a piece of leftover roast lamb. Talia would cook breakfast later, near-kosher porridge, eggs and toast. Slinging a towel around his neck, he went outside. Dawn grey seeped up the horizon as he ran under palm and eucalyptus trees. He sniffed the stimulating scent of the eucalyptus, feeling intensely alive. A woman was walking a beagle. It barked at Jake and barked again. A kookaburra cackled, and white cockatoos screeched. In the distance, a dog answered the beagle. Jake cocked his ear. It wasn't a real dog but a lyrebird imitating the beagle's bark.

The beagle didn't get the joke. It broke free, trampling a garden-bed of peonies. Jake chased it, grabbing its leash.

"Lyrebirds are such comics, they even fool dogs," he laughed, handing the leash to the woman, who clucked in dismay at the broken flowers.

She thanked Jake profusely. Eyeing his bare ring finger, she looked him up and down with frank interest. *Not bad. Is he available?* he imagined he heard her thoughts click. Her calf-length skirt suggested she was conservative. *War changes manners, along with everything else,* he mused as he disengaged and began his run.

Lampposts sported new recruitment posters for the army, the Second Australian Imperial Force. *More colourful as the war drags on,* he mused. He stopped to wipe his sweating face at one amusing poster: a clean-cut fellow with a pearly-toothed smile, the spitting image of Clark Gable. *Better than a long-faced Not-Gary Cooper,* Jake thought.

Not-Rhett-Butler wore a black business suit and fedora hat. His jacket had large-patterned blue stripes. Some advertising expert must have said that blue stripes were just the right touch to attract volunteers. Not-Rhett's right hand hoisted a rifle, while his left carried army khakis. The caption read: *We're Coming! Join the AIF Now!*

Jake ran on. Other posters featured a smoky seductress handing her hapless suitor an infantry digger's slouch hat with the caption *Here's your hat, Mister*, and *Make Your Mother Proud*.

He didn't have to volunteer. There was no conscription despite the war being eighteen months old. Even if there were, his concussion could have got him an exemption as an essential worker at home. Yet he was certain of his decision. It wasn't Blue Stripes or the hope for some femme fatale's approval that brought him to his certainty. It wasn't the car crash, despite his anguish. But Grace's death had clarified things. When his cotton ball brain allowed thought, the absurdity of wasting death and injury in Colac overwhelmed him. In wartime, casualties should be like ration coupons, redeemable for worthy items in war service. He loathed fascism and loved the British democratic system that provided dignity and safety to Jews. Any future accidents involving him must happen in uniform.

He stopped at a traffic light at the main road, Beaconsfield Parade. Military lorries rumbled by, passing clopping horse-drawn carts that would deliver fresh milk and hot bread to individual homes. While he waited, he pulled out a folded paper where he'd noted that the Army was seeking volunteer doctors, which he'd heard at the University of Melbourne's Department of Medicine. The call sealed his decision and his sense of urgency.

Crossing the road, he ran past an empty playing field to the esplanade and beach. Stripping, he ran into the waves. There was an undertow. A faint tang of industrial metal and sewage hit him as he dived into waves to get further out, to clean water. A few people were fishing from the pier. He hoped it was sport, that they'd throw the fish back and not eat them. Otherwise, they'd turn up at his office with food poisoning.

A child squealed, "I saw it, Dad, a fairy penguin!"

Yes, there were some among the rocks.

He rolled on his back, imagining he was in the pristine waters of Queensland, with their scrubbed, dazzling sands. He often lived superimposed realities. At St Kilda beach, he thought himself to the Great Barrier Reef. During Queensland monsoons, when all was sodden and rotting, he thought himself to dry Colac. A wave broke over him. He spat out foam and swam against the current for forty minutes. He had to get fit for basic training.

A big military parade was advertised for later that morning. Well, an infantry march, no tanks or planes. He would meet Talia there—Simon worked in the barracks at logistics. After the parade, he'd tell her he was enlisting.

As he punched through the waves, invigorated at last, Esther's face, the curve of her ears, and the reassurance of her touch on his shoulder took shape in the foam. She was his most intimate friend. A nurse in the obstetrics ward, half-Jewish by her Sephardic father, she was the only woman with whom he felt at ease. Her stocky, muscled torso felt manageable, unlike the perfumed opulence of the single women at his shule.

Esther was good-humoured, efficient, kind, and loved children. They'd drifted together, two lonely Jews in Christian farm country. He'd succeeded in making love to her three times in one night. In the morning, blushing with relief and pride, he'd proposed. He confessed his teenage passion for a high school football champion and occasional attraction to men, but she wanted him despite his ambiguous nature; they were united in the desire to make a family. They considered themselves secretly engaged—secretly, because having a Jewish father didn't make Esther Jewish in the eyes of Jake's orthodox community. Jewish blood passed through the mother, and Esther's was Methodist. "Jake married out," the gossips would complain, and he wouldn't be there to protect her. They'd agreed on discretion until after the war.

When he'd shown her the army's call for doctors, she'd cried, "You rotter, you're abandoning me!" Hurling a vase at his still-concussed head, she'd thrown him out of her flat. He'd had no idea she had such temperament, but he loved being wanted. She'd left a remorseful note in his mailbox the next day, writing that she'd volunteer when her contract ended. He imagined her being in the same battalion. But that wasn't reality. Her contract ran another six months. She'd be posted thousands of miles away. For Australians, everything was always thousands of miles away.

Jake dog-paddled ashore, towelled, then ran home. The family was still asleep. He didn't want to see them at breakfast, as his head was buzzing with colliding thoughts. After showering, he left a note for Talia to meet him on Princes Bridge at 10:00, and then he took the tram into town. At his favourite side street cafe, he wolfed down steak and one egg—rationing kept eggs to one—and washed it down with a milkshake. *NOT kosher,* he chuckled as he read the newspapers. *Mark today with Aussie fare.*

When his meeting time with Talia neared, he strolled along the city's main road, Swanston Street. Crowds were spilling out of the central Flinders Street Station. Its great old clock showed 9.50 a.m.

CHAPTER 2

• • • • • • •

T HE TRAMS had stopped running, and the street was filled with women in floral dresses and perky hats, men in summer suits, and uniformed soldiers and sailors. Some children played hide and seek, bumping and squealing, while others unfurled streamers. Jake pushed past the town hall, where the governor general would accept the salute. He made his way along the footpath of Princes Bridge and climbed onto the base of a broad lamp standard. He craned his neck for Talia. As church bells tolled ten, he waved her over.

"Nothing beats a musician for being on time," he grinned. "Did you get that pun?"

"Bad one." She wrinkled her nose.

They found places in the second row. It was near 90 degrees. Everyone was fanning themselves between waving away flies. A few opened umbrellas to curses and clutching at eyes. A vendor pushed a cart selling ice cream and lemonade.

Talia frowned. "The paper says it's for the Great War Victims' Fund. Hasn't that been done? What about our boys today?"

Jake fingered the note in his pocket about the Army calling for volunteer doctors. "They're brewing up enthusiasm for this one with a good show. Look at that recruitment booth..."

He was drowned out by cheers from people waving Australian, New Zealand and British flags. Talia stood on tiptoe to look at the object of excitement: several young men at a booth near Flinders Street Station. Soon, martial drumming and tunes boomed from the Shrine of Remembrance, the new war memorial on the tree-lined throughway of St Kilda Road leading to the city centre. Brass bands led a few thousand lean, tanned soldiers in summer khakis marching three abreast. The infantry wore digger slouch hats, officers in caps. Rifles sloped, and boots pounded the pavement. Unit badges marked each company. Confetti, streamers and torn paper whirled from upper-floor office windows.

A purple triangle on top of an inverted red triangle adorned the shoulders of the band leading the 2/22 battalion. To delirious approval by the sweating crowd, this band swung into the "Wizard of Oz", the hit movie of 1939. Since Oz was a nickname for Australia, the crowd sang along. "We're Off to See the Wizard" was followed by "The Merry Old Land of Oz" and "Ding Dong the Witch is Dead". A single voice behind Jake chanted, "Ding Dong the Kraut is Dead". Hundreds of voices took it up. As the band marched out of view and neared the reviewing stand at the town hall, the band changed to "God Save the King", but a version enriched by exotic harmonies.

Jake stared intently at the men of the 2/22, wondering if, by any chance, this battalion was seeking doctors; they had a new demeanour. Talia followed his stare. She frowned, and he felt her anxiety spatter over him. He tensed. Had she known about his teenage lusting for Izzy, the high school football champion? She'd been ten, he'd been fifteen. They'd never spoken about it, but she may have overheard his quarrel with their dismayed father. Those were years when his stutter was worst, which he'd conquered by winning every elocution contest he entered. He'd won control of his tongue, but not his desires, not for a while. Or had she sensed his intention to join the army? He put a reassuring hand on her shoulder.

She brightened. "They're great musicians."

"They've been written up in the papers for original arrangements. Salvation Army blokes volunteered together, hoping to serve together. It worked. *Perhaps she'll accept me doctoring army musicians, even if they're Salvos.* Her support was vital, given the troubles of the Friedman family. "Salvos, who are a bit of a wag," he added.

"Salvos and humour? Oxymoron," she retorted. "I can't stand them and the other proselytisers who knock on our doors and tell us Jews are damned." She sighed. "Maybe these are different since they do joke in sound. Thickening *God Save the King* with chromatic harmonies is pretty daring. 'Don't generalise', Mum always told us."

"Tal, let's go to the riverbank. I've got something to show you." It was time.

The parade was nearly over. They ran down stone steps to a footpath that followed the river's contours. Vendors were selling fish and chips, ice cream, meat pies and Cornish pasties. Talia bought fish and chips wrapped in greasy newspaper while Jake took a pasty. Benches were filling, so they walked down the grassy slope and sat. On the river, oarsmen in eight-man racing shells were practising. Their competitive focus offered a lulling illusion of normal life. The grass was a sad end-of-summer beige, but sprinklers kept the shade trees green. Children squealed with delight as they ducked in and out of the spray.

Jake and Talia ate in a silence prickling with tension. Jake felt a heart-pounding dread of upsetting his family again when he revealed he was volunteering for the army; they'd never liked his far-flung doctor contracts. Talia knew something was coming; news was rarely good these days. He could smell fear in her sweat.

When they'd finished, he handed her his paper. She read it, crumpled it and tossed it on the grass.

Leaning over, she ruffled his hair. "It's your concussion, Jakie. Your brain's still fuzzy, I can tell. The crash wasn't your fault. Simon says even only Jewish sons can't be expected to see around road bends. You can't go and do dangerous things to make up for guilt you shouldn't feel." Frightened coal-black eyes willed his hazel ones to drop in compliance. When he held her stare, she sighed. "Men!"

Inwardly, he smiled at Simon's irony. It took one Jewish son to recognise the expectations draped on another. "It's not the concussion. I'm the doctor here. I'm fine."

"But why now? There's no conscription. It's overseas, isn't it? Please don't. We need you here."

"There will be conscription eventually. You're right about one thing, Tal. I decided after the car crash, but not because of my guilt. I feel that death and injuries shouldn't be wasted on a peaceful Saturday night. We're at war. What do you think it was like telling Grace's Mum and Dad over the phone? She's from Western Australia. Every time a telegram comes or the phone rings, they think it's their three sons in Egypt. Grace was the one they didn't worry about. 'Was it sudden?' 'Yes,' I assured them, though it wasn't. 'At least she didn't suffer…' I let them think that, but I don't know. Future injury to me has to be when I'm in uniform."

"Do you have any idea how *alone* I'll be?" Talia shouted the word 'alone.' "With Miriam sick, insane really, and you away, it's just me." Her face was stricken white.

Jake sighed. That was the impediment he'd struggled over. The Friedmans had been an energetic family of five a few years ago, but now were shrunk. Mum had died after a stroke in her forties in '37, and Dad of a heart attack just ten months ago, at 55. His death also felt premature. Jake was the head of the family, supposedly its protector. Their older sister—Miriam the beautiful, Miriam the lawyer and violinist, Miriam the advocate for women's rights—had had a mental breakdown after her divorce. Her husband—a revered spiritual leader—turned out to be a street angel/house devil, a vicious abuser. Untangling their marriage had been especially excoriating because the failings of a man so deeply entrenched in everyone's lives had to be covered up. Miriam took the blame. She now veered from vicious verbal abuse to hysterical giggles; three years of medications hadn't helped. A close-knit family, the Friedmans felt that trust was only possible between blood kin. Talia was right; Jake's enlistment would be a burden on her. *Having one foot in the modern world and the other stuck in ancient orthodoxies makes life very difficult,* Jake mused.

"Jacob Mordecai Friedman, it's not those tan, lean blokes, is it?" Talia shot at him. There, in the open. Every muscle in his back knotted. Poking his stomach, she rushed on, "You're not fit. You'll look funny in a slouch hat. You're shorter and rounder than all of them."

"I won't be infantry, Sis. Doctors are officers with caps and pips on their uniforms. I know it's hard, but Simon's a good husband with a large family. Ask them to help. Look at the big picture. We know what the Nazis are doing to Jews. England's just holding on. Imagine Australia surrendered to Hitler, swastikas on the town hall." He gestured in the building's direction. "You want to be like Paris, Amsterdam? You own a rental house..."

"Mortgaged."

"Yes, but if tenants don't pay or damage it, you've got a remedy in good old British law. In the Depression, we Jews suffered *like* others, not *more.* That's precious."

Talia pivoted. "Don't *you* want to own a house?"

He smiled at her effort to tack. "No. The Depression cured me of wanting things. Medicine and travel, those are my riches. I won't be shooting anyone; I'll be in a hospital. The Geneva Conventions protect army medics. Even the Germans signed them."

She sighed. "Jake, I'm so sorry. I was horrible. Put yourself in the other person's shoes..."

"Mum's mantra. Dad's was 'look for an option; there usually is one'."

They squeezed each other's hands. Jake stared at the river while Talia looked down, tears on her eyelashes.

"It's hollow being orphans," she began, "even though we were grown up when it happened. What's your favourite memory?"

Jake thought. "Dad asking the Passover question: 'Why is this night different from all other nights?' Turning the service over to me, just Ba'mitzvahed, me struggling not to stutter the Hebrew, which felt like blasphemy." He smiled wryly as he let her hand go. "I still smell his bleached shirt cuff and smoke-fugged wool jacket as he leant over with the prayer book, the feeling of solid safety in him. With Mum, it was her pride when Miriam graduated Law School and was admitted to the Bar; how she cheered Mirrie on the dais. Her breath exploded out as if her destiny was fulfilled. She was too sick to glow when I graduated. You?"

"Mum was a not-too-bad pianist. When I dream, she's accompanying Mirrie at her violin exams, that cherubic smile on her lips, always late turning the page." She laughed. "Dad in the shop, returning imperfect fabrics, teaching me good from bad. They lived for us to go a step higher. We tried." She looked at him. "You'll be a very handsome officer."

"Not true."

"Yes, true. You have a lovely face." She reached over and kneaded his back, iron pianist's fingers loosening knotted muscles.

"I do?" He didn't think he was handsome. He lived in the shadow of sisters who were acknowledged beauties, shapely brunettes with dark eyes and fine features.

"Yes. Rudolf Valentino, with Ashkenazi Jew fat reserves."

He laughed, sucking in his stomach.

"Not those silly Rhett Butler and Gary Cooper look-alike posters"—so she'd noticed the recruitment posters—"they're delivering types. Rudolf, he's looking for something." She stopped, puzzled.

Jake wondered if her intuitiveness had just outrun her words. "Well, thank you, I think. Rudolf, righto. But I hope to deliver value." He rolled his shoulders. He'd won her acceptance of his enlistment. The second hardest task was accomplished. Now, the hardest: "There's one more thing," he ventured. Her frown tightened as her shoulders stiffened.

"I know you've read books saying that insanity's hereditary, that after Miriam's breakdown, you can't risk having children. It's nonsense." He pointed at the children splashing through the sprinklers. "Don't you want a few like them? Grow more Friedmans? Mirrie won't, of course. Simon's from a big family; you know how much he wants children, and before Mirrie's troubles, you did, too. You can. I'm the doctor. Friedmans don't have a madness gene."

"When Mirrie went off, I said you go first. I still do. You're older. Show me it's safe."

Their discussions on the topic hadn't lessened her fear. Whether Miriam was in their living room, screaming that they were poisoning her with the pills and that her family wanted her dead, or living quietly in her own flat, the deterioration of a sister who'd been the pride of their Jewish community haunted Talia like Banquo's ghost.

Avoiding her gaze, Jake stared at the rippling river, recalling years of consultations with Miriam's doctors, the unpredictable resilience of some patients and the frailty of others.

Talia's nudge jerked him back to her. "You're dreamy. The waves can't be that interesting. You're not Monet." The French Impressionists were her lodestar.

He reeled back their conversation. He was to have children first and show her it was safe. "I intended to go first, love, until I decided to volunteer for the army." He squeezed her hand. "There's a Jewish nurse, Esther, in Colac. We have an understanding for after the war. I can't bring forth a perfectly sound baby right now, but I know Esther and I will produce good-looking geniuses with kind hearts and healthy minds."

Surprise, relief, and then a touch of suspicion crossed her face. She sensed when she wasn't hearing the whole story. "Have you spoken to her father? Should I plan an engagement party?"

"No." It wasn't the time to burden her with the complication that Esther was only half-Jewish. "It's fairer to wait. Only tell Simon. She's the one… I'm easy with." His body gripped in a fervent wish to do this magnificent traditional thing with Esther. "You'll love her."

"I suppose you know what you're doing. Thanks for telling me, though it sounds a bit theoretical. Look, I'm willing to read the books on insanity you recommend."

"Good, love. I'm glad. You'll feel better."

"But I won't tell Miriam you're enlisting. Spare me that."

"Of course. I'll say you need her protection. Maybe that'll jolt her out of her self-absorption. *Family life's so complicated. The army will be simpler.*

They watched the racing shells, now on the leg back. Jake pointed. "Isn't that your poet friend Rex, the leading boat's stroke?" The oarsman in the bow seat was chisel-featured and loudly repeating the coxswain's orders as he powerfully wielded his oar.

Talia stared. "Yes." They stood, waving their hands. "Rex! Rex! It's Tal and Jake!" Others started hailing rowers. Some rowers inclined a shoulder or hooted. Rex didn't; he kept urging his team on.

"He's fit. Will he enlist?" Jake asked.

Talia was quiet for a moment. "Don't tell anyone, but while Joe Stalin has a non-aggression treaty with Hitler, he won't enlist. He trusts Uncle Joe."

"Peacock Rex a commie? You're ragging me!" Jake didn't

like Rex, but he'd married Talia's closest non-family friend, a soprano named Stephanie.

"He reveres Stalin for destroying feudalism and capitalism. Communism appeals to lots of young people. You know that."

"Stalin's just a butcher. Rex is a preacher's son; he has to know that."

"He says that's propaganda." Talia sighed. "Look, if you're posted overseas, I'll make you a going away party. Be nice to Rex."

"Deal," Jake promised. Watching the last racing shell pass out of sight, Jake frowned. "If you're set on a party..." Talia mixed very different people at her parties, hoping that loving hospitality would lead to new friendships. It wasn't his idea of fun, but the least he could do was to be a model host. "Can I ask you to be careful about mixing Zionists and anti-Zionists? The shule board's at loggerheads with our Rabbi and could split apart."

Zionists advocated an independent Jewish homeland in Palestine. Papa Friedman had been born in Palestine; the family were Zionists, as was Simon. But Rabbi Jacob Danglow, an Englishman and the shule's rabbi, advocated a permanent British Mandate there. German persecution of Jews heightened the dispute.

"Jake, I know far more than you do about who's on what side. That's what we talk about in the women's section while you gents daven, looking self-important."

Jake laughed. "Caught in the act. How could I doubt you?"

In the street, trams were rumbling again. They brushed confetti off their clothes and took a tram home. The soaring "Shrine of Remembrance," part Greek columns, part pyramid, part Mayan-inspired stairs, came into view then receded. They fell quiet. *How long before we pass this monument together, again?* was their common thought.

CHAPTER 3

· · · · · · ·

F EBRUARY'S COOL CHANGE from the late summer heat had hung around, allowing the flat to breathe. On city streets, hints of autumn brought smiles to people's faces, their lips no longer having to clench out flies. Now, on Sunday, 30 March, Talia and Simon wanted a photograph of Jake in uniform, so he put on winter khakis. Under his captain's pips and unit badge of red triangle on purple, a blue rectangular patch with a red band and centred inverted red V adorned one sleeve.

"This'll be the only time I wear wool," he called as he emerged from the flat's spare room. He'd been posted to Rabaul, the capital of New Britain island, the northern tip of Australia's mandated territory of New Guinea. Its sleepy heat was legendary.

The spare room was a jumble of leave-taking. His backpack and suitcase lay open on the stripped bed, underwear and uniforms folded, and shaving gear and boot polish in tins. Medical texts sprawled on the carpeted floor, Kenny's protocols for treating polio among them. A primer on Pidgin English lay next to books of poetry and philosophy. He hadn't decided what to leave; each book was part of him.

By contrast, his medical kit, an army-issue brown

fibre case with exterior steel clips and interior partitions, was organised: pristine honed scalpels, along with scissors, needles and safety pins; a thermometer; syringes; wool, cotton and gauze bandages; a tourniquet; oiled silk; and bottles and tubes of disinfectant powders, morphine, quinine tablets, tubes of tannic acid jelly, Vaseline, Epsom Salts and Sulfamate.

Sitting on a chair, cap in hand and head cocked, Jake smiled gently. After Simon clicked once, the doorbell rang.

"You look at peace," Simon remarked, putting the camera away.

"Truth is, I love the army. Private chat before I go?" Jake responded. He straightened his jacket again—coats never fell quite right on his stocky frame. He locked the spare room door and went to greet the first guests. *May I be stammer-free,* he implored himself.

"Jakie, dear, how handsome you look! You've lost weight. Is it really you? I swear, you could be Valentino or some other brooding film star. Tal says you're already a captain." The admirer was their cousin Sylvia, a diminutive young woman who curled her hair in Hanoverian-style ringlets. She kissed him on both cheeks. Her equally-ringleted mother followed with a dish of pasta. Sylvia was holding hands with a red-haired woman he didn't know. "Say hello to my close friend, Rosalind Mclean. She's a legal secretary. Rosalind, meet my cousin, Captain Jake Friedman."

Jake chuckled inwardly. Sylvia had married *in,* to a wealthy Jewish lawyer. But she urged the rest of the family to marry *out.* "Too much purity weakens a race," she'd proclaim, thrusting one Christian girl after another at Jake, the family's only remaining bachelor. He hadn't dated any of them. Sylvia was beginning to have suspicions about him.

"Delighted to meet you, Miss McClean," he said as they shook hands gravely. "I'll get you a drink while Sylvia and her Mum help Talia." Rosalind winked at him. Officers posted overseas weren't good catches. She was probably as little interested in him as he was in her.

Families from the shule bustled in. Behind them were Jake's doctor colleagues. Everyone brought food, excluding meat, to accommodate kosher guests. Bangs and rustles came from the kitchen, and repeated, "Oh, wonderful," from Talia, as she organised, and re-organised, platters.

The living/dining room filled with bodies, voices and tobacco smoke. Smells of fried fish, stewed vegetables, cheese, and devilled eggs with parsley mingled with the tang of sherry and beer. A side table displayed cakes. A trifle made with passion fruit, Talia's speciality, emitted a distinctive scent that drew guests to it, visibly repressing the urge to dig a finger in and lick.

Talk was a rolling ocean of risk-free cliches: "Fine man, doing your duty," or "Bravo, Jake, doing your bit for us oldies," interspersed with, "You look well," "You're handsome in uniform." "Marvellous tropical ulcers and fungi. I'm jealous," from a doctor friend. A former patient pulled him close and whispered a new urgent ailment, as if draping him with need could postpone his departure. Jake was moved by the clumsy affection. He didn't realise how woven into the community's fabric he was, despite his jobs outside Melbourne. Everyone avoided the word *war*. Rosalind made the rounds with hors d'oeuvres. With an eye for available men, she lingered at the group of doctors. *A go-getter like Sylvia,* Jake noted, amused.

The Zionist shule group crammed onto the lumpy sofa and armchairs. They were modern orthodox, the women with fashionable hair styles, the men without yarmulkes. They talked vegetable gardens; what to do about the bloody bush turkeys, whether their eggs were worth the destruction they wrought on gardens, and the novelty of hearing radio news in the blackout. And determined murmurs of optimism, "Next year in Jerusalem." One woman whose son was Missing in Action since Dunkirk nodded absently, lips clenched. Unspoken was the collective terror: *Will his German captors see he's circumcised?* Her friends hemmed her in with a palpable *We won't let you go to that dark place.*

Ashtrays filled, were emptied, filled. Talia opened the windows. Rose and marigold scents wafted in as a few guests left and others arrived. Some of her piano students trooped in. Her star pupil, thirteen-year-old Tommy Whipple, a tall boy with brown hair, slouched in holding the hand of his sister Sally. Their mother, Monica, a pale, freckled, red-haired automaton, trailed them. Sally, fourteen, had blue eyes, a classic nose and blonde curls. Craning her neck for Talia and not seeing her, she made for Jake. Shyly, she gave him two folded drawings. Their father had recently been killed in Egypt, crushing the family emotionally and exacerbating their strained finances. Paying for Sally's drawing lessons and Tommy's piano lessons was impossible. They sold their piano. When Talia insisted on teaching Tommy for free, Monica began giving her Sally's drawings. "I accept them so that Monica feels less guilty," Talia explained to Jake as drawers filled with her art. "I'll give them back when she's older. You can't tell with child talent. Some go on, others fade."

Talia had explained that Monica, once a bubbly optimist, now glided through minimal daily tasks in a daze. "The poor kids are left to grieve in their own ways."

Lack of effect exerts its own centripetal power, Jake mused. Tommy had become taciturn, muttering only to his belt or socks. Sally, not by choice, struggled to be the family's liaison to the world. "Captain Friedman, good luck. We will pray for your safe return," she chirped.

Her first watercolour was a bowl of seasonal fruit with puckered skins and a crust of mould. Jake whistled. "Amazing. I can smell the rot setting in." He showed her where Talia kept her drawings.

"I made the second one for you," Sally blushed.

"How can I be so honoured?" Jake protested. He'd only met her a few times.

The painting featured a stocky man with a plump face, a thin moustache, black hair, and an officer's cap. Jake smiled:

him before his weight loss from military drills. He was angled on one leg looking up, the other raised to suggest running. One arm thrust skywards, flicking a huge middle finger at an aeroplane with German black cross markings in a blue cloudless sky. A different face, small, pale and angular, also with black hair, gazed down from the heavens. The distance between Jake and the other face was filled with brown dots in an upward swirl, the colours of khaki uniform and boots. Sally's father had black hair and an angular face. The painting's talisman purpose was clear.

"It's brilliant. I'll keep it on me always." Jake was moved to tears. Putting it in his coat pocket, he kissed her cheek.

Tommy took possession of Talia's upright Ronisch Grand piano and rippled through Beethoven's "Rage Over a Lost Penny." At its end, everyone cheered and clapped. Ignoring them, he muttered to his belt, then launched into a bangy piece by Khatchachurian that obsessed and obsessed over its ack-ack theme. He played it again. Talia wouldn't let anyone ask Tommy to stop since he had no piano at home. People drifted to the kitchen or passage to talk while Sally and the shule children ran out to the garden to play.

Sated with Khatchachurian, Tommy relinquished the piano and started looking through Talia's scores. Gentler Schumann filled the air, duets played by her other students. Distracted from the scores, Tommy Whipple listened. "Under-fast, in my opinion," he told his belt. His voice was breaking, so everyone heard the squeak/growl. Blushing, he went outside.

The first guests began to say goodbye, crowding Jake with hugs. Rosalind left with a group heading for the beach for a late-season swim. Jake returned her earlier wink as she wished him the best of British luck in the tropics.

The flat wasn't large, so guests were invited in two shifts. Jake and Simon were enjoying a quiet smoke, along with Monica, who'd been invited to stay all day. Talia had just joined them with a cup of tea when the doorbell rang. Time had flown. It was the first afternoon guest.

"Rabbi Danglow," Jake exclaimed. "Wonderful, please come in." Jake looked at Danglow's car, parked at the curb. Clergy were among the essential workers who could get petrol. He was alone.

"Mrs Danglow is indisposed," the Rabbi explained.

"Sorry. Nothing serious, I hope," Jake said quickly, affecting a physician's concern to cover his amusement. Mrs Danglow was so anti-Zionist that she was uncomfortable around those with different views. The rabbi was anti-Zionist, but he loved everyone. More afternoon guests were approaching from the tram stop. Jake left the door ajar.

Once inside, the clean-shaven, open-faced Danglow bounded from guest to guest, booming, "Call me John, not Jacob," in an English accent. He moved like a soldier. In fact, he was an English veteran, having served as an army chaplain at the Western Front of the last war.

"Good decision volunteering, and captain no less," he said, clapping Jake on the back. He whispered, "I've got news, not public. I'm appointed chaplain for next year. Guess where? New Guinea! You'll treat my malaria when the mossies get me. Keep the metaphorical candles lit. Next year in New Guinea, before Jerusalem, ha, ha!"

Jake knew not to take the anti-Zionist barb in bad part. "Ahhh," he murmured. He searched for words to express his delight, but they didn't come. In fact, he was ambivalent. Although he went to shule, he was agnostic. Not wearing a yarmulke for a while appealed to him. And Danglow often visited Miriam; he had a knack for calming her paranoid outbursts. If he went to New Guinea, Miriam and Talia would lose a support system.

Sensing Jake's embarrassment, Danglow talked to other guests. The party was winding down when Rex and Stephanie arrived. Rex was in the oarsman's outfit he'd worn on the Yarra River. His clothes were tailored to emphasise his athletic build. Pipe in mouth and with faux-military bearing, he shook hands with the men and flattered the women, showing his first published volume of poetry at every chance.

"Trust Rex to come late and mix master everything," Simon muttered to Jake. Indeed, the newcomers brought a jagged energy to the room.

Sensing Jake near him, Rex turned. In a voice he thought was low but wasn't, he harangued, "Jake, you can change your mind. You weren't called up. What's the matter with you? Got a death wish? The car crash, right? Guilt. But you're ruining your sisters' lives. Stop this 'all for my country' rubbish. That's the past. And don't give me a 'Palestine for Jews' look. That land's populated. Let capitalist-imperialists tear each other to pieces. We'll build a new equal society, including for Jews..." He looked around. Faces twisted in amazement, contempt, amusement. "I mean, Jake, you don't have to..." He tailed off as Stephanie pressed his hand.

Jake exchanged glances with Simon.

"Bloody commie," a doctor snorted, flexing a hand aching from Rex's grip. "A poet commie who swans in dressed as the stroke of a racing shell. Puka Sahib imperialist commie named Rex, king, no less." He laughed.

"You can't destroy truth by labelling me. Let's debate the issues." Rex was unfazed.

Simon clapped his hands. "Good idea."

Jake jumped in. A theoretical wrangle could soak up the anxiety. "As host, I set the proposition. Rex, are you a Marxist or Stalinist? You can't be both. And brandy all around before the man answers."

After wiping his lips, Rex said, "I can be both. They're one continuum. First theory, Marx; then revolution, Lenin; then a transition requiring the will of Stalin, as Russia industrialises. Different leaders shepherd one process, a new Holy Trinity."

Everyone gasped. "Ouch, and you a preacher's son!" Jake exclaimed, seeing Danglow wince.

"Stalin's nothing but a butcher," the rabbi retorted,

"madder than Ivan the Terrible. Social progress must be won without bloodshed, or it becomes worse than the abuses it pretends to correct."

There were murmurs of agreement, except from Rex. "No pretence. Stalin's atrocities are mostly capitalist propaganda. The same capitalists who joined White Russians against Lenin's Reds and killed thousands. Where's your outrage over that? Many White Russians live high in Shanghai, exploiting starving Chinese coolies. Spare me your moralising, Rabbi."

Danglow tugged his chin. Jake knew shule members with White Russian relatives in Shanghai. By all accounts, they'd done well financially.

"The party has to get rid of traitors," Rex expanded. "Exorcise the cultures of capitalism. Women get official jobs; children go to school. There's free medical care. You doctors should cheer that. No more seeing dying cancer patients who couldn't afford your fees when they first felt a lump."

Simon countered. "Rex, table-pounding doesn't resolve your self-contradictory positions. Jake's proposition was that you can't be a Marxist and a Stalinist. Marx said workers must own the means of production. Stalin's farm and factory workers don't own their own bodies, let alone the means of production. They're slaves to the State."

"Temporary," Rex retorted, "until industrialisation is complete. That's why Uncle Joe isn't fighting Hitler. He needs time to industrialise. Party leaders know what's best for the proletariat. This transition is the blink of an eye in human history."

"Who's the mug for propaganda now," a shule member demanded. Owner of a hardware store, he was everything communists despised. Rex gave him a condescending glance.

Jake expanded Simon's argument. "Intrinsic to workers' rights is the right to strike. Marx stressed the right; Stalin eliminated it."

"Good point, Jake," Danglow interjected. "Let's

first consider the madness of Stalin's bloodlust. You know what I heard?"

Everyone leaned forward, knowing that Danglow had connections in intelligence. Would they learn a morsel beyond the censored news?

"This non-aggression treaty between Hitler and Stalin that you comrades love? The Nazis have been whispering in Joe's paranoid ears tales about his best generals spying for them. So easy to forge documents. These generals have disappeared from official photographs, murdered by Joe. Who does that help? Russia has oil. Germany doesn't. You're deluded, Rex. Communism's a beautiful ideal, but it can't be realised because it contradicts human nature. Religion's concept of original sin, and the laws it spawns to regulate our basest instincts, is the best chance to help humanity. Lord Acton said: 'Power tends to corrupt, and absolute power corrupts absolutely.'"

"Good on Lord A, whoever he is," the hardware store owner enthused. "Whoever heard of the head of anything giving up power, except by law? I always vote out whoever's in."

Rex focused on Danglow. "Religion has nothing more to offer. It has led only to the privileged giving *surplus* to the poor. They jigger things, so they even get tax deductions for it, depriving the state of resources. Why were we so unprepared for this war? Capitalism's venality, that's why. Your charity doesn't even feed the hungry. Religion's original sin is profiting from sharing the surplus." He pumped his fist in the air, face red with sincere passion.

He'd hit home. The mindless excesses of the Roaring Twenties and terrible deprivations of the Depression were still raw.

"You're partly right," Danglow conceded. "But you denigrate our generosity..." He stopped, losing his thread.

Jake had always seen his rabbi as a master debater, but he'd just made the beginner's error of personalising. Coming to Danglow's rescue, he prompted, "Generosity, Rabbi? You were saying?"

"Yes. Sorry. But the back-breaking dedication of our soup kitchen volunteers, our congregants who take in orphans as their own, and the communal love underpinning religion are my life. Our sins of omission are great. But we *must* progress without tyranny, which turns evil to sustain itself. The selfish drive of capitalist imagination has created our modern comforts. But it needs to be tempered by sharing profits. Socialism. Capitalism and socialism will always struggle to prevail, the balance tilting one way and then the other. Resolution is impossible because of the sin of greed. There's no simplicity in this life. Simplicity belongs to the afterlife."

Rex looked at Danglow with the beginning of respect. He opened his mouth, but Talia spoke for the first time. "Rex, dear, our workers already own the means of production. Think of the brownouts when electricity men go on strike; even army ships aren't loaded if the wharfies walk off the job. Strikes end when the workers vote to work. That's owning the means of production. We already have Marxism."

"Good on ya, Tal," the hardware store owner clapped. "You won the debate. Armchair commies have no idea how hard business is."

Jake was suffused with benevolence. His cells were liquefying; his skin felt like a wafer-thin cover holding in his bursting universal love. Here he was, in improbable army khakis. He'd enlisted to defend arguments like this. It was radiantly clear. Everyone here was an idealist. He stood. "I l... love you all. In Germany or Russia, we'd be shot for this debate. Our government is good..."

He was about to add, "it is us", but the back door banged. Heads turned. Billy Cadranel, a boy of twelve, charged in, followed by a screaming Sally Whipple.

"He called me pimple-face and pulled my hair." Sally grabbed for Billy's sleeve.

Billy dodged around the table. "Didn't mean to hurt," he yelled.

"Liar, liar!"

Billy made for the grandfather clock and half-eased around it. On the wall, near the clock, was a dinner plate secured by a bronze frame. It was Russian, Simon's heirloom, part of an ancestral dowry from the time of Tsar Nicholas I. Bearing the Romanov crest, it had been made by ceramicists with a Royal licence. Simon's ancestors had taken the dinner service when they escaped Russia ahead of the pogroms, then Poland ahead of the pogroms, then to Germany, England, and then Australia. During these wanderings, plates broke in heaving ship holds and on wagons. This plate, the lone survivor, had pride of place above the chair that stayed empty during Passover Seders, waiting for Prophet Elijah.

Billy refused his father's order to come out. Things happened too fast for adult minds still locked in debate to grasp. Sally grabbed the silver soup tureen with its drippings—carrot and salmon specs—and hurled it at her tormentor. Food spattered the white tablecloth. Adult hands reached for the tureen. But it sailed high, higher, seeming to hover for a millisecond, a raptor choosing its prey. Then it smashed the Romanov plate. The pronged frame held the plate's rim, now jagged edges, in place. Ceramic pieces spattered the carpet.

Simon turned sickly grey. Sally burst into hysterical sobs as she realised what she'd destroyed. Tommy wandered in from the garden. He rolled his eyes but said nothing. The war always intruded.

"Atta girrrrlie." Rex's eyes were wide with admiration, eyes on her budding breasts. "Magnificent self-expression!"

The grandfather clock tolled 3.30 p.m. Billy poked his face out, holding his ears. Monica stirred from her apathy and tugged Talia's sleeve. "How can I make this up to you?"

"It's my husband's plate." Talia looked at Simon.

Simon pulled his stomach in and stood tall. "Dear Mrs Whipple, it's only a thing. With its jagged edges, its symbolism of survival is even stronger. It will stay above Elijah's chair, wounded but indomitable." He knew he had to absolve a suffering child who'd lost her vibrant father. He hugged Sally.

Sally convulsed with louder sobs. "The cheap frame's indomitable, not the plate. Oh!" Simon wiped her tears with his handkerchief.

"There's grace in action," Danglow murmured to Jake as they picked up the pieces

"Tal's in good hands," Jake agreed. He poured another round of drinks.

Billy's father made him apologise. Simon refused the Cadranels' offer of a replacement plate, and they left with a waterspout of "Sorry"s.

"Well," Rex said when the door shut, "I'll now prove the Rabbi wrong."

Jake looked at his watch. "No. We're done. I must get ready." He went to his bedroom to change into civvies and finish packing. He retrieved a yarmulke from his sock drawer and packed it in preparation for Danglow's posting to New Guinea. He took Esther's photo from his wallet, kissed it, and then returned it. The sounds of leave-takings floated into his ears.

When he returned to the living room, everyone was gone except Rex and Stephanie. But it wasn't calm. Stephanie was complaining, "How could you cheer that poor girl's misery as self-expression?"

Talia took Stephanie's hand. "Let's have some music." Rex sank into an armchair with what looked to Jake like a guilty smile.

It was time for Jake's private talk with Simon. Tapping his watch, he pointed in the direction of the spare room. They sat on the bed.

"Oh dear," Simon began, "parties are so hard these days." They started laughing.

"Are you alright?" Jake asked, concerned. "I know how much you treasured that plate."

"Yes. Sally didn't mean any harm, poor kid."

"In the past, everyone knew how to behave," Jake mused. "Our generation makes it up, rather badly. "

Simon pivoted. "So you like the army? I'm surprised."

"Me too. But there's comfort in rules and schedules, the illusion of muscle b...beating chaos. Good mates..."

Simon was waiting for him to finish his thought. But how could he convey the inundation that was basic training? The manic drills, the mushing of different personalities—he, the plump Jewish doctor, the weedy man next to him, a paroled safebreaker or worse—into a new whole. Then, the psychological dimension: hate of the enemy whipped into a frothing frenzy to kill. But then its opposite, when the enemy threw down his weapons, a duty of care. Could he manage the spiritual gymnastics? What he finally managed to say was, "I cherish the togetherness. Herd power. Jews don't often get that."

Simon nodded. "Herds of Jews roaming their own acres instead of cowering in ghettos. Oh, for a Jewish state! Will you keep your moustache? It's hot there. Clean-shaven is the fashion now." He touched his own scabbing chin.

"Yes. Makes me look Pukka Sahib, and it'll impress the Tolai hospital boys. We've been warned that they don't understand the need for constant sterility, floors and surfaces, as well as linens. The *Rabaul Times* is full of complaints that you can't scare them by threatening to fire them because they're 'landed proprietors.' They go home, farm their land and sell the produce to us in the market. But they're supposed to be proud and competitive. I'm hoping a little subtle shame will do the trick on hygiene. It'll be interesting. Tolai are the majority population. This will be a new experience for me, true colonialism."

He paused. "To things here. Tal's my sole executor. There's some insurance and savings, half to Tal and half to Mirrie. But Mirrie's portion will be in a trust, Tal sending her a weekly allowance. I've stipulated the minimum two weeks' mourning. Don't let the shule rope Tal into longer. She has to teach."

"Jake, please. This is purely academic. The war will bypass Rabaul."

"So many say. Our blokes are bitter that we're not going to Egypt. Still, Rabaul has the best harbour in the southern hemisphere, and Nazi policy is to retake it. After the volcanic eruptions of '37, the government moved the Administrative Centre to Lae, on New Guinea proper. But Rabaul is still vital. By the way, you shouldn't have spent all that money on my goodbye present. I'm embarrassed, but I love it—postcard quality photos." He patted the glowing leather cover of the Ensign E20 camera.

"Send us photos of...um... locals?" Simon blushed.

"You mean indigenous?"

"Do they look like Aborigines there?"

"I will," Jake noted Simon's awkward curiosity and pressed on. "Now, don't tell Tal or Mirrie this. My assignment isn't in the Field Ambulance Unit with the other doctors. I'm the sole medical officer for a new heavy battery unit. Rabaul's getting cannon. A captain's pips came with the posting. I wasn't promoted because of my push-ups." He smiled wryly.

Anxiety twisted Simon's face.

"Stop worrying. Nothing will happen, as you say." Jake drew a breath. "A final thing: I've done my best to convince Tal that Miriam's mental illness isn't hereditary, that you can safely have children. She's agreed to read some modern psychology authors I recommend. Karen Horney and Erich Fromm are good."

A car horn honked; Jake's ride. He stood. *Rotten topic, my Will.* Eager to get the goodbyes behind him, he slung the camera bag around his shoulder and picked up his kit bag and medical case. Simon took his suitcase to the car while Jake made the rounds once more. When he passed Rex, he murmured, "I don't have a d..death wish, you quack. I have a freedom-for-all wish, even for commie peacocks."

At the door, Talia thrust a bag of leftovers into his hand.

She grabbed his sleeve. "Our family core leaving." Tears flooded her eyes. She gulped, embarrassed.

"What do you mean?" Jake was astonished. "How can I be the core when I'm away so much?"

"You always come back. You know what to do."

"Listen, love, do you remember that poem you helped me prepare for an elocution competition? John Donne. 'Inter-assured of the mind, we care less eyes, lips and hands to miss.' You have inside you most of what I could advise. You're stronger than you know. Make a family with Simon. He's a good man."

The car honked again, its impatient occupants familiar with last sleeve-clutches. He kissed Talia, then strode to the curb. *Life will be simple now.* Care dropped from him as he joined five soldiers in a single-seater Holden, all with picnic baskets from loved ones. Jake climbed into the dickie seat. His mates cheered as the car engine coughed and revved them toward an unwritten future. Jake heard Stephanie singing the page-boy Cherubini's aria from Mozart's "Marriage of Figaro": *Is it pain, is it pleasure that fills me?* He waved to the closed front door.

CHAPTER 4

•••••••

J AKE STRETCHED LAZILY in the narrow bunk in his cabin on the troop transport ship Zealandia. One thing he didn't mind about being short was that his feet didn't poke over the edge. He'd slept well, without dreams.

Re-entering reality on the transport ship was pleasant: the chugga-chugga of pistons driving the ship reliably through bad or good weather. Its engines were veterans of Pacific and Indian Ocean crossings. SS Zealandia was a converted 1909 cargo ship, a refrigerated Australian and New Zealand food transporter. It had also carried coal, oil, and a few rich passengers, for whom the state rooms and saloon were reserved. That is, until the navy requisitioned it. Now, the hold bunked over five hundred infantry. One stateroom was allocated to junior officers like Jake for washing and crammed-in meals. Elbow to elbow was still more comfortable than the infantry's deck-hose showers and kitchen galley.

Another stateroom housed the six army nurses of A company of the 2/10 Field Ambulance Unit, turning spacious luxury into shoved-together coping. The third stat room was inhabited exclusively by the nurses' superior officer, Officer in Command Major (and doctor) Ted Palmer. Hierarchies on land transferred to sea. Sturdy but shabby, Zealandia was like a favourite aunt who wore Edwardian-era lace while mopping the floor. Jake chuckled softly at his image; he'd become fond of the 6,683-ton metal tub. The fact that he didn't get seasick certainly influenced his affection. It's hard to love when you're heaving up your guts.

His three doctor cabin-mates weren't as lucky. Two were seasick non-stop. In the kitbag of the third, a middle-aged surgeon, Jake had spotted cocaine pills. The surgeon's posting was to a different island of New Guinea. Jake was relieved he wouldn't have to assist this man at the operating table—his haunted face reeked of over-use. Cocaine was legal, but Mothersill's Seasickness Remedy was the military's approved treatment of motion-sickness. Its hyoscine compound suppressed the nerves that triggered vomiting. And there were better pain killers now. Jake never judged addicted patients, but he'd seen botched surgeries by addicted doctors, which disgusted him. He was doing his cabin mates' shifts in the ship's sick bay as well as his own. He liked the extra work but wished the nurses aboard could help. He'd heard they wanted to, but the OC Palmer, for unknown reasons, said no.

The sounds of ship life and the work were all good. Smells were another matter. Zealandia ran on coal and had transported tons of the stuff. Not on this voyage, for the cargo were two coastal cannons and ammunition for emplacement over Rabaul's harbour. Still, coal residue swarmed up nostrils, flavoured the mush the army called "meat stew," and tainted the custards, tea, and even the beer. His mouth was never free of it.

He looked at his watch. 4.30 a.m. Sunrise would be in a half hour. He wanted to get ahead of the soldiers who'd pound up the staircases from the hold to the deck for morning callisthenics, which he intended to join. He yearned for fresh air. His cabin was stuffy, but better than the near-airless hold. *Amazing how one defines luxury, as long as it's comparative.* Quietly, he pulled on shorts and runners, and washed his face.

As he shaved, holding up a hand mirror, he mused on

army life. He found male patients fascinating, how their egos met frailty. He was taking notes for an article after the war. Tough adventurers fainting at the prospect of ether and the knife: "Don't write 'pendix stuff in me file, Doc." Women were braver in this regard. Most amusing were the protests of victimisation when he diagnosed syphilis.

"But she was a virgin, Doc. I paid triple."

"Big business, s...selling virgins over and over," he'd retort, pointing at the poster on the wall of packets of rubbers. "You're lucky it's 1941, not 1881." He'd then describe the horrible mercury tortures their horny ancestors suffered.

"Doc, promise *it* won't fall off?" The inevitable plea got him laughing as soon as the patient left the clinic.

Australia's defence now depended on such unformed material since seasoned troops were fighting in the Middle East for the Motherland. But Jake was sure the men he knew would face any human enemy heroically. During basic training, he'd worked as a medical officer at the heavy battery at Fort Queenscliff, the fortress guarding Melbourne's Port Philip Bay. Men like his patients boasted that their gun fired the first Allied shots of both World War I and World War II. They led him to the very gun, stroking it as they described how, the moment war was declared, it lobbed shells across the bows of escaping German freighters in 1914 and 1939. Did the fact that Australian time was eight hours ahead of Greenwich Mean Time affect these first-shot honours? Did Polish riflemen in 1939 count? Still, Jake believed that if a Pacific war were to break out, Aussies would again fire the first hostile shot.

He'd come to realise, with surprise, that he was popular. Despite being a Jew, despite his avoidance of gambling and drinking parties, despite his moralising over venereal disease, he'd heard that the soldiers called him a good bloke. "Gives it t'ya straight, fixes y'up." He was happy in the army.

Finished shaving, he wiped his razor and put the hand

mirror down. His cabin mates stirred and turned over as he eased himself out of the door. He relieved himself in the washroom at the top of the staircase, then opened the deck door, pushing through curtains to the deck.

Nirvana! Fresh tropical air. The blackout was still in effect. Bright starlight on a moonless night guided him to the bridge, where he named himself to the ship's officer of the watch, a second lieutenant who was his army counterpart, and the army messenger, a staff cadet standing rigid. Jake leant against the rail. Venus was blatant but close to setting. The constellations of Castor and Pollux fuzzed as grey intimated its presence, then challenged the black of the sky and its silver canopy of winking stars.

"Never gets old, eh?" the army officer murmured, joining Jake.

"No. I worked in Queensland. Can't get enough of tropical mornings."

"We can smoke at sunrise," the officer said pleasantly. "Want one?"

"Not today. I'm doing the huffin' puffin' routine."

The officer laughed. Companionably, they gazed over an ocean empty of ships.

"Are we as alone as we seem?" Jake asked, suddenly uneasy. German and Italian raiders were a constant threat.

His companion's jaw clenched for a moment. In silence, they watched the stars fade to hints as purple asserted dominance. "Can't say, Captain Friedman. Maybe there's friendly eyes..." His voice held a question. He sighed. "Maybe not. Planes'll be by soon."

"Ah, one of our submarines escorting us?" Jake suggested.

Another silence. The tip of an orange-ball sun poked up, its rays spreading.

"'ssume that makes an ass of you and me, sir," the officer blurted out. "There's no subs! We sent 'em back to England, couldn't afford to maintain em. The Depression. No, sir, it's our civvie two-legged observers on the islands with their radios. Hope they're awake. Hope their batteries aren't dead."

Jake was startled. A doctor's silence elicits confidences, he thought, realising the power of saying nothing. As a captain, he outranked a second lieutenant with one pip on his shoulder. He must have felt compelled to fill the sound void. The second lieutenant's unarticulated fear was: are we five hundred troops and crew worth less than a destroyer's petrol? *How easy it is to get unauthorised information. In another life, I could have been a spy.*

The sun jerked up, painting the bridge windows orange-red. The sky morphed from purple to brilliant blue, marred only by filthy grey smoke pouring from the funnel. Slow-moving clouds offered a future breeze. Chugga-chugga went the engines. Far above the ship, a white tropicbird soared while a school of dolphins played in the distance. A large triangular fin matched the ship's progress, an opportunistic shark waiting for kitchen carcasses.

"We're goin' 14 knots, hopefully faster than an enemy," the second lieutenant said more cheerfully as he put out his cigarette and returned the butt to his case. "Time for your huffin' and puffin'."

On cue, whistles blew. Boots pounded up the two metal staircases. Companies formed up on the fantail and the open space behind the bridge. The soldiers gulped the sodden air as if starved. Agitated, the tropicbird fluttered its wings and fled. Two soldiers vomited over the rails—Jake knew he'd see them later in the sick bay for Mothersills, not cocaine.

"Sissies, fags," sailors jeered.

The ship's officer took the names of the taunters and stopped a brawl. The smell of unwashed bodies mingled with the salty air. To a loudhailer, the exercises began: running in place, jumping, push-ups, squats, and kicks while standing on one leg. This class finished with a drill called "war club." Jake picked up a concrete-filled fruit can with a handle. It weighed twenty pounds.

The drill sergeant yelled, "Back over the shoulder, right, left! Quick!"

The clubs flew over alternate shoulders with a continuous motion. Jake's heart thudded. *I will not yield,* he told himself.

"Across the chest. Don't hit your pretty little nipples. Right, left!"

Finally, the hardest part. High in the air over one shoulder, then to the ground at the opposite foot but without hitting the deck. A blow to the deck cost a man a half-day's pay. This exercise required discipline and strength, the drill sergeant's favourite strength trainer for cooped-up hordes. Jake's neck veins were bulging, his body oozing sweat, but he'd done it and felt wonderful. He'd do it every day; well, maybe once more before they disembarked.

Zealandia was two days out of Sydney, where Jake had embarked, and one day out of Brisbane, where the last soldiers and doctors came on board. The schedule for the remaining seven days was tight. Exercise rotated with small weapons training and lectures on island customs, the town amenities and rules of conduct. Doctors learnt map reading and a little Pidgin English, so they could supervise Tolai hospital boys. Censored war news was read out at the two daily meals. Today was Saturday, and a film was scheduled. Sunday would offer the one church service before they reached Rabaul on Friday, April 25, the national memorial ANZAC holiday day—a full colonial welcome was promised. For what free time remained, the men were encouraged to put on a play or make music and dance, anything to keep them out of trouble.

Officers were permitted to date the nurses—Jake had noticed bonds forming. He was shy and serious with them. *They must think I'm a wet blanket, but God made me this way.* One nurse had looked his way for support during a dispute with the overbearing OC—Cal or Priscilla her name was—he'd given her a sympathetic wink, but avoided getting involved in disputes beyond his unit.

After exercise, he showered in the state room, put on his uniform, and ate a breakfast of powdered eggs, bread, marmalade, and tea. The gaunt surgeon was there alone, mopping up egg clumps with bread, swallowing with relish.

"Glad you're feeling better," Jake offered, working up his courtesy.

"First class. See the flick poster?" The surgeon's voice was muddy gravel, stronger than Jake expected.

"No. What is it?"

"*Prairie Moon*, a western with Gene Autry."

"Never heard of it."

"It's been around a while, which is why they could get it. Singing, galloping horses, gunfights, pretty women, cute kids..."

"A good bang-bang'll keep the men too busy to puke." Jake laughed.

The surgeon laughed with him. "There's a booze party for medics after. Bet our mates will miraculously recover. My niece saw me off in Sydney, came from Melbourne no less. No telling when we'll see Oz again."

Jake was envious. None of the flower-tossing ladies or cheering men waving flags had been his family. No petrol, little money. He'd stammered his goodbye through a soon-cut-off phone call.

"I'll join your shift, help you out," the surgeon continued. "They *begged* me to volunteer. I saw you putting your nose up at my cocaine. You thought I was asleep—ha, ha! I lived in New Guinea for over ten years. Broken pelvis, malaria, dengue, I've beaten them. Tougher than you, hazel eyes. The coke is for when the old pelvis acts up. I never use on the job."

Jake blushed. "Honoured to have your help."

In the sick bay, one youth twitched on a cot. Jake looked at his chart: Henry Lee, Seaman, Australian Merchant Navy. A mixed-race Chinese-Australian by the look of him: olive skin and slanted eye folds told the Asian part of his story, a lanky frame, deep green eyes and long narrow face told the Caucasian part; the kind of male beauty often harassed by white bigots. Lee's eyebrows were blood-crusted, his nose a pummelled mash, wispy nostril hairs glued to his upper lip. He gulped in air through a mouth missing one tooth. One arm was in a cast, and his chest and back had large reddening patches. The chart noted he was pissing blood.

"He was fit when I boarded," the surgeon said, clicking his tongue in dismay.

"Who did this?" Jake asked.

"No one." Lee's voice was indistinct, almost a purr. "Fell down... staircase."

"Liar," the surgeon said.

"Bad cliché, Seaman Lee," Jake agreed. "We're not drips. Why were you beaten?"

"I wasn't, sir, a crate in the hold fell on me."

The doctors exchanged glances. They couldn't force a crew member to talk, so they set about cleaning Lee's injuries.

"You any good at anaesthesia, Friedman?" the surgeon asked.

"First rate," Jake responded over Lee's dubious eyes. He injected Novocain and epinephrine just left of the broken bones between them and the injured cartilage. To the surgeon's approving glance, he stepped back. Jake admired the surgeon's deft realignment of the nose bones; obviously, he was used to patching up brawlers. They shoved pain pills down Lee's gaping mouth. Jake told the orderly to ice the injuries every twenty minutes. He prescribed one night in the sick bay, then light duties for two weeks. Lee slumped back and dozed.

After this, the shift went quickly. There were minor cuts and burns among the crew, five humiliated seasick soldiers and one broken finger. They processed blood and discharge samples from a suspected venereal for the next doctor on shift to analyse.

When Jake went to dinner, the doctors' state room was full. The surgeon motioned Jake to a corner. "I liked working with you, Friedman. You're good. Going to the bang-bang?"

"Haven't decided. I liked working with you, too." Jake smiled. "You saved Lee's nose."

"Listen." The surgeon whispered in Jake's ear. "The bang-bangs and sing-along will cover more than blokes puking at the rail. There's a boxing match scheduled. Unsanctioned. An artillery captain took up Lee's cause. This white knight challenged Lee's attacker, an Able Seaman named Joe Bruiser Collins. You're the medical officer for Praed Point Heavy Battery Unit, right? Artillery. This white knight's your man, even if you don't know him yet.

"Drat," Jake muttered. *Shit, fuck,* he thought.

"I recognised Collins when I boarded. He was a welterweight champion. I saw him box in Melbourne, his wife and kids hollering loud as everyone. He retired from the ring and joined our Merchant Navy. In a Rabaul pub, I saw the degenerate bully he's become, always picking on weaker blokes. Brain's off, but fists are as good as ever."

"My man, whom I don't know, challenged this bastard?" Jake sighed. "How do you know who beat Lee?"

"Before dinner, I went to see Lee. He's a bit, you know?" The surgeon flapped a hand to suggest effeminate. "Fey. Don't know if he's a shirt-raiser or just looks the part because of his hairless chest. Don't care. But that's why he was beaten. Two things set Bruiser off. Effete is one. Mixed race is the other. To Bruiser's addled noggin, Lee's both. When I came to the sick bay, Bruiser was stomping out, growling 'piebald fairy'. Lee was covered in kitchen slops. The orderly cleaning Lee up said it happened fast while he was in the dispensary inventorying drugs. Lee 'fessed up then. It's not his first beating by Bruiser."

"Hmmm," Jake mused. "The man supports his family punching and being punched to amuse brutish crowds. Something 'Fall of the Roman Empire' here. Are we better than the Romans?"

"Don't shove Gibbons at me, you prude,"

Ah, he's one of the hollerers. "Sorry," Jake said hastily. "I was empathising with a bashed head. I had a concussion last year, car crash."

The surgeon nodded. "Rookies don't offend me, apology accepted. Anyway, Roman or not, your man'll be pulped. "

"Should I report it? Stop it?" The artillery men in his unit hadn't been at camp. He didn't know them.

"No. If you do, it'll happen anyway and could end worse. They'll clear space in the hold and fight during the flick. I'm going to watch *Prairie Moon*. I like a good song and a hero. Thought you should know. If your man gets hurt, you'll be called."

After dinner, Jake cleaned and re-bandaged Lee's cuts, telling him about the fight.

"I didn't ask anyone to stand for me," Lee insisted, alarmed.

"I know."

"You're so skilled and kind. Be assured I won't forget. I'll repay you." Lee's tone was pompous, odd for his low rank. A tear pooled on one bruised eye socket and burst over. His soft green eyes pooled again. Straightening his back, he rasped louder through two broken teeth. "Yes, sir. I will repay this obligation."

Jake patted his shoulder, feeling the muscles under Lee's singlet bunch relax. He saw deep sadness sag his face, as if generations of discrimination had shuddered his psyche. A young man reaching for dignity. Jake understood the feeling.

"No obligation. It's my job, Seaman Lee. We're all outsiders, you know. But you have a protector. I've changed my mind about your staying here tonight. Here's your discharge from the sick bay, pain pills and a sleeping pill. Get out before the fight ends. Keep a low profile, avoid Collins's mates, but have the surgeon check your nose. Here's our cabin number if there's trouble."

Through the metal doors, Jake heard a bugle sound for the film, which was to be screened in the refurbished saloon— refurbished downscale to accommodate hundreds of soldiers rather than a few rich passengers. A big sheet hung from the ceiling in the middle of the room. Men crammed rows of chairs on either side of the cloth, jostling to sit near the nurses. A projector beamed the credits and tinny soundtrack. One group would watch *Prairie Moon* in regular images, the other in reverse. They'd swap rows during the reel change. Because of the medicos' party, Jake knew he'd be alone in his cabin if a call came. He stood, watching. Audience whistles accompanied swelling orchestral music. The men stamped and sang along with Gene. They applauded the trademark horses galloping diagonally across the screen, the men and women seeing it in reverse laughing uproariously as if it was the funniest caper ever. "Ohhhhhs" amplified the ambushers' bang bangs. Jake smirked at the frontier damsels in distress, ridiculously well-groomed, a brunette and a blonde, a glamorous twofer braving evil gangs, needing rescue by honest Gene.

CHAPTER 5

$\cdots\cdots$

A SHAKE OF JAKE'S SHOULDER jerked him from his dream: he was an intern on call at Royal Melbourne Hospital, his patient a girl of about thirteen bleeding out from a botched abortion. The long-ago nurse's face, twisting in pity, faded as a male voice called, close to his ear,

"Captain Friedman to the sick bay."

Jake rubbed his eyes—no, Zealandia. His watch read 11.26. His cabin mates weren't there; they must still be partying.

"Hurry, sir." The staff cadet's face had recently been visited by acne.

"How old are you?"

"Nineteen, sir."

"Balderdash. More like sixteen. Lied on your intake form," Jake grumbled. He straightened his rumpled uniform. "But sally forth," he told the astonished cadet. His brain was slow to leave the Royal Melbourne's dirty lino floors. A steep metal staircase lurched him back to the present. He was relieved he wouldn't have to explain the facts of life again to the dead girl's appalled Catholic parents.

When he reached the sick bay, Lee was gone. A soldier and an irritable orderly—undoubtedly also roused—were shifting a grumbling lump from a blanket to the steel examining table.

Jake didn't know this man in his unit. The orderly got his file from the cabinet while Jake soaped his hands and forearms and cleaned his nails. His mind sped: the doctor in him itemised injuries to treat while his imagination tried to take in the person. He and his patient were captains. What did this mean for hierarchy? Jake's rank had been awarded because he was the unit's sole doctor. He hadn't earned it in action. His patient could be a veteran of the last war—grey tips sprinkled among the matted honey-blond hair suggested he was old enough. As Jake angled the patient's face to the bright light, noting scabbing gashes on his scalp and forehead, the man began to grin.

"Tough bloke, huh?" Jake said, letting the man sit up.

The patient gingerly pulled up a bloody singlet, his head disappearing then re-emerging, "Oof! Not my blood, though." He coughed.

Jake probed two ribs—could be cracked—and patches of reddening skin on his chest that would blossom into vivid bruises. Under a sock, one ankle was swelling.

"Breathe in, out."

The patient winced as he complied.

Not too bad; the ribs would heal.

He went back to the scalp gash, which had stopped bleeding. The patient gulped as Jake gently pulled the skin apart and then closed it. The skin was springy.

"Good," he said. He saw pride flick across the patient's face. "It needs a good cleaning—dust and rat hair, no doubt—and three stitches."

After pulling on gloves, Jake injected Novocain into his patient's scalp. Waiting for it to take, his mind wandered. The patient's seamed face and dark freckles suggested sun exposure. Bleary cornflower blue eyes would be compelling when his forehead healed. A chin dimple gave him an air of cling-to-youth mischief. Despite Jake's irritation at the unsanctioned fight, he smiled. An anomaly struck him: the patient's classic nose looked unbroken—*is he careful to shield it? Odd for a fighter.* Raw, bloody knuckles abraded through boxing gloves presided over long-fingered hands with tended nails. A hard-living but husbanded body with no sign of substance abuse. *Never gets old, the story a body yearns to tell.* He fell in love with medicine all over again.

His hands took over. He cut away hair clumps, cleaned the wounds, then stitched and tied off the thread, handing the patient over to the orderly to bandage. While he wrote up the chart, he wondered: *Why didn't I respond to Lee with this level of curiosity? Do I look down on other races?* A thought rattled him: *Or, oh God, is this attraction? Is he, well, sending something out?* Shaking his head, he expelled the thought.

The patient began to smile again when the painkiller took hold. Jake continued musing while the orderly finished bandaging. He couldn't help comparing his olive Ashkenazi skin, which tanned evenly and retained its oils, to the patient's freckled dryness. Ashkenazi skin covered a propensity to heart attacks, strokes and cancer. Who was healthier? He glanced at the man's history. The name looked familiar—Whipple, John Alexander, Captain, Royal Australian Artillery—but the connection escaped him. He had a vision that this man was born with a slender build. Had he transformed a reed-like frame into a fighter's bulk? *Stop being fanciful.*

"How did it go down?" he asked the soldier who'd brought Whipple in.

The soldier shifted from one foot to the other, no doubt worried about his involvement in an unsanctioned fight.

"Sir, Captain Whipple challenged Bruiser. Couldn't stand his bustin' on Lee, Bruiser being welterweight champ. Cap was an hour dodgin' the worst Bruiser threw at him. Bruiser couldn't believe all the weavin' and skippin' outa range, gettin' tired. Bastard cheated. Between rounds, he threw a weight at Cap's ankle. Cap landed kicks on Bruiser's crotch and jaw then collapsed; ankle'll be swolled."

"Yes, I saw that. Scalp gash?"

"Sir, Cap hit his noggin on a crate edge when he fell after Bruiser hit his foot criminal like."

"I see. Where's this Bruiser?"

"Comin' in. Cold-cocked, stone out!"

"Find Whipple's superior officer," Jake told the cadet, who left, eyes agog.

"Worth every blow," Whipple spat out. Jake had leant close to hear him. He was wiping pink spittle off his cheek when the door swung open. Two sailors, arms around a hairy, tattooed hulk's waist, heaved Bruiser in. He was leaning on them, starting to come to, awakening rage imbuing every shuffle.

"Keep Collins and Whipple apart," Jake ordered. He studied this man who'd punched and been punched to amuse crowds. The pain from Bruiser's testicular contusions was obviously penetrating his semiconscious state. He cradled his crotch with a huge, callused hand. He had a broken jaw, his mouth dripping blood; he probably had a concussion as well.

"Collins stays here. Morphine. Whipple's ambulatory, has to be elsewhere."

Whipple's superior officer, a major, stomped in, beery and irritable. He ordered Whipple and the soldier who'd brought him in to be confined separately, pending an inquiry. Jake updated his charts and went to bed, too alert to sleep.

When day broke, Zealandia was in the Solomon Sea, a lick of land in the distance. At last, a plane was patrolling. It had two propellers and droned ponderously over the horizon, returning thirty minutes later. Over the ship, it dived and wagged its wings. On deck, they could see the pilot, one hand raised in a Churchill V sign.

"Yay, Hudson!" Everyone cheered. It was Australia's new bomber, made to an American design. Cheers continued until the plane was out of sight.

Jake skipped callisthenics and went to the sick bay. Bruiser was asleep, an orderly watching him. After checking his vitals, Jake nodded. "He'll live, but won't be up to much. Lower the morphine."

He updated the chart and then took out Whipple's file. Something in his army intake exam had seemed odd, but he hadn't had time to analyse it. He held the X-ray to the electric light and saw what he suspected he might: faint old fractures in several ribs and a forearm. Were they accidents, fight injuries, or abuse? Jake winced, recalling his vision of Whipple bulking up a willowy frame. If he'd been bullied as a youth, he'd fought back and now took on the cause of others. Jake couldn't help admiring the chivalry. Whipple was single, two brother beneficiaries crossed out, leaving a sister-in-law—a stark history of losses. Jake thought of his own shrunken family. Whipple had served the last year of World War I as a gunner. Before joining the army again, he'd managed a coffee plantation in the Finisterre Mountains above Lae, on the New Guinea mainland. He'd survived malaria and had a tattoo on each foot. *A nomad like me,* Jake mused.

When Zealandia rounded the Gazelle Peninsula of New Britain two days later, everyone permitted on deck gazed at dense green forests, strips of radiant sand, sparkling bays, native log huts with what looked like thatched leaf roofs, and native fishermen in canoes. The ship passed a coconut plantation, its rows of palm trees waving in the wind. This plantation had a dock, a schooner and a motorboat tied up. A handsome house stood on the hill overlooking the dock. Glinting rail lines linked a warehouse to the dock. Efficient. Rabaul was a tropical paradise; everyone said so.

Jake checked Whipple's wounds again. "What do you like to be called? Captain, John, Alexander, Whipple, Whip?" he asked, distracting Whipple as he unwrapped the bandages and cleaned the skin. He was pleased with his work.

"Alex," Whipple rasped. "But Whip, that's new. I like it, but without the *h*, please." He winced as he smiled, the dimple hinting at a joke beyond Jake.

"Four days, and the stitches can come out. A doctor on shore will do it. You'll have new scars."

"I've had worse."

"Yes. Your X-ray showed that."

Jake thought Whipple retorted, "My bruises hurt less than the wondering in your eyes." But Whipple's lips hadn't moved. Jake pivoted, embarrassed. "I know Whipples in Melbourne. My sister teaches Tommy piano. His sister is Sally. Any relation?"

Wip straightened up. He opened his eyes wide and gulped a breath that swelled his diaphragm, causing him to cup his ribs at a stab of pain. *Oh no, what did I trigger?* Jake wondered.

"I'm their uncle!" Wip sat back, smiling as broadly as his mouth allowed.

Joy, Jake decided, relieved.

"Long-lost. Haven't seen them since they were baptised. God be praised."

"You're an observant Christian?" Jake didn't know why he was surprised.

Whipple snorted. "One doesn't say observant Catholics. You're devout or lapsed."

Jake laughed. "Right. We Jews are observant or secular. You're talking well, by the way. Healing."

"You're a good doctor. I give credit to the Almighty when human causes aren't discernible. Another deity is the pagan god of coincidence. You knowing my family is a gift from that jolly god. When you've faced gas in the trenches, lost a brother in that war, lost another in its damned sequel, no, I'm not devout anything."

"I'm less observant than my parents wanted," Jake offered.

"I never met Jews 'til the last war. They killed Jesus, was all we heard as kids. The one Jew I met was Pukka Sahib, who could've passed for an English toff. He was the chaplain for Jewish soldiers. We called them "kikes", but they fought as well as anyone."

"We call you gentiles 'goys'." Jake was irritated. "I told goys all the time I didn't kill Jesus and that he was a Jew. Walking home from school being taunted, 'You killed Jesus', hurt." He stood, old anger flaring. He rolled his shoulders to ease his tension.

"Ah," Whipple murmured. "Sorry. I might've shouted that myself. Bloody unfair."

Jake sat, his amazement at a second coincidence linking them banishing his irritation. "That chaplain you met? I think he's my Rabbi, Jacob Danglow. He *is* English. Always says, 'Call me John.'"

"That's the bloke!" Whipple almost shouted. "The 'Call me John' rabbi. I can see him now, handsome, square face, open-minded, for a cloth fellow."

"What are the odds of two coincidences on one troop transport?" Jake exclaimed.

The silence was thick, nervous, what-comes-next. Jake reverted to medicine. "Your X-ray shows old breaks. Were you bullied when you were young? Bulked up to stop it? Is that why you took Lee's cause? Bruiser's crew, not army. You're a captain, he's a sergeant. The fight wasn't sanctioned. Your superior officer could punish you."

"I know the rules. Bruiser's pro champ and I'm an amateur. That's the rank that matters to me." His eyes grabbed Jake's. *How handsome he is, those whorls of blond hair crisscrossing his legs,* Jake thought. He scowled his response away to the basement of his libido.

Whipple leaned forward. "Yep. What Bruiser did to Lee brought back the bullying. Why are you scowling? Did I offend you again?"

"No offence. What are the foot-tattoos your file mentioned?" Jake asked.

Whipple slipped his sandals off and raised the soles. One tattoo was a perfectly built man in an impossible skyborne leap. "Nijinsky. I saw him dance. Paris '17. His farewell performance.

He's my personal god." The other was an open hand with a torn heart on the palm. "My broken heart's dream of being a professional dancer."

"Ah." Seeing the man's stricken face, Jake noisily closed his bag, wanting to spare Wip embarrassment from the intimacy. *A natural dancer bulked into a boxer; my instinct was right.* He wanted to ask how Wip had kept his nose unbroken through his fights but sensed a boundary. "Get witnesses to Bruiser's assaults on Lee for the inquiry," he concluded, opening the cabin door. "I'll check on you tomorrow."

"They won't discharge me. We're at war. They'll demote me. I might be saluting you soon. Screw rank!" Wip called out. Suppressing his grin, the guard saluted Jake.

The next day, after Jake pronounced the cuts clean, Wip wanted to talk. "You knowing Tommy and Sally and me knowing your rabbi, doesn't this say we should know more about each other?"

Blushing, Jake nodded. "Tell me about Captain Whipple."

Wip launched into a sketchy family biography: four brothers and a sister widely separated in age. The brothers all gone now from sickness or war, a military family. Wip wanted to get through this war so he could be a proper uncle to Tommy and Sally. "I'm their last adult male relative. Every family needs a mature bloke, even um, a... flawed one." He *had* been bullied as a sissy at school. He'd read every article on Nijinsky, copied his moves and practised in the street. "The street was my stage. I was damn good. Learned to fight to stop the attacks."

They were sitting on chairs, leaning forward to hear each other over the whistles and busy footsteps outside. Their bare knees were angled close as if drawn together by magnets, but not touching. Retreating behind a doctor's neutral smile, he disengaged and left.

On the last night of the voyage, Whipple was allowed on deck. Urban lights from Rabaul smudged the horizon, bringing the promise of welcomes and adventures. Jake joined Whipple at the rail, waving his guard away. Wip was smoking a cigarette, wincing at a scabbed lip, but happy. He scratched his bandage. "Bloody itches. Can't wait to get the stitches out."

"Patience," Jake urged.

Wip was right-handed. So was Jake, but he was nearly ambidextrous, like his musician sisters. He shifted his pipe to his left hand, leaving his right arm on the rail near Wip's left arm. Tobacco cut the humidity. Chugga-chugga, the engines purred. Soot poured from the funnel, obscuring emerging stars. *Soon, I won't taste coal in my spit,* Jake thought. *Will I miss its association with a happy time?*

"Doc," Wip began. "You know Tommy, Sally, their Mum, Monica. How are...what are they like?" Jake sensed he had a stake in the answer, although he hadn't seen them since their baptism, probably by choice. But the intensity emanating from Wip meant that Jake's answer mattered.

He tiptoed through his words. "Monica's in rotten shape, sleepwalking through life since their dad's death."

"Egyptian front," Wip interjected.

"Yes," Jake agreed. He'd seen the recent beneficiary change on Wip's file. "Her detachment hurts the kids, but they have support. My sister teaches Tommy piano for free. He's a prodigy. Sally's a gifted painter. She gave me an amazing watercolour as a goodbye present." He described Tommy's ferocious piano playing of Beethoven and Khatchachurian, and Sally's painting of an officer giving the finger to a German aeroplane. Then, at his goodbye party, how a stupid boy cruelly teased Sally. "She lost her temper and hurled a tureen at the boy but missed. She shattered my brother-in-law's heirloom plate instead. She understood what she'd destroyed and was devastated."

Light from the bridge illuminated their faces. Whipple's eyes were glistening. "Monica can't understand them." His tone was urgent. "They need me. I *must* survive this brouhaha."

They were standing stiffly at the rail, Jake feeling his arm glued to Wip's and both breathing shallowly. As one body, they peered at the cresting waves.

"It's my job to keep you healthy," Jake assured him. "But you say you didn't visit for years, why now?" He wondered if the thwarted dancer in Wip wanted to live through talented kin. If Tommy fixed cars and Sally baked cakes, would Wip express the same urgency? Jake knew artistic elitism from Talia. "Because?"

"Because nothing." Clearly uncomfortable, Wip changed the subject. "Why did you volunteer?"

The magnetism between them dissipated slightly, and they moved apart. "Australia's been good to Jews; one of the few places we can survive until there's a Jewish homeland. Parliamentary democracy and the rule of law are the only systems that check our vilest impulses. Lord Acton said, 'all power corrupts, and absolute power corrupts absolutely'." To Jake's surprise, he saw pity on Wip's face.

"How abstract!" Wip exclaimed. "I'm not up on the Jewish homeland stuff, but signing up for dead old Acton? Doc, democracy doesn't give a fig for you or me. Judge by actions, not words. I don't like being the skunk pissing stink all over your fine principles, but I owe you. You're a… terrific doctor. Hopefully, Zeus, or the Tolai's evil spirit living in Rabaul's volcanoes, Kaia, or our Almighty God, will keep us a backwater, just parades and parties. But if war comes, get ready for a shock. You don't understand the farce you signed up for."

"What do you mean, farce?" Jake bristled. "Our government is good, democratic."

"You got people to live for?"

Jake nodded: family, his future with Esther, his Jewish community. He'd re-read Esther's latest letter today. At this moment, he had trouble calling up her details. His affection for her was infinite, but she herself was going fuzzy. He frowned.

Wip sensed his realignment of feelings and chuckled. "The tropics do that, Doc. Supercharge some, er, feelings, smother others. You don't know yourself til you've lived here, sweated malaria, got lost in the jungle, dependent for rescue on a kind savage who would've eaten you eighty years ago." He checked that no one could hear them. "I owe you a glimpse of a possible reality. We have four army divisions, right? Three are protecting Mother England's interests in the Middle East; the fourth's protecting Mother's fortress in Singapore. Who's left defending Oz and its sprawling Pacific-mandated islands? You docs did map reading, right? How many miles of coastline are New Britain island and Rabaul?"

"Over 1000."

"How many are we?"

"1,300 plus 150 local militia."

"How does that work? Now, the cannons in the hold: two 1913 guns, throw just six-pound balls. It's 1941. Artillery a whole bigger game. These guns guarded one river at home. Now they'll guard Saint George's Channel and Blanche Bay, which we just sailed through. Good enough for the island's defenders, our government says, which is us. God forbid enemy spies get close enough to see how puny they are. Our Hudson bomber everyone cheered? They're teaching planes—a couple of bombs, room as a transport, a gun or two for aerial fighting. Same with our fighters, the Wirraways. All we could afford. Our pilots are good..."

"The best! They flew me to outback care calls, lots of treacherous terrain," Jake said.

"Agreed. But this is the age of specialisation. You're a fighter or a bomber. Against German fighters or bombers, our planes are...well..."

And we have no subs, Jake remembered. He chewed his lower lip. Wip's facts rang true.

"Our Lord Acton government knows this," Wip continued. "Keep that in mind, Doc, when you ponder the purpose of your life. Love smaller and, ah, closer. That's as real as you can get." He moved to put an arm around Jake but drew back. Jake thought he looked older than his 40 years. "I've said my piece. Enough skunk at the picnic," Wip pivoted, smiling. "Did you bring Sally's painting with you? Will you show me?"

"Yes, and yes. But our government is good. Surely, they'll send reinforcements. If you believe all this, why are you, Captain World-weary, in uniform?"

Wip grinned. "I'm a veteran who knows New Guinea. Oz is worth defending despite everything. Military family."

"You hypocrite! That's Lord Acton-light." Jake couldn't resist clapping Wip on the shoulder. They laughed together, a subtler affinity opening. Exchanging glances, they said goodbye. In Jake's cabin, he found a surprising order: he was to stay on board while everyone else disembarked tomorrow. He was to leave the next day.

Zealandia entered a crowded Simpson Bay. Schooners and launches were crossing on business; rowboats carried passengers and officials to cargo ships; canoes paddled by natives were selling fruit to the new arrivals. A whiff of sulphur overlaid the smells of lush foliage, fresh and fried fish, coal and diesel oil. On deck, the soldiers gazed as wharves, warehouses and offices gained definition. Jake saw faces fall as some pointed to local sand, grey from volcanic ash, not the pristine yellow of the previous day. Native workers stood ready to unload cargo and luggage while dignitaries waited to greet the army. A band played while women in floral dresses and businessmen in tropical whites clapped and cheered. Newspaper reporters snapped photographs and wrote in notebooks; it was a full colonial welcome.

Jake saw Whipple led off under guard and Bruiser carried down the ramp on a stretcher. The other doctors and nurses followed. Then eager soldiers stepped fast, brimming with energy. Bugles blew as they formed ranks for the three-mile march to camp. Five hundred men recoiled from the heat as if they'd been blasted by artillery. The first welcome speech began. Jake returned to his cabin, puzzled by his instructions.

CHAPTER 6

· · · · · · ·

JAKE FOUND A STRANGE MAN in civilian clothes sitting on his bunk. Middle-aged, lean with tropics-battered skin, he wore the moustache and monocle of an English colonial officer.

"John Smith. Pleased to meet you." His accent was broad Australian.

"Really?"

"No, but that's how you'll know me."

"What do you want with me?"

Smith smiled, a wintry affair of lips spreading under appraising blue eyes. "Here's how you'll contact me." He passed Jake a telephone number and the address of a camera store in town. From Jake's memory of the map of Rabaul, the shop was in Chinatown.

"Mr. Smith, I'm a doctor. If you're not sick, why should I contact you? Why a camera store?"

"You have a British E20 camera; easy to get rolls. And you'll be at Praed Point."

Jake was shocked. Smith, whoever he was, had searched his luggage.

"You're more mature than most of this bunch of Salvation Army marching band types. You've worked in subtropical Queensland, the outback, and our capital cities. Varied experiences, and no complaints. Just a sad car crash."

Smith had read his file. But what sounded like a compliment, wasn't. Smith's smile was even more wintry.

The visitor straightened up. "Here's what worries us. Sit."

He motioned Jake to the next bunk. Jake sat, annoyed by his instinctive compliance. What was the use of captain's pips? "There are German sympathisers here. We interned the planters when war started, but their families are free. Some Lutheran missionaries wear Hitler arm bands. The Nazis are lovey-dovey with the Japs. Jap traders and pearlers come and go, photographing our harbours here and at home. We're at peace. We can't stop them..."

Japs? Jake couldn't quite stifle his smile. No one in basic training had mentioned a Japanese threat. Wickedly, Gilbert and Sullivan's "Mikado" popped into his mind:

Our great Mikado, virtuous man
When he to rule our land began...

Smith glared. "I see you need a history lesson. When the League of Nations gave us these islands, the mandate said we shouldn't fortify them. We removed the German cannon and under-invested in security with virginal purity. Not the Japs. Their mandated islands bristle with fortifications and weapons. Rabaul has the best harbour in the southern hemisphere."

Jake nodded, serious.

Smith pressed on. "The Japs are pummelling China. They're vicious. Chinese traders are the backbone of Rabaul's local economy. Some have family in China. So, what do you know? Jap traders complain about orders going wrong. They wander up to our camp and aerodromes, jolly good at getting lost, bowing and boo-hoeing about broken merchandise. Click-clicking their cameras. Are they working for their buddy Adolf or their own emperor?"

"You can't have them getting near our Praed Point

cannons, and you want photographs of anyone who tries," Jake ventured. *Wip was right about the inadequacy of our guns.*

"Bright boy. Yes. The Yanks'll fortify us in '43, but they're currently busy supplying England. Keep Jap gawkers away. Some business types may do a caper near Praed, need medical aid, and demand to be taken to your tent. They won't be traders, they'll be Kempeitai, Jap Gestapo. Treat them far from the guns. Give them Aussie hospitality and photograph them. Patriotic duty, Friedman. Britain's been damn good to you Jews." He stared into Jake's eyes, "and I'll stay quiet about your little foibles." He got up and stalked out, banging the door shut.

Jake stared at the closed door. Fear, amazement, and a very old shame turned his face purple. He'd just been blackmailed! Had Smith known about the old scandal from high school, his attraction to Izzy brought to a dramatic stop? It didn't seem possible. There was no written record. Was it a guess based on his aloofness with the nurses on board, or did he know something about Wip, heard they'd spent more time together than medically required? Rage banished shame. He would have done what Smith asked without pressure. Smith had jerked the kike/fag bell then left.

He spent the day finishing his charts while Izzy came and went in his mind, fuzzing his notes on drugs dispensed. Izzy had been nineteen, Jake fifteen, when the scandal broke. Izzy had been blond and handsome, a Jewish football champ, which was unusual. He'd been in the same B'nai B'rith group as Jake. Izzy's parents were rich, and when they'd gone on cruises, Izzy had thrown parties. Izzy couldn't do maths and had had to repeat a year; pudgy, admiring Jake had done his homework. He'd felt chosen when Izzy had kissed him at one of his parties, and he'd experienced ecstasy at their first mutual masturbation. *Is Whipple like Izzy? No, he's deeper and more decent.*

The group gropes at the parties had been heterosexual, apart from Izzy and Jake. They'd happened in dark, smoke-filled, beer-sodden rooms noisy with radio dance music. But someone had reported the two boys to the school. Izzy had been expelled from school. Jake's record had been kept clean because, as a minor, he was the perceived victim, although he'd been eager at the time.

He'd never forget his father summoning him to his study, staring in horror at his only son, raising a hand to strike him but dropping it in impotent confusion. "It's a stage, boy"—not "son" or "Jake"—"Grow out of it."

Nor could Jake forget Izzy's face the day he'd collected his schoolbooks. Half of his face had drooped, inanimate. He'd been much frailer than his muscled bulk ever suggested. His family left town. Jake never saw or heard from him again.

For months, whenever Izzy swarmed Jake's consciousness, he ate a tablespoon of mustard. He threw himself into study, then work. He danced with girls at balls. Then he found Esther and was relieved to consider his romantic future decided. He knew his feelings for certain men were more than a phase, but they didn't have to dominate him.

That night, Jake's last on Zealandia, he woke several times, feeling irrationally free. Why? Smith was a predator. But then he heard father's mantras: "look for options," or "re-interpret the event for positive potential." "Watch for improbable Jap spies and do what you like," was Smith's message. Oddly, this nasty bully was giving him a green light. What had Whipple said? In the tropics, you meet yourself. *Who am I? Will Rabaul answer that?*

BOOK TWO
PARADISE ATOP AN EARTH HEAVING APART, APRIL-DECEMBER 1941

CHAPTER 7

· · · · · · ·

STEPPING DOWN Zealandia's gangplank, Jake craned his neck for his escort. Behind him, the ship buzzed with the rush of imminent departure. A native hospital boy working for the army camp was supposed to walk him to Rabaul Hotel, where an officer would drive him to camp. Jake was relieved about the lift, rather than marching three hot miles like the soldiers had done yesterday.

No hospital boy was waiting at the foot of the gangplank. Checking his watch, Jake realised he was early, so he took a moment to orient himself. *My God, I'm here.* Flashbacks of home almost made him dizzy: his car crash in Colac, where Grace had been killed; Esther's goodbye embrace; fumbling the loading of his pistol under the drill sergeant's mocking glare; Rex spouting communist slogans at his goodbye party; Talia clutching his sleeve as he left.

I'm really here. Excitement suffused him as he watched the loading of a cargo ship at the next dock. Both sides of the wharf were lined with white men in long white trousers and shirts. One white man directed native men—Jake assumed they were Tolai—wearing only loincloth lap-laps. They were hauling huge logs, perfectly cut and numbered, onto a crane bed. The crane winched each log up and over the ship's hold, where other Tolai men muscled it into position for lowering into the hold. The sun flashed white on some of the labourers' ears. *Shell earrings?* Jake wondered. With admonishments and praise from the supervisor, loading proceeded efficiently. *True colonialism.* The realisation jolted Jake.

"Masta Dokta?" A piping drawl with downward intonation addressed him. Jake turned. He nodded at the wiry, lean youth of about eleven wearing a lap-lap and a white singlet. The boy slung Jake's backpack of books over one shoulder as if it were a feather, then picked up his kitbag. He held out his other hand for the medical case. Jake clutched it. He didn't know what crime was like—the lecturer hadn't mentioned theft. The boy seemed alarmed, which was puzzling. But he fell in behind Jake as they walked along a paved lane leading to the business district.

Jake had worked in five Australian cities. He liked to memorise the main streets before he took his first step. Today, he expected a short walk to the main west/east road, Malaguna Road, where he'd turn right for six-plus blocks, depending on how you counted intersecting side streets, to Rabaul Hotel on Yara Avenue. Lines on the map didn't prepare him for the explosive smells, feel and sounds of an entirely foreign place.

He picked his way between narrow gauge tram lines, the boy behind him. Yesterday, when the troops disembarked, it was the memorial Anzac Day holiday; businesses closed for several hours. They were certainly open today, a Saturday.

"Hairiap! Hairiap!" Older voices. Pidgin for "hurry" got Jake and the boy jumping to one side, backs against a warehouse wall. Jake put down his medical case and wiped his forehead. Four Tolai boys were push-pulling a careening bogie wagon laden with sacks along the tram lines to the wharf. Smells of dead fish and the oily sweetness of what Jake assumed was the processed coconut product called copra mingled with rotten egg foulness blowing up his nose. He identified the culprit as sulphur fumes from the active volcanoes. *Is this scent and taste better than the ship's coal? Like it,* he ordered himself. *It's harmless, and it's your world now.*

The lane emptied. Jake bent over to retrieve his medical case, but the boy grabbed the handle first. He looked up, eyes anxious. "Lusim na mi karim! Em wok blo mipla ol wok boy. Yu Masta, yu wokabaut." Jake understood Masta and wokabout, heard the fear in the boy's tone. Sighing, he let him add his precious instruments and drugs to his load. *This colonialism will take a lot of getting used to.* The boy breathed easier, obviously relieved.

The lane met Malaguna Road, a wide tree-lined throughway. Its spacious footpaths on both sides were bustling with pedestrians. On the road, bicycles weaved between slow, honking cars. Giant casuarina trees along the centre, dividing east and west-flowing traffic, blocked the sun, emitting a delicious fragrance after the harshness of the docks. Jake's body relaxed in delight. The lush, if somewhat stifling coolness, soothed his soul.

They passed a shipyard on the right side of the road. Jake noted with surprise that its name sounded Japanese: Komini, while two marine supply stores on the same lot had Chinese-sounding names. He reminded himself to ask about how different racial communities mingled. There was reportedly strict separation.

The sensory assault of a new environment got him reaching for the familiarity of home. In dry Melbourne, bushes, trees and grasses struggled to survive. Droughts were frequent. Nature had adapted with a myriad of small flowers in muted blues, ochres, maroons and purples, differentiated to attract the right pollinators. He revered the miracle, but one had to crouch to appreciate it. Here, abundance was a pummelling affair. Beneath the great trees, the sky would disappear. He'd know blue was up there, but wouldn't be able to see it. Growth here would be corralled, not nursed; gardeners would crop, rather than dribble rationed water on parched soil.

He came back to the present when they walked into a noisy cosmopolitan crowd moving in both directions. Their bodies obscured his view of a steepled church separating residential bungalows set back on lots abutting the footpath. *Shipyard, houses, church? Weird zoning.*

"Maket, Ol man meri wok long go kam long maket," the boy interjected, meaning the people were leaving or going to the native market, the Bung. He waved vaguely south. Jake took in the pedestrians: weary-looking Caucasian women in floral dresses escorted by husbands in casual whites and houseboys loaded with baskets of fruit, nuts, vegetables, or fabrics. A few happy Australian soldiers in khakis carried bottles of hard liquor and tourist knick-knacks. People moved slowly, trailing insect repellent. Jake realised why the hospital boy had been agitated at not carrying his medical case. No civilian whites carried packages.

Chatter floated around him in BBC English, broad Australian, European-accented English—*German holdovers from Germany's rule?*—and melodic Chinese. Some young Chinese men wore traditional tunics, while older men wore Western suits with high-collared shirts, not the casual tropical whites Australians favoured. Chinese women wore cheongsams with slits in the sides, revealing undulating skin. They kept their eyes under their umbrellas. Jake noted an incongruity, to Western eyes, of modest demeanour and the hint of eroticism. The Chinese all wore good fabrics; Jake's draper father would have approved.

Tolai locals seemed to have two dress codes. Some wore European shorts, dresses and blouses, while others were naked over their lap-laps. One woman's bare breasts bounced as she walked two leashed brown pigs with bristly hair. Other women slung full baskets around their shoulders or carried them on their heads. Their bare-chested men watched them work, chewing betel nut and eyeing each other competitively.

The bare-breasted Tolai were villagers, Jake decided. He'd

read that a Public Health edict from the 1920s forbade them to wear European clothes because they didn't understand how wearing and sleeping in wet fabrics exacerbated the endemic tropical skin fungi and ulcers overwhelming native clinics. Missionary youths, hospital and domestic servants could wear European clothes; it was assumed their employers had taught them how to change and clean them. Artificially bleached blond streaks in their hair seemed common to both village and urban Tolai. Jake hadn't seen Australian aborigines bleach their hair; this was a different culture.

Jake noticed some Chinese businessmen interacting with village men. They seemed to be on more familiar terms with villagers than the Europeans. Up ahead, a Chinese man offered a Tolai man a cigarette. They chatted, waited for traffic to ease, and then trotted to a shade tree. A Tolai woman with a basket joined them. Intrigued, Jake stopped, lit a cigarette and watched. Jake's escort, walking behind him, lowered his load and waited.

The Chinese man took out a string of white shells. After gesticulating and measuring, the villager beckoned the woman, who handed over a bolt of coloured fabrics. The Chinese man bowed. The men smoked down their cigarettes, put the butts away in pouches then went their separate way. Jake stiffened. A tall, young Chinese-Caucasian man fell in behind the fabric buyer. He wasn't in uniform, but the white tape on his nose made him look remarkably like Seaman Henry Lee. *Why the civvies?* Jake wondered.

His thoughts turned to the deal he'd just observed. Australians were ordered to transact only with cash or trade tobacco. But he'd read that Chinese traders accepted shell-money, *Tambu,* which retained religious significance in Tolai culture and presumably endeared them to the tribes.

The Chinese were a subordinate social class here, but so integrated economically that the Australians couldn't govern without them—a bit like Jews in Melbourne. Jake had grown up in a subordinate class. Now, he wore the military uniform of the ruling class. What does dominance mean? He'd depend on the Tolai and Chinese for basic services. Rabaul's vibrant complexity engulfed him as he dodged people with "Excuse me, ladies, gentlemen." He now understood the city's reputation as the jewel of colonial postings.

Suddenly, the hospital boy spoke. Jake turned around. "Masta dokta bilong dispela dokta? Missus bilong Haus Sik krai, krai."

"What?" Jake's brain reeled. He wiped his forehead with the back of his hand. Insect repellent stung one eye as he retrieved his beginner's Pidgin. 'Dispela' was 'chief.' "Put your packages down."

The boy complied happily, then pointed to a shop, made sharp-angled gestures with his hand, and then waved it in a curve. Did the curve mean an opposite kind of building, like a tent or something else soft? 'Bilong' meant 'belong to' or 'choosing a side'. 'Haus sik', mixing German and English, meant 'hospital'. Nurses crying because of OC Palmer? The nurses, orderlies and doctors were in the same unit under OC Palmer.

Was the boy repeating something he'd heard? He couldn't know that Jake was a doctor in a different unit. On Zealandia, they'd been warned that native servants were prodigious gossips and often played pranks. On the other hand, the OC Palmer hadn't let the nurses work in the ship's sick bay. There was some issue here. He had to say something. But what? Certainly not take a side in something he didn't yet understand.

The boy spread his lips, exposing gappy pink teeth. He'd been chewing the mildly intoxicating betel nut. That was a fact. His bleached hair streak was another fact. All else was guesswork. Still, he couldn't admit ignorance. What was 'this' in Pidgin? Right, 'Qo.' Jake pulled his bushy eyebrows together to make a forbidding impression. "Qo dokta not tell...buksop!" There. 'Buk' was boy, and 'sop' was soap. He was pleased with himself.

The boy shrugged, then giggled. Jake suspected the laugh was at his expense. They resumed their walk.

Malaguna Road segued into an obvious Chinatown, with shops on the right side of the road sporting Chinese awning signs. They were more crowded. To the left was a curved iron gate to the Botanical Gardens. They looked spectacular and lush. Jake looked at them ruefully; he was hot. But his escort, behind him, didn't break stride.

A minute later, the boy put down Jake's medical bag and pointed at an intersection. Two handsome two-storey hotels occupied opposite sides: the Cosmopolitan Hotel and Hotel Pacifica. Turning right on Yara Avenue, Jake saw the sign for the Rabaul Hotel and the BP Club a block south.

When they approached the hotel, an officer leaning against an idling truck in the parking lot uncurled from his slouch, stubbing out his cigarette and saluting. He looked familiar, if thinner.

"Corporal Jim Robinson, sir, 2/22 'Little Hell' battalion. Welcome to Rabaul, sir, belching sulphur complimentary."

He laughed, then turned away to sneeze. After wiping his nose, he paid the boy, who ran back toward the Native market.

CHAPTER 8

••••••

The Bung, April 26,
half an hour earlier.

"I AKUMU, take your eyes off that man. He's Chinese-white and a stranger. Get back to work."

Her maternal aunt's words snapped out in their tribal language without curiosity about the stranger. IaKumu, just fifteen, heard the implied threat: her aunt could complain about her wandering eye at the village moot; this stranger wasn't her intended husband. As a big man's daughter, much was expected of IaKumu.

Under a broad-leafed shade tree, the two women sat on the ground at a low bamboo table where IaKumu's aunt displayed her baskets and tapas cloth, and IaKumu sold bush medicine plants. They'd stopped seeking customers for this moment of discipline, while all around them, the hubbub of bargaining proceeded with gusto.

Open most days, Rabaul's celebrated Native Market occupied a dedicated block of land near Chinatown. On one side, an open rectangular shed stood, where a long table displayed local produce grown especially for Australian and

European tastes, as well as local. The rest of the block was dotted with shade trees and bamboo tables, where vendors piled more fruit and vegetables, coconuts, fabrics, dog's teeth jewellery, baskets and other artefacts. All the vendors were women, who clustered near other vendors from their village, some with children and babies.

IaKumu grew the best green vegetables in her province—her nickname, IaKumu, meant 'green vegetables'—which she sold in the shed mostly to foreigners. She also had an outside mat next to her aunt, where she sold medicinal plants that Tolai sought when they didn't want to go to the government-run Native Hospital: aiting sap for asthma, matmat plant for skin disorders, and marmar for malaria. She loved seeding, staking, picking off beetles and harvesting produce in her own garden. Even better was walking into the jungle with the village healer to find a certain tree bark for ailments like falling-down fits.

At the Bung, IaKumu's aunt stayed on her mat outside. But IaKumu, with her varied produce, worked both inside the shed and outside. In the shed, she could escape supervision. She was a joyful person, except for this proposed husband.

She nodded demurely to her aunt. While her aunt sold cloth to three tourists, IaKumu found the stranger with half-closed eyes. He fascinated her. He'd left her section of the shed table after buying her green beans, lettuce, spring onions, parsley, a mustard plant and an Aloe Vera cutting. He seemed to be in a hurry, barely looking up as he counted out Australian coins. He didn't bargain with vendors or gossip with other Chinese. *Does he fear someone?* Noticing unusual things was tradable currency with Tolai houseboys. You never knew when impressions became opportunities to sell more produce or learn a secret.

He had Chinese eyes and golden skin in a white man's tall frame, a white man's long face and a square jaw. His black hair was springy, like the shorn grass on Europeans' game fields, but shorter than the hair of Chinese traders and longer than the bristles of the white soldiers now crowding the town. A strip across his swollen nose showed he'd been fighting; he wasn't a coward. He was handsome.

A between-person like me? Baptised Anne, IaKumu wore a white meri blouse at the market and church, but went bare-breasted the rest of the time. She didn't mind practising the modesty Christianity required at these places—she set herself to wear the cleanest, whitest garment around—but the kiss of sunlight or rain on her warm flesh, and the conversations between her bare feet and the varied surfaces of bush trails, gave her more happiness. She and her family bellowed Christian hymns with full fervour at church but kept many traditional customs.

Her relatives were negotiating her marriage with relatives of a big man's nephew from Naguluna, a village two rivers away. From a different tribe, they'd fought blood feuds before Christian times. But mingling descent groups was now thought a good idea. The former enemy's lands had a slightly different growing season for vegetables and produced betel nuts. The potential mutual benefits were clear. IaKumu's aunt loved the match, which involved a big bride price for IaKumu; these days she hardly let IaKumu out of her sight. The problem with this fine blood-mingling was that IaKumu loathed the groom. She knew in the depth of her bowels that he would bring wretchedness and pain to her, and shame to her tribe. She was bewildered that her family didn't see it her way.

As her eyes followed the stranger out of the shed, IaKumu heard a spirit whisper inside her head and above her. She hurried outside. A gorgeous white-tailed tropicbird was sitting on a yara tree branch. 'See him,' the spirit chirped in flat-toned raps. 'He can get you out of this marriage. I hear you weeping at night.'

A good spirit. IaKumu steepled her fingers and bowed to the bird. No one else had seen it. Tropicbirds belonged on oceans or cliff faces, so if its spirit came here, it must mean that the stranger came from the sea.

Now back on the mats, her aunt was packing up their shell money, coins and tobacco from the day's trade. IaKumu glanced at the woman's stringy frame: 'empty tin' was what the boys called women past their 'mun sik'. By contrast, IaKumu knew that she bloomed with first fertility.

"You think I don't see you ogling him? You have a fine proposed husband," her aunt snapped. "I'm your eldest maternal relative. Ignore my status at your risk."

IaKumu craned her neck for the stranger, who was leaving the market and walking along Mango Avenue. Three slouch-hatted Australian soldiers were on the other side of the road, preparing to cross. They were laughing at something. Her stranger slipped behind a tree. *So that's who he's avoiding?* She looked at the soldiers, blinked, and then her jaw dropped open in shock. The three soldiers were bloody cloth scraps and skinless bones. *Aren't masta white warriors invincible?* She'd watched a hamlet's worth of them yesterday marching to join the ones who'd come a moon ago. A houseboy had said they were here to stop enemy white soldiers from landing. She blinked again. The three soldiers were halfway across the road, whole, laughing, and full of life.

"Lee Henry, over here!" a middle-aged Chinese man yelled. The stranger ran toward him.

Struggling to absorb the spirit messages inundating her, IaKumu was even more amazed. She'd met the older man— her father brought their trucks to him to fix. Now, these two men were leaving together. She thrilled again at the tall golden beauty of the man who now had a name: Lee Henry.

A connection! And a warning? IaKumu went to the shed to collect her unsold vegetables. She heard more flat-toned bird trills. "He is the right man for hard times. Get your father to introduce you to him on his next visit to Rabaul." She looked at the yara tree, but its branches hosted no birds; the spirit's work was done. Jittery, she veered from hope to fear as she accompanied her aunt to the village truck, where her elder brother waited to drive them home.

In the truck bed, her black-plumed pet dwarf cassowary growled for its reward. Reward for what? For being itself, an indulged pet few people could love. While her brother drove, the bird wrestled onions and chicken pieces from a fraying sack. IaKumu chatted to it about her visions. The bird, ToMuruk for 'Mr Glutton', was her number two friend, a discreet listener when he'd eaten his fill. She often told him details of her secret life ambition to help many native people beyond her tribe, something no Tolai woman had done. Her number one friend was her younger brother, ToSaina. She'd tell him about the Chinese stranger, the spirit bird's messages and her horrible vision of dead soldiers when he returned from a mission school in the mountains.

She held up a finger to catch the breeze. *Help me, ToSaina,* she mouthed, hoping the breeze would choose to float her words over trees and hills to him. Baptised John, he was a catechist and worked part-time at the Cosmopolitan Hotel. Nicknamed 'Saina' (China), he spoke some Chinese, Pidgin, some English, and their village language. *Get Papa to end the negotiations,* she sang softly. Perhaps she'd confess to him her secret life ambition. She hoped he wouldn't laugh.

CHAPTER 9

· · · · · · ·

BACK IN RABAUL HOTEL'S parking lot, Jake returned Robinson's salute. "Now I recognise you. I'm bloody glad of the lift. Thanks. Less hellish."

Robinson's eyes crinkled at the battalion in-joke. The nickname 'Little Hell' had been given to the 2/22 battalion by its commander, Lieutenant-Colonel Howard Carr, a poker addict. Three twos (2/22) were the lowest group of three cards, but could win; a 'little hell' of a hand. Jake had never liked the nickname; he wondered if Carr was subconsciously betraying class bias: was his volunteer battalion the lowest military material? Three twos *could* win, but usually didn't. Still, the men loved it, adopting "Little Hell, here we come" as their chant. Jake concluded that he was oversensitive to any hint of being lesser.

"You a poker player?" he asked Robinson.

"No, sir. Chess and cricket at Scotch College. I do bet on the horses."

Jake studied Robinson's face, etched with weariness. "At Bonegilla, you were a private. I arrived just before you left. Congratulations on your promotion."

"Yes, sir, thank you. We came last month and set up camp."

As Jake swung into the passenger seat, he looked at the parked cars: a Mercedes, two Rolls Royces, modest Fords, Humbers and Holdens, evidence of the town's love of cars. He saw no horses. Most cars had corroded metal; a few had holes. "What's happened to the cars?"

"Sir, Tavurvur, that bloody volcano." Robinson pointed at a mountain on the Rabaul side of Matupit Harbour. "It sang last month." He laughed again, hollowly. "Not funny. Civvie cars have thinner steel than ours do. Still, we sanded day after day, painted and painted. You begin the beginning of the same job all the time here. I was promoted because I saved a mate from drowning in a downpour. Monsoon goes 'til June."

There was no sign of rain as they drove down Yara Avenue, a narrow tree-lined street with one-storey businesses, government offices and bungalows on one side. The other side was a recreation centre with a school, tennis courts, cricket and bowling fields. Games were in full swing, with barracking spectators. Rounding the east side of Simpson Bay, the avenue opened into side streets leading to more docks. Robinson pointed out the Yacht Club. "Local poohbahs invite senior officers to parties, sir. A doctor captain's high enough."

"I'll see," Jake said, and fell silent. Did his moustache make him look imperial Pommie?

The heat was building.

Robinson didn't like silence. "Sir, some of us are going to Ah Chee's pub in Chinatown next Saturday. Gambling's all night, free liquor, other treats, um, like massage. Like to join us?"

"Nope. Thanks. Don't get suckered, Robinson. In Brisbane, the Triads run Chinatown's gambling and prostitution, and make a fortune off rubes. Lose your money? Your business. But I don't want to send any of you to a venereal ward, or wean you off opium."

Robinson reddened. The truck bounced over patches of gleaming tar, followed by ruts. A sign, "Detour. Rabaul

Department of Public Works." forced them to drive along residential streets. Jake admired the raised houses with wide verandas. Hedges or garden beds marked property boundaries, and shade and fruit trees were plentiful. Cultivated gardens dazzled: hibiscus, frangipani and bougainvillea were bigger than in Australia, and their colours and scent more explosive. The butterflies were more vivid, and he got a fleeting impression of large bees. Jake inhaled the sulphur-tinged blooms, feeling intensely alive. Some streets housed official buildings like the Land Office and Travellers' Office.

"Not getting the hang of the zoning," Jake remarked.

"Higgledy-piggledy, sir. No rhyme or reason. Fun, really," Robinson laughed. "Except, natives have to live on the outskirts, Chinese around Chinatown; separate black, white and yellow hospitals."

Along the road approaching the camp, Robinson pointed at a mountain overlooking Saint George's Channel and Blanche Bay: Praed Point. "Public Works are busy on the lower slope, sir. That's why street repairs are delayed." His voice held a question as he offered Jake his binoculars. Robinson would have seen that Jake's badge put him in the L Heavy Battery Unit of the Royal Australian Artillery, not the 2/10 Field Ambulance Unit.

Jake peered at the site where the coastal guns transported by Zealandia would be emplaced, where he'd be the sole medical officer—red-brown soil surrounded by impenetrable green, major jungle clearing.

"Checkpoint already on the new track, sir," Robinson prompted.

Jake smiled. The sinister John Smith on Zealandia had told him to photograph unauthorised strangers who tried to get to Praed Point, and that details of the guns had to be concealed. The fact of the guns wasn't secret, but their quality—puny— was. Robinson wasn't cleared to know.

Handing back the binoculars, Jake grunted appreciatively at the dappling turquoise water. White egrets and a blue heron stood in the shallows while a lone black cormorant commandeered a rock. Fishermen, knee-deep, were holding a long rope, presumably with nets, competing with swooping gulls. There were enough fish and crabs for all. "Paradise," he murmured.

This was too much for Robinson. "Sir, if your notion of paradise is taking a shit on top of hell opening up. That's how it was last month. Dust and debris everywhere. The volcano didn't shut up between eruptions. Blokes couldn't sleep. Bangs all night." He bit his lip. "But we do swim in the town pool and beaches on days off. In town, the food's marvellous, and the films at the Regent Theatre change often enough. If a town family notices you and takes you home for home cooking, you're in for a treat: chicken, fish, mangoes, paw paws, more kinds of bananas than anyone knew existed. I even got used to sweet potato and the weird breadfruit, which doesn't know if it's fruit or vegetable. Tasty nuts, too. If that volcano would just shut up, it'd be perfect."

They turned onto a dirt road as the humidity increased. The camp was hemmed in between a glowering extinct crater, The Mother, and the harbour. Surprised, Jake looked at elevated plains on the other side of Rabaul. They would be cooler and breezier.

Robinson read his glance. "Commanding Officer's decision, sir. That volcano was quiet for years. Seems it heard we were a-coming'. CO Carr insists we stay, ours not to reason why. He's a Sat'day Afternooner, sir. Cares most about spit and polish. Blokes call him a blodger."

Jake stiffened. Blodger was slang for loser. Robinson, a graduate of the elite private school Scotch Col, was too clever by half, almost insubordinate. 'Sat'day Afternooner' was code for rising in the ranks of the part-time militia; he'd never faced battle. Gabby Robinson wasn't the right person to ask about strife between the nurses and OC Palmer

"Sorry, sir, out of line. I got a King's Scout merit badge

for bush survival. The camp's placed wrong for permanence. But here we are."

Robinson helped Jake carry his luggage to his tent, saluted him, and then left. Clothes lines strung between some tents held underwear, shorts and shirts jerking in the breeze. Tolai boys were taking down clothes, folding them in labelled baskets, and then pegging others up. They kept glancing at the clouds, expecting rain, Jake assumed. Clay drains partially lined with piping were laid to drain off excess water. Based on the mildew edging the canvas, they weren't up to the task.

Jake's tent was in the third of about twenty neat rows. Supported by a front pole, the tent's side flaps were open, and a net was keeping out insects. Inside, there were two beds with mosquito nets. Jake's tent mate wasn't there, but had moved in. His gear named him as Derek Egan, Captain, Royal Australian Artillery, the same rank as Jake. Jake carried his luggage in, dumped it on a mat, and unrolled and inspected his net. Priority one: no holes. Each bunk had a small table with a battery lamp and a tin bowl for washing.

After rolling the net back up, he went to find the latrines and showers. Once cleaned of grit, he climbed the two steps to the mobile hospital tent. He stood on plywood boards for a moment, assessing the space. Two rows of cots were separated by sheets or screens, some presumably occupied by sick soldiers.

Two men stripped to their underwear were sitting on stools waiting to be examined. The Officer Commanding doctor was supervising a masked doctor tending the cots. Orderlies wheeled trays of medicines and instruments, taking temperatures, dosing and marking charts. Two Tolai boys brought clean linens in and took dirty ones out. A third Tolai boy was sterilising instruments in a cauldron of boiling water under the watch of an orderly. There was a flushing system, water pipes connected to a tank outside. Bright lightbulbs hanging from the roof attracted flies. When they reeled back from the heat, they slammed into sticky fly paper. The boy sterilising the instruments stopped and replaced a full fly paper, laughing as he swung his squirming victims into a bin. Four tall fans stirred air to little effect. The mobile tent was spacious and efficient. The only thing missing was nurses.

Jake saluted Major Edward Palmer, chief doctor and OC of A Company of the 2/10 Field Ambulance unit, who'd disembarked Zealandia yesterday.

"Time you got here, Friedman," Palmer rapped out crisply. He was stocky and radiated bull-in-his-prime confidence. He had receding black hair and a thin moustache. His trimmed beard emphasised a square face and thick neck.

"Yes, sir. Orders," Jake replied. Palmer wasn't his superior. He didn't need to explain his order to meet John Smith, or his disembarkation date.

Palmer nodded. "We've got pneumonias, tropical ulcers, and two malarias staying overnight. No dengue, fortunately. The two waiting ones are yours. I'm off, big do at Government House. Inspection tomorrow at 6.00 a.m. Be ready to dose the boys with quinine."

He and the other doctor left. Jake was the only doctor, supported by the orderlies and laundry boys. Slipping into a white coat always felt magical, the fabric releasing his craft and competence.

Jake diagnosed mild dysentery in his first patient. He ordered drinking plenty of boiled water. "Let's watch it for a week. You can do light duties, but don't share towels or sheets. If you're not clear by then, I'll have to transfer you to the civilian hospital in town for intravenous fluids. You don't want a tube."

"You're wrong, Doc," the dysentery said loudly. "At the civvie place, there's nice nurses, better'n here."

"What do you mean? Our nurses arrived yesterday."

"OC Palmer won't let'em in."

Jake scratched his head, puzzled. Why? He hadn't let them work on Zealandia either. He saw nods of agreement from a couple of other patients. The orderlies looked down—a mystery.

His second patient's face scrunched as he scratched desperately at his back. "Turn around." Jake sucked in his breath at a sprawl of blistering brown-pinkish circles, pale spots on several. Then he ran a gloved finger down a leg with two glaring red, ulcerated sores. The itch on the patient's back seemed to bother him more than the pain from his ulcers. Jake had never seen scaly fungi as big as this; it sprawled over most of his back.

"Crikey, you let it go too long," Jake remarked. "I'm sorry. How did it happen? Did you wear a dirty wet shirt? It's slow, curing fungi in this humidity."

While he was treating both conditions—mercury for the ulcer and a powder of boric acid, zinc oxide and starch for the fungi—he heard thudding boots, a bugle, and orders bellowing though a megaphone. He let the sound of the end-of-the-workday parade wash over him as he worked on his patients' charts. The unit's excellent band played martial songs. He heard orders to present arms. Eventually, the bellow "Dismiss!" and whoops from men heading to town. Fifteen minutes later, trucks revved up and roared off, leaving an eerie quiet outside.

Jake felt he'd lived several days since stepping onto Rabaul's soil. But it was still Saturday. He hadn't eaten since breakfast, and his stomach growled, but he wasn't ready to stop. He wanted to check all the other patients and read the observation notes.

He noted a change in handwriting starting yesterday. It became clear that the OC Palmer might be unpleasant, but he was a superb doctor—new instructions for at least one shower daily, fines for men caught wearing wet socks, daily preventive quinine dosing, frequent disinfectant of common areas, and instructions to hire a better laundry company. Jake admired his near-religious devotion to prevention. Still, the nurses would have been an asset.

It was a purplish twilight when he finished, the moon an orange saucer sliding between garish clouds. It hadn't rained, but it felt like it would soon. In the mess, men who hadn't requested passes for town were drinking beer and playing cards with an intensity that suggested high stakes.

"Beware of blokes with three twos," Jake called.

The men laughed, appreciating the battalion in-joke.

On another bench, Robinson was playing himself at chess. Jake declined the corporal's invitation to assume his opponent's position. Jake's chess was rusty, but he could see that Robinson had set himself up for imminent victory.

"No invitation for home-cooked meals?" he asked.

Robinsons smiled wryly. "Not tonight, sir. Next week, for certain."

Rubbing his eyes, Jake realised he'd wandered into the sergeants' and enlisted men's mess. He found the offices' mess, picked out a meat pie with beans, two bananas and an apple, and ate quickly, quietly, and alone. He took a mango and chocolate bar for later and found his way to his tent by torchlight.

His tent mate was bent over, putting away a thick notebook. "Drongos, fuckwits," he growled at the notebook, "bugger off an' wanker. All yer fit for. Let me do me job. Spare me old war stories, meddlin' morons, drips!"

"Bonga, bonga, bonga, all the drips are in Tooronga," Jake chanted. "Enchanted to meet you, Egan. I'm Friedman. Bad day?'

Egan swivelled, reddening. "Blimey, Friedman, ya gave me a fright. Yeah, bloody bad day. The drips aren't in Tooronga, wherever that is. No sirree, they're runnin' Rabaul."

"Drips in Tooronga too," Jake said. "Melbourne. We played their footie team. Our chant."

"I'm so pissed off, I forget my school chant. Hobart."

They shook hands. Egan flung himself on his bunk, lit a cigarette and launched into his problems. "Praed Point, now nicknamed The Fort…"

Jake was all ears. His posting was Praed.

"Local vets, Returned Soldiers' League, never fired

cannon, just Vickers machine guns in the last war. Blah blah, they say the cannon shouldn't be at Praed, but where the Kraut cannon were, Keravia Bay, other side of Rabaul. Cheaper, right? Costs less. But the Kraut guns only covered Blanche Bay. Couldn't reach the approach of Saint George's Channel or Rabaul's critical Simpson Harbour. Useless. Worse, land's flat at Keravia, sittin' ducks for attack from behind. That's how we took'em in '14. Krauts didn't fire a shot. Praed's so precipitous, surprise's impossible."

"Is there a negative to Praed? I'm the unit's medical officer."

"Yeah, the flip side of its advantage. The narrow slope means the guns have to be placed one above the other, vertical like, not side by side. Not what the manual advises, but the only possible position. Wide slopes here don't overlook anythin' worth firin' at. Location was set months ago. But the vets yak, yak, yak. Upshot: I have to write a technical justification before Public Works continues construction. Writing's not me talent. How was your day?"

"Good." Jake frowned. How to convey his fascination with Rabaul? Egan raised reddish-auburn eyebrows, peering at him with anxious green eyes. *He's wondering if I'm a bore,* Jake realised. "Fine hospital tent; I treated a marvellous fungus. I want to ask you something about the hospital, but first, the guns. You said their positioning isn't what the manual advises. What do you mean?

Egan laughed. "Oh dear, you *are* a city civvie. I'll show you for the mango. Looks good."

Jake handed it over. He chewed the chocolate bar slowly as Egan placed one hardcover book above another, separated them by a postcard and held them.

"Voylay! As the poor occupied Froggies say," Egan exclaimed, withdrawing his hand. The edifice tumbled to the ground with a thud.

Jake stared. "My God!"

"Now don't go mother-cluck-cluck on me," Egan said.

"Like them vets. The manual recommends *generally* against vertical placement. But topography rules. In Rabaul, Praed's the only possible site, and at Praed, near-vertical's the only possible placement. You'll see when you're there."

"What's the odds?" Jake asked. The chocolate's aftertaste was sour.

"A bomber pilot would give you a better estimate, but I'd say….5-10%. Remember, the uselessness of placing the guns anywhere else is 100%."

Jake brooded while Egan peeled the mango with his knife and ate it. Jake imagined two Leaning Towers of Pisa, one collapsing on the other, then both hitting his little canvas medical tent with him in it.

After Egan put the skin and pip into a sealed tin for the rubbish dump, he said, "You wanted to ask me something about the hospital tent?" His voice was cheerful. The gun positions didn't seem to bother him.

"Oh, yes. A mystery." Jake decided to adopt his tent mate's nonchalance about Praed Point. 90-95% were good numbers, better than he'd scored on some medical exams, and he was a good doctor. "Why aren't the nurses working? I don't know who to ask without getting in the middle of something."

"Oh, I can tell you. A big fight blew up the moment the nurses arrived yesterday. They ended up in tears. It's about the new hospital structure. Everyone expected a fixed building of 60 beds, fully staffed with doctors and orderlies of the 2/10 Field Ambulance Unit, the Regimental Officer staff and the army nurses. But Major Palmer, OC of the 2/10, refused any construction of a fixed building. He insists on keeping the mobile tent you just came from, which is modelled after front-line tents in the last war. He sees himself as a battle-station surgeon."

Jake recalled the hospital boy pointing to a shop, then making contrasting round gestures with his hand. He was repeating something he'd heard, not pranking. "But why be against a comfortable fixed building, nice and dry? And what's that got to do with the nurses? Palmer's a good doctor. What am I missing?"

"Yeah, you're volunteer, not regular army; no reason you'd get it," Egan sighed. "Nurses are automatically designated non-combatants, see. They don't carry pistols like male docs and medical corps do. So, if nurses work in a medical structure, that structure follows their designation and becomes a non-combatant building, relegated to the rear of front-line battle. Theoretically safe. I reckon OC's terrified of bein' stuck in the rear of any action; reckon he dreams of miracle surgeries he'll do in battle, become famous, like docs in the last war. But he can't say it direct like, too selfish, so he table-pounds about nothing. Got the highest rank in his unit, so his decision sticks, unless Commanding Officer Carr, a lieutenant colonel, overrides him."

"What ego," Jake exclaimed. "There's no war yet."

"Technically, there is, against Hitler, so the rules on designation apply. As long as he keeps his nurses out of his tent, he keeps his tent combatant status. They're miserable, poor sheilas, nothin' to do. Nice ladies, great tits, some of 'em. Hated to see them in tears."

"The patients need them, matter of health. Palmer's wrong." Jake liked Egan. He was about to describe the hospital boy's gossip when a percussive slap above his head stopped him. Slap, slap. Rain slapping the canvas. "This'll be intense," Jake predicted. "I know tropical rain. Tie up our dry clothes and towels."

After doing their best to protect their essentials, they pulled on boots and ran out, joining a crowd dragging clothes off lines and stuffing them in sacks to be rushed to the administrative tent for sorting and drying.

The wind drove from the west. Lightning split the sky, striking trees at the camp perimeter. Rain pounded in slanting barrages, then, when the wind shifted, disgorged billowing dumps. The drains swelled, drained, topped, and then gave up. Mud sucked boots, causing trip-ups. Some returning trucks got stuck in the mud, engines revving furiously before being turned off.

Jake ran to the hospital tent. Its elevation should protect the patients, but he had to be there. The Tolai workers had left for the day; he was in charge with one orderly. An hour in, the roof sprang a leak. He and the orderly filled buckets, emptied, and filled again. When they opened the door, they heard the crack of coconuts slamming truck cabin roofs.

A coughing pneumonia and two wobbly malarias heaved out of bed to help.

"Back," Jake ordered. "We can cope" The absence of nurses was idiotic.

A patient cranked up his radio. Reception was erratic, but men laughed uproariously at an old schoolboy spoof: *Yes, What?* Between advertisements, the news anchor announced six inches in an hour; then, Allied progress against Rommel in Egypt. Chatter erupted from the cots: whose relatives were in the fight? A tinny Rossini overture, then the announcement that eight inches had fallen, the season's record. "We won!" everyone cheered. *What good sports*, Jake thought.

Dawn broke on Jake's first full day in Rabaul. Inspection was cancelled. An innocent yellow ball in a pristine blue sky beamed on the mess as if amused by the nocturnal mischief of its counterpart heavenly body. Sweet morning fragrances of tropical grasses mitigated the smells of man-made debris. Blinking aching eyes, Jake sloughed through water up to his ankles. The latrines were foul, and truck beds full of water stank of petrol. He waved away mosquitoes as he dodged floating bits of wood, a clock, a framed photograph.

Some tents had collapsed, but Egan had kept theirs up. The beds slumped in mud. As he and Egan upended them to start the cleaning marathon, a sea snake trapped between Jake's mattress and sheet hissed bewildered, yellow-skinned fury. Jake carefully grabbed its neck with both hands, tight as a clamp, waded toward the perimeter and threw it in the direction of the beach. By some miracle, their spare clothes and towels were dry, the books only smeared. Both of their cameras were wet.

Jake started laughing. Nature's joke. What would John Smith say about his damaged camera that was supposed to record would-be Japanese spies?

Egan stood cross-armed, heaving with exhaustion. "Are you mad?"

"I love big weather." Jake straightened up and rolled his shoulders. "Someone who'd lived here said that Rabaul seems elemental, brings one to the heart of creation, destruction and regeneration. Look on the bright side, Egan; there usually is one, no sermon today."

Egan laughed. "You're alright, Friedman, lover of magnificent fungi."

CHAPTER 10
• • • • • • • •

THE RAIN LET UP. Jake got used to sulphur fumes floating up his nostrils. Life began to feel like a blend of basic training and weekend resort living. Mornings began with inspection, weapons maintenance and daily quinine dosing. Rotating chores around the camp followed: cooking, latrine duty, litter pickup after storms, and tent repair. Jake did several shifts in the hospital tent. Workdays ended with a parade and Lieutenant Colonel Howard Carr's inspection of the spit and polish of uniforms. Soggy pants creases and smudged boots earned withering rebukes.

Carr conducted military drills per the Army manual, which got Jake puffing and sweating through zig-zag crouching runs over open ground to plunge into ditches. The drills seemed designed for trench or field warfare, like battles in the 1914-18 war. Since fighting here would be on beaches with narrow sand spits or in the jungle, the drills made no sense to Jake. A few soldiers, including Robinson, explored the jungle if they found a guide. But for most, the impenetrable green was a no-go barrier.

"The manual's the bible," Egan explained, when Jake asked him why they continued to sweat through open field exercises. "Has to work the manual."

"Do I hear sarcasm?" Jake asked.

"Big word for a simple bloke. Dunno. Just lesson one from my civvie militia days." Egan had told Jake he'd had to leave school at fourteen to work at a horse farm to support his family. He'd attended night school to learn radio and telecommunications. As soon as he had a certificate, he'd joined the civilian militia on weekends. "No time for sheilas. I was a good boy. Now I'm owed some love." He'd pointed at a cloud and declaimed, "Almighty, time to pony up. I'm a decent bloke at heart."

Jake noticed his eager offers to fix anything the nurses wanted repaired. So far, it hadn't secured him a regular girlfriend.

What Egan couldn't fix was the OC Palmer's decision to exclude them from the hospital tent. Palmer only allowed them to help with the daily quinine dosing during inspections.

One morning, Jake noticed that all the nurses had jettisoned their army-issue long stockings and sleeves. "I wondered how long you could endure all that cloth. Ridiculous accoutrements in Rabaul's humidity," he murmured to the nurse next to him as they dosed their way along a line of reluctantly opening mouths. "Chief Doc approved?"

"I'm Priscilla Evans. Good morning, doctor. He says it's up to our matron in Sydney, so we don't know. This is what civvie nurses here wear."

"Sensible. We're in short sleeves. I'll write you a note if you need a doctor's opinion. Matter of health."

Priscilla flashed him a grin from a strained Celtic face florid with sweat. "In South Australia, I never felt heat like this. And it gets hot in Clare and Adelaide. Clare's lush farmland, miles from ashfall Addy, but boy, the summer still sears."

"Dry heat's easier," Jake agreed. "My sisters'll send me to Coventry if I don't help you."

"I love your sisters already." He saw her eyeing his bare ring finger. "Can I make you tea?"

After dosing, they sipped from tin mugs, sitting on chairs outside her tent. Priscilla took off her white cap, shook out auburn curls and vented. "The other docs treat us like we're the first women they've ever met, like we're Martians. But they've got sisters and girlfriends who work. We enlisted because we're professionals. AA NS, Australian Army Nurses Service. We sailed on Zealandia, just like you and Major Palmer. We just sit and pout with no one to treat and comfort. Nor are we sent anywhere else to work. But Major Palmer's the highest-ranked doctor here. Only someone above him can change it."

Lighting a cigarette, she breathed in the tobacco and talked fast. "My parents ran a hardware store in Clare. Suffered like everyone else in the Depression. I did a lot of caretaking. Diapered and rubbed cream on my sibs' nappy rashes, took temperatures, cut and sucked snake bites, and even injected Granny with insulin. At Adelaide Children's, I got my midwifery and operating room certificates. But the moment my younger brother put on his doctor's white coat, it was like he grew an extra inch of nose to look down on me."

Jake laughed and touched his nose. "I think attitudes like that are institutional shorthand for getting through hard days. You nurses don't have the burden of wrong diagnoses, the catastrophic life or death mistake..."

He paused at her tightened her lips. *Enough.* Hastily, he returned to what bothered the nurses most. "My tentmate Egan explained the hospital tent's automatic non-combatant status if Palmer lets you in. I don't agree with him excluding you." Finishing his tea, he stood and shook hands with her. "The patients and orderlies want to see you as much as you want to be there. Let the word get to Carr. A lieutenant colonel trumps a major. Carr's a card player, likes trump hands." He laughed, then turned serious. "Look, I'll be at Praed. Just a captain, but I'll add my voice if you need it. It's a matter of health. Major Palmer's not my superior officer," Jake offered. "Thanks for the tea. It was delicious."

CHAPTER 11

·······

Mid-May 1941

THE NEXT MOON-FLUSHED NIGHT, when IaKumu and ToSaina judged it was too bright for evil spirits to wander, they slipped from their siblings' arms and crept out of their house to the river. There, ToSaina continued teaching IaKumu English. The priest had given him a torch so he could study at night. Together, they scratched letters in the dirt with small sticks. "You understand more than you say," he observed.

She sighed." So slow."

"Enough." He reverted to their native language. "Tell me why you've been crying at night. Our baby sister said you wail a lot."

"Oh, how can I not wail? I've seen the right man for me, and it's not the man from Naguluma. Nothing good can come from our marriage; I know it, know it, know it. A good spirit told me. Why can't Papa and Auntie see it?"

Her brother shifted uncomfortably, then scratched his head. "His relatives say he's strong, healthy and handsome. He can hoist big logs on his shoulders and build houses fast. Papa says he did his time in the bush and killed a wild pig with his hunting dogs and just one spear. He's suitable. You know how enthusiastic Auntie is about the bride price. Surely, you'll like him in time."

"I hear what everyone says, endlessly. I'm sure Auntie gave ToStonehet my hair for his magic. She criticised my looks last moon. 'Hair ragged. You're a disgrace.' But I had just done my hair. She cut one of my black curls and a bleached one. Instead of burning them so a sorcerer can't use them against us, she gave them to him. I've heard he's living in the Men's House and paying shell money for spells to get me to long for him. But his magic doesn't make me desire him. I feel my hair in his boastful smile tickling my cheek; his gaze turns my spine to sickly sap."

She began crying. ToSaina put a hand on her shoulder. "We men sing over secret plants and animal teeth because we want our chosen girl to find us handsome and sweet, to desire the closeness and love us. Bride prices are contracts; we call on magic to give the contract heart. How is that bad?"

IaKumu was distraught that she wasn't getting through to her number one friend. Wiping her eyes, she said more calmly, "I know about my intended's strength, but there's little going on in his mind. He's all belly feelings, quick to anger. He won't hire the greatest singers and dancers for our sacred ceremonies—you know how important that is to our reputation—not because he couldn't pay for them, but because he won't know beauty from shoddy imitation. He's a braggart. Stonehet (obstinate) is his nickname by his own tribe. It's our nicknames, not our birth names, that follow us to the Abode of Death and pass to our descendants. What skill is obstinate? The women from Naguluna say that his father taught him to kill by neck-cracking, which his ancestors did to some German planters. What if his belly rage at some white official makes him neck-crack a district officer?"

"He'd never do that!" ToSaina exclaimed.

"How do you know? Tell me true, do you like him?"

"My feelings don't matter. Someday, I'll move away." ToSaina looked down, his body hunching and tense.

"Mine do! I could never sing an honest prayer to the spirits when he's away. He'll be a wife-beater. I can tell. 'Ooee, Lalala, good spirit, bring him back, my sky, my sun, I am nothing without you…ooeee."

"Stop!" ToSaina cut her off. "Never begin an invocation without the true context."

"I'm sorry. I was wicked. The man I could make honest prayers for is the man I have my eyes on. He's Chinese and white, a stranger, but from the best Chinese family. His legs are as long as ToStonehet's, but he moves gracefully. He's not all corded thickness, but a palm tree that will bend with storms but not break. A good spirit, in the form of a white-tailed tropicbird, told me that he's the man for me. I was filled with hope. I can love him, and the appearance of the spirit tropic bird is a sign he can love me back."

IaKumu saw her brother's moonlit jaw clench. "Which came first? Your liking of this stranger or the spirit bird's advice?" His voice was stern with disapproval.

IaKumu sobbed again. "You sound like our priest. I yearn to have children with him. Listen. On the nights ToStonehet sings his magic, the spirits he invokes make me dream I should go to the bush to meet him. I feel his wooden split drums vibrate my body. I roll off my mat and stand. But a good spirit at the door counters his spell. I fall back on my mat and cry. Surely, you can be on my side. Don't you love me?"

"Of course; you're my sister. But what can I do?"

"Contest the match at the moot. You're educated. You know our ways and the white people's way of thinking."

"I'm just good at the tongues people speak. I'm younger than you." He was silent. "This is a big burden you put on me. He's passed all the tests. You haven't given me enough."

"Then hear my dreams. Always brown eagles. You know they mean death. They fly over our land in a sky full of big metal bird machines. They're like the balus the government sends with people and things. But these are only terrible. They don't land. None of our boys carry things out of them. Everything is fire that turns day into night, and night into day. The fires aren't Kaia, the spirit in the volcanoes; we know them. I see ToStonehet and me, but only our backs; that can also mean death. It did when Papa dreamt of seeing his brother from behind, and then we learnt he'd died. When I wake, I go to our fields and watch the sunlight waking the leaves. The dreams walk with me, making the leaves garish and twist the wrong way. The dreams say that if I marry ToStonehet we'll both die, leaving orphans. What mother can want this? Another visitation…"

ToSaina interrupted. "Stop. Let me think."

"Just this. At the market, I saw three white soldiers, sweaty and laughing. I blinked, and they became cloth scraps, skinless skulls and jaws. When I blinked again, they were laughing and whole. What can that mean?"

ToSaina turned his eyes away from her and up to the moon, then he followed its rays illuminating the river's meandering waters, up to the light, down to the water, his body still, transfixed and quiet. She tapped his shoulder. "I don't know," he said. "Your sadness could be making you rebellious, with your mind seeing things, or it could be more." He paused. "Papa told me that he saw the white Australians come with ships and guns and defeat the white German soldiers who ruled us. He was your age." He fell silent again.

He's listening.

"Why didn't you tell me about these visitations first?" he exclaimed. "I think they're not dreams, but visions, an ancestor's shadow soul or a spirit warning." Gently, he touched her hand.

Near melting with relief, she pressed on. "The Elders harangue you men to copy the Chinese; learn how they turned labour into trading. Why can't I marry a Chinese man? Others have. I like my stranger. I've watched him several times. He's kind. He leans down to pet the vendors' dogs. He's not all passion and pride. He's polite to the women even when they laugh behind his back for buying without bargaining. But he's not a spendthrift; that would be bad. He hurries away when he sees the soldiers."

"What's he hiding?" ToSaina scrawled random shapes with his stick.

"He's from the Chinese family Papa trusts to fix our trucks. He's alright." IaKumu watched ToSaina make increasingly ornate designs. The moon sifted in and out of the clouds.

She paused and took a gulping breath. "I have a life dream, an ambition." She plunged forward, her secret no longer. "Of many greens of leaves—dark, pale, near blue-grey roots, bark-coloured seeds, red sap, gifts of our rich dark soil, all on wooden shelves, all for healing. My dream is to have a store. Instead of me walking my vegetables and bush medicine along jungle tracks to village markets, or being driven by Papa to town, everyone coming to our store in Chinatown. I'm already respected in the province. Nothing makes me happier than a coiled face relaxing when pain flees after my leaf wrap; the relief in dancers' eyes when my crushed seeds and leaf salve the leg ulcer, so they can leap and crouch, both legs equal without shame; the joy of the mother when my chewed stem cleanses her afterbirth for burial, and she suckles free. I dream of helping so many of our people. I can't do this living in ToStonehet's village."

She waited for her number one friend to laugh, to mock her. He did not. "You're best known for vegetables the whites buy. You don't do a lot of bush medicine," he objected.

"But I can do much more and bring us honour. Our village healer will pass on one day.

My store has a red awning like hibiscus, and the metal pole catches the sun in a bright flash.".

Finally, ToSaina threw the stick away and offered his

hand. They shook hands solemnly. "I want you to be happy," ToSaina said. "Your dream has beauty. I'm no sorcerer to explain your visitations that seem to warn of evil coming, but at the moot, I'll protest that marrying ToStonehet should be taboo: his blood ties are too close to ours for union. His maternal grandmother's afterbirth was buried on what was our land. Before Christian times, their tribe took our women and land. You can speak, but don't mention visions. Auntie's brother will have to come home for marriage negotiations."

IaKumu nodded. "I know." Their sole surviving maternal uncle was a cook on a cargo ship owned by the Australian company Burns Philps and rarely visited. They walked home as moonlight imbued tree canopies with an eerie radiance. IaKumu thought, *my number one friend is a treasure,* but *he'll fail. I may have to resort to more desperate measures.*

CHAPTER 12

· · · · · · · ·

Friday 9 May 1941.

OUTSIDE THEIR TENT, Jake and Egan frowned as they dismantled their wet cameras.

"Need a repair place," Egan grunted.

A shadow falling on them pulled their eyes up from the stools outside their tent. A middle-aged Chinese man in a business suit bowed and offered his card. The Australian officers jumped up.

"Did you come with that van?" Jake asked, pointing at the laundry van from town. Its driver was sitting at the wheel, watching Tolai boys unload and load bags. The camp's new contractor was doing laundry daily at an industrial scale and very well.

"I fix good, honoured sirs," the visitor said, pointing to the cameras. "I came with the van. My company." Jake and Egan looked at him, curious. His grey western suit with wide lapels over a starched white shirt and patterned tie must have been miserable in the heat. But that was how Chinese traders tended to dress. Beads of sweat shone on a smooth forehead. The visitor's clean-shaven face was round, his nose small and broad, his black eyes calm. Jake got the impression of intelligence and thoughtfulness. One front tooth had a gold filling.

Egan read the card out loud. "Ah Kuan Ho, Proprietor, Ah Kuan Ho Laundry Co. Pty. Ltd." The shop's address was off Malaguna Road in Chinatown. He turned the card and whistled at the affiliated companies: "Ah Kuan Ho tailoring; construction; tea house; watch, camera and jewellery repair; automobile repair and sales, two regional addresses."

"Mr Ah, you are a significant entrepreneur," Jake said, impressed. He exchanged glances with Egan. "Thank you for the card. We'll try your shop."

Ah Kuan Ho bowed, then worked his way around the other new officers.

*
**

On their next morning off, Jake and Egan parked the truck at Hotel Pacifica, walked one block north and searched for the shop. Jake peered at the card and then pointed at a white storefront sign with slanting black capital lettering. "That's it. Ah Kuan Ho, Pty. Ltd. (1928)."

Carrying their muck-damaged cameras, Jake and Egan stepped over an open drain stinking with waste and eased between the awning poles of a two-storey wooden building. Ah Kuan's store was between a laundry/tailor store and a dry goods and spices store. Down the street were a tea shop, two restaurants with outdoor chairs, and a pub. The old structures and mature shade trees spoke to a settled presence. A hand-printed sign on Ah Kuan's window read, "Good Price Everything!"

Inside, they removed their caps, mopped their faces, rang the counter bell, and called for camera repair. A misshapen Chinese boy in metal leg braces heaved himself through the inner doorway, his braces rapping the cement floor in an uneven rhythm. Grimacing, Jake helped him hang the camera straps on his bony shoulders, and the boy clinked back. They heard adult males talking in Chinese.

"Sounds like they'll fix'em," Egan rumbled. "What's up with that boy? That why you scowled?"

"Polio, wrongly treated by splinting too long," Jake muttered. "Wish I'd had a go at him."

"Your bugaboo. I saw Kenny's book on your table and dipped into it. She's some Boadicea."

"We all have our outrages. Yours is veterans of trench battles telling you where to put coastal cannon. In Brisbane, I saw a polio paralysis case from Rabaul, treated for months here in splints. The desperate parents sent him to Kenny's clinic. White boy, of course, about four. I watched her recover his mobility in a few weeks. Too late for this kid."

They fell silent and looked around. The walls were crammed with photographs of different Chinese traders and German administrators in nineteenth-century suits at a construction site with an Australian army officer, plantation managers and Tolai chieftains.

"Ah Kuan's relatives?" Egan asked.

"Clan credentials," Jake said.

Wooden cabinets with locked glass doors had exquisite lacquer boxes, ivory carvings and Chinese miniature landscapes, while the counter cabinet displayed cameras and film. A magazine rack offered local newspapers in Chinese and English, as well as Life magazine. Prominently displayed was a yellowing framed article in *The Manchester Guardian Australia* reporting massive Japanese atrocities in Nanking, 1937, by their China correspondent Harold Timberley. Even older was a photograph of a young Ah Kuan standing next to a white-haired Chinese man in a western suit under the blue sky, white sun on red earth flag of the Republic of China. The caption read: "Local resident Ah Kuan Ho with visitor King Tse Lai from the Shanghai Theosophical Society, at Rabaul's new concrete Kuomintang Hall. 1927." Ho liked his customers to know what his values were. The smells of old paper and metal cleaners clogged the air.

An elderly woman bustled out with a tray of steaming teacups and sweet rice balls. Jake and Egan sat on stools while they ate. Customers came in, looked around and left. One imperious white woman in a pale blue dress looked, stayed and rang the bell. Jake twisted his neck and saw a houseboy outside carrying two parcels and a furled umbrella. Presumably her servant. When help didn't appear immediately, she called, "Sairviss!". German accent, Jake decided.

The emerging helper wasn't the hobbling boy or the old woman. He was a tall Chinese-Caucasian with a scab on the ridge of his nose and dark circles under his green eyes. Jake jumped up, almost knocking over the teacups. He called out, "Hey there! Glad you're recovering."

The youth went ashen and scurried to the back. They heard a door bang. Egan pushed outside and shouted, "Wass 'up, mate?" He came back, scratching his head. "Sandals slapping down the side alley fast as he could. Well?" He asked Jake.

Jake's mind buzzed. The fleeing youth was Henry Lee, the seaman he'd treated on Zealandia. The ship was long gone. Lee wasn't hurt enough from Bruiser's beating for medical leave. He must have deserted.

Ah Kuan strode out red-faced, his composure gone. He sold the woman two Indian ivory statues and then left, barely acknowledging Jake and Egan. The woman gave the Australian officers a hostile glance.

"What's with our Oriental gent? Last week, he was all bows and smiles," Egan prompted.

"Mistaken identity on my part," Jake murmured. He wasn't ready to report Lee.

Egan frowned. "Thought you docs could tell one coloured bloke from another, unlike the rest of us."

"We're not perfect." Jake laughed uneasily.

"Doesn't make sense," Egan persisted.

Five minutes later, Ah Kuan brought out their repaired cameras, full of smiles and solicitousness. The charge was tiny.

"Why the discount?" Egan asked, slinging the camera bag over his shoulder.

"Good price, everything," Ah Kuan replied, pointing to the sign in the window. "Sign true."

"Get me bargains like this, and I'm your shadow," Egan laughed to Jake outside. He was too excited about his date with a new lady friend in town to give the strange ways of "Oriental gents" another thought.

Back at the truck at Hotel Pacifica, Jake was about to open the door to drive to camp when he stopped. He stared, jingling the keys. Surely not? Lee again!

Lee was now standing on the wide veranda with two men and a native girl. One of the men was Chinese, in a traditional long tunic—aged anything from 45-65. He was talking to a Tolai village man with grizzled grey curls, wearing a red lap-lap. He had a roll of shell money around his neck. His head was thrown back and jaw thrust out. Jake couldn't see more details, but registered substance. Behind him, a young Tolai girl stood. Lee was about to greet her, but instinctively glanced at the street. Seeing Jake standing by an army truck, his mouth opening in surprise, Lee bolted inside.

The men followed, leaving the girl. Calmly, she lit a pipe. Jake was intrigued. He'd been looking for a village girl to photograph for home. Living in urban Melbourne, most Australians had no idea what a colonial city looked like. His brother-in-law Simon had asked for photographs of Rabaul people. There was something compelling about this young woman. Jake waved his camera, took off his cap and bowed. She put down her pipe and sauntered down the two wooden steps and onto the grassy footpath in front of his truck. He clicked and clicked. His camera was black and white, but she was so vivid he hoped to capture the neat blonde streak dividing her crinkly black hair, a joyful cry of varied colours in the patterned lap-lap under her bare breasts. The shape of her nipples suggested she hadn't suckled babies, so she was the Tolai version of a maiden. But hardly modest; she basked in his attention. When he finished the roll, he clapped his thanks. "IaKumu, Anne," she called, obviously expecting him to name her on the prints. *Where's Lee fleeing now?* He wondered as he turned on the engine.

*
**

A few minutes later, Lee reached his uncle's car repair shed, two blocks from Hotel Pacifica and rarely visited by Europeans. Panting, he sat on packed earth and slumped against the shed's wooden wall. Bile filled his throat; he leant over and retched into spiky, shorn grass. Slapping away a mosquito, he rested, roiling with conflicting voices. Accusation: *Ungrateful shit, running away from the doctor who treated you.* Excuse: *No choice after jumping ship.* His most dreaded voice: *A real man would have toughed it out in the Merchant Navy and trusted the hierarchy to stop the beatings.* His cousin's and uncle's consolation: *After Bruiser's beatings and his mates' hatred of us Chinese, only a fool would stay.* Lee let that voice stand for now.

His bruises were fading, the pain just an episodic twinge. But what had stolen his soul was the destruction of his diary, the men's wrong reading of him. Bruiser had shown it to his mates, yelling that the images were all 'fairy', pissed on it and tossed it overboard. Lee felt like nothing. When he'd protested that Bruiser was wrong, the beatings began. Growing up, he'd been a social outcast, left out of everything. His Chinese-white looks came from a white missionary great-grandfather. By contrast, his parents and sister looked pure Chinese. Chinese and white families alike had decided that his family was scandalous, so Lee wasn't included in parties or the football team; he turned to marathon running, a solo affair. This was passive discrimination by exclusion. On Zealandia, he'd suffered active, violent, unprovoked hatred.

'Piebald fairy?' He dreamt nightly of a model's catwalk of beautiful women. The doodles Bruiser called 'fairy' were something else entirely: scrawls expressing the conflict between what his parents wanted him to do and what he dreamed of for himself. Filial disloyalty was a failing too painful for words. They needed him to run their laundry, but he was allergic to the chemicals; he longed to study theoretical science at university. Measuring the world and explaining the measurements to others felt like control. So he doodled: cross-hatched hemmed-in shapes were his parents' needs; wide looped curves were his own.

When war was declared, he'd joined the Merchant Navy out of a surge of patriotism, the expectation of camaraderie, and to postpone the reckoning over his future. It hadn't worked out. Somewhere in Lee's ancestry was a dignified high official whose forbearance of pain made him wise, strong and generous. Lee longed to be that shadow whose blood ran in his veins. As yet, he hadn't been able to touch his spiritual inheritance. He was on a journey but didn't know where. He knew what he didn't want; what he sought was as misty as today's monsoon air.

"Fairy!" He considered the charge. His body went cold and still as he visualised the act. Slightly repulsed, he knew it wasn't for him. Then he remembered his favourite high school science teacher bringing flowering plants to class to demonstrate the range of reproductive techniques. Roses were bisexual; one cucumber plant had male flowers while the other had female flowers; squash had flowers of each sex. "Sex exists on a continuum, with variety," the teacher had enthused to tittering adolescents. After a parent complained, the teacher lost his job. What's good in plants is bad in humans, not to be spoken of, was the message.

The sudden creak of sandals on rickety outdoor stairs cut his reveries. He stood and bowed. His aunt, bent and wizened, was trudging down from the flat above the shed carrying his lunch hamper. She gave him a piece of paper with the licence plates of trucks he was to clean. Her bright eyes twinkled affectionately as she handed him fried fish, paw paw and tea.

He got to work sanding off rust, cleaning and polishing. He felt his muscles ripple wetly under a singlet drenched with sweat. Pausing, he removed the garment, got a drink of water from the shed hose and resumed working. A phrase from childhood ran through his mind.

'Would you tell me, please, which way I ought to go from here?'

'That depends a good deal on where you want to get to,' said the Cat.

'I don't much care where—' said Alice.

'Then it doesn't matter which way you go,' said the Cat.

Alice in Wonderland was one of his favourite books.

Suddenly, he laughed: at life, at himself. He was happy to be alive. Anything, everything, was before him.

An hour later, he uncurled from his stoop and massaged his back. The morning's embarrassment flooded him again, especially that of the Hotel Pacifica, where he had been bowing to the tribal big man, his family's most prominent native client, and his daughter. He'd glimpsed Captain Friedman at the curb and fled.

Sweat ran down his back and groin. His eyes stung, and he was filthy. He missed the bracing sea air and the deck shower hoses, but at least it was time for his lunch. The hamper was on a tree stump beyond paint spatter. As he stretched, a prolonged guttural rattle startled him. Another long rattle, belch-like but not. Was someone about to throw up on his lunch?

He swivelled to grab the hamper. The rattle wasn't coming from a sick human but from a big wingless bird. As the beast pranced at his lunch, Lee's eyes registered black plumage and a long neck with blue and pink patches. He was too late to save his food. The beak wrenched the paper bag open and gulped down the fish and paw paw whole. The bird upended Lee's tea; that drink evidently wasn't up to its standards. "Bastard!" Lee wailed.

"Sori...!" an un-avian voice purred.

Lee turned again. The voice's owner hurried from behind the casuarina tree. Lee stared in astonishment. Here was the Tolai girl, the daughter of the big man he'd greeted at Hotel Pacifica. Had she looked for him? How odd. She was carrying a basket made of coconut leaves. Shyly, she looked away from his gaze, but a rich, full-throated laugh bubbled out of her belly.

The bird had finished Lee's lunch and was pecking at vegetable peelings and dry dog faeces. The girl made rattling guttural sounds. The bird looked up and then pecked at more rubbish. So, the girl and the bird were acquainted. Clearly, it didn't fear becoming anyone's dinner.

Lee began to see the funny side. He started laughing, wincing when his nose hurt. He tried Pidgin. "Pisin bilong yu emi no hairim tok bilong yu!" (Your bird won't listen to you) He wanted to get one up on her, but had no idea how much English she understood. He was hungry.

"IaKumu," she purred, pointing at her heart.

The relentless sun that had tired Lee out while he was working now gave him a crystalline view of her. He hadn't seen her clearly on the shaded veranda. She was breathtaking. He gasped, instinctively bowing. Her face was symmetrical, upper and lower lips equally full under a straight nose, her ears delicate, and one blonde streak on her scalp made her black hair glisten. She showed no shyness about her naked breasts. Her lap-lap was tied below her belly button, and her ebony body was barely sweating, unlike his melting skin. She'd never walked his dream catwalk of beautiful women, but she was better, and she was real. Why was she here? He swallowed, feeling the beginning of an erection under his shorts.

She pointed in the direction of the Bung. "Hairiap na

yumi go baim kaikai." Reaching into her basket, she pulled out a string of shell money. "Food!"

Thanks to God, an English word. She was going to buy him food. It felt pre-determined that he'd follow her.

He attached a hose to the garage tap and washed grime, rust spatter and ash off his bare torso and hair. He felt her black eyes on him. He straightened, letting her look before he put on his shirt. He hoped his slender, well-muscled frame and hairless skin didn't repulse her. Could she possibly like him? Her eyes had eagerness, but what did he know about Tolai feelings?

"Anne," she said, making the sign of a cross. She took a stiffly starched white blouse out of her basket and put it on. "Meri," she said with a grin.

Baptised, he thought, relieved, as they walked to the market. The market vendors, all women, wore white blouses or dresses and were called "Mary" by white shoppers and vendors alike. As they walked, IaKumu managed to convey that her nickname was given to her because she was the best at growing green vegetables.

The bird pranced behind them. At a large truck parked under a tree, IaKumu rattled a low sound as she lowered the back. "ToMuruk, kalap insait lo car" (go into the car), she kept saying. The bird lumbered into the truck bed, folded its legs and hunched. The girl's father must be wealthy, Lee thought. Perhaps he'd bought the truck from Lee's uncle and came to him for maintenance. "Muruk," IaKumu said, pointing at the bird. She puffed out her stomach, one hand shovelling air into her mouth. "Muruk" meant glutton, Lee assumed. He laughed again, delighted that she had a sense of humour.

At the Bung, hectic gossiping and bargaining were in full swing. He looked for Australian soldiers, periodically half-turning as IaKumu/Anne guided him away from the shed where he did his usual hurried shopping. He began to relax; there were no soldiers here. They bypassed piles of cassava, sweet potatoes, carrots, sweet corn in sheaths, tomatoes, and tropical fruits displayed on green palm leaves, past coloured fabrics, baskets, bracelets, sugar cane, nuts and betel nut vendors.

She stopped at a low bamboo table on a patch of grass. Two naked village boys played under a tree. IaKumu greeted the woman. They seemed to know each other. After what sounded like banter, she bargained hard, finally unthreading half her shell money for one huge, boiled egg. She peeled it and pushed it at Lee's mouth. His eyes widened as he chewed and sucked the rich yolk, savouring the scent of palm frond and grass. It was filling, better than his lost fish. *Must be the local delicacy, a brush turkey egg.* Then she bought him roasted chicken wings cooked in coconut sauce. She'd more than made amends.

"White sorcerer emi wokim rong poisen?" (White sorcerer makes a poison against you?) she asked, mixing English and Pidgin.

They were now walking back to the truck. *White sorcerer?* Oh yes, Dr Friedman. Lee's uncle must have explained that the man Lee wanted to avoid was an army doctor.

She mimed taking photographs. "White sorcerer, IaKumu."

That made sense. Any man of taste would want to photograph this compelling girl. IaKumu/Anne's father must have asked about him. "No spell. Very good doctor, heal my wounds." He touched his bruises. "I run away." He made a military salute. Her father would find out he'd deserted; no point in concealing it.

"Emi wokim bigpela, IaKumu, rong poisin." (He is casting a spell to seduce me).

"The white sorcerer? Never. He's a good man."

She shook her head, it seemed impatiently. "Na. Brait prais, bikpela, mari."

Oh, a different 'he.' Is she fifteen, seventeen? Tolai men paid "big fellow" bride prices with financial help from their relatives and were reputed to turn to magic before the marriage. One of their drivers had boasted that he and his friends sang incantations of his noble body parts all night in the Men's Hut over dog's teeth, a pig's tail and secret substances he'd never reveal. The magic worked; his bride couldn't get enough of him. Well, that wasn't working on IaKumu because she called her buyer's magic poison. Lee wished he could save her. "So sorry," he said, suffused with sorrow. Female beauty could be a curse.

At the truck, she took off her blouse. The bird belched from the truck bed. Screened from view by the shade tree, she willed Lee close. He clasped his hands behind his back, forcing himself to resist touching her breasts. He leant forward to brush her lips, his heart a percussion orchestra. She drew away. He stood, leaning, in a bubble of coconut butter, tropical flowers, sweat and pipe tobacco. She rubbed a strand of his hair, an expression of curiosity on her face. Then she stepped back and offered a hand to shake, purring, "Church Michael...Sande?"

She *had* followed him. He was smitten. St Michael's Church, Matupit Island, Sunday.

CHAPTER 13
· · · · · · ·

J AKE WAS EAGER to make the most of his solitude to mull over Henry Lee's extraordinary behaviour and finish his letter home. He opened his tent flap. No solitude; someone was sitting on Egan's bunk. Flinching, he expected the shape to clarify as John Smith, with his fantasies of Japanese spies. A bigger shock: instead of disdain and a monocle, a hunk with cornflower blue eyes, honey-blond hair and a chin dimple uncurled and saluted.

"Captain Alex Whipple!" Jake's heart sang. The nearness of their knees on Zealandia, not touching, pulsed through him. Then terror. Then, a febrile joy. "Why the salute?" is all he managed to say.

"Protocol. I was fined and busted down to lieutenant, which means I salute captains. See, two pips, not three." Ruefully, Wip touched his shoulder. "Two weeks in the brig, dumped into truck maintenance. But it's worth it to put Bruiser out of action. I came to show you how well I've healed. Your stitches were as fine as an oriental tapestry." He leant over, head down.

Jake studied his work. New bristles masked puckers from his stitches. Wip's suntanned skin looked smooth, but that was an illusion; on white skin, a scar would show. However, pale wasn't in the foreseeable future. "I did well. You're a fast healer. But age'll catch up with you. Doctor prescribes less Sir Lancelot."

"Fergetit, mother," Wip chuckled. "Caution is for caution's season. 1941 isn't it. How are you settling in? Sir?"

Jake felt his cheeks grow hot at Wip's implied sarcasm. "I don't have brandy or beer, but let's smoke."

They lit up: a cigarette for Wip and a pipe for Jake. Smoke cut the humidity.

"Medical work's good. I treated the biggest fungi I ever saw. Marvellous. Dickens of a storm my first night." He described the deluge Wip had sat out in jail.

"Camp's on the wrong site," Wip's scoffed. "Glad I'll be at Praed's construction." He paused. "Though I'll be thinking of you."

Thinking of me or the weather? Inside his boots, Jake's toes clenched. *Is he sussing out if I still feel attracted?* Flustered, he coughed out Dunhill smoke. "Well," he said.

"Well," Wip agreed. Pause. "What other news?"

Matching his elusiveness, Jake said, "Listen, we um… became acquainted after Bruiser beat Merchant Seaman Lee. I saw Lee in town today. No uniform, ran away, didn't want to know me. I thought he appreciated us both, and the surgeon who saved his nose. Could he have deserted?"

"Didn't think he'd go that far," Wip exclaimed. He got up, stretching his arms. Jake felt a quickening excitement at the patch of skin the rising shirt bottom exposed. "But now I think about it, I'm not surprised. Not enough support. Desertion's the wrong word. You're civvie, not regular army," Wip continued. "I need to explain that Lee's Merchant Navy, and there's no conscription, so he broke his civvie contract by jumping ship. Very bad in wartime, but not legally desertion. Here's what I know. Bruiser got a medical discharge. I think the kick I gave his jaw finally dished his grey cells. You can only survive so many concussions. Of course, you're the doc." He looked up at the tent roof, lost in thought. When he resumed, Jake heard a bitter edge in his tone. "What's the formula? X blows by Y position divided by .013 time between blows?"

Fear for himself? Jake wondered.

"You had one, right?" Wip asked as he sat. "Our refined doc in a fight? I'll teach you better moves." His sudden smile curved appealingly over his chin dimple; mischief replaced darkness.

"Car crash," Jake said tersely. "I told you." How could Wip have forgotten a single word of their conversations? *Stop being presumptuous,* he checked himself.

"Right, I remember now."

Jake put his pipe on his side table and leant over, head in his hands. He saw Grace crushed by the overturned car he'd been driving. He hadn't told Wip the circumstances of the crash, his rush with the nurses to polio cases; he'd just said, 'car crash' and 'concussion.'

Wip started flicking through Egan's radio communications textbook.

Giving me space. Jake appreciated Wip's finesse. Taking a few breaths, he reverted to the safe topic of Bruiser. "The world's better off with that thug out of the service."

Wip shut the book and lay back on the bunk, puffing contentedly. "He won't have an easy retirement though, not enough service for a pension. He can't do much more than sitting and bellyaching. Got kids. His lawyer told a sob story at the hearing. Tried for a work injury classification. Absurd."

"Hell, yes, after what he did to Lee."

"You haven't heard how it began. Bruiser stole Lee's diary and tossed it overboard, saying it depicted fag stuff. When Lee protested, the beatings started."

"Brute," Jake exclaimed. "The surgeon on Zealandia said that Bruiser sees sparse chest hair on Asian men and says 'fairy'."

"Seems so. Bruiser's lawyer hammered Lee. Did he provoke Bruiser; was his conduct prejudicial to good order?

Military code for naughty boys who like boys..."

Jake was pinned by Wip's blue eyes; he met them.

"Bruiser's defence," Wip continued, lowering his eyes, "was that he was protecting crew discipline. But Lee was definite. 'I'm not that way.' His diary had no English writing; the first page was a Chinese character for a beautiful woman, and the rest were doodles. Bruiser looked at the Chinese character and saw a slatted bed frame and two dicks, and the doodles as phallic. Lee said at the inquiry that if he drew an Australian flag on a flagpole, Bruiser would say it was 'fairy' because of the pole. That dished Bruiser's defence." He paused. "Lee's inclinations were always obvious to me."

You can tell? Jake raised his eyebrows.

"Lee's a good bloke," Wip exclaimed. "He praised you and me. I heard he's AWL."

"Clever retort, the flagpole. I'm glad Lee's feisty. What did the Seamen's Union say?"

"Moment of sanity. Stayed quiet." Wip grinned—the dimple spread.

"So, he jumped ship. At Hotel Pacifica, he was talking to a Tolai village girl. I photographed her."

"Not to report him?"

"No, no. My family wants photos of locals. There was something compelling about her."

"Permission to speak? Sir?"

"No need for sarcasm." Jake grinned. "I'll promote you with Egan's dress coat pips, so we're equal." He reached for Egan's trunk. "Speak, silly."

"Let Lee go." Wip was serious. "He'll have relatives here and disappear into the labyrinth of Chinese businesses. They came as labourers but are now the island's economic engine. Lee's future in the Merchant Navy isn't pretty; Bruiser's got nasty friends. I hate ship-jumpers, but beating Lee wasn't initiation or hazing; it was just plain fag-bashing."

Jake fiddled with his pipe. *He's so comfortable in his skin.*

What about me? "You came to, um, show me you've healed. I'm glad you're here."

"Yep. I'm here. Very nice. Yep."

Jake was on his bunk, Wip was on Egan's, and both of them were breathing lightly. Wip leant forward, his blue eyes giving Jake a message, it felt, of wanting, yet not committed beyond deniability.

A bandicoot scuttled into the tent. Small eyes above a long snout stared wildly at them. It froze and hugged the floor, pouch flopping. "Gravid and confused," Jake mouthed. He pulled a biscuit out of his bag, turned toward the tent entrance and hurled the biscuit outside. The animal trembled to life and charged out after the food. Jake and Wip suddenly burst out laughing in the same second. "Oh dear," Jake giggled. "It'll get diarrhoea." As they laughed, Wip shifted his hips. Invitation?

Jake forced his cement-weight body upright and stood behind Wip, teetering on the bank of his Rubicon. *Can I swim?* He massaged Wip's shoulders, then ran a finger down his spine, feeling a delicious, slow arousal in himself.

Wip twisted into Jake's palms with a deep sigh.

Heart bashing his ribs, Jake closed the tent flaps. "Derek's got a date; gone for hours.

Wip's face radiated relief. "Ah, I wished and wondered and wanted, but wasn't sure."

Jake's heart raced faster.

Their lips brushed, and then tongues pushed into welcoming mouths. Wip's complex scent thrilled Jake— deodorant powder escaping his shirt's vinegar/rice of laundry starch; shower water tainted with sulphur and rough army soap on his skin; tea and tobacco on his tongue. A forest of the smells of *him*. He put his hand on Wip's chest, feeling the crinkly hairs move beneath the cotton. "Yes," Wip murmured.

As they began to undress, Jake's every pore was alert with desire. They took in each other's naked wholeness and hugged, ears attuned to the sounds of work outside, the risk of discovery adding titillating anxiety. *This can't be happening.* Jake felt he was in an alternate existence, a character in a scene cut from a Hollywood movie, the spools of forbidden love strewn on the floor. Wip guided Jake back to his bunk.

Shyness. *What now?* With a sense of wonder, they kissed and stroked for magic pleasure spots. Shivering with excitement, Jake spread Wip's foreskin.

"Ah, my first Jewish man," Wip groaned. "Your touch is exquisite, strong, earth-shaking…"

The bunk shook slightly. Startled, Jake took his hand away. "Noooo, sorry. It's an earth tremor. Not your Jewish Don Juan." Elemental Rabaul joined them in bed.

They lay still on the unstable bunk, lust fighting to stay alive, adrenalin telling them otherwise. Soft rattles sounded under the earth—had sensing the tremor sent that bandicoot into the tent? Wip drew Jake to him "This isn't bad. There's time."

After, they collapsed into an entwined tangle, Wip lying on Jake's arm, Jake's ankle over Wip's calf. Time stopped for Jake as he savoured the whole scent of Wip's salt/sweat/musk, the delicious weight of Wip mixed up with him. But it was seconds. The bunk shook. It felt impossible to drag on shorts and boots, but they had to.

"Gotta rush to Praed, sorry, fix dangerous loose wires," Wip muttered, tying his boot laces. "You're wonderful. Find a private place?"

In a daze, Jake nodded. "Is it alright for sex to be… a bit silly?" He felt somehow the earth tremor was his fault; a sense of separateness and differences tiptoed in, settling on their boots.

Wip embraced him. "The best." He ran outside.

Jake tried to take in what had just happened. Could he really have a boyfriend after all those hopeless adolescent dreams?

"Wowee!" Wip's voice came from several yards away.

Jake joined him. The field was a tangle of fallen tents and clothes lines. Everyone was picking up. Beneath their feet, there was a rumble, then another tremor. The flagpole rocked and settled. Wip ran to his truck, gunned the engine and manoeuvred around a rut.

Tremors intensified over the next few days, beginning a cycle of damage and repair. Jake treated cuts and sprains so repetitively that he lost track of what day it was. But his focus wasn't on the calendar, the injuries or the weather. In every spare moment, he called up Wip's kisses. What a discovery for a 30-year-old who thought such pleasures could never be his. With Wip in his life, he felt, was it invincible? No, invulnerable. No, *complete.* He got a discreet message from Wip at Praed Point saying he'd found a place. The note sent him into visions of a lifetime together: Wip creaky with arthritis, Jake grey-haired and asthmatic, but both happy. Where are they? Rabaul: a house with paw paw and mango trees, far from the volcanoes. He has a medical practice, while Wip grows rich from coffee and runs a dance school.

Then he'd push the visions away. Why was he so quick to commit? *Who am I?* He'd proposed to Esther after two nights of successful lovemaking. He loved her. Or did he? How much was gratitude? He'd told her about his conflicted desires, but she wanted him as a family man. Making a Jewish family was the ultimate virtue. Esther/Wip: he was a walking contradiction. As he went from bandaging to drills, he thought, *This'll be sorted after the war.*

CHAPTER 14
· · · · · · · ·

H ENRY LEE BARELY SLEPT on Saturday night, excited about his Sunday meeting with the fascinating IaKumu. A date at a church; what would that be like? Ever since she'd asked him to go to Matupit Island, he'd been the good sailor and studied the map. A mile long and narrow, it was near the natural hot springs—would she take him there for a soak? There was a stretch of warm, heaped volcanic soil across Matupit Harbour, where certain Matupit men had the right to dig out buried bush turkey eggs. Perhaps a fresh egg? His mouth watered, re-tasting the richness she'd pushed into his mouth. Did her relatives have title to egg-lands harvesting? Otherwise, Matupit looked crowded: three churches of different denominations, schools and a cemetery; a few descent groups in different villages; rocky beaches busy with fishing canoes. He did not let himself dwell on her tantalising breasts, which he'd worked hard not to touch. By Saturday night, he was tingling with tomorrow's mystery so much that he turned, sweated, and couldn't calm his breathing.

Before dawn, he gave up and went to the kitchen to make tea. To his surprise, his cousin Ah Kuan Ho was sitting at the table in pyjamas and a dressing-gown. Tea was brewing, and there were a few newspapers in front of him. Reading upside down, Lee got an impression of thick black headlines screaming

Japan-occupied Indochina. The usually genial Ah Kuan greeted Lee with only a frown.

Lee waited for his cousin to speak, praying that nothing would disrupt his day.

"You can do more than polish cars," Ah Kuan finally said. "Now I think, you're a sailor, the right man for what I need today."

Bile soured Lee's mouth. "Sir, I'm honoured to help you. Um, I'm due at St Michael's Church this morning."

His cousin gave him a speculative stare. "Due? First Sunday you've shown interest in attending church; Catholic at that. Aren't you Church of England?" He drummed his fingers on the table. Lee had noticed that Ah Kuan spoke smoother English at home than when he interacted with Europeans or Australians. Strategy? He was a man with many layers. He held his breath, hoping Ah Kuan wouldn't ask for an explanation.

After a minute, Ah Kuan took a photograph from his dressing-gown pocket. "See this broken fishing float? I want you to go to Nordup and Vulcan Beach. Show native fishermen the photo and ask if they've picked any up. I'll buy them. Come to my bedroom, and I'll give you a string of shell money."

Nordup and Vulcan Beach were miles from Lee's meeting place with IaKumu, respectively east and west of Rabaul. Desperation closed in on him like an ellipse blotting out the sun. "Sir, have you inquired at Matupit? They fish both sides of the island." His pulse raced as his eyes met another appraising stare. After an awkward silence, Ah Kuan nodded. "Very well. Start there."

Lee tried to conceal the immensity of his relief. "Sir, may I ask why you would pay for this rubbish?" He hadn't seen any sign of whimsy in his driven, practical cousin.

"No," Ah Kuan answered snappishly. "It may not be what I think." The electric light accentuated puffy dark circles under his eyes.

"Should I worry, sir?"

"No." Ah Kuan collected himself. "Enjoy your Sunday."

An hour later, it was low tide, and the causeway linking the mainland to Matupit Island was walkable. Grateful that his cousin had given him absolution to relish the day, Lee took the three miles from the house in Chinatown to St Michael's on foot. Early morning fragrances teased his nose—sweet grass, salty sea air and dead crabs.

Fishermen were already at sea. He found one old man sitting on the sand, mending a net. When Lee showed him the photo and shells, the old man drew away, rolling his eyes. *He thinks I'm a mad foreigner,* Lee decided, turning toward the church.

Despite his good looks, Henry Lee had never been with a woman. Growing up in Melbourne, he'd faced discrimination from whites and Chinese alike. His green eyes and Caucasian physique came from a white grandfather in mainland China, but his parents and sister looked pure Chinese. The disparity in their looks fed speculation that the family was scandalous; people avoided socialising with him and the family. He knew there was a freer world out there. When war had broken out, he'd enlisted in the Merchant Navy. His parents had hugged him tearfully and given him the names of relatives in Rabaul, perhaps even relieved to see him go. Now, he sensed that this beautiful native girl might actually like him. It was an unfamiliar delight.

He reached the simple, wood-framed church after the service had begun; wood and glass vibrated with exuberant song. Nervous, he walked around the Parish building and looked at the nearby houses with their cultivated gardens before entering. It was a pleasant spot.

Pulling in his trim stomach muscles, he entered a full church: men and boys in lap-laps, white singlets or shirts; naked toddlers; and women in lap-laps and blouses or dresses. But no IaKumu. During the two-hour mass—hymns in the local tongue, an interminable sermon in Pidgin at which adults nodded wisely—he craned his neck for her. He had a terrible thought: was she there and he didn't recognise her? What an insult! But tumbling into the sunshine at the longed-for end, he realised that she truly wasn't there.

He cursed himself for a sucker; she'd played him for a fool. He cursed himself a second time. The tide would have risen, and he couldn't walk back; he'd have to pay for a ride. He patted the photo and purse in his pocket. There were fishermen on the other side of the island, Simpson Harbour.

Depressed, he started walking. After a few minutes, he stopped. Beyond the last garden, someone was waving a white cloth. For him? Straightening from his slouch, he followed the figure into the woods. His body came to life again; he recognised the slight swagger of IaKumu's hips. And there she was. She'd quickly climbed a tree again. She was sitting on a v-shaped branch of a frangipani tree, waving her blouse. Once on the ground, she led him into an enveloping world of palm, banana and kapok trees, the trunks hugged by parasitic vines. She'd cleared leaves under a solitary bukubuk tree and set out a cloth and woven basket. The fierce sunlight outside the church filtered through layers of leaves, draping them in a dappled magic. A secluded jungle spot on this crowded island seemed improbable, yet she'd found it. She hadn't brought her bird.

While she set out nuts, cucumbers, bananas, and sugar cane juice, Lee looked from her bare-breasted torso as she bent over the cloth, to the tree canopies, and then back to her in wonder. He roused himself to swat away insects. His heart banged, stopped, banged. Here was the compelling beauty of his memory, not his imagination.

"I looked for you at mass. Where were you?" A breeze whiffled and shifted leaves, allowing sunlight to hit her face. He looked into her eyes. Was it his fantasy, or were they thirsty? For him? His brain was gritty with a lack of sleep. Had she understood his words? He longed to hear her full-throated laugh again.

Instead of laughing, she crossed herself, smiled and looked down. "Anne forr..i..en a'ready."

He burst out laughing. *What a marvellous girl! Forbidden/ Forgiven? She'd come earlier and got absolved.* Their lips brushed, nibbled, and then opened. She sighed with pleasure. The nuts and fruit lay untouched. *Could this be the day I lose my virginity? Oh, bliss!* Tentatively, he put a hand on her breast, stroked, and then kissed her nipples. She pulled him close, arms around his shoulders, buried her nose in his hair and kissed his head. He thrilled to her touch. He felt himself getting hard and very long under his trousers.

He pulled away. "I've never done this," he muttered in Pidgin.

She touched her crotch and said, "Mary," meaning virgin.

In magazines, he'd read something about withdrawal. She was encouraging him, but no, he must be honourable, a gentleman; he'd never take advantage of any woman, especially a virgin. And what about the intended husband she didn't want to marry? He widened the physical distance between them. She looked down, sighing. *Shamed?* he wondered. He steepled his hands and bowed his head. She nodded and smiled. They brushed away ants exploring their food and ate in shy silence, allowing their desire to subside.

He felt a stab of alarm when she put on her blouse. "Meet here Sunday?" he stammered, "Please?" It felt like a life/ death question.

After offering her hand to shake, she laughed a "yes" and then strode toward St Michael's Church. He watched her disappear into a thicket of flowering bushes. *A perfect frame for her beauty,* he thought, trembling with excitement, adoration, frustration, regret and fear. *What am I getting into?* He spilt his lust onto a banana leaf and used dripping moisture from above to wash.

On the beach, he found four fishermen killing their catch. He pulled out the photo. After shrugs, puzzled looks and giggles, one man struck his forehead with his palm. He began talking excitedly to the others and then pointed out to sea in the direction of New Ireland island. Lee paid him for the information and a ride to the mainland.

Back at the house in Chinatown, he found Ah Kuan in his office. He tried to paint seriousness and dignity on a face suffused with the thrills and possibilities of the day. "There may be one of these floats picked up on New Ireland, sir. Here are the unspent shells."

"Well done," his cousin replied, offering no explanation of his need for broken stray fishing floats. He gave Lee an appraising glance and waved him out. "You have happy day at church, huh? No scrapes. Your uncle making plans for you."

He saw right through me? Lee's stomach clenched. *Plans?*

CHAPTER 15
·········

FOR THE MEN of the 2/22, June 6 started unremarkably. The groundwater felt warmer, and the tea tasted more metallic than usual, but no one thought much about it. Wip was still at Praed, and Jake waited impatiently to hear about the place he'd found. Other soldiers daydreamed about girlfriends, boasted about being sports champions, and compared parties in town.

Then everything changed. After morning inspection, with a cataclysmic roar, thick grey-white ash whooshed out of Tavurvur volcano. Soon, warm ash swirled and fell, draping vehicles, tents, radio antennae and telephone cables with a toxic blanket. The phone went down, and the radio was all static. Whooshing eruptions continued.

"Black silver," Egan rasped to Jake, coughing spasmodically after an emergency cleaning of the antennae and cables. "But the geo bloke says lava won't reach us. First call Carr made after I fixed the wires." Egan tended to overhear things after a repair. "Hafta check it works. Perk of the job," he'd grin as he repeated some titbit. He and Jake were in ponchos, scraping viscous muck off their tent. Then, they cleaned and oiled their guns for the second time. "That Ah Kuan's getting rich off our laundry. No wonder he flashes his gold-tooth grin at us."

"C'mon, you liked him when he fixed our camera for pennies," Jake retorted.

During the second night, clattering, bangs and rumbling woke them. "Was the geo bloke wrong?" Jake yelled in alarm. He and Egan rushed outside. A garish red glow tinted the tent's sides. They joined a crowd of soldiers staring in wonder. Against a pitch-black sky, a white-orange flame soared skywards, followed by gush after gush of molten red. It seemed to reach 20,000 feet before falling back on the mountain slope.

They alternated between the canteen, for company, and running outs to see more blows. The lava didn't look like it would reach them, but it inspired awe. In the canteen, Jake joked, "I hear that the natives say evil spirits live in Tavurvur and the other blowers. Is night the spirits' mating hour?"

"Some foreplay," Egan laughed, slapping his thigh. "You have funny taste." He blew his nose, showing the black snot on his handkerchief around.

"Train rattling across a rickety bridge," a soldier said. "When will we get a proper night's sleep?" Everyone grumbled, "hear, hear!". Faces sagged in exhaustion.

"Why aren't we on higher ground?" Robinson demanded—everyone's question.

In the morning, they met novel debris: blobs of pink glassy lava on just-cleaned trucks, tents and paths. "Let's paint'em and make checkers sets, sell to tourists," a soldier grumbled as he picked balls off the path.

Rumours fluttered and swirled that the camp would soon move. "That elevated plain the other side of Rabaul you noticed, sir, the morning I drove you to camp," Robinson told Jake, when he limped to the hospital tent with a sprained ankle.

"I hope it's not just a wish," Jake responded.

Egan hadn't heard anything yet over the wires. Still, morale improved as work crews slogged through daily cleanups.

After a third exhausting day and night, Jake was inspecting a stalk of dried kunai grass at the camp perimeter when he saw

Priscilla, the nurse, walking swiftly toward him, deftly dodging the hardening lava blobs that strewed the ground.

"Look, sister," he exclaimed. "Ash is killing the vegetation. But here's something exquisite." He pointed to a wild orchid nestled at the base of a palm tree, a rich blooming purple amidst brown. "That little critter found a refuge. Go, brave orchid! Hey, what's up?"

"Can you help?" Priscilla blurted out. She started crying noisily.

"Come now," Jake murmured, embarrassed. "You'll feel better in time." The nurses were still forbidden to work in the hospital tent, but Jake, a traditional male, attributed her new distress to a broken romance. "Forget him."

She glared at him. "There's no 'him'."

"Sincerest apologies. I misunderstood. I'll help in anything medical."

"We have two problems. First, we *must* work. The new camp hospital is our chance."

"I agree. The second?"

"We're facing dishonourable discharge when we go home."

"What?" Jake was shocked. "What? How can that be? What on earth is someone saying you did wrong?"

"The uniforms. We cut the sleeves and got rid of the stockings."

"Exactly the right thing in this heat," Jake affirmed.

"A horrid planter's wife who knows our matron complained that we'd defiled the King's uniform. Defiled! All we want is to nurse patients. Matron in Sydney wrote that we must reinstate army-issue uniforms or...as I said. Chief doc won't intervene."

Jake couldn't help himself; he laughed at the sheer absurdity of the complaint. "Your matron's an ignoramus. No idea of tropical fungi and ulcers. Alright, it's gone too far. I'll write you a note."

In his tent, a small shake rattled the table. His pen stabbed across the paper. "Séance," he chuckled.

Priscilla laughed at the jagged scrawl, her green eyes crinkling amidst drying tears. "Or the mountain's evil spirit," she offered.

It took him three tries to get a clean note. He recommended short sleeves and bare legs for health reasons and added that soldiers' recovery from tropical maladies and injuries from volcanic activity could be accelerated by help from the nurses. "Seance done. Did I channel Pasteur? Good luck."

Priscilla gave him a grateful kiss. After an awkward second, she said, "We're going to the Regent for a film tomorrow. Would you like to come with me?"

Jake hesitated. He was on edge, waiting to hear from Wip. "How kind, but please don't think I wrote the note to, um, t...take advantage of you," he murmured. Nonplussed, Priscilla left, letting the misunderstanding stand.

The next evening, Jake had an encounter as enchanting as seeing his orchid. At the camp tip, he was dumping rubbish from their tent, balancing against shaking ground, when a big flightless bird charged out of the ash-spattered forest. It ran about several times in a daze, then stopped and gave Jake an appraising stare. It was a small cassowary with a bright blue and red neck. *The island's native species*, he recalled, the dwarf cassowary. It uttered a long guttural rattle and advanced on him. *Has it been feeding here? Oh, I get it: ash is covering its scraps.* "Not my fault," he said. Another low, long rattle. *We're talking!* Jake thought, delighted. *I'm supposed to do something.*

He fished at the bottom of the tip for worms, beetles and maggots thriving since the army came. He grabbed a handful of squirming somethings and offered them to the bird. It hopped warily from one powerful foot to the other. Then, with a swift swoop, it grabbed dinner with a rough snap on his hand and ran into the trees. Jake inspected his palm; the skin was reddening—he'd have a bruise. Chuckling, he decided to add a pet dwarf cassowary to his fantasy life with Wip.

Back in his tent, he found a note: "Back. W." Jake's skin tingled.

CHAPTER 16

"Y EP," WIP PUFFED, sliding out from under a car chassis, his face oily and red. "Gotta place."

Jake had looked for him at the vehicle maintenance shed near Q Store so they could coordinate their time off. "Vegetable or mineral?" he asked, meaning a secluded place in the woods or a vacant house in town. He hoped for a house. Privacy was hard to come by; the normal solution of a hotel room was too dangerous for them.

Wip laughed. "I've been busy. A leafy retreat near Praed."

He'd slashed a track up South Daughter to where he thought he might find volcanic caves. Having run a coffee plantation on a mainland New Guinea mountain, he believed he could read the terrain. Creepers and ferns angling inward were his clue. He'd poked and ripped, and found the entrance to a cave. His labour was an act of faith; he had no idea if his fastidious doctor lover would go inside. He did a preliminary sweep, apologising to scuttling beetles, centipedes and nipping spiders whose webs he swatted.

Two days later, Jake's eyes widened at the diamond-shaped hole and moss-slicked rocky entrance. "In here? Well, there won't be competition for a bed. At least I know how to treat snake bites."

"No snakes, promise. Bats are over there." Wip pointed at a dead tree trunk and a distant tangle of rock and ferns.

After manoeuvring over uneven rocks, Jake turned and looked wistfully at the sunlit green abundance they were leaving. Wip's torch pulled them deeper. Finally, his feet found flat ground. Arms outstretched met air in every direction.

"You found a biggie," Jake marvelled. Wip shone his torch around the oval space. He'd erected a one-sided tent supported by a six-foot pole, covered the ground with a tarpaulin, and put a sleeping bag inside the tent. Sweet-scented frangipani flowers lay around the sides.

"Romantic. A threshold?" Jake grinned.

They touched palms. "You're a tad heavy for that," Wip said, pulling Jake into a hug. Jake buried his face in Wip's soft neck and shirt collar.

"Truthfully," Wip continued, "frangipani mask decomposing insects."

"You did all this on faith?" Jake asked as they stepped into the tent and sank onto the sleeping bag.

"Faith in your desire, at least." Wip lit two Tilley kerosene lamps outside the tent. They sat, watching the lamplight dance shadows across the dark rock.

Jake pointed at a tall bottle. "What's that?"

Wip handed it to him.

"Huvet cognac? Not medicinal brandy. Where did you get it?"

"New Guinea Club, town's most exclusive." They drank, passing the bottle back and forth. The smoky sandalwood/jasmine liquid slid silkily down Jake's throat, leaving a pleasant coating on his tongue. What's the other bottle?"

"Lemon musk oil from Hotel Pacifica; didn't want local coconut stuff for this, um, not baptism of course...um, debut."

"Man knows how to court," Jake murmured, feeling flushed.

"Circumcision's magnificent," Wip giggled. "Ruined me for Christians forever."

"Playing aficionado today?"."

Wip looked down, busily opening the massage oil.

Secrets, Jake realised. He unbuttoned Wip's shirt and worked oil into Wip's back.

"Remind me—" Wip purred, "oh, that's *so* relaxing—to tell you about Lee. Resourceful bloke, I had to laugh. Later…" Wip turned. Tracing a finger across Jake's lips—lower, upper, pause; upper, lower. "Pagan god's mouth," he murmured.

Jake's lips moistened under the soft pad. Touching Wip's belt buckle, Jake asked, "Yes?"

"You bet." Wip slid his pants and underwear off and lay down. "Don Juan, I succumb to your charms…" He arched.

"Are you sure?" Jake asked, nervous.

"Yeah, oh yeah."

"My first time…I hope…forgive me…" Jake probed Wip's arse with his finger—it was pristine and becoming slick. *He gave himself an enema. I didn't even think of it.* Jake was three people: a bumbling kid terrified of doing badly, an erotic animal meeting Wip's heat with his own, and a doctor registering a tiny something. *A well-trafficked passage.* He was awed, not jealous; Wip lived in a world he didn't know.

"Nirvana," Wip gasped when they reached satiation.

Wrapped around each other, they dozed. After a while, still drowsy, Wip stretched his arm for the cognac, and they drank again. Blood thrummed in Jake's veins. Light-headed, he risked a question. The desire to understand Wip scuttled around his brain like a wary mouse; ask it this way, no that. Not about the tiny internal scar he'd felt—not perforation but atypical—that would be using his professional knowledge to take advantage of Wip. "Umm," he drawled, his voice an octave lower than normal and gritty, "I've always wondered how you kept your nose and cheek bones unbroken. I've never treated a fighter with an intact face."

Wip eased away, not meeting Jake's eyes but pinning his gaze on the orange-yellowed rock near the Tilley lamps' flames and the eerie blue-blackness beyond. Jake felt Wip curl into himself. With an edgy grin, Wip said, "There's a clearing nearby. Let's barbecue fish next time." Unspoken was "I don't question you."

They smoked, Jake's pungent pipe tobacco mingling in his nostrils with Wip's bland Camel.

"Oh, for a Gauloise!" Wip suddenly snorted, spitting out a tobacco flake.

"Players not good enough?" Jake quipped. He felt bad for seeming intrusive and frustrated. *Paris secret,* he decided. *I haven't mentioned Esther,* he reminded himself, as a psychic distance between them opened.

He'd written to her, hinting that something he'd relegated to his past had resurfaced, staying oblique enough to beat the censor; he wanted absolute honesty between them. The letter came back "Moved. Address Unknown." He assumed she'd enlisted. Since their engagement was informal, he had no one to ask.

He was relieved when Wip pivoted. "About Lee. I told you he'd have relatives here. I saw him when I bought the oil. He couldn't have been friendlier; he must realise you didn't report him. He's found love, so happy he glows neon, hinted it was the daughter of a Tolai big man…"

Jake sat up. "Bet she's the girl I photographed. He won't be able to boss her around. She has a determined look." He laughed.

"Chinese-Tolai marriages aren't unprecedented," Wip commented. "Ah Tam, the first rich Chinaman, married a chief's daughter last century."

"Is the name a coincidence? The owner of the camera store where Lee was working is Ah Kuan Ho."

"Could be a descendant," Wip mused. "Or Ah Kuan could have taken the name 'Ah' as a business brand. Ah Tam's a local hero. Lee's smart." He looked at his watch. "Sorry to tell you, but your fungi and my broken brakes await."

"Nooo. Can't be. Ahhh, it's been…words are useless."

Slowly, reluctantly, they dressed. Navigating the track, they turned periodically to watch branches for pythons.

"How do I say goodbye?" Jake pulled Wip into a long kiss at the track entrance.

"You don't. Say ninety-five hours, fifty-four minutes to reunion, less every second."

Jake let Wip go ahead of him. Watching the swing of Wip's lanky frame, Jake didn't feel alone; his whole body tingled with the imprint of Wip's touch. It was wondrous.

CHAPTER 17
••••••••

LIEUTENANT COLONEL CARR announced that a fixed-structure base named Malaguna Camp would be built on an elevated plain on the other side of Rabaul, the place Jake and Robinson had spotted as a good site. It would be complete in October. Palmer's hospital would move into Government House with full staffing of doctors, orderlies and nurses. Tavurvur's eruptions were so disruptive that the civilian headquarters was moving out of Rabaul. Government House would be given to the army. The nurses were ecstatic.

Priscilla found Jake updating his charts and hugged him. "The patients always wanted us, as you said. Now we learn that the orderlies and other doctors wanted us, too, but couldn't petition openly. Only Palmer's miffed. You helped us."

Jake beamed, patting his captain's pips. Back in his tent, he settled down to write home.

June 22,

Dear Tal, Mirrie and Simon,

I am enjoying Rabaul, although that will seem strange to you if you've read about recent volcanic activity. It keeps me humble, being up against nature. Many Melbourne boys are here, so I expect The Age *and* Argus *have written exaggerated articles about lava. Don't worry. There are few serious injuries because we know what to do. We're moving to a regular base soon. Sometimes, I wonder how anyone could attack us; they'd be too busy brushing ash out of their eyes. Those Salvo bandsmen, you heard, play here in parades, and they're the town's darlings...*

He paused, pen raised. Should he mention Wip? He had to, for Tommy and Sally Whipple's sake.

Do you still see Tommy and Sally Whipple? I met an Alexander John Whipple, who said he's a relative. He said he wants to help them after the war. Let me know if Monica wants me to give him their address.

There was a disagreement between the army nurses and higher-ups, not a medical issue. I can't say more, but rest assured, Tal and Mirrie, your well-trained brother supported the nurses. Their righteous cause prevailed. I took the enclosed photograph with the camera you gave me. Fairly typical example of a village woman I saw in Chinatown. Her demeanour impressed me. Note the bleach stripe in her hair and bare torso. Tolai employed in town or at missions cover their chests. Simon, I hope this satisfies your curiosity. Rabaul is very different from Melbourne...

He was about to sign it when Egan burst in, his body vibrating with excitement, his face blue from holding his breath.

"Breathe! It's free," Jake exclaimed.

Egan exhaled. "Listen. You know I'm Mr Fix-it, cables, right? Well, what I heard this morning... War Cabinet in Melbourne talkin' to Carr. Checkin' reception, see, make sure all's working...didn't mean to eavesdrop, but this changes things...Had to hold it in 'til confirmation...just came. Another check, see? It'll be broadcast in five minutes. Come listen. Gotta find maps." He rushed out, heading for the Salvation Army stack of books, maps and magazines.

Whistles, shouts and a bugle sounded outside. "Broadcast! 1700 hours. The Mess!"

Jake put the letter on his table. News that couldn't wait for the morning newspapers? He wished Wip was at camp, but he was back at the Praed gun emplacement construction site. A few seconds later, he was propelled by bodies pounding into the mess. To cheers, the music tag for the Australian Broadcasting Commission News came over the radio. Egan had done a good job cleaning the antenna. Some of his mates clapped him on the back. Mercifully, Tavurvur cooperated, emitting just one cough.

The announcer's voice was plummy BBC English, but with the flattened vowels that pegged him as Australian, despite his careful consonants.

"Yesterday, on Sunday, 22 June, at dawn, German forces crossed the Russian border. They appear to be mounting a major offensive. The Wehrmacht had been massing at the Polish border with Russia for some time, but due to the non-aggression treaty between the Nazis and the Soviet Union, this blitzkrieg appeared to be a surprise attack. The treaty was signed in August 1939 and was believed by the Allies to serve the temporary interests of both dictators.

"There are unconfirmed reports of heavy Luftwaffe bombing and Russian divisions already fleeing. The Soviet leader, Josef Stalin, has not made a statement. His whereabouts are not known to the Allies. There has been no statement from the Politburo...'

"Blimey!"

"Bloody amazin'!"

Exclamations drowned out the droning account of cataclysmic events. "Shut ya gobs!" finally quietened the excitement.

Egan waved an atlas. "Map. We'll look after…"

"In other war news, our heroic 9th Division led by Lieutenant-General Sir Leslie Morshead is still holding Tobruk in Egypt. Our boys alone have stopped Rommel's Panzers and Luftwaffe from capturing the strategic port city, denying the Nazis open passage to Cairo. In April, our 9th Division was ordered to hold Tobruk until Allied forces under General Auchinleck could counterattack. By God, they're, we're, doing it! Pray for them all."

The announcer's voice shook. It sounded like he was choking back tears.

"Rommel's second assault last week seems to have failed. Donations to the Red Cross are urgently needed for our prisoners-of-war." He gave the addresses of the charity.

There was static, a pause, then a local announcer read local news: expected shipping, estimates of the year's copra revenue, scheduled road repairs, festivals and upcoming events in town, and the winner of the last swim meet. Rail service between Rabaul and the Native Hospital had ended, affecting mostly natives; a bus would replace it.

An officer turned off the radio, and the cook announced dinner. Everyone in queues or on the long benches became an expert tactician, shouting over their mates.

"Isn't Kraut doctrine no two-front wars? They just opened a second front with no provocation."

"What second front? Europe's under Jerry's heel. Heil Hitler will cut through Russia like bayonets through butter."

"Won't be that easy..."

Egan made the round of benches with his map. Hitler's priority targets were boisterously disputed. "Hush up," he yelled, standing on a chair so he could be seen. "My opinion: we're the first front, Russkies the second. The RAF beat the Luftwaffe last year, kiboshing Jerry's invasion for a year. Brits got 300,000 regulars back from Dunkirk in ordinary blokes' boats. Saved the country. Our 9th Division's holding Rommel, first time Wehrmacht's stalled on land. Our boys are showin' Jerry can be stopped."

"C'mon Egan," Corporal Jim Robinson cut in. Jake turned and nodded to the chatty officer who'd driven him to camp on his first day. "Not being invaded doesn't make a front. Motherland can't do anything active. More to the point, how does this Russian invasion affect us?"

Egan ran his finger across Russia, "Place's huge. They'll fight their women, too. There's weather. Russkies'll see from us to stay the course. I say party up! Jerry's busy up north. I know Nazi doctrine is to retake New Guinea, but they won't right now."

A voice from the back of the canteen drawled flatly, "Some Lutheran missionaries wear swastika armbands."

Jake turned. He stiffened. It was John Smith from Zealandia, complete with monocle and wintry expression.

"We'll keep an eye on them," Egan declared. "No worries."

Smith said nothing more. Egan sat next to Jake. "Odd bloke. You know him?" Jake rolled his eyes as Egan downed a beer. "Glad that's off me chest."

Groups argued and drank for hours. Tobacco smoke swirled while fly papers filled with squirming insect bodies. Jake joined some of his recent patients. Instead of the brag "Little Hell, here we come," he heard: "Shit. I wanted to ram this,"—a middle finger—"up Jerry's ass!", "9th boys'll grab all the medals!" and "Fuck this backwater. Local sheilas aren't even kind." This with a sour wink.

"You're spoilt kids who got your sister's present from Santa," Jake retorted, surprised by the vehemence of their let-down. "Tobruk's no gift from the reindeer's basket." He stayed far from Smith.

"Now, now," a major said, walking between benches. "We're here to protect the pounds, shillings and pence of copra, vital to the home coffers that pay you. Russia's misery lessens the German threat here, which is good for business. Don't think I don't know a bunch of you signed up for the six bob a day, twice what your British brothers get paid. I know you want to fight. That's commendable. But when you accept party invitations…" He waved a handful of name cards. "No whining." He handed out the cards, repeating his orders.

During a pause—everything that could be said about Hitler, Stalin, Mussolini and Churchill had been chewed over—with yawning men and some nurses getting up to leave, a lonely high-pitched voice cut in, "What about Japs?" It was Robinson again. "If Jerry's busy up north, the south's open."

Egan turned several pages to Micronesia. "I read up on it this afternoon." He pointed to former German island colonies in the Pacific Ocean given to Japan by the Treaty of Versailles of 1919 as colonial mandates. "Mariannas, Palau, Marshalls, Carolinas, Truk." Tiny dots strung like a sagging washing line north of the equator. "Poor land made by underwater volcanoes." He pointed to French Indochina. "Now under Japanese control."

"Exactly," Robinson affirmed.

"Nuts," another officer laughed. "Those little men with thick eyeglasses can't threaten a European army. Time for bed." With that, many yawned and left.

Egan turned to Robinson. "OK, Corporal, the floor's yours."

Robinson took the map, swelling with his minute of fame. "Do either of you ladies have lipstick?" he asked the two nurses still here. One pulled out a stick. Facing his audience, the atlas page facing them, Robinson traced with his finger a shoe-like shape around the Japanese islands, with their internationally recognised waters. He paused, then drew a red circle on each island. "Red dots are the Japs' Rising Sun flag." Holding the book by his chin, he used his other hand to point northwest of the Japanese possessions: "American Philippines," then southeast, "British Singapore, Malaya, etc." He fingered an imaginary oval west, "French islands." Blobs south and southwest, "Australia's and New Zealand's mandated territories.

"Crazy quilt of colonies stupider than a five-year-old would draw. Jap possessions are the only coherent bunch, a bit like a shoe: toe nudging the Philippines, heel the Brit colonies, sole, us. Jap islands are poor in natural resources compared to the others. That's alright while everyone's on the same side, as we were in 1919. Today? Maybe geography means more than resources."

Jake leant forward, fascinated. "Are you suggesting that

if the toe kicks up and the heel and sole stamp down, we could be the front line?"

"I don't know, sir." Robinson shrugged. "It was a school project. I learnt map reading in the Scouts. I'm sure our government has it under control."

Everyone became an expert tactician again: "Japs are eviscerating parts of China.", "China's backward.", "Japs illegally fortified their islands. No one's allowed to fly over or inspect. We didn't fortify, obeyed the rule.", "Don't worry. We're the 2/22, Little Hell. Bring it on!", and "Robinson, you can put lipstick on a shoe, but it's still a shoe. Maybe even a slipper, ha, ha! Japs can't do diddly-squat; supply lines are too long. Yanks are sittin' hard on'em."

The nurse retrieved her lipstick, scraped off the top layer, and put it away. The nurses left after a last beer. The remaining debaters passed the map around. Jake saw John Smith leave quietly, smoking a pipe.

"I'm just a doctor," Jake asked. "I don't know about a Jap problem with America."

Egan retrieved the atlas. "Simple, Doc. When Heil fartin' Adolf beat France, Japan allied with the Axis. Demanded French Indochina for bein' so friendly; wanted the rubber. After some bloodshed in the jungle, the puppet Vichy government agreed. The Americans hated it. Motherland did too, close to Malaya, but couldn't lift a plane or ship in protest. Cheered the Yanks on."

Robinson, who'd sat down facing Egan, said, "Seems the Japs sent 125,000 troops to Indochina. Agreement with Vichy was 40,000. The first week, Japs violated their own treaty."

Egan agreed. "Last year, right? Our Yank friends say, 'Hey Nip, give up ya new resource-rich toy.' 'Nah,' Nip says. Yanks anger up and embargo rubber, steel, and scrap iron, close the Panama to Nip shipping, everything but Hollywood movies. Worst for Japan would be oil. If the Yanks embargo oil, somethin's gotta give."

"I say Nips are up to something. We should wake up," Robinson concluded, slapping his hand on the wood. "Others disagree."

"Supply lines, Jim," Egan retorted. "Hafta jaw-jaw, not war-war. We're safe in our backwater."

With this, the meeting broke up. Jake strolled back with Egan. It was misting, a cloaking moisture rather than rain, atmosphere more than event. Jake had developed new words to capture the varied qualities of moisture. Tonight's mist turned planets and moon into hazy blobs and draped the camp with the smells of sulphur-tainted wet grass. Their lean, fit fellow soldiers were fuzzy.

"Giant floating pupae cases," Jake laughed to Egan. "Every night's different. I didn't realise the spread of our island mandates. By square miles, Australia's an empire."

"Few of us to defend it," Egan snorted.

Suddenly, a tremor underfoot. "Shiiit!" boomed curses, the mist amplifying the voices of soldiers looking for their tents. A thickening wisp might be from Tavurvur, but it was hard to tell. There were no more shakes.

"It'll blow soon," Egan predicted. "God, I'm lonely! Wish there was action. Betty won't see me again, even for dinner."

Jake's tent mate wasn't a confiding man, but he'd told Jake he was dating a woman in town, not naming her, just praising her tits. Jake took this as bravado. Egan was capable of dog-like loyalty under his crassness, thrilled to have a girlfriend. *In the dissolution of the affair, good tits become Betty,* Jake mused. *Will he tell me all about the whole person?* "Mate. I'm sorry. What happened?"

"She can't let herself get fond of another bloke in uniform." Egan sighed. "I thought she was already fond of me."

"Everyone's in uniform. Is she going to be a nun? Didn't you say her husband's serving in Singapore?"

"Yup, marriage on the rocks for years. Coast's clear for me, but she won't have it."

"Sorry. I didn't realise..." He tailed off. "Married women are a bit chancy…"

"Don't you get lonely?"

Jake gestured at the hospital tent.

"Come on," Egan scoffed. "You're not that self-sufficient." But he was too sunk in his loss to pry.

Relieved, Jake returned to the Japanese, thinking about John Smith's sudden appearance. "Do you think we have contingency plans?"

"Carr and the town pooh-bahs don't seem worried; lotta islands between them and us. Plus, ten of our home-built Wirraway fighter planes and four Hudson bombers may come. I heard that on the wire."

"*We're* the contingency plan? Just our 'Little Hell, here we come' battalion?" Jake said dubiously. Wip had said that the Wirries and Hudsons were just trainers. Back in the tent, Egan seemed embarrassed by his personal confidence. He made a show of falling sleep.

Jake retrieved his letter. By torchlight, he added:

We just heard that Hitler attacked Russia. A great buzz, arguments about who'll win this one. There's a run on maps, as everyone wants his own. It must be the same for you. Will Rex enlist, now that Uncle Joe's our ally, us depraved imperialists? Dramatic weather here, but otherwise bucolic. Love, Jake

CHAPTER 18

• • • • • • •

W HEN JAKE AND WIP next hiked to the cave, they hurried to be alone together, dodging under low branches and exchanging sideling glances. Wip's warmth so close to Jake radiated through him.

And yet... The radio broadcast they'd heard in the canteen about Hitler invading Russia clutched at Jake, constricting his breathing. Halfway along the track, he slowed. Moodily, he said, "My rabbi predicted it."

Wip slowed. He looked down then joked, "Your 'Call me John' rabbi foresaw *this*?" He yanked Jake away from a fallen tree branch. Between its green leaves, a long green shape coiled.

Jake stared at the snake. "Pit viper with great camouflage! Don't worry, I've got a knife and antivenom. Metaphorically. He predicted Hitler's invasion and said the non-aggression treaty was just a ruse. While it held, viper von Ribbentrop convinced Stalin that his best generals were spying for Germany, whereupon Stalin killed them. Russia has oil, and Germany doesn't; he said only deluded commies could have missed the obvious."

"It's terrific for the home team. Nasty new ally and Jerries butchering each other will give us a breather," Wip responded.

"I'm torn," Jake confessed.

They stopped. Insects hovered as Wip touched Jake's eye sockets. "Puffy. Tell me."

"The Nazis have new Jews to persecute. One part of me cheers—I'm a British citizen wearing her pips—while the other part dreads every Russian inch the Nazis take as my people's death knell. My grandparents left Russia because of the pogroms, but many stayed. I ask, 'do I have divided loyalties?'"

Wip hugged him. "You're ethical. I love that. Let's stop feeding mossies."

The comfort of Wip's enveloping arms calmed Jake. He brightened as they scrambled over rocks to their private haven. "We should name it. I'm getting fond of the spider webs. 'Ardent Grotto'?"

"Grottoes have human decoration, not just gifts from our eight-legged friends," Wip chuckled. "But I like the sound of ardent."

After long, slow and tender lovemaking, Jake lay on his back, hands behind his head, feeling lazy, stretched and sated. Wip got up, brimming with enthusiasm. "Come on," he urged. "Time to eat. I found a curious place."

"Slow is nice; fast is nice; getting up is *not* so nice," Jake grumbled. He dressed and followed Wip back over the rocks.

They hiked a few yards uphill through conifers, beech and tall banana trees to an unexpected clearing of ferrous soil covering pumice stone. A thin stream of water snaked from an animal track above them, collecting in a pool on the indented stone below, the spillage seeping into a fern grove. A lonely flowering bush had branches with clusters of white orchids in late bloom.

"Amazing place," Jake remarked as they unrolled the tarpaulin. Wip lit a fire, and they barbecued smoked fish, washing it down with brandy.

"Aren't men of, um, our inclinations supposed to tell of our first loves?" Jake ventured, picking a fish bone from his teeth. He was eager to fill in the gaps in his understanding of

Wip; his sense of Wip was almost all gaps. Surprised to see Wip's jaw clench, he went first.

At the sorry end of Jake's adolescent debacle with Izzy, Wip's eyebrows knotted. "This Izzy had a half-paralysed face and was expelled? How awful. God, how hard to be young."

"Tragic for Izzy and rough for me. For months, I ate mustard every time I thought of him. To repress what now feels so right."

They watched the sun plop behind the treetops. Wip reached over and kissed Jake's hand. "Our desires are natural to us. Mustard. You poor blighter. Did it work?"

"Obviously not; I'm here." Jake began to see the funny side of his struggle. "I *hate* mustard!" He turned serious. "Fear got me through medical school. With locums, I was busy with new places, colleagues and paperwork." *I've left out Esther.* He looked at the pool below. *He called me ethical, but I can't bring myself to say her name.* Perpetuating his omission, he related family history. "Ma died four years ago, Pa last year. I couldn't disappoint him by hinting I wasn't quite a traditional Jewish son. He and my grandmother were born in Palestine. Friedmans have a homing instinct for family and a Jewish homeland. My younger sister senses my nature, but keeps quiet. She's a musician, familiar with...flexibility. My older sister's not well, mentally." Mentioning Miriam gave him a stab of anguish at leaving Tal to cope with her. After a pause, he asked, "Your first love?"

Jake waited, but Wip chewed his lower lip, staring at the bare skin between his trousers and shoes as if there was a new freckle he had to find. *What's so hard? It was eons ago.*

Abruptly, Wip asked, "What's the purest emotion?"

Automatically, Jake responded, "Family love."

"Did your Ma and Pa love each other and you purely?" Wip persisted.

"Of course."

"Describe this love," Wip continued. "What's it like?" His tone curled with a sneer.

Jake stroked his moustache. No one had ever asked him to define 'For better or worse'. *What's he after?* "Maybe it has layers," he conceded. "Ma's and Pa's love for me felt more like expectations than unconditional. I never dared to test them; being a tolerated racial minority weighs on one. 'Don't put a foot wrong, and you'll do alright.' Yet there was also joy in the feeling of a closed-in tribe. Sexual passion initially; they had three of us. I saw agreed values, a defensive front against bad times, and habituation to each other's presence. I've made your point. Your family?"

Wip sighed. "Ma was always pregnant, lots of miscarriages and stillborns. The priest prayed for her and praised her as an ideal Catholic wife. We kids brought each other up. We had raucous fun at times, but we were so separated by age that we went different ways. I loved my younger brother, Ron, Sally's and Tommy's dad, but I lost touch with him over the years. Melbourne's hostile to…our kind, so I mostly stayed away after the war. And now Ron's dead, his kids in need. Pa was a utility man, a bitter drinker full of opinions and always short of money. To me, family love is an organism that does what it's designed to do: procreate and provide temporary shelter until the young can physically defend themselves. Ma and Pa were once good-looking—full of energy, perfect complexions. My chin dimple's hers, my nose his."

"What about those adorable freckles?" Jake touched Wip's forehead.

"Ma's. Her high school photo showed a sprinkle on her forehead. I barely saw them through her wrinkles. I never knew them carefree. No, the purest emotion is dominance/submission, one person's power over another."

He moved away, arms around his knees. He seemed suddenly desolately self-contained.

"Oh, my love, you must have been terribly hurt to say that," Jake exclaimed. Afraid to close the distance between them, he waited. He yearned to cradle Wip from behind, sink against the muscled back, nuzzle his neck, sniff his cologne/army soap scent and feel the springy hair with his lips. Uncertain, he let the silence stretch.

"Not by… any one person," Wip finally said.

"Then by circumstances?"

"It's a long, boring story. Some other time."

He wants to talk. Jake fought down frustration. Wip dangled a shock-proclamation in front of him, then withdrew, almost a tease. *Let it go. He can't talk yet.*

"I see you as a magnificent tree," he offered tentatively, "forced to grow bark ring upon bark ring abnormally fast. I long to know each ring; see what it saw, feel what it felt." He sensed Wip's tension easing. He was looking at Jake. "For me," Jake plunged on, "I cling to optimism. If you'd delivered babies, you'd know what I mean. Each delivery feels like a miracle of possibility. Wip, I hold out this tiny squalling human, fragile but amazingly strong at the same time—it's the most beautiful thing—to the exhausted mother, anxious father and relieved nurses. We're strangers, but we share one thought or prayer: *Maybe we can make the world right for* **this** *one?*"

"But we don't." Wip's eyes were moist. He edged back to Jake.

"No, we don't. But the hope hits me fresh every time. Who was your first, um…male love?"

"Ah, required ritual, I suppose," Wip relented. "I was eleven. My first blow job was in Melbourne's Botanical Gardens. An unshaven old bloke pulled me into a fern grove. It was twilight; the gates would shut soon, but I could squeeze between the bars. He begged me to rub him and then suck. He didn't seem scary, just sad. It was gross, but better than being bullied at school. He hugged me a lot. I was less lonely with him than at home. We met a few times…He…" A pause. "He admired my dance technique and told me to follow my dream."

Jake thought, *that's an evasion.* He knew the Botanical

Gardens well. Full of winding paths and uneven surfaces crammed with trees and bushes, it was an unlikely place to demonstrate dance moves at night; clandestine trysts, yes. He tucked the lie into his box of mysteries about Wip. "That old man exploited you disgustingly—a boy of eleven!—but I'm relieved you didn't resort to mustard and reject me. I can't believe the risk I took."

Wip kissed Jake's hand. "Let's enjoy the rising dark. Darkness doesn't fall, love, it rises. The poets are wrong."

On-top-of-things Wip had returned. His hand on Jake's thigh was beyond sexual, solidly comforting, the soft fingers pressing then releasing Jake's flesh under his trousers. "We won't be disturbed by any Tolai. They believe evil spirits rule the night. Glad I'm a modern man." He patted their torches. "The fire's about dead, but we can do without our artifice."

Night pulsated with energy. Arms around each other, they watched, entranced, as bats poured out of their cave or pulsed up from the hollow tree trunk, fluttering wings against the dense black foliage. Moonlight was implied by slants of light on tree trunks and an almost ominous shine on the upper side of leaves. The winged predators gorged on mosquitoes, ignoring the gyrating fireflies lighting up the small patches of the dark.

Tavurvur coughed, throwing up grey-pink smoke high enough for them to see. Jake leapt up. "Gotta rush back. Camp could be in danger."

Wip stood and put a finger in the air. "Relax, love. wind's shoving stuff out to sea."

Jake licked his own finger and put it up. The fiery detritus was drifting east.

Wip grinned. "Weren't sure you could trust me?"

Jake felt his cheeks grow hot with embarrassment. They sat again, enjoying the spectacle as if it was being put on especially for them. Their fire had gone out, but the pink-red-greyness swirled around the stars, making a mysterious garishness Jake had no words to capture and preserve. "What a privilege to be here. Wish I'd brought my camera."

"You can't stuff paradise into two dimensions and one sense," Wip murmured, ruffling Jake's hair. "Gauguin got it wrong." He sat up, leaving Jake's hair spiky.

"Gauguin?" *Paris secrets again.* "Where did you see modern art?" He patted the strands into place.

"Gauguin never painted Tahiti's night fireflies or luminescent tree fungi," Wip expanded, ignoring Jake's question. "He missed the jungle's true enchantment and went for flat and gaudy. Which reminds me, are you going to show me my niece's painting?"

"When we have good light," Jake promised. He smoothed wrinkles in his army khakis, and the discussion about Japan's fortified Pacific islands came into his mind. Despite the mellifluous cricket song and distant bat clicks, war intruded; the night's magic was dissipating.

"What do you think Japan's intentions are?" he asked Wip ."Robinson showed us that their positions are grouped in a cohesive shoe shape, while the allies' islands are spread out. Some blokes said our government has it under control. But before I disembarked from Zealandia, the day after you did, a nasty fellow with a monocle, a hush-hush type, ordered me to watch for Jap spies." He stopped, uncertain if he was permitted to say more. Then he rushed on. "He sort-of blackmailed me, Wip. He said to photograph unauthorised strangers who try to see our coastal guns at Praed by using some invented medical emergency. He knew what make of camera I had and hinted he knew about me. If I don't do what he wants…"

"Bloody pig," Wip snorted. He thought, then smiled. "Relax. He won't hurt you or us. He needs your help. Actually, what he asked you to do supports the idea that our government's onto the threat. The Japs will have supply-line problems if they take southern hemisphere ports."

After a companionable silence, Jake suggested, "I'd like to climb the Mother."

"Ask, and genie Whipple will grant your wish. Saturday; supposed to be a great view."

It was their first trek back in darkness. Clouds must have blotted out the earlier moonlight because they were enveloped in a density of night that swallowed up the puny beams of their torches. White fungi glowing on fallen logs signposted the edge of the track. A little nervous, they whistled to let the wildlife know they were leaving their turf. Acutely aware of busy rustles, energy and purpose around them, Jake whispered, "I see why Tolai believe the night belongs to evil spirits." Wip pressed his hand.

When they reached the grassy slope end, they relaxed. Spotty starlight returned. Wip's almost nihilistic view of human relationships seized Jake again. *My life has had its difficulties, but Wip's must have been exponentially harsher.* He wanted to make love to Wip again and feel the merging into one body and heart. *But who am I? Who is he? I don't know.*

*
**

On Saturday morning, they hiked up the extinct volcano, the Mother. The trail was notoriously arduous, so they knew they wouldn't bump into their mates, who preferred beaches and beer stands on their day off. The trail began gently, but soon they were hemmed in by spiky kunai grass taller than Jake, temple-height for Wip. The dry season had begun, but the foliage was still dense.

They shrugged off knapsacks and studied the grass for the easiest way through, a path someone had trodden recently. A mistake, as sandflies and mosquitoes swarmed them. There was no depressed grass.

Jake looked at the summit as he slapped a mosquito.

"Come on. I must send a photo home to prove I did the climb."

Wip chuckled, white teeth gleaming. "Another risky photo? But no native girl."

"I headed off Mirrie. Telegrammed her 'no marriage, no legal work. But visit, spend money hotel and market.' She won't spend her own money. No worries."

"Onward to the summit, then. This photo will be won with the heroism of infantry charging an enemy hill," Wip puffed, his face wet with sweat. They took out their knives and hacked. Spikes of grass nicked their chest through their shirts.

"Glad I brought disinfectant," Jake grunted, worrying about infected sores.

When the vegetation thinned, the insects gave up. Finally, with whoops, they reached the summit. It was a varied expanse of yet one more grassy hill and flattish spaces. A few spindly trees framed sweet-smelling grass, some calf-high, others short and velvety under their blistered feet. The slope of the terrain implied an ancient crater long overgrown.

Jake pinched himself. *Am I dead, looking down on Paradise? No. Pain, proof of life.* They walked, gazing over Matupit Harbour and Simpson Harbour, across the sea to the Duke of York Islands glistening in the distance. Jake pinched himself again. What a vista! Focusing back on Rabaul, he saw town buildings etched in the radiant morning. Fishing canoes and motorboats bobbed on rippling waves. He took a photo and then gasped, pointing at a huge crater below them, a tangled mass of bushes, oval cliffs and deep water. A fragment of his psyche wanted to plunge into it, into oblivion. He stepped back to higher ground, startled.

"Yep, another extinct one," Wip said. "Long name, starts with 'R'. And that…" Wip pulled Jake around to face west. A distant peak glowered. Jake took another photo. "That's sin…" Wip grinned mischievously. "Mount Sinewit! Highlands. Pray you never have to go there."

Wip pulled out his own binoculars. Suddenly, he swore—

all seriousness now. "Goddammit, love, look at that splash of yellow with grey blocks." He pointed past Tavurvur's gauzy smoke. "Praed Point Battery, our posting."

Jake looked. The new fort gleamed on cleared ground: four grey wooden buildings, two concrete and steel gun emplacements, and the winding black access road. It couldn't have been a contrast with the dense green surrounding it. "How exposed!" He shivered despite the heat. "Any plane can spot our crown jewels!"

"Bollixed up. Our Lord Acton government protecting us." Wip sounded bitter.

"Let's enjoy the moment." Jake shook pleasure back into himself. Through the binoculars, he admired egrets in the shallows of Simpson Harbour. Turning toward Matupit Island again, he saw native women climb out of a canoe with baskets. "Look. Are they carrying mud snails to make shell money?"

Wip grunted but pointed in the opposite direction at North Daughter, the biggest of Rabaul's three extinct volcanoes. It felt cheek-by-jowl to Jake. "Heard we'll put an anti-aircraft battery there in September. Hope it's more up to date than our coastal guns." Wip couldn't let military issues go.

They unrolled a sheet. "Here's Sally's painting," Jake said. Wip brightened as Jake tenderly withdrew a waterproof envelope and slid the painting out.

"Oh, my God, a talisman for you," Wip breathed. "You before joining the Army, a tad plump; my brother's face at the top; and the distance between filled with an upward swirl of brown dots." He ran his fingertip over the lines. "Such dynamism. Shades of Magritte, I swear. My own kin, I must survive this war to help these kids."

"I hardly know her." Jake put the painting away carefully. "I don't deserve it. Magritte?"

"René Magritte, 1920s avant-garde," Wip said testily. "Sally could be his student."

"Tell me."

Some thought twisted Wip's face into a haunted mask of misery. "Ta for showing me. You do deserve it. Let's eat."

The sun seeped through them, dissolving worries and memories. They grabbed each other with quick, deft intensity, then dozed. When Jake woke, the sun was slanting from the west. Wip was reading the *Rabaul Times*.

"What's news?" Jake asked drowsily. He'd needed the sleep more than he realised.

Wip was frowning. "Oh, welcome back. Coffee sales down, crop infestations by berry." His face creased with anxiety. "Pneumonia and dysentery delayed picking, so the beans spoiled. Bloody shit, literally!" He jabbed the offending newsprint.

"You must be a part-owner of a coffee plantation to be so upset. I can solve the problem of small fever for you," Jake said, awake and excited. "I've been reading about tropical diseases.

Wip looked at him intently. "Actually, I do part-own the plantation I managed."

"After the war, I can treat it."

Wip was silent. His eyes followed the scudding clouds, and then he lowered his eyes to appraise Jake. He seemed startled, even shocked. "Everything's always after the war," he sighed. "Very well, tell me."

Jake sat up. "At medical school, we didn't learn tropical diseases, just urban ills. In basic training, we did quinine for malaria, remedies for fungi and ulcers, and preventive hygiene to keep army blokes healthy. We didn't study native illnesses because there's a hospital here for them. But for trade, you need workers, and here, they're mostly natives. That's why you're fretting, right? Beans ruined by delayed harvesting.

"Rabaul's so beautiful, I'm staying after the war. The Liverpool School of Tropical Medicine has a graduate certificate. There are parasites here I can research. They're developing drugs and water purification for parasites. The cost would be repaid in spades. This is what I want to do when I grow up. I'll make you rich!" He rattled on, unaware of the breathtaking continuity he was offering Wip.

Wip paused. "After the war," he said again. "It's a kind thought, but dream on. Your enthusiasm is medicine. Apart from coffee, mine's particle physics, splitting the atom."

Puzzled, Jake said, "Why care about atoms? It seems very abstract right now." He hadn't pursued physics beyond required undergraduate courses, though he admired colleagues who were at home with that language.

"No more abstract than the chemical formula for strychnine," Wip retorted. "Physicists recently proved that chain reaction by multiplication of neutrons from fission can be engendered. Physics instantly leapt from equations to a potential weapon. A nuclear bomb could vaporise a city. Rotten timing. Who'll weaponise nuclear energy first? Us Lord Acton types, on the side of angels? Or the Jerries?" He pointed at Praed Point's guns. "*Those* are the irrelevant abstractions."

Jake exhaled. "That's your pure emotion—the power of one nation of people over another?"

"Gives me nightmares. Sorry for the doom and gloom."

Jake grabbed Wip's hand. He felt an answering throb from the slender fingers he was getting to know so well. Had Wip's dread of a new weapon sealed his view that dominance was the strongest human desire? He wouldn't talk about his experience in the last war, or the years after. But his pressure on Jake's hand meant something. Maybe he needed Jake's care to reshape his vision.

A hawk hovered, watching for a careless...something. Jake withdrew his hand to point at it. His hand felt clammily alone. "Desperate predator. Look how hard it has to work. It's sad it never learned to like ferns," he joked. "Wip, dear, if you believe we're about to bomb ourselves to extinction, you wouldn't hate losing money from coffee. Lost money implies a future need for it."

Wip laughed. "Touché. Thank you. I'm two people,

both so intense I can't manage them. This is a great day. Tell me about Sally and Tommy. Our youths will have to clean up our mess."

On the slithering, slipping hike down, even more arduous than the climb up, Jake exhausted his memories of Sally and Tommy in ten minutes. They continued in companionable silence. Jake reflected that one Wip was the boy blasted by war's carnage to expecting the end of humanity; the other Wip fucked, made money, intended to help his relatives, and fought bullies for victims like Lee, whom he didn't know.

CHAPTER 19
· · · · · · · ·

July 1941

W AVES SLAPPED the merchant ship Caroline Maru against its dock at Rabaul's main wharf, causing it to rock. In his cabin, Toshio Hisanda, wearing only underpants, was shaving. He worked deliberately, steadying his feet as the ship moved. The waves were erratic, as if they resented the metal disruption of their progress. Accustomed to instability underfoot, Hisanda didn't flinch; his country, Japan, was prone to earthquakes. He never cut himself or anything else accidentally with a razor.

Hisanda was a sho-i, a second lieutenant in the Kempeitai, military and secret police. He and his comrades solidified Japan's control of conquered Chinese territories, penetrating resistance groups and interrogating prisoners. His orders today were more peaceable: to gain access to and evaluate the new artillery batteries Australia was emplacing at Rabaul with rumoured American help. His source in Manila had reported there would be four batteries with two guns each. Success today would bring him a longed-for promotion. Of course, he would be honoured to die for his emperor, whatever his rank; that was the sacred debt he owed his sovereign. But his desire for seniority also burned hot in him. With a high reputation in Tokyo, he could get his son into the coveted pilot training school and arrange good marriages for his two daughters.

Finished trimming his moustache, he studied himself in the mirror. Plump cheeks, thick lips and eyeglasses made him look younger than his 35 years, a youthfulness that belied his decade of experience. He sometimes wondered if his soft looks had slowed his rise in rank.

He glanced at the neatly made bunk where his business suit was laid out, with a card that read Toshio Iijima, Import/Export. His plan was to have a car accident at the checkpoint to the new coastal guns at Praed Point, the battery he had confirmed already existed. Employing a little strategic razor cutting, he'd demand immediate medical treatment by the medical officer at the battery's Regimental Aid Post. Wistfully, he looked at his trunk, where his Kempeitai sword and uniform were packed. He was going to feel naked without the red and white armband that gave him authority. Still, every step that advanced his country's cause was sacred. The image of his good-luck purse danced in front of him—the cherished tasselled bag soldiers took into battle; it was with his uniform. *Why not wear it?* Today wasn't a physical battle, but it could be a contest of wits.

Snapping open his trunk, he felt between the layers of cloth and pulled out his small, brocaded purse, full of good-wish messages on folded paper from family, friends and dead comrades. As he tied it around his waist, he murmured his favourite lines. He felt their support surging through him.

He'd got his start in China. After some success there, he'd sailed with Japanese pearling fleets. When they docked in the Philippines, New Guinea and Australia, he photographed harbour facilities and made contact with local Japanese traders. Moderately capable of speaking several languages, he was qualified for today's task, his first not as a subordinate.

He resented European imperialists in Asia with a

contempt that flowed just beneath his surface politeness. It was a reservoir of purpose that sustained him when he most ached for home—for family and the precise rituals of an ordered life that fostered a still spiritual centre. However, his career was to serve his emperor overseas, and serve, he would,

He knew Japan's Pacific islands well. Their paltry resources he considered to be proof of Caucasian bad faith, hypocrisy and greed. During the last war, Japan had secured many of the Pacific Ocean colonies for its European allies at the time, who were too busy bleeding in France to defend their territories. Despite this magnificent contribution, and although Japan's need for natural resources was well known, it didn't get resource-rich Pacific plums in the peace. It got spits of land with sugar, not rubber; kava, not gold; rocks, not palm oil. The allocation was a betrayal of his emperor. When Japan moved into China and Indochina to secure natural resources, the white colonials embargoed Japan's oil imports. Their ruthlessness delivered a collective shock to Japan, inspiring an unshakeable determination to correct the wrong.

He'd read his army's plan to rid the Pacific of white parasites. *Now is the time,* he thought. *Whites have grown timid. They eat so much red meat their breath stinks. But the meat hasn't strengthened their blood. Look how they twisted to avoid war with Germany, where we've been fighting since last century. What right do last century's empires have to deprive a nation of such spirit as Japan?*

As he buckled his belt, he gave a soft sigh. The beauties of home felt far away. But what travelled with him were Haiku poets; the wisdom of Iio Sogi and Basho was never far from his lips. He ran over a haiku he was working on. Entranced by the southern hemisphere's constellations, he'd written: *Southern Cross, oh fabled star, prostrate yourself to my Rising Sun.* It should be attached to a season, but in this part of the world, the seasons were wet or dry. He hadn't solved this aspect of his creation. Still, the thought was correct. *Work your plan*, he told himself, as he knotted a red and white striped tie matching his good-luck purse and the arm bands he had to forgo.

When he came on deck, he glanced across Simpson Harbour. There was Kpmini's Japanese shipyard, and, like an insult, Chinese-owned marine supply stores on its lot. How did these inferior people make themselves so indispensable? *Time to correct this.* Hailing a taxi, he went to Rabaul Hotel to meet his driver and servant, Chai Hoon.

*
**

Chai Hoon was a young Korean. His family name meant brushwood. He was taller and thicker-boned than his master, but he lived in fear of the smaller man's temper and absolute right by rank to punish him.

Chai had grown up as a farm boy, hunting and fishing when harvests were poor. He revered the domestic and wild animals that sustained life. When a visiting shaman sang of the divinity of tiger, bear and golden frog—God-animals that had assumed human form to be the founding ancestors of the regional clans—Chai's heart soared with adoration for the creatures' transcendence.

He was almost equally transfixed by motor vehicles. Their smoke, noise and speed were magic gifts from a more available god. He had seen his first motor vehicle when a squadron of Kempeitai military police riding motorbikes raided his village. The raid had changed his life.

The Japanese were hunting rebels who'd ambushed one of their patrols. The rebels had dispersed into mountain hideouts, leaving the villagers to bear the brunt of Kempeitai rage. The raiders had decapitated several men, taken two young women captive, and burnt huts and fields, including the Chai farm. They had offered to spare the lives of villagers whose sons looked strong and accepted conscription. Chai, then sixteen, had volunteered to save his parents' lives.

His new masters had sneered at his belief in animal sky gods. They had tried to beat their spirits out of him. But he had cleaved to them, taping a gold-painted wooden frog to one ankle and a red wooden talisman that warded off evil spirits to his chest. His consolation in these hard days was that he was getting closer to the magic smoke-belchers. For them, he endured the face-slapping and beatings with bamboo sticks, which Japanese officers routinely inflicted on subordinates. After cleaning latrines and digging trenches, he had spent every free moment polishing the unit's vehicles. He had graduated to driver, then mechanic. By 1941, he'd come to a grudging acceptance of his life. His bucolic childhood and his parents' faces had faded to a dream.

It was a radiant morning, with tropical scents from lush shade trees providing shelter from the heat. It was a day on land to relish. Chai had learnt that Rabaul was a car-heavy town with an infinite variety of models to gawk at and stroke. Now he stood by a rented taupe 1938 Ford. It should have been a thrill for a car worshipper, but Chai was miserable. Uncomfortable in a cheap western suit, he was almost in mourning. His sho-i had made him *adjust* the car's mechanism in a destructive way. "It's my *plan*," Hisanda had insisted. Poor Chai had the skill to create exactly the incident his master demanded. Gloomily, he bowed and ushered Hisanda into the Ford's back seat.

"Crash only at the checkpoint, not before," Hisanda repeated. "We'll get minor injuries, which will make them take us immediately to the medical officer at Praed Point Battery. Five yen if you do it right. You know what's coming if you don't."

Starting down Yara Avenue, Chai concentrated hard. Having the steering wheel on the right side of the car felt unfamiliar, as did the cars and trucks passing them on the left. It was so long since he'd driven English-style that he felt like a first-time learner. Cars honked, and drivers looked at them with curiosity. He was acutely aware of a warning rattle beneath him.

They followed signs to Lakunai Aerodrome. Five minutes out of town, they turned left on Battery Road. Hisanda laughed at the freshly painted road sign. "How kind to help me find the new coastal guns by naming its road 'Battery'!"

Chai sighed in relief; his master was in a good mood. Then he watched through the car's front mirror as Hisanda removed his tie and made a knotted circle with its end. He slipped one arm out of his suit coat, pulled out a razor and sensuously flicked his thumb over the edge. Chai gasped when Hisanda sliced his forearm through his shirt, casually, as if he didn't care where he cut. With his other hand, he made a tourniquet and put his coat back on. His shirt had bloody fingerprints, and there was blood splatter on his suit sleeve. His face was impassive throughout. He sat back, smirking but pale.

Traffic thinned as the road wound between Tavurvur, the active volcano, and South Daughter, the extinct volcano. This was the access road for authorised personnel. Hisanda took the opportunity of the car being out of sight of other vehicles to throw his razor out of the window. A moment later, a truck with Australian soldiers in shorts and digger slouch hats passed them. Chai saw mouths opening and heard harsh flat sounds, a laugh and hand-waving.

"Ignore them," Hisanda rapped. "They shouted 'Go, Grandpop.'"

Chai nodded, seeing the spread of blood on his master's arm. Tavurvur receded. The rattle beneath his feet came again. He slowed, stomach churning. More shouts from another truck: "Granddads, shove along. It's not Sunday, ha, ha!" Hisanda translated.

As the dot of a distant checkpoint came into view, Tavurvur suddenly spewed smoke. Wisps of smoke fogged visibility. Through the swirling greyness, Chai saw a big dark lump of a living creature ahead. He had no idea such a being existed. It was longer than the car's width, and its humped body on two powerful legs was windscreen height. He slowed more, trying to listen for the mechanical rattle. The smoke cleared to reveal a bird with glossy black plumage and a brilliant blue neck with pink patches. He sounded the horn, but the bird didn't fly or run. Instead, it uttered a harsh, low, guttural rattle of a cry and darted at the car. He was mesmerised. Was it an island God indicting him for hurting the car?

He braked hard and turned the steering wheel. *Don't hit a god!* With a wild crack, the car slewed, one front wheel turning, the other straight. The driver's door flung open. Chai tumbled out as the car rolled to a stop off the road, hundreds of yards from the checkpoint. He lost consciousness to Hisanda screaming, "Stupid traitor!"

Hisanda's head smashed against the door's side. His glasses fell off. They lay on the floor twisted, one lens broken. He tried opening the back seat doors, but they'd jammed shut. He had to watch, helpless, as a sentry with field glasses flopping against his chest ran to pull him out. "Gotta get ya out before petrol tank blows, mate," the Australian shouted.

The dwarf cassowary pecked its bruised flank. With majestic indifference, it hobbled into the tall grass, leaving behind two bloodied black feathers.

*
**

In his medical tent at Praed Point Heavy Battery, Jake was sponging a tropical ulcer on his patient's calf. The tent was more of a first aid station than a mobile hospital tent; complex cases would be taken to the army hospital tent at camp.

A messenger burst in without asking permission. "Sir..."

"Wait."

"Urgent phone call, sir."

Jake's first thought was *Miriam.* He continued cleaning

the ulcer. *She ignored my telegram and is on a ship heading here. Or she's having another mental breakdown.* But in that case, Talia would have telegrammed him. There was nothing he could do quickly. He reached for sulphanilamide powder.

"From the checkpoint sentry, sir. Car crash near the checkpoint, the victim demands to come here for treatment."

Jake looked up, suddenly alert. "Our boys?"

No, sir, Sentry says two Orientals in toff suits."

"Elevate the leg," Jake told the patient. "Explain," he said, taking the messenger out of the tent for privacy. John Smith's warning on Zealandia that a spy might use him to see the Praed guns rushed back to him. Smith had instructed him to be hospitable and photograph the individual, but away from Praed Point.

"Lots of blood, maybe broken bones, . Sentry says he got them out of the car—a miracle the petrol tank didn't blow. One bloke demanded to be taken to the medical officer here, not to call a town ambulance."

"Enough English for demands, huh?" Jake was excited and scared. "Tell the sentry, in no circumstances, bring them here. I'll go there. If they need surgery or X-rays, I'll drive them to the civilian hospital in town. Tell the sentry not to call a tow truck for the car. We need a look. Double quick, then come back."

He stepped back inside to apply the powder and a pressure bandage on his patient's leg. The soldier limped out, disappointed he couldn't tell his mates what the fuss was about. The messenger ran to the communications hut, returning a few minutes later. "All set, sir."

"Righto. Who's on car repair?"

"Sir, I think I saw Captain, I mean Lieutenant, Whipple."

Jake turned away to hide his pleasure. He breathed slowly to steady his pulse. He and Wip were snatching scattered moments of bliss in their cave. Now, in a dangerous encounter, they'd be working partners. "I suppose he'll do,"

Jake said, putting on a show of indifference. "Tell him to bring refreshments as well as tools. Is there a water heater at the checkpoint?"

"Yes, sir. It's dank after storms. Night blokes like a cuppa with cards." He hesitated, not having meant to let on about the cards. "But they're always on the job, sir. That's why they get wet. Outside, storms be damned."

Jake frowned. "Sentry duty isn't party time."

"No, sir."

Jake filled a thermos with ice, checked there was no mildew on the bandages, and packed his case. The messenger looked around. The only decoration was a map of the Soviet Union glued to the top of the small, humming refrigerator. Pins showed the latest reported German positions at Smolensk. Grimy abandoned holes told the grim tale of German progress.

Picking up his camera and case, Jake ran toward the parked vehicles. "Get Lieutenant Whipple now," he shouted at the messenger. "What do you think of the Russian front?"

The messenger ran ahead of Jake to open the truck door and salute. "Sir," he puffed, "I wouldn't sleep if I were Stalin. But there's two million Red soldiers around Leningrad. Russia's bigger than Oz and millions more people, room to regroup. Supply lines are everything."

Jake started the engine of a truck with a clean bed. "Good answer," he shouted. "Hope the Russkies hold."

The new road was a joy to drive. No potholes yet. He parked behind the checkpoint under two palm trees, then trotted to the two injured men. They were sitting off the road, shifting uncomfortably on scythed kunai stalks. The sentry's rifle leant unattended by the hut.

The sentry standing over them was trying to reassure them. "Our doc's the best, fix ya'up very nice." From their frowns, his solicitousness seemed to be irritating them, Jake thought.

The smaller man was holding a bloody handkerchief to

his face. A pair of twisted glasses lay at his feet. His stained red and white tie was knotted around his left arm.

Jake asked the sentry, "Did you make the tourniquet?"

"No, sir."

The other man, taller and stockier, slumped over, hugging his ankles. *Who's the boss?* The smaller man had slicked glossy hair with flecks of grey, but his skin seemed young. It was hard to guess his age; the taller man looked in his twenties.

Jake glanced at the wrecked car, Wip's job to examine. Turning back, he pointed at the red band on his shirt sleeve. "I'm the medical officer. Captain Jacob Friedman, certificated doctor. Let me help you with these injuries."

The smaller man paused, his face expressionless, then nodded at the taller one. *Knotted tie's boss.* Both men heaved to their feet with an effort. The taller man's face strained with pain; it must have been agonising to be upright, even at a slant. Knotted tie glanced at the sentry's unattended rifle. Jake noted surprise passing across his face, followed by blandness. He inclined his head and shoulders slightly. The taller man copied him but deeper, confirming Jake's impression that the smaller man was senior.

Jake was ignorant of their customs. He didn't know that the shallower the bow, the less respect was being accorded the recipient. Afraid of making a mistake in etiquette, he got to work pulling bandages and disinfectant out of his case. He didn't know that his lack of any reciprocity was an insult.

He and the sentry helped the men onto a blanket on the truck bed. The sentry couldn't help smirking at the dirty green stains on the men's trousers from the kunai grass. His grin earned him a glance of coal-hot rage from the smaller man, quickly suppressed. Jake worked quickly: cutting clothes, disinfecting, numbing skin, stitching and bandaging. He kept his own expression neutral at the purse tied to the smaller man's waist under his shirt, but he memorised its details. Likewise, he showed no interest in the broken bits of red wood that pierced the taller man's chest or the gold-painted wood at what was probably a broken ankle. Talismans, he assumed. Tears snaked down the taller man's coarse face as he watched a stranger pick broken wood from his skin. Jake smiled at him sympathetically.

Authorised vehicles passed toward the checkpoint, ogling the wreck. Trucks and motorbikes roared from the base in the opposite direction. The smaller man turned, apparently counting. *Not subtle,* Jake thought, splinting the taller man's ankle. He slipped the broken pieces of red and gold wood into the man's surprised hand. Puzzlement shaded the taller man's face as his hand closed around the wood. More tears.

"You're lucky these injuries aren't more serious," Jake told them. *Or was that the intention?*

He gave them painkillers washed down with brandy, then motioned for them to hold ice packs on the injuries. *Where's Wip?* "We'll stay here while the ice lasts, then I'll drive you to hospital."

"Hotel, Rabaul Hotel only," the smaller man said, "no hospital." The first words either man had uttered.

Jake raised his eyebrows. The sound of a single motorbike grew louder. Wip parked and handed Jake a rucksack. "Food," he said, saluting. He stared at the injured men.

"Thank you, Lieutenant Whipple. Your turn to diagnose and treat," Jake said, pointing at the car. Wip saluted and sauntered off.

Turning to the smaller man, Jake continued. "Your driver needs an X-ray at the hospital in town." He pointed to Chai's foot. "I will do my duty as a medical doctor. After I leave you, if you take a taxi to your hotel, I can't stop you."

"Private," he turned to the sentry. "Boil water for tea. We need to feed our guests."

The bemused sentry lit a primus stove and put a pot of water on to boil. He took three tin mugs from a shelf. Opening a jar, he dumped handfuls of coarse brown leaves into the mugs. No teapot, apparently. Jake was pleased that the mugs had handles on the tops, not the sides. That meant he could brew Billy tea, an outback speciality. The method involved holding the handle of a near-full mug of boiling water and tea leaves and swinging it around in a circle for a couple of minutes to steep the leaves without anyone getting burnt. Billy tea virtuosi believed that they put refined tea-making to shame. "And pick up your rifle," Jake reminded the sentry.

From where Jake and the intruders were, they couldn't see their wrecked car. He walked down the road and around a bend. Wip was photographing the car. He strode up to Jake, lips twitching in amusement. "I have a wicked theory of what happened, but I need to hear the sentry's version."

The water hadn't boiled, so Wip and the sentry walked out of Hisanda's earshot. After a minute, Wip beckoned Jake. "You've got a situation here. I don't like it at all, but I'll help you. We can fix the car. I'm off, explain later."

Jake walked into the grass, cut a bamboo stick for the taller man to use as a cane, and then returned. "Good news, gentlemen. Our mechanics can fix your car. We'll eat while they work. Food will help your shock and loss of blood."

He pulled meat pies, chocolate, and bottles of beer from the rucksack. The sound of Wip's motorbike receded. Jake made Billy tea for three, doing his mug swinging a few feet from the two Asians. "This is Australian tea. The trick is speed and rhythm to avoid burning your hand or your guests." He didn't spill a drop. The smaller man grimaced at the meat pies, but the taller one ate ravenously. Both men ate the chocolate.

For Jake, time passed in a blur. Wip returned with three mechanics. Clangs, "damn mossies", and other curses floated back. Then, triumphant whistles and yelps. Eventually, Wip returned to say that the car had been fixed. He opened a beer bottle. "Is alcohol prescribed with painkillers?" He winked at Jake.

"The very thing," Jake answered solemnly.

When the three mechanics joined them, toasts began.

Wip crooned "It's a Long Way to Tipperary", *a* song from the time when Japan was allied with Britain in the First World War. All sang along.

Jake watched the smaller man. He thought he saw wary resignation as the man launched into "We're Off to See the Wizard" in an unexpectedly sweet tenor, the words thickly accented. The taller one mumbled unintelligibly. Hollywood was the universal language, and Hollywood products were freely exported to Japan. The three mechanics sang "Waltzing Matilda", which the Asians couldn't grasp. After more beer, Jake sang "A Trip to the Moon on Gossamer Wings", which everyone knew. He looked at Wip, whose face softened.

The smaller man sang a Japanese song to blank Australian faces. Jake suspected he was testing if they knew Japanese.

"A love song from your country?" Jake asked. He was now photographing the group, his clicks capturing linked arms and stupid grins.

"Love, yes, greatest love," the smaller man smirked.

"Look," Wip said slowly to him. "I don't know you, but those big native birds get very confused by our new roads cutting their territory. Be careful on the others." He held up the two black feathers. "That's what caused your crash."

Jake fought to hide his surprise. *What's Wip doing, hinting at non-existent new roads?*

The smaller man pulled out a business card: Toshio Iijima, Kyoto. Import/Export. "Thank you for good care. We Japanese count being clean greatest virtue. Not clean, shameful. I implore you, take us to your base to relieve ourselves and wash. What I get you? Girl? Opium? Money? Have all."

Jake refused several times. The Asians had to settle for a hobble into the kunai grass. When their backs receded, Wip grabbed Jake's camera. He came back, lips pursed, after three minutes. The Asians followed two minutes later, the taller one ashen pale. Jake drove them to Namanula Hospital and left them on the veranda. He didn't stay to watch if they went in or to their lodgings. Wip drove the repaired rental car to Hotel Rabaul.

When Jake picked Wip up at the hotel, Wip was excited. "So, here's the story. I had this theory. One wheel had turned, the other not. Unusual. I'm sure those fellows would have killed me if they saw me photographing the car."

"They couldn't see you from my truck. The little fellow didn't like our happy act." Jake started laughing, then stopped. "It's not funny, is it?"

"It's not. What caused a well-maintained car to come apart with one braking? Didn't look like brake failure 'cos both wheels would've been involved. I've done a bit of insurance investigating; I know sabotage. Those slant-eyes didn't know who they were dealing with in old Whipple! I suspected suspension failure. And Bob's your uncle, there it was. They cut the tie-rod almost through. They planned to crash at the checkpoint, then be taken to you for treatment, where they'd see the coastal guns. I bet they drove like grannies along the way. That's something we could check. Also, the tank had little petrol. That's why it didn't blow; they weren't planning to drive far, see? But the big bird foiled them, and yours truly, genius Wip, worked it out. We've got Fords at the base, so I replaced the tie-rod. I've photographed that, too."

Jake whistled. "You know mechanical sabotage. I know self-inflicted injuries. The Toshio bloke slashed his own arm with a razor before the crash. The cut wasn't consistent with the crash. Not a suicide attempt either; he avoided arteries."

"No razor in the car," Wip said.

"Doesn't matter. I'm certain. Puts a sinister spin on it. So determined." They fell quiet.

Wip was the first to speak. "Let me tell you what I photographed when they went to piss. The little one stood on a stone and slapped the big one, slap, slap; thought his neck would break. Hissed in Japanese. Terribly angry. More slaps. Then he kicked the big bloke's cane, big bloke went down, uttered not a word, stayed in an awkward kneel. How he kowtowed with a bum ankle is beyond me. Kicked again. Then they shake themselves off like ducks coming out of a lake, piss and hobble back, faces blank. What do you want to do with the film? It's hot stuff."

"There's a store I'm supposed to leave it, hush-hush. Why did you hint to Toshio about other new roads? There's only one battery."

"These people need to save face. You're not the intelligencer type. You're a great doctor, a patriot and a dope."

"You know spies?" Jake asked.

"Met some," Wip said, then looked away. "Japs have an ancient tradition of disembowelling themselves if they perceive they fail or exact revenge, which is noble to them. They weren't registered at the hotel, by the way. I checked. I bet they're on that Jap cargo ship."

"I read about seppuku, like ancient Romans," Jake mused. "But that's medieval. Japan's modern."

"Sure? Toshio's in the old mould, I reckon."

They drove in silence. In April, when John Smith had ordered Jake to keep a look out for Japanese spies, Smith didn't know if the Japs were helping their German allies as a courtesy or themselves. Hitler's invasion of Russia clarified this. German needs were in the north, not the south. Would Toshio Iijima, or whoever he was, slash his arm for distant German whites who had temporary mutual interests with Japan? No. The arm slashing was for Toshio's emperor. Jake chewed a lip. Maybe still medieval.

Wip looked at him. "Stop brooding. Today we won. You had fun getting the better of them. That's the problem. Don't ever do it again. You told me to stop playing Lancelot. I'm telling you, no more Pimpernel."

*
**

Back on the Caroline Maru, Hisanda slapped Chai hard on the face four times. "You see that I went calm when you ruined my plan," Hisanda snapped. "Intelligence officers adapt. Your stupidity prevented us from getting to the Battery today, but I learned three things. First, how careless these oafs are with their weapons. We don't tolerate that. Second, they know no Japanese. When I sang "Bullets, Tanks and Bayonets', our army song, they thought it was a love song to a woman. And third, that blond soldier mentioned other new roads. That confirms my Manila informant that there are four heavy batteries at Rabaul. I won't execute you today despite your uselessness." He sent a messenger for the ship doctor to tend Chai's foot.

Chai leant against the cabin wall, face bowed, breathing raggedly. His fingers in his pocket stroked the broken bits of gold and red wood that the white doctor had pressed into his hand. His talismans had saved him from his master's lethal rage. If he glued them, they might still have power. A dim childhood memory of receiving human kindness returned to him, a strange, foreign sensation. He'd felt it from the doctor. He knew he was right to avoid hitting the bird god.

CHAPTER 20
• • • • • • • •

24 August 1941

IAKUMU'S FATHER, ToBalamat, entered the house where the family's and village's shell money, which was not needed for everyday use, was stored. He lit a kerosene lamp, sat on a mat and studied the wheels and strings of shells. As the owner of the greatest number of shells, and big man, he decided which loans to make to enterprises that the village men proposed, and which projects to invest in. He also controlled who could enter the house, which didn't include females. He chewed a betel nut and shone the small flame around the dark circular room.

He was content and humbled at his village's success: they'd built four western-style houses and owned three trucks that villagers leased out for fees. He wasn't the first big man to buy a truck from the Chinese instead of chartering it, but he was second, and the villagers owned more vehicles than his rival. They had a church, school and coconut plantation; the gardens were fertile, and the women sold produce, baskets, jewellery and fabrics at markets around the province. Some villagers had bank accounts, including his daughter. He meticulously avoided corruption, while his subordinates enforced tribal law firmly but fairly. Servicing the new Australian troops was bringing jobs for village men subcontracted to Ah Kuan Ho's construction company, and he knew the gardens could increase their produce to feed the arrival of more people in Rabaul. He was here today to think about which enterprise to approve next: machinery and a shed to dry coconut meat into copra, or a bus to drive Tolai and other natives to and from the Native Hospital.

He was still achingly lonely since his wife had died, a weight of stone that suddenly pressed on his stomach or heart unpredictably. Mentioning her name brought him to tears, and he'd resisted those urging him to take another wife. Instead, he threw himself into being the best leader he could, taking on his shoulders the indignities of "Boy, pick up that load and find me ten carriers!" from colonials as he shepherded his people through tumultuous change. His nickname 'Balamat' meant 'brave' and 'confident'. Everyone said he'd earned it, but he was often uncertain. *My ancestors' shadow souls have guided us, and we're blessed by Jesus, the saviour,* he thought, but what would next wet season bring?

"These are happy times for the province," he said aloud. "Everyone has enough food, and no one is poor." The moment the words left his mouth, a *feeling* clutched him, a dim memory. He jumped up and beat his chest. He'd known this feeling of sweet plenty when he'd been a young man, for just several wet seasons. The tribes had been making the best of German rule, learning typesetting and machine repair, and coconut sales constantly increased. Then, the Australian soldiers defeated the German soldiers, and things got worse for most of his life. The changes were bewildering, and sometimes people *were* poor. He rubbed a finger over his face, feeling deep lines of crises trodden into his skin. Then, the last four dry seasons had been sweet with plenty. What could this mean? He walked around the room, sat, stretched over his legs to rub a toe, then sat straight, thinking. He must honour his memory's reminder; he'd wait before approving either the copra-drying tools or a bus.

With the decision made, his satisfaction returned, albeit tinged with the loneliness that never left him. He was pleased with his two sons: the elder one ran their coconut plantation, while the younger one was a catechist and worked at Rabaul's best hotel, the Cosmopolitan. He hadn't paid much attention to his daughters' upbringing—he'd left that to their maternal aunt, as was proper after his wife's death. He liked the result: IaKumu was a glowing beauty with a kind nature and celebrated skill with vegetables. She'd soon marry a man from a former enemy tribe. He touched each shell wheel and then opened the door to find his daughter crying.

*
**

IaKumu had been waiting for him for a long time. She stood barefoot, kneading the dirt with aching toes, overwhelmed by the enormity of her gamble, of her deception of him, beginning with getting him to introduce her to Henry Lee without saying why. The village moot had rejected her brother's argument that ToStonehet's blood ties were too close for marriage, and to her plea that he was stubborn and violent, they said he'd mature with responsibility. Her desperate measure was to make love with Lee and become pregnant.

Her sole maternal uncle, ToBahin (a nickname for being 'after'), was required for this session of confession and negotiation. He wasn't here yet. With his usual warm smile and ready tears, he'd promised ToSaina he'd come; as usual, he was late. A cook on a cargo ship, he was carefree and uninterested in cultivating gardens or building anything. He worked and spent. Most people didn't respect him. Still, he was a man and her maternal blood; he was necessary.

She and Lee were meeting twice a week in secluded forest groves. They had learnt the intoxication of sensuality together, with deepening attachment. Days apart now felt like being cheated. During their cross-language talks, she'd told him how she dreamt of having a fixed-building store in town filled with her medicinal plants and vegetables. Far from scoffing, he'd embraced the idea. "I can show you how to run a good store. I know all about it," he'd enthused. On several occasions, he'd mentioned different locations for the store where the metal pole of her red awning would shimmer in the rising sun. IaKumu had been astonished; she'd never imagined that a man could inhabit a woman's dream. He'd dutifully used condoms after a hasty withdrawal spill. But when Ah Kuan told him that his family had selected a fine Chinese girl in Hong Kong as Lee's wife, he and IaKumu agreed, with torrents of tears, that they couldn't be apart and that pregnancy was the best way to stop their families' plans. Now, she'd missed her 'mun sik,' her moon bleed. *Will I have to break the news to Papa alone?* She wondered with clutching anxiety. She burst into noisy tears from fear, not regret.

The closed door opened. Barefoot and in a black lap-lap, a whistling ToBalamat backed out and turned. When he saw her, he smiled a mouthful of teeth blackened from chewing betel nuts.

"Papa," IaKumu called. Tears flooded her face.

"What's wrong?"

Rigid with fear, she looked up at the man who'd given her life. His black eyes were fierce, but she'd seen them soften when he was puzzled; she needed to appeal to his capacity for reconsidering things he'd considered settled.

"Come now. ToStonehet isn't bad. He passed all the requirements for your hand." He threw his head back and thrust out his jaw, his habitual stance.

IaKumu felt a conceding pat on her head and felt the bored *Stop making a fuss*. His smile faded as she stood braced. Her expected compliance hadn't come. "Papa, a secret? Please." Her esteemed father was no different from any other Tolai; he loved a secret. She started for the bush. As he followed, his whistling grew tentative.

"Papa, I missed my mun sik. I'm so terribly sorry. Oh, oh, it is bad, what I've done. Papa, I'm with child."

"Ohhhhhhh!" he roared. He slammed his fist against a tree trunk. "Who raped you?"

"Papa, I'm so ashamed. Not rape."

"ToStonehet, then. You like him more than you pretend—bad behaviour, but not a crisis. We'll advance the marriage date. That's settled." He started back to his house.

"Stop, Papa. Please listen. Not ToStonehet. Listen. Advancing the date won't help."

He turned. "What do you mean? A village boy?"

She stood silent, her skin prickling with terror, watching as, infinitely slowly, realisation dawned on him. He coiled with rage like a snake.

*
**

Back at the house, knocking on wood, a male call. The sounds filtered into the heavy-leafed track. *ToBahin at last,* IaKumu thought. Her father's large, callused hand crashed on her cheek. Again. And on the other cheek. She didn't dodge the blows. *Not his fists,* she thought, breathing hard and holding her stance.

A muscled man in a white lap-lap on silent, bare feet joined them. ToBahin had a soft, pleasant face. He stood by, head down and impassive, while ToBalamat grabbed a stick. IaKumu made no effort to seek her uncle's intervention. This was a father/daughter matter. ToBalamat hit her on the back of her neck and shoulders. "Oh, you evil one. My daughter, a whore. Mixed race? Not a white boy? No. No. No. Make it not so. It's against our rules and theirs."

ToBahin wept openly, then spoke. "It's a sad, bad thing. But my niece says he's not white."

"No, Papa, I promise." IaKumu cried.

"This boy is from the best Chinese family. Will you make her an outcast? Some Chinese have married daughters of great men. Ah Tam…"

"Don't give me Ah Tam!" ToBalamat roared. "That was in Great-grandfather's time! Oh, the shame!"

"We love each other, Papa. I won't take the leaf to flush his life from me."

He stared at her. She saw incredulity fill his face, a softening. "Who are you, daughter of my blood?"

IaKumu's heart banged, thumped and thumped against her ribs. Before he could collect himself, she rushed on, "Papa. I have horrible, terrifying dreams. What do they mean? Oh, please explain them. I never had them before ToStonehet negotiated for me. You always tell us that Jesus is our saviour, that Christian ways have brought many benefits, but that Jesus isn't familiar with our land. We should hear messages from our own spirits and ancestors."

She described the flocks of brown eagles flying over their hamlet, the metal bird machines in the sky pouring fire, and her other dreams. "When I sit under the trees at dawn after these dreams, the leaves look sick and turn the wrong way, away from the sun."

While she was talking, a wind snatched dead leaves from their branches and whirred them high before settling them with a crackling rustle on ToBalamat's head. He raked his hair with his fingers. Nothing had fallen on ToBahin's head. IaKumu's uncle stared at ToBalamat with wide, frightened eyes and an open mouth. The leaves didn't move. ToBalamat put one large hand over his heart, growing sombre. Iakumu held her breath; the gesture meant he was recalling tribal legends.

"Brown eagles are rare. A flock flying over our land must mean death," he said slowly. His rage began to dissipate. "Maybe you had visions, not dreams."

"There's no track but negotiation with both families," ToBahin said, his eyes still on ToBalamat's leaf-crusted head.

ToBalamat thought for a long time, chewing his lip as he looked up at tree canopies and slivers of sky between the foliage. When he hissed at a shrieking parrot, IaKumu noticed that the sun's angle had shifted; her father had been thinking that long. The stinging pain in her neck and shoulder was diminishing to a throbbing ache. "Lee's family will have to pay off ToStonehet's relatives. It will be very expensive. Ohhh, what a mess you brought me," he finally said. "What will you contribute, brother of my beloved wife?"

ToBahin looked at his lap-lap. Everyone knew he had no savings. He sighed. "I will work extra days. I will give you three months' wages." Feeling his duty was done, he offered his hand to ToBalamat and IaKumu and quickly disappeared into the bush.

ToBalamat snorted at the man's back and went quiet again. Father and daughter stood apart, toes gripping muddy roots, face to face but silently speaking their separate thoughts.

Suddenly, he chuckled, a shallow guffaw that became a full-throated roar. "You scheming vixen! Your great-grandmother's shadow soul is in you. She ran off with a man who was not the tribe's choice. You fooled a big man and your very determined aunt, who raised you. I could never cast you away." He paused. "There's a way to lower the bride price, an old quarrel. When ToStonehet's great-uncle bought land from my grandfather, he paid with counterfeit shell money. The Germans made shell money in their homeland factories but never cut them right. Most of us can see and feel the difference between coconut husk cuts and steel cuts. But grandfather was blind, his fingers callused. The quarrel was never settled. The land's now valuable. I'll revive the dispute. I kept the shell wheel as a lesson not to be a fool. I touched it this morning, wondering when I'd find a use for these fakes. Don't tell anyone."

"Papa, never. I love you. I'll be perfectly obedient now."

"Ha!" ToBalamat spat to keep bad spirits away, then

strode off without looking at her, without a handshake or sign of affection. The leaves slid off his hair.

Watching his angry, receding legs, IaKumu clutched her belly, crying with relief and marvelling at the new life inside her. How glorious pregnancy was. The blows were less than she'd expected. He was furious with her, but he'd negotiate a solution with ToStonehet's relatives and Lee's family.

*
**

Two days later, Lee was on his way to the negotiation to marry IaKumu. The location was a mystery; he'd find out when he arrived. His escort was a mystery too: a relative of his cousin Ah Kuan Ho, whom Lee hadn't met, Ho's manager of interior trade. He was to meet the mystery man on one of Ho's motorboats.

Ever since Lee had arrived in Rabaul, he'd grown increasingly astounded by the number of relatives Ho had, which meant that he had them, too. Lee's family numbered four. When his father had written down Ho's address, he hadn't mentioned extended family. However, with each branch having five children or more, family ties proliferated. When would he know all their names and not greet someone inaccurately?

Excited and nervous, he turned off Malaguna Road onto an industrial lot near the main wharf that contained two Chinese marine supply stores and the Japanese shipyard, Komini's. Lee assumed Ho had some equity interest in the supply stores. Despite Japan's invasion of mainland China, these businesses co-existed. *How uneasily? Is sabotage going on?* Passing two sheds where a launch and a schooner were on hoists for repairs, he approached the one motorboat tied up at the dock.

He'd formed a mental image of a manager of interior trade. A clerical type wearing thick spectacles, stooped, young and single—most Chinese men would stay in town or at a plantation when married, he theorised.

Reality met theory only with a stoop. The man who nodded dourly at him was over fifty. Though bent, he was wiry, with corded muscles on his arms and legs. His hair was wispy white, his face like corrugated cardboard into which his nose and brows slid with little definition. But his black eyes were fierce. A red and gold Koi tattoo symbolising family ties and business prowess poked above the back of his singlet. A scar ran from his cheek to his neck, knife probably, belying frailty. *What does managing interior trade for Ho entail?* Lee wondered. He thought he was a man of the world, with his callused sailor fingers and healing nose, soon to be a father. He touched his skin and felt like an innocent.

Before starting the engine, the old man turned and growled, "I'm Quong Kuan Yu. Are you sure about this girl? You can't change your mind after the agreement. They're baptised Catholic. No divorce."

"Life's nothing without her, sir. She's magnificent."

The old man snorted. "You're costing the family a lot of money. If you'd grown up here instead of Australia, you'd marry a Chinese girl your parents chose, with good character, good health, and family properties." His scar bobbed as his head moved, emphasising his words.

"Anne is all these things," Lee protested, omitting their pregnancy. "She went to a Mission school. She knows more languages than I do: Tinata Tuna at home, Pidgin and more English every day. Her people follow matrilineal descent, so she has land from her mother, who died when she was young." He paused and took a breath. "She wants to have her own store in town with produce. Our family should like that..."

"A Tolai woman with a store? Unlikely."

Hearing the old man's snort, Lee flushed with anger. "Sir, you are speaking of my fiancée. She'll do it. Her brother..."

"Yes, yes, that little catechist boy who interprets for us

sometimes. She's still native. How you'll live in harmony, I don't know. What name will she answer to when she comes out of her dreams, IaKumu or Anne? I bet she didn't tell you what Tinata Tuna means."

"I didn't ask," Lee admitted.

"It means the real language. Everything else is for convenience. You'll have to observe both Christian and Tolai rites. Marrying a Chinese girl would be simpler. You're a handsome fellow with a lot of choices. Are you certain?"

"A hundred times yes. Mr Quong, I've never known oneness. But thank you for saying I'm handsome. That's news to me."

Easing the boat away from the dock, Quong spat in the direction of the Komini's sign. He was muttering "youth" as the boat put-putted to sea. Finally, he smiled at Lee over crooked, brown teeth. "I do what Ah Kuan tells me."

"Where are we going? Can you tell me now?" Lee asked.

"Kabakada Village, then a hike."

Lee studied the map. "That's about twenty miles by boat, around Saint George's Channel to Ataliklikun Bay. It's eight miles by road."

"Less eyes on us this way," the old man grunted. "You'll understand later." His tattoo undulated as he turned the wheel.

Surveying a storage area crammed with crates, Lee's eyes widened at the prices for canned meat, steel knives and dried fish; they seemed high, as did a commission to trade in shell money. Perhaps Quong had earned his scar. From then on, the journey continued in silence, except for exchanges about local currents and treacherous coral reefs. Two hours later, they tied up at a small dock. The old man lifted a tarpaulin off two bicycles. They walked them over sand through beach ferns and bushes to a paved road. As they cycled to the village, they passed a Methodist Mission. Lee admired the sprawling residential house, school and medical clinic, presided over by the tall spire of a white wooden church. Native girls were working in the gardens while native families in the driveway crowded around women missionaries.

"It looks settled," Lee said, hoping the old man would stop for a break and tell him about it. "A lot of land."

"Bloody history," the old man replied, riding on.

Past the village, they turned onto a dirt road for twenty minutes, bumping over stony ruts. The old man finally stopped at a clump of bushes. They pulled the bikes into bushes screening an animal track. "Hush now," he ordered. They hiked uphill, wading over a fast-running brook, sometimes angling between thorny vines. Lee dabbed a scratch on his arm. The vegetation was dense above hip height. *Are we intruding on a wild boar's turf?* Nervousness swelled his bladder. He motioned to Quong, then stepped over bushes and vines to piss. When he turned to catch up with the old man, he could no longer see the track. This was a remote place. There was obviously some need for all this concealment.

After about forty minutes, they emerged from the dense, tangled forest into a cultivated forest of totally different growth. The old man showed no sign of fatigue. Lee admired him as he mopped his own sopping face with the bottom of his shirt. The old man strode off to join five Chinese men who appeared to have pistol and knife holsters at their belts. No one spoke. Nods only.

Why the secrecy? It's a meadow of trees. A few yards away, Lee saw Ah Kuan Ho in a white short-sleeved shirt, beige pants and brown boots standing quietly while a tall, stocky elderly tribesman in bare feet and a lap-lap bent over a gangly teenage native boy, who then turned to whisper in Ho's ear. They must be IaKumu's father, ToBalamat, and her brother, ToSaina. *My God, they'll be my kin soon. Am I doing the right thing? What is this place? He* fretted. *Yes, yes and yes. Don't let that old man infect you.* He waited to be told to approach.

After a while, Ho beckoned Lee. IaKumu's father shook his hand, scowling. Then Ho waved him away and pointed to the next hour on his watch. Perplexed, Lee left him. He saw the three heads bend to each other again.

For an hour, Lee wandered about the clearing of about three acres. Tall trees with narrow round trunks and bowler-hat canopies were planted with plenty of space between them filled by lush bushes. The bark was reddish brown, nothing like the forest surrounding them. It was eerily peaceful, with no human sounds. He began to feel encased in a fecund abundance of green with its own language of sighs and multi-pitched rustles.

At one point, Ho came over to him, "Do you have any quarrels or debs of honour you'd bring to the union?" He murmured.

Lee matched his cousin's volume. "One, sir. To two Australian officers from Zealandia. Captain John Whipple fought for me without my asking after Collins, a professional boxer, beat me up. Whipple was injured and demoted from captain to lieutenant because he stood for me in an unsanctioned fight. The doctor, Captain Jake Friedman, treated me with exceptional care and kindness. I promised Dr Friedman I'd repay the kindness. If they're in trouble, I must help them."

Ho shook his head. "You shouldn't have promised any such thing. Let the ruling class take care of itself." Ho returned to ToSaina and his father. Lee saw him pull out a sheet of paper, and ToSaina scratched his head as he puzzled over it.

Bored, Lee scratched at the reddish bark. These trees were different from the pine, coconut banana or mango trees of the primary or secondary forest. The bark was fiercely astringent to the tongue. *What is it?*

He saw IaKumu's father scrape his hand through his grizzled curls and stand very still. ToBalamat craned his neck at the sky, looking left and right, then down. He seemed shocked. Then, the meeting broke up. IaKumu's father and brother left, moving fast. Ho beckoned Lee again. They hiked down the trail in silence and retrieved the bicycles. Ho led Lee to a different motorboat.

Finally, normal speech. When Lee's breath of relief exploded out of him, he realised he'd been holding it in the whole time.

"I was hoping the chief would reject you over this theoretical debt to two army officers," Ho said as they climbed aboard. "But he accepted it. He's reconciled to the union. You're getting your way, Henry."

Lee stood stock still, visualising IaKumu's village, with heaps of shell money being deposited by his relatives at the feet of her relatives; IaKumu walking from her people to stand at his side, her visible skin painted with exquisite geometric designs. In a separate ceremony, a Catholic priest joining them in perpetuity. No mystery between them on their wedding night. But after? His breathing grew shallow with joy and anxiety.

"Untie the rope, dreamer," Ho snapped. Lee leapt to it, and Ho started the engine. "Listen," Ho continued. "I need to explain the bride price. What you saw and where is secret. Do you swear?"

Lee nodded. "I swear. But why the silence?"

"You take the boat while I talk." Lee took the wheel. "This forest above Ataliklikun Bay is regarded as a sacred place by the tribal chiefs who sometimes allow hunting there or the use of the land. The spirit Kaia is in that forest and Ataliklikun Bay. If you are there, you must be silent so as not to anger the spirit.

"Now, those trees, my trees, are mature cinchona trees. The bark will yield quinine for malaria. I bought the land from ToBalamat ten years ago, explaining that what I would plant was a special medicine. I bought seeds in Java and grew the trees. As part of the bride price, I'm returning the land and trees to your bride's relatives for free. I thought it would be hard to convince the chief that the trees are valuable, but he was amazingly quick to agree. I wonder if he had some information or prophecy of his own. You know I follow Japan's atrocities in China?"

"Yes, sir. Everyone knows you keep up to date."

"What everyone doesn't know is that I have a nephew with the mainland communists. His group killed a Japanese Kempeitai officer in '31. They found a copy of the Japanese war plan to conquer South Pacific islands. My nephew knew enough Japanese to translate it. Rabaul is the number one target. He got word to me. I've made plans for our family's survival if the worst happens. If it does, you'll be here taking care of the trees with your wife. A couple of village men will supplement my guards."

Too startled to sort out his emotions, Lee asked. "Sir, where will we live? I saw only trees."

"A short hike through dense bush, you'll find huts, a well, an outhouse, potential vegetable beds, and kerosene lamps. There's a well-stocked cave nearby."

Lee's mind buzzed. This was wilder than his wildest fantasies. Was he excited, distraught, terrified, resentful? All four emotions churned inside him, along with a speck of scepticism. Was his cousin exaggerating the danger? Still, his self-doubts dominated his questions about Ah Kuan Ho's reliability. "What if beetles eat the trees? I'm just a sailor."

Ho laughed. "The trees are sturdy. This is fertile soil. Your bride is reputed to be clever with plants. She'll learn. I'll send a botanist to give you lessons. The main thing is to control the earthworms and ensure the trees stay rooted in subsoil, not the topsoil earthworms aerate."

"Why the secrecy, sir? Do you really think the Japs will attack?"

"Oh yes. Look." From his bag, Ho took out two heavy glass balls attached to a rope. There was also a watertight transparent rectangle with a numbered note attached to the rope. "I'll take the wheel while you look."

Lee fingered the rope and rotated the ball. "So, you *did* buy stray floats. This looks Japanese. There's a note. I've never seen anything like it. Is someone lost on an island? A new Robinson Crusoe?"

"Read the note, fool," Ah Kuan snapped.

Lee read the English block letter words aloud: "If you write to the following address with the time and place you found this note, with its number, you will receive a gift of a Japanese doll in national costume." The address was a Japanese Government department in Tokyo. Lee gasped.

"A native fisherman sold me this instead of taking it to the police," Ho explained. "You're a sailor. Why are the Japs giving away dolls?"

"My God, they're learning how the tides and currents move without arousing suspicion." Lee's doubts vanished.

"Exactly. These floats have been washing up for a year. How many stupid whites have dolls on their mantlepieces by now? The Japs are coming, and the war will be long. Manufactured quinine will quickly run out. We Chinese have an ancient curse: 'May you live in interesting times.' That's now, Henry."

In the choppy waters under the unforgiving radiance of a dry season sky, Lee's mind jumped back to the dark jungle and cinchona trees. An infinity of physical tasks and blank time, interspersed, maybe, with moments of terror and danger, opened before him. And faintly, a sense of his destination: it wasn't a place or achievement; his journey's end was coping. He felt the spirit of his ancestor caress him. Then epiphany. The jungle around the cinchona trees was perfect for his beloved to collect and grow bush medicine. He'd teach their child, somehow very quietly. The guards, too, if he could find a way. There must be a book of sign language at one of the Mission libraries. He'd get all the books he needed before they moved here and find a dry cave to store them. His new diary would be lesson plans. And the guards would teach him to fight. He hadn't fulfilled his parents' needs to run their laundry or repaid Dr Friedman's kindness yet. But this was his moment. He felt inspired purpose settle on his shoulders. He squared them and smiled at Ah Kuan. "Thank you, sir. I'm ready for 'interesting times'."

CHAPTER 21

●●●●●●●●

Lull: *To cause (someone) to feel safe and relaxed*
instead of careful and alert
(Britannia Dictionary, 2022).
Lullaby: *A folk etymology derives lullaby from*
'Lilith-Abi.' Hebrew for Lilith Begone.'
(Wikipedia, 2022).
'Lilith' is a soul-stealing demon.

ON THE MOTHER, Wip had been careful not to show his reaction to Jake's astonishing offer of permanence in their relationship. But he cherished it. As days passed, Jake's tossed-out, assumed continuity became Wip's reality. And as nights passed without him jerking awake holding his ears—his recurring nightmare of a jackhammer clattering through his skull—he imagined the unimaginable: an affair between men with a happy ending. They'd worked together against Toshio Iijima, or whoever that nasty piece of work was. Wip's nihilistic view of human attachments was lightening.

Now, scrubbed and barbered, his uniform cleaned by the best laundry in town, Wip whistled as he approached Jake's aid tent at the end of the day's shift. He had a gift equal to his dream: an advertisement for local land they could buy.

As he neared the tent, he suddenly felt uncertain. An

atmosphere encased him. It had a bad taste and smell. He took a breath and sat on a bench outside to calm himself.

When he finally pulled in his stomach and walked in, his eyes hit shifted pins in a map before he took in Jake's scowl. Wip's subconscious wanted to delay what it sensed was coming. *How little I know the heart of the body so intimately familiar to me.* The body's hands fidgeted with a round cloth skull cap that Wip recognised as Jewish. Jake's officer's cap was on a wall peg. *But he's agnostic,* Wip's hope cried. He waited.

Jake put the skull cap down, tapped a letter with a pencil, glanced up in bleak acknowledgment, and then looked at the letter again.

He's not ready for whatever this is. Wip seized on Jake's cue and studied the map, something they could share. The map showed Ukraine and Russia. Pins were in a city named Tallin, a railway line between Leningrad and Moscow, and a pin not far from Moscow, the latest known Nazi positions.

"So, Hitler's panzers are on the move. They were moving when we hiked the Mother. That's not what's upsetting you, is it?" Wip couldn't let his inhaled breath out.

"No," Jake sighed, "though the capture of Ukraine's industrial heartland is appalling. My great-uncle came from there. Better close the flap." He set his jaw.

When it slapped shut, he gulped then rushed out, "I will marry Esther..." a hoarse whisper but loud in intent, 'will' being emphasised, "...after the war."

"What! Who... is... Esther?" Wip crunched the newspaper advertisement of land for sale in his pocket. Then he pulled his hand out and clenched his fist. "You have no right..."

"Right?!" Jake's voice tightened. "We've never talked about personal stuff much, you not at all. Deflect and deflect. I never asked you...certain intimate details...when I sensed reserve. I had an informal understanding with Esther before I left Melbourne. None of this...makes us...makes my... I...my feelings for you... less."

"What? You went on and on about Izzy of the half-drooped face, taking my whole heart, and left out a woman named Esther, to whom you made promises!" Wip stared into Jake's eyes.

Jake looked down, his expression stricken. Wip saw his sensuous lips twist with... what? Shame? Grief? Confusion? But Jake raised his eyes and met Wip's stare, implacable. It was as if nothing else human was in the tent.

But Wip *was* there. He pointed at the letter. "That's from this Esther. She's fat with your child, sweating and breathy."

"The letter's not from Esther. I haven't heard from her since....she's posted somewhere, don't know where." Jake gave Wip a pleading look as he tried to explain. "The letter's from my rabbi, Jacob Danglow, the chaplain you met in the last war. Look!"

He pointed at Hitler's pins. "Massacres of Jews. See?" His finger jabbed at town after town. "Danglow got a telegram from a refugee who'd escaped Tallin. Wherever the Nazis raise the swastika, murders of Jews follow. Industrial scale. Far worse than the pogroms my ancestors fled; worse than what you goys did in your Inquisition." His face was red, his breath shallow.

"Go low, why don' cha?" Wip snorted. "I'm no more an Inquisitor than you're a Christ killer."

"Can't you see?" Jake persisted. "Try. Please. Tens of thousands of Jews, men, women and children, are being shot in pits they dig themselves. Kids! Because they're Jews. Many of the murdered men fought for Germany in the first war. Doesn't matter. They're Jews. Esther is a Jewish nurse I met in Colac. I could...um...perform with her. If I survive, I must make Jewish children. It can never be enough, but I *can* make some. I told Esther about my attraction to men, which I thought was in the past. She still wanted the engagement. It doesn't change...*us.*" He put his head in his hands.

"Bet you cried over Izzy and got her sympathy. How does this work, exactly, in your peculiar mind? Your research on parasites, my coffee plantation? Does Esther treat my native workers between birthing your Jewish litters? All sing and dance together?"

Jake was silent, his cheeks pink.

Does he feel like the scrub he is? "I had happy news for us. Now it's garbage. All bloody over. I don't know how you can...I've never screwed a woman. Can't... bouncing breasts, god-awful makeup. They're always coming on to me. They're alright at a dance, but oh God, I quake when hopeful, mascaraed eyes wait for me to ask them out."

"Of course," Jake mumbled. "You're so handsome and rugged. No one would ever guess."

"How can you think of bringing more children into a world on the verge of a weapon of total annihilation?"

"We differ on that," Jake said flatly.

With his blood a frozen river of bleakness, Wip gazed at the man he thought he knew. Jake's hazel eyes—when they shone with joy, when they focused in intense thought, or burned with disapproval, when they clouded with an unshared thought; he'd ruffled every strand of Jake's bushy hair, and seen Jake pat it down for inspection; and the wanting curve of his lips, Wip had thought he could interpret—all these he'd charted, and internalised as the one who meant the most to him, ever.

And now, this body inhabited a world of possibilities unavailable to Wip. Jake's body was a liar, and he, Wip, a sucker, his 'forever' dream gone. His world would revert to a different forever: wondering, *is that a signal?* The jackhammer nightmare again. The Paris years flashed before him—his secret humiliations, extreme experiments. Why had he imagined this time would be different? *So be it. God, how smug he looks.* But the implied racial purity test Jake was displaying? That he wouldn't let go.

"What's this Jewish compulsion?" Wip pressed. "You said you're agnostic. It's not faith. You hate what your traditions did to your elder sister. It's racism, the very idea of race purity that you attack in others. Look at me. Look! Am I less than you? What's so superior, so to be conserved, about you? My freckles you said that you adored, my blue eyes and crinkly groin hair. Where are they from? Celts? Picts? Or wanderers like the Partholonians, whose myths the Celts absorbed. Look at me, Jake. Am I, a mutt, less?"

"Never," Jake whispered, with his jaw still set.

Wip saw his eyes shift. *Is he uncertain?* He fought down hope. The gulf between them felt to Wip as wide as that between duke and peasant. "Last thing I'll say..." Wip pointed at Jake. "Your Esther's a fantasy. You don't know where she is, if you're not lying. If it means so much to you, go plant your frigging precious Friedman seed, vastly overrated, in my opinion, in a Jewish woman here. I meet the town's comers and goers. A Jewish family from Singapore, business types, is here, soon sailing to Argentina. Getting far from what they've decided is trouble coming; don't know what. They have a daughter, very pretty to a bloke like you, I reckon soon in heat. Go have your ordinary life, you skulking bourgeois coward. You don't deserve a man of honest emotions."

Open-mouthed, Jake watched Wip wrestle an imaginary ring off his finger, throw the mimed shape on the floor and grind it with his foot. That wasn't enough. He stamped on it.

"You're no Jean Louis Barrault!" Jake shouted, his voice raised for the first time.

As Wip stalked out, he had a sudden inspiration. "Mixed marriages don't work!" he shouted. With a malicious laugh, he ran to his truck, passing a soldier clutching a bleeding arm and walking to the aid tent. Wip gunned the engine. *He'll assume that refined Doc Friedman's been tupping a native girl, got her pregnant and wants to marry her. The handsome, mature artillery officer, me, is trying to give his friend good advice.*

Jake cleaned and bandaged the soldier's arm like a robot. Stunned by Wip's accusation of racism, he was running excuses in his mind: his cousin Sylvia's dictum that Jews should marry out, that too much purity weakened a race. He knew Wip was wrong, that the loss of a people and culture did matter. But he had no counterargument without demeaning the beauty of Wip the mutt, with Wip's heart and soul. Wip was unfair; he'd done his own withholding—Jake guessed what he was hiding—but Wip's anguish tore Jake at his core.

Over the next weeks, he didn't see Wip. At the maintenance shed, Jake learned that Wip was helping to set up the anti-aircraft battery on North Daughter. Obviously, he was finding tasks off base when Jake had free time. Jake's days passed in a cloud of shock and confusion; nights were a jumble of piles of Jewish corpses as high as skyscrapers, accusing dead eyes, severed limbs, pooling blood; Wip's imaginary ring glowing in the air, Jake reaching for it but the ring whirring away; Esther alternately embracing him and spitting in his face; his father's horror long ago at his son's "phase." He saw his mother's coffin being lowered into the grave and his father's soon after, Mirrie's electric shock treatment, and Tal's terror of having a child who might go insane. It was up to him to make a new Jewish family. He had no capacity for perspective; only helping his patients stabilised him. Dimly, he sensed Wip was terribly hurt, but his own sense of martyrdom for jettisoning his personal happiness for a principle spoke much louder. His turmoil screamed so constantly that he heard nothing else.

A few weeks later, he went to their cave, hoping to find Wip or traces of him. Jungle fecundity was reclaiming the track; he cut his wrist on a bramble. The cave was musky, beetles scurrying from his boots. Their tent, tarpaulin, sheets and lamps were gone. There must be *some* evidence of our joy, Jake thought. He didn't give up. At the back of the cave, he shone his torch on a sliver of brown and white. It was a Camel cigarette butt, Wip's. He'd missed it in his annihilation of all they'd shared. Jake picked it up, brushed away a spider and kissed it. After putting it in his pocket, he wrote a note and left it at the cave entrance. "I guessed what you did in Paris. I don't care." A heart and the initial J.

As the peak turmoil subsided, he just felt alone, lonelier than he'd ever imagined. Scholarly sentences about tropical parasite articles danced in front of his blurring eyes. During hard-working days, the spirit of Wip was everywhere, the man nowhere. When he inhaled his Dunhill pipe tobacco, he tasted Camel flakes. When the breeze rustled leaves, he'd swivel, hearing Wip unbutton his shirt; a falling coconut was Wip slapping a fly on a wall. *It can't be over.* But it was.

CHAPTER 22

Mobile Hospital Tent, Friday 8 August 1941.

JAKE TAMPED DOWN his pipe, lay back on his bed, and glared at the gold-edged invitation in his hand. This party he couldn't decline. He was in hospital pyjamas, having faked nausea to avoid seeing Wip at the Officers' Ball tomorrow. The event promised to be spectacular, put on by the battalion to thank Rabaul citizens for their hospitality and construction work on the aerodromes and artillery bases. Jake had checked himself in on Thursday night and planned to discharge himself on Sunday, working extra shifts to make up for his deception.

But this event, which Wip would also attend, he couldn't dodge. It was a ball scheduled for Wednesday, August 20. Sir Joshua Cohen, a visiting Singapore businessman, had rented part of the Cosmopolitan Hotel to reciprocate the army's hospitality at the Officers' Ball. For Captain Jacob Mordecai Friedman, a Jewish physician, to snub an obviously Jewish merchant who'd earned the king's honours would be grist for gossip. *Wip's not worth the embarrassment,* Jake told himself.

He wrote an acceptance note and sent it by the hospital boy to Sir Joshua.

Five evenings later, he watched his tentmate Derek Egan don the mess dress of a Royal Australian Artillery officer. Egan shimmered in a black jacket with red lapels, a white shirt and black bow tie. He was so scrubbed he could have been an advertisement for Colgate soap. Jake was equally shining in his best khaki tunic, captain's pips and unit badge. His shoes were mirrors. Miraculously, they'd kept their formal dress free of mould. Jake's cheeks glowed pink, his curly hair and moustache were glossy black, but dark circles under his eyes betrayed his insomnia.

The guests would be the same as at the wildly successful Officers' Ball—the island's governing and merchant leaders with their wives, veterans who'd captured Rabaul from the Germans in 1914 and stayed, and current military officers—an all-white crowd, of course.

Jake's bowels braided as he stepped onto the veranda of the two-story Cosmopolitan Hotel. Above him, hotel guests on the upper balconies leant against the rails, watching city leaders emerge from their cars.

The hotel had a beer garden and car park under the shadow of the picturesque Mother. Jake vaguely remembered that a Chinese entrepreneur had built and owned it for years, then sold it to a plantation owner. The Cosmopolitan was the preferred social hub in Rabaul. He'd arrived early. He hadn't meant to; anxiety must have made his body rush as much as his mind. *How will I handle seeing Wip?* No part of him allowed Wip to be indifferent to him; his gut expected it.

Lively talk wafted from the beer garden. It stopped suddenly when the news broadcast began. Grateful for a distraction, Jake sat at the bar, took off his white gloves, and sipped a glass of bitters.

"'I have no son,' the Soviet Dictator, Joseph Stalin, is reported to have replied to German ransom demands for his son, Yakov. The Germans have apparently captured Stalin's illegitimate son and are using his purportedly eager surrender to urge Russian soldiers to defect..." Jake recalled Rabbi Danglow telling him that Yakov's mother was Jewish, and Stalin kept her out of sight. "...So far, Russians soldiers don't appear to be defecting. They've learned that it is possible to be even more brutal than Stalin..."

Disowning a son is why he's **Uncle** *Joe, not Father Joe.* Jake was amazed he could still pun. His mind leapt to Australia. What did armchair commie Rex think of this? Talia had written that he didn't volunteer when Hitler attacked Russia. He'd won a poetry prize and said he would stay home to elevate Australian literary language. *I'm in khakis to protect the likes of him? No. It's for family and democracy.* For a moment, he was having breakfast with Talia and Simon. *I have a loving family. Wip doesn't. That's why he couldn't understand me.* He kicked himself. Always, his thoughts reverted to Wip.

He re-focused on the news. "Our heroic outnumbered troops are holding Tobruk against Rommel. Negotiations between Japan and America may be at a stalemate." The news ended with sports scores and horse race winners. The instant cheers and boos told Jake that the bar's patrons had money at stake.

He went to the dining room. The doors were closed. He opened them and saw the room was empty. A Tolai boy hovered behind him, anxious. "Go. No worries," Jake muttered. Tables were set with white tablecloths, cutlery for several courses and place cards. He found his card and stared at it, breathing shallowly. A minute later, he found Wip's on a different table. He switched the cards so Wip would be sitting opposite him. *This will clarify everything. Surely, he can like me again...*

He tapped his lip. Their closeness was beginning to feel like a treasured memory, a framed photograph from an earlier era. Sighing, he returned Wip's card to its original place. *I can't control this.*

He left the dining room, nodding to the boy. "Sorry," he said, not knowing if he understood. In the ballroom, a local band had set up. It swung into "Begin the Beginning" by Cole Porter, "How Deep is the Ocean" by Irving Berlin, and "The Wizard of Oz". The host, Sir Joshua Cohen and his family—a plump middle-aged wife, two sons and a daughter—bustled in and clustered around the band. Town guests drifted in: men in tuxedos with bejewelled women. Some men had brought their house boys, intending to change shirts during the eating, drinking, dancing and sweating hours ahead.

Excitement grew when the military officers arrived in uniformed splendour. Five pilots swaggered in, spectacular in short navy-blue jackets with wide pale blue lapels over white shirts and black bow ties. They were in town to assess the aerodrome facilities for the planned squadron of fighters and bombers. Jake held his breath when Wip strode in with Egan and companions from the Royal Australian Artillery. They wore short black jackets over black waistcoats, snow-white shirts and black bow ties. Their wide lapels were red. Athletic yet graceful with his blond hair speckled with grey, Wip looked like a mature Adonis. His stiffened shoulders showed that he'd seen Jake. He headed to the other side of the room, where he was surrounded by admirers, mostly women. *I guess hostility's better than indifference,* Jake thought.

Older uniformed veterans arrived. A voice behind Jake rasped, "More medals on us than them pretty boys here to defend us." Jake turned. A middle-aged man with a row of medals on his chest and a single pip of a second lieutenant was leaning on a cane. The rasp spasmed to a hacking cough. His companion put an arm around him. "Relax, mate." *Doesn't sound tubercular,* Jake diagnosed. *Maybe a gas attack from the last war.*

Jake looked at the "pretty boys," which included him. There was an abundance of gold braid on fit men with the crowns and pips of rank, but few medals. *Limper's got a point,*

Jake thought uneasily. *Must be Returned Soldiers' League, the fellows who made Egan's life a misery over gun placement at Praed.*

He turned to the door and saw the nurses of the 2/10 Field Ambulance Unit come in. He waved at Priscilla, his army nurse friend, glad to see a woman he was comfortable with. Saluting the veteran, he went to introduce himself to his host, Sir Joshua, and his family. Three Jewish officers from the battalion were lined up behind Jake to pay their respects.

Jake made for the mobbed bar. Ceiling fans mingled the scents of beer, wine, smoke, sweat and tropical flowers. Tolai boys in western suits offered trays with salmon patties, cheese pastries, salami, boiled shrimp, and bread with spiced taro paste. Conversation roared above violins and brass.

A crash of cymbals called for silence. Florid-faced and beaming, Cohen led the immaculately tailored battalion commander Carr to the microphone. Cohen gave a short speech of thanks to the army for last week's entertainment, and especially for lending him the celebrated 2/22 brass band to play "God Save the King" and the early dances.

Cohen led his beautiful young daughter to the floor for the opening foxtrot, while Carr partnered Cohen's wife. Cohen's sons, young men in their twenties, led out merchants' wives. Rumbas and waltzes warmed up the crowd. Jake danced with Priscilla. He hadn't gone to balls since his undergraduate days, and began tentatively: slow, slow, quick, quick. Priscilla's responsive moves were severely neat; he visualised her ferociously taming bedsheets. After the first dance, he relaxed. *I'm good enough.* He began to enjoy the exertion.

But he couldn't help it; his eyes always swivelled to Wip. The epitome of gallantry, Wip guided a middle-aged woman through a flamboyant twirl, pressing a protective hand on her back to keep her within their half-circle. At the dance's end, Jake noticed him detaching quickly, as if recoiling from static electricity when she pressed against him. *He's working hard.* A tendril of hope? He smothered it and danced on.

The music shifted to swing. Lights dimmed; couples clung and undulated. The 2/22 band, former Salvation Army musicians, kept playing with the local orchestra, tossing melodies into the air and then making wild embellishments. *They're having a fantastic time.* Jake grinned. *Kids out of school.*

A singer crooned a love song by the British band Six Swingers, "Bluebirds in the Moonlight". Jake thanked Priscilla for the dances and turned toward the door to go outside for fresh air. "You seem... absent," she murmured. He hadn't asked her to accompany him. She saw his eyes touch and recoil from an artillery officer's back, looking away hurriedly when she pursed her lips. He walked fast, his shoes rapping the wooden floor.

In the garden, a stew of scents from tropical flowers and bushes hit him. It was the dry season; there was a taint of decay in his nostrils. At the end of the garden, a lone palm tree shaded a table and bench. War felt a world away. He walked around the parked Rolls Royces, Fords and Chevrolets, a Tolai guard watching him. Jake laughed. His mind was on Wip, not stealing a car.

When he returned, the musicians were taking a break. Recorded music blared. To his relief, Priscilla was jitterbugging with an orderly from her unit. Sweating freely, her set hair straggling, she twirled with abandon, transformed. *How we exist in separate desk drawers,* he reflected. At the bar, he downed a glass of the night's kai punch, a blend of dark rum, paw paw, sour breadfruit and lemon. "Punch" was the right word for its kick. He exchanged pleasantries with a guest who turned out to be a local doctor. They turned to watch the dancers. Wip was in the centre of the floor. He lifted a cheerful teenager with blonde bobbing curls and lipstick that matched his red lapels into his arms, spun around with her, and then set her down gently, not missing a beat. Jitterbug was made for him. Pummelled by loss, Jake bit his lip.

The gong for dinner sounded, and the music stopped. Guests found their place cards. Chairs scraped the floor, and the hubbub of strangers introducing themselves boomed. Military uniforms were dispersed among the civilians.

Jake had been placed opposite another doctor, who introduced himself as "Tim Blackwell, general practitioner, Native Hospital." He looked a jaded forty, his twang Western Australian. Jake took an instant dislike to him; he was in Wip's chair, if Jake had had the guts to keep the place cards switched. His other companions were a square-jawed corporate executive with wavy brown hair, a gold watch and a heavy signet ring, and his pretty blonde jewelled wife. They introduced themselves as George and Jennifer Beaumont. A lean and corded plantation manager with his equally corded wife were Bill and Gertrude Blitzer, she with a European accent, from New Ireland. Both emanated a jittery energy. Jake recalled that New Ireland was poorer than New Britain. *No easy living there,* he thought. The table was completed by a clergyman named Tom Rowland, who wore a white collar. Jake was the only army officer.

Trying to rise above feeling out of sorts, Jake asked the doctor in Wip's chair, "How was your day?"

"Two tuberculars," Blackwell replied, unfurling his napkin. "Labourers from a plantation compound—not yours, Bill, you two space cots correctly. I can't get the other managers to give their employees enough living space. And a beriberi and ulcer from a village near Talligap Mission. Fortunately, no new polios."

Jake sat up, activated. "How do you treat paralysis polio?" He remembered the Chinese boy working at Ah Kuan Ho's store heaving his splinted body to the counter and back.

"Splints. Immobilise until well past the acute stage. Only thing to do." Blackwell looked surprised. "But what shattered lives! If they survive, they're useless in their system. The boys can't build huts, and the girls can't garden or gather shells for money. Patrol officers sometimes bring in a poor dumb blighter accompanied by an adult from their tribe, equally dumb." He puffed his cigar as they waited for the first course.

"With respect, sir, I disagree." Jake leant over the table. "I've seen Kenny's regimen of hot compresses, massage and exercises restore mobility in and after the acute stage. Splints d...debilitate." *What's got into me?*

Blackwell frowned. "Kenny isn't standard protocol. The idea that a villager could learn the hygiene for hot, wet compresses and re-training flaccid muscles is absurd. They run to their sorcerers if a cure isn't instant. With respect, sir, you don't know what you're talking about." He turned to Jenny Beaumont, the executive's wife, for support. She patted his arm but said nothing.

Her silence encouraged Jake. He looked at his table companions. The priest had a pixie-like angular face. Under white hair, his expression was good-humoured. The plantation manager couple were staring at him with quizzical curiosity.

Jake persisted. "I think they could learn. Look at their motor skills. The boys shimmy up palm trees as easily as drinking a glass of water. The intricate bamboo fishing nets they make take great skill. The girls balance loads on their heads and make fine crafts. You're imposing low expectations on them. I believe a doctor like you could help paralysed polio patients if you wanted to." *What am I doing?*

"By God," Blackwell exclaimed, jumping to his feet, "You're picking a fight with me. In earlier days, I'd demand satisfaction."

Jake half-stood.

"Terrible outbreak in villages near us recently," Gertrude Blitzer offered. "There's another way?"

The priest wagged an age-spotted hand. "Please, everyone. We all want to do the right thing. Polio's a scourge. Let's enjoy dinner. Give thanks to Our Lord that we have the option." He crossed himself.

Jake heard a chair at the next table scrape. Turning, he met the eyes of Cohen's daughter. She looked—what—vindicated? More than excited. She jumped up and shrilled, "And no one should impose low expectations on young women!" She stayed there, blushing but determined.

"Miss Cohen, I don't," Jake said. "My younger sister's a virtuoso pianist, and my elder sister was the first Jewish woman admitted to the Bar in Melbourne." He was proud of Talia and Miriam despite Miriam's illness.

"I apologise," he said, turning to Blackwell. "I abused my duty to represent the army and was unfair to you. But I believe what I said. Tell you what, let's have your duel. After dinner, let's shimmy up the garden palm tree, no rope. The first to fall loses." His cheeks were hot. *I'm drunk!*

Cheers came from nearby tables and a promise of bets. Blackwell had to agree. As they sat, Jake realised he had no idea how to climb a palm tree. He noticed the girl also sat after trying to catch his eye.

Toasts and speeches were interspersed with dinner: shrimp coconut soup followed by a salad, then roast beef with local vegetables, ice cream, cheese and port. Jake felt woozy. *Did I lash out at Blackwell because I want Wip in that chair? Or is it the car crash, Grace's ghost never letting me forget the polio call I didn't reach?* He looked down, loathing himself.

"Let me widen the discussion to my area of knowledge," the priest began with a kind smile. "Both of you excellent doctors are right. Early missionaries found the Tolai amenable to our doctrines because they resembled their own founding myths. They believed that two brothers were the first men and that they created the sea and land. They had a first mother. One brother created all the good places, the other all the bad places and ugly people, though more from incompetence than evil. Because of the bad brother's mischief, man lost immortality. Interesting, yes? Some Tolai are now catechists."

"I never heard these myths, Father," Jennifer Beaumont said, draining her wine glass. "A Trinity?"

The priest's Catholic. Jake contemplated Jennifer discreetly. She was heavily made up, but skin bloating suggested alcoholism. Her eyes expressed defeat. He'd read in the *Rabaul Times* that executives' wives in Rabaul drank excessively; they had so much native help and no jobs of their own, that they were reduced to rounds of boring formal parties.

"No Trinity. Their beliefs differ from ours."

"If the bad brother was incompetent, do they have a myth of evil, like Eve eating the apple?" Jennifer Beaumont pursued.

Jake interjected, "Ma'am, some Hebrew scholars say 'apple' was a mistranslation of pomegranate."

"Really?" the priest said, his face alive with interest. "My Hebrew isn't good enough to comment; I know local languages better. As to evil, the bad brother first killed a man against the good brother's order. For Tolai, the worlds of spirits and ancestors' souls coexist with the world the living inhabit."

"So every day is Halloween?" Gertrude asked with a grin. "That I believe."

"In a way," the priest answered. "They have an Abode of Death where the dead enjoy a happy afterlife if they've distributed enough shell money at death. There's a place of eternal torment if they haven't. They always had a trading system and shell currency for accumulating wealth, to qualify for their Abode. When Tolai elders saw material benefits in not killing each other, most converted. They're adaptable. Dr Blackwell's right about village hygiene. I see far too many preventable diseases there. Dr Friedman, things can backfire if you deviate from government manuals. But you're right that some Tolai could learn anything."

George Beaumont cut in. "They're buying up soap from our Burns Philps store. We had to triple our orders." *Gold watch works for the Australian conglomerate,* Jake noted. "But," Beaumont pressed, "you missionaries should be careful. Preaching that God creates men equal causes discipline problems for us coves who keep the place running. Last thing we need is another strike."

"As in labour strike?" Jake asked, eyebrows raised.

"In '29," the priest explained. "A young Tolai ship captain heard from American Black sailors that Tolai wages were too low. Tolai are competitive. He felt shamed. He organised a walkout of 3,000 Tolai workers in Rabaul when senior officials were away. He planned it in total secrecy. Europeans woke up one morning... no workers."

A Tolai waiter refreshed their drinks while Beaumont continued. "Luckily for us, the Americans hadn't told this captain what to do next. The workers assembled at two missions outside Rabaul, expecting missionaries to mediate— Christ's mercy and all that sermon stuff—but the missionaries told them to go to work; they were under contract. The strike fizzled and the ringleader captain was jailed. But the natives won't make that mistake again."

"Impressive secrecy," Blackwell conceded, "But as for buying soap, I bet they're trading it for shell money. Not for hygiene, as far as I've seen."

"George," Jennifer Beaumont said, grabbing her husband's arm. "Didn't Ricky Miller here get polio bad? He was splinted for months and then sent to Kenny's clinic in Brisbane. He was three."

George loosened his bow tie, grunting, "If you say so, Jen. Can't say I recall."

Jake turned to her. "Mrs Beaumont, what a small world. I saw Kenny treat a boy of three from Rabaul. He came in crippled and left a few weeks later, climbing stairs. Kenny posits..."—he locked eyes with Blackwell— "that muscles in spasm are the ones affected by the disease; the seemingly paralysed opposing muscles are usually not diseased. Standard theory says the opposite. Splinting without treating the initial spasms damages viable muscles."

"Kenny's methods can't work here," Blackwell snapped. "Leave off."

Jake went red and pivoted. The account of Tolai conversions was intriguing, and the priest seemed broadminded, up to a tease. Despite his devastation over losing Wip, part of him was coping. "Father, reasons for conversion are complex, no? Early Jews converted for a simpler life. St Peter wasn't kosher."

The priest's eyes twinkled. "We accept mixed motives for conversion but offer absolution when the heart is pure. It's been a successful formula. Look at our numbers!"

"Touché," Jake conceded, laughing.

After dessert, card players drifted to the game room to gamble while other guests had a last drink and left. Battalion commander Carr showed no sign of leaving, so the military stayed.

"Right, Friedman, time for your duel," Blackwell grumbled. He and Jake walked outside, accompanied by boisterous bettors. Two grinning Tolai boys, one of whom Jake thought had waited on their table, followed. In the corner of his eye, Jake saw Wip on the veranda. He felt stupid; Blackwell wasn't a bad sort. But he was committed.

The temperature was cooler, and the air was sweet. As Jake and Blackwell shrugged off their coats and unlaced their shoes, Jake eyed Blackwell's athletic physique. *Use will. You only need to last a second longer. You're doing it for oppressed Jews in Europe. You want it more. If it hurts, remember Pa's dictum—call pain Balm-of-Gilead sweet.*

They tossed a coin to see who'd go first. Jake won and deferred.

Egan clapped his shoulder. "Good luck! My bet's on you, mate." He called the time, shining a flashlight on his watch. "On the count of three, Dr Blackwell, begin. Remember, the longer time on the tree wins."

Blackwell stood beside the tree, gripping its thin trunk. The bark ridges were narrow and flaky from the dry weather.

"One, two, three!"

Blackwell sucked his stomach in, heaved his arms, then thighs up a few inches, heaved a second time, rested and heaved.

A puff of wind dislodged a coconut. "Shit," Blackwell yelled as his socked foot missed the ridge. He clung with his arms for a second, then slithered down.

"Eighteen seconds," called Egan.

The two Tolai boys had edged to the front of the crowd. Gleaming white teeth showed their amusement.

"This is bad for discipline," Blackwell hissed. "God forbid they go on strike again." He put his shoes and coat on.

Jake clutched the trunk with his thighs and arms. On the count of three, he heaved hip-first. The bark scraped his skin through his trousers. *Feels good, I'm made for this,* he willed himself. He intuited the dimension of the next ridge, the resistance needed for stability, and heaved again. Bark seared his palms. *Feels sweet.* He pushed one thigh up, leaned in, pulled with his arms, pulled the other thigh up, and with the momentum, heaved once more before falling backwards, landing on the grass.

"Thirty-one seconds," Egan shouted. "Friedman wins."

One of the native boys stripped to his underwear and scampered up the tree with an antelope's grace. He seemed to spend a long time there, but brought down a perfectly ripe brown coconut. He offered it to Jake.

"A prize?" Jake asked, still lying on the grass. "Thank you."

"ToSaina mi," the boy said, pointing at his chest. He dressed, and both boys went inside.

Jake felt soft, bare arms helping him sit up. Rubbing the back of his head, he found himself staring at Cohen's daughter. "You're magnificent," she said, "to do that for the oppressed people of the world." Then, in a whisper, "I'm Sarah. My family will be hours at this dance. Come to my room." They were standing face to face now, almost touching.

In the hotel, the music was starting.

It was a frank invitation, generous and brave. Perhaps she was rebelling against her family; perhaps her hormones were raging with frustration and rage. None of that lessened her astounding courage. He felt a stirring in his groin. She was gorgeous, with tumbling brown curly hair, a slightly aquiline nose, flashing dark eyes, full lips and high cheekbones. She was in the pink of health, her figure a 36, 24, 37, if he had a tape. *If it means so much to you, go plant your frigging Friedman seed in a Jewish woman here,* Wip had taunted, fingering him for a racist. Jake had a flash of what children of his seed and her egg would look like.

After a moment, he shook his head. It wasn't him, after all. "I'm incredibly honoured," he said, "but I must decline. I'm on duty." He kissed her hand, feeling her grow hot with embarrassment. She ran inside.

Jake walked to the cloakroom, tossing the coconut from hand to hand. He put it in a bag and then returned to the ballroom. In the ballroom, the dancing was wilder. A screen had been put up, and the recorded acid voice of Josephine Bradley, England's leading dance teacher, was introducing the American Lindy Hop, a dance new to the colony. A film showed the moves. Jake stood at the side, watching.

"Oh no," a voice drawled from the ballroom floor. "Yank negro moves filtered through Rule Britannia's staidest old hag." It was Wip, quite drunk.

Live musicians returned and duplicated the Lindy Hop beat. Several couples tried it, with the inevitable collisions and laughing, "Sorry, mates."

Jake looked at his watch: 2.30 a.m. The ball wouldn't wind down for some time. He stalked the perimeter, longing for it to end.

The band reverted to waltzes. Wip was still an Adonis in his black, red and white uniform and glowing blond hair. But Jake could see him losing composure. His face creased with dread when a jewelled woman moved determinedly in his direction. Anxiety, repulsion? "Cossack dance," Wip shouted. "Honour the Russkies keeping Jerry busy!"

The band launched into eastern-sounding folk songs.

Wip danced alone. Every bit the feral Cossack, he jacked his legs, leapt while spreading them, then down, supporting his bulk on one hand. A few officers joined him, clumsily mimicking his moves.

Jake hardened under his trousers. He was flooded with a yearning to be close to Wip, in their cave, saying the things they'd withheld. He felt tears singe his eyes. He'd pushed to the front row without deciding to and was hemmed in, a shoving minute from the bathroom. Distracting his mind, spelling 'onomatopoeia' backwards, he worked his way through to the veranda. To his relief, his tears dried, and his erection subsided.

The priest spotted him and pressed a card into his hand: Father Thomas Rowland, retired, with a local phone number. "If you want to talk more about the island you're here to protect, do call me. A caution, if you'll permit me: for Tolai, accepting a gift can imply reciprocity. Sometimes a coconut is just a coconut, but the gift of a perfect coconut figures in their creation myths."

Jake pocketed the card. "Thank you, Father. I appreciate it." *Reciprocity? Balderdash.*

The final dance was a conga around the room, up the stairs and down again. At 4.30, the musicians played "God Save the King." It was over.

Grimly proud that he'd survived the night, Jake collected his bag with the coconut and headed for his car. He was embarrassed by his fight with Blackwell but, mostly, desperately lonely. At the car, he smelt hard liquor behind him, too many kinds to identify. His hand was grabbed and fiercely kissed.

"God, Jake, I'm a jerk. I saw the whole tree caper." It was Wip. "Can you forgive me? Please. I owe you explanations. Sunday? I can get a vacant house. Every moment should be precious."

The last thing Jake had expected was a perfect night. He was reborn. With the lightest of touches, they separated.

CHAPTER 23

· · · · · · · ·

O N SUNDAY MORNING, Jake bounded up three wooden steps to the veranda of a two-storey bungalow on Naramula Avenue. Before rapping on the front door, he paused, listening to the agitated crump of his heart over the birdsong. He turned and looked downhill, past elegant government buildings built by the German Administration, to the shimmering harbour and quiet docks. A medley of church bells tolled eleven. Turning back, he knocked. Inside, shoes hurried, slapping on wood. The door flung open.

"Ahhh!" Wip exclaimed, arms outstretched and face alive with mischief.

"This is nicer than our cave," Jake said approvingly as Wip showed him around the ground floor.

The living room had sofas and chairs upholstered with cheerful floral fabrics, a grandfather clock that had stopped, and a covered grand piano. It was stuffy and stale-smelling, and the fans were off. They walked through a dining room to a kitchen equipped to cater parties. A sticky flypaper hung from the light fixture; Jake saw two flies.

"Changed it this morning," Wip explained.

There was a billiards room, library, bathroom and a locked office.

"I met the Collins family in New Guinea years ago," Wip explained. "He's a buyer for Burns Philps and visited the coffee plantation I was managing. When we ran into each other at the Post Office last week, he asked me to keep an eye on his servants while the family was away. He gave me the key and said, 'bring your friends,' with a wink. Little did he think..." Wip laughed. "They won't return from Australia until Tavurvur stops smoking. The kids have bronchitis, and their Rottweiler—I kid you not—has a tropical fungus that nothing could fix. The cleaners and gardeners are off on Sundays, and their houseboy and cook have gone to their villages. It would be an empty luxury without you. This is the first of my trinity of surprises."

"Hardly holy." Jake grinned.

Wip lightly punched Jake's arm. "Let's have a drink on the balcony, get to know each other, really, this time."

Jake elbowed him back. "'Really'—good word."

On the balcony, they sat on bamboo chairs sipping a Tom Collins cocktail Wip had made to honour their absent benefactor—gin, lemon juice, sugar and soda, with grated rind and salt on the glass rim. The local lemon was explosively fragrant. *Lavish with sugar. Does he think I need an aphrodisiac?* Jake had to restrain himself from pulling Wip onto his lap for a kiss.

But they had to talk, and this was a good place. Tall poles supporting the roof allowed a breeze to provide fragrant ventilation. Jake looked over a tree-shaded lawn sloping to the property boundary, marked by hedge bushes with glossy green leaves and delicate white flowers about thirty feet below. The gardens were a riot of yellow-white frangipani, blatant red hibiscus and purple crocuses.

"This is like the house I imagined us living in." Jake reached for Wip's hand. "The only thing missing is a guest cottage."

"Guest cottage is out back, and a cook's quarters. Did

you really think of life with me?" Wip toyed with Jake's hand, stoking it.

"All the time. You age very fine." Jake sighed. "But don't get conceited. I commit quickly, perhaps too quickly. I know you're, have been, different. I don't care. I guessed you were a prostitute. That explained protecting your nose through your fights and the tiny scar I felt. I was awed then, not jealous. Now I'd be a mauling tiger of jealousy."

"Heavenly, to be so wanted." Wip leaned back, arms behind his head.

Jake saw the lines around Wip's soften, and he continued, "Wanting to cling close and long is new for me—all terror and thrills." He gazed at a butterfly resting on the red flower of a potted fern near their feet, unready to meet the eyes of the cause of his unmanageable emotions. His stare disturbed the butterfly; it fluttered away, blue wings with a white stripe and pale blue dots beating. A flock of parrots with red breasts and blue heads whirred from branches into the dappled sky. "Every living creature here is a masterpiece," Jake declared.

"I'll 'fess my... complicated tale later," Wip said. He wriggled seductively. "What do we do in this life?"

"Well, I have a medical practice run from our house and publish research on tropical diseases. The house is like this, but further from the volcanoes. You get rich from coffee. I help you succeed by keeping your workers healthy. You run a dance school for talented youngsters, including Tolai. We give scholarships." He sat up. "Yes, see, they have their traditional moves. How amazing it would be to mix styles with the moves of your beloved Nijinsky. A new art form..."

"Hmmm." Wip shifted in his chair. "Tolai elders won't allow European pirouettes to pollute their sacred steps, not in our lifetimes. But it's a charming vision. Clearly, I put too much gin in the drink. Who stays in the guest cottage you say we must have?"

They had fun, initially, deciding which family members

would swallow their prejudices for a month in paradise. But what began as choices on their part quickly turned into rejection. Tal, Jake's sister, would visit. But would her husband, Simon? What would Rabbi Danglow think? He liked Jake risking his life in uniform, but Jake unconventionally settled and happy? Would Wip's niece and nephew be allowed to make the trip, the youngsters he wanted so much to help? Jake's tears pooled when Wip insisted that his mentally ill sister, Miriam, could live with them as long as she wanted. Taking a breath, Jake wondered, "How did we get into this? I swear, my visions weren't specific." He wiped his eyes. "I can't tell you how much your support helps me with my guilt over leaving Mirrie."

Absorbed in thoughts of family, they were silent. Then Jake cleared his throat. "Wip, fantasies aside, I can't promise never to seek a Jewish marriage." He tightened his lips, anxiety supercharging his pulse. *Is this the end again?*

"But isn't life with me what you want most? We just decided who'll visit us," Wip protested.

"Yes, but the need to have Jewish children is also my core. I dream in Hebrew."

Wip drummed his fingers on bamboo: tap; tap-tap-tap; tap; for what felt like forever. Finally, "I accept that. I love you," blowing Jake a kiss. "Learning about Esther crushed me. You were my... chance for a happy ending. In a second, you slashed my future like an axe through lace." He looked up. "But the weeks apart changed my perspective."

Jake stood, touched Wip's moist eyelashes and licked his finger. "Nice. I was empty, a blubbering fool without you. Thank you, thank you, thank you."

Wip pushed Jake to sit. "We know things our mates don't. That Toshio's up to something. I've been in a war. Its horrors,"– he shook his head. "The moment. That's all that matters." He finished his drink. "Did you hear from the hush-hush bloke who wanted the film?"

"Unsigned note under my sheet, said I'd bagged a real

one. Forget Toshio. You said you had three surprises. I count this house, unless the amount of gin in my drink counts?"

"I'm not *that* cheap." Wip snorted. He pulled a crumpled scrap of newspaper from his shorts pocket. "The day you broke up with me..."

"Darling, you dumped me. Do let's be accurate." Jake took the paper from Wip. "Crikey! You meant us to buy land? Stunning. Marvellous."

"It's gone now. I don't know why I kept the ad. Dumb faith that one day I'd prove that I dreamt your fantasy." Wip chuckled. "Third surprise later. Um, what do you say to going inside?"

They'd entered the balcony through a room with a sewing machine and shelves of fabrics, buttons and thread. Holding hands, Wip led Jake along a wood-floored corridor to the master bedroom.

Jake burst out laughing at the four-poster bed with netting, thinking of their cave. Wip turned on the white ceiling fan. *Tuk tuk tuk,* a grey and black-spotted gecko chirped in warning, shifting its position on the wall to escape the fan breeze. A white-tipped dropping on the wooden floor showed it had recently dined. Sunlight angled through a five-foot window, hitting light primrose walls. Between two upholstered chairs, a potted green fern stood, and on the dresser, Wip had put a decanter of water and a vase of hibiscus. Jake saw an eyeglass case behind the flowers. He reached for it. Wip grabbed his arm. "Later," he whispered.

Tentatively and slowly, they undressed each other. Wip's fingers marked Jake's cheeks, jawbone, and neck; his tongue danced a tango with Jake's ears: lobes, outer and inner. Easing onto the bed, Jake pulled Wip toward him, his eyes opening and shutting on the topography of this man he'd tried to forget after their quarrel. Jake desperately wanted Wip inside him—and was terrified. At Wip's caresses, he dissolved into a lake of want and lubricating. Wip pushed in, Jake clutching the filling, pulsing warmth. "Home. Home," Jake wept when they came.

"Home," Wip echoed, falling on his back. They lay still, stupefied and separate, arms behind their heads, letting their hearts slow. The fan blades laboriously shot puffs of air that separated the sweat on their chests into rivulets dripping onto the sheets. Jake put a finger on Wip's ribs, tracing the rise and fall of Wip's lungs and matching his rhythm. "My hands have in them every gorgeous inch of you," he murmured.

Wip turned, suddenly somewhere else in his head. He supported himself on his elbow. "I don't think of bodies that way…"

"How then?"

"I hear what a body wants." He got up and started massaging Jake's feet, pressing points in the heels, each toe and the flesh of his soles between.

Jake stretched in a supine stupor. "How did you know what I needed when I didn't?"

"I listen."

A twitch of distance between them. *He knows because he's been a pleasure boy.* "Wip, every time we make love, and I'm meshed with you, body, heart, the depths of my soul and imaginings—where do I end and you begin—you go away with your mind, you make us different. I've guessed a lot about your life, but it will be so much better for us if you say it all. Out loud. Now. Please. It's time."

Rain whacked the house and streams of snake patterns down the window. Wip nodded. "Yes. In a minute. You think you've guessed my past life; you haven't. Last surprise." He got up and brought the eyeglass case. "You open it," he said, tense with anticipation. "I'll get the sheets laundered," he added prosaically. "Can't have servant gossip."

Jake opened the case. Inside were two rings.

"To make up for the imaginary ring I ripped off my

finger and stamped on. Pick one that fits." They were the same material and design, just different sizes.

"Oh, God," Jake breathed, looking up at Wip, "how... generous spirited." The setting was gold around an oval of an off-white substance mottled by brownish-yellow specks. He didn't recognise the matter; it wasn't a jewel. He touched its varnish. Some gold specs had dripped onto the oval. He turned the ring over. Crudely scratched in the back were intertwined letters J&W.

"What is it?" Jake slipped a ring on his middle finger. "I've never seen anything like it."

Wip grinned over his dimple.

How childlike; I adore him, Jake thought as Wip sat.

"It's rough because I made it myself after Cohen's ball using the maintenance shed tools. Yours truly, who replaced a car tie-rod, thought he could make jewellery. Ahhh, harder than it looks. Everything's local: the gold's from the new mine, and the oval is a wild pig tusk I bought in the Bung and shaped."

Beyond words, Jake rubbed the oval. He could feel the feral pig rise from the dead and infuse him with energy; he felt his fingers trawling cold river water for alluvial gold. The connection with Rabaul was profound. "I'll wear it on my finger or under my shirt, always. Tiffany diamonds are rubbish compared to this."

They held hands. But Jake kept twisting his hand, admiring his ring. "I want to make love again."

This time, they were quick. After washing in a bathroom down the corridor, they sat wrapped in towels on the bedroom chairs. Jake ventured, "You have things to tell me: why you say the purest emotion is dominance of one person over another, what happened after the war, and what makes you Wip?"

"Yes." Wip lit a Camel, and Jake filled his pipe. Silence. "This is hard," he complained. "Impossible. It's such a lovely day." He got up and paced the room; the towel fell to the floor.

"It won't be if you just do it. I've guessed a lot."

Wip picked up the towel and sat again. He spoke fast. "I stayed in Paris after the war. I had army pay. As I told you, I've never screwed a woman, can't function with them." His face creased with puzzlement. "This is the first time I've said the word: impotent. Perhaps the doctor can explain the will of a cock..."

"You're all stud with me. Sex is, well, mysterious. Scientists have observed animals and plants being exclusively same sex."

"I'm related to pervy plants and what, squirrels?" Wip's laugh was bitter. "Anyway, I knew in '19 that home would be all hiding and pretending. My family would press me to marry, except for Mum, who wanted me to be a priest. Holy orders would have given me a hiding place. Our priest fumbled me when I was an altar boy, the same priest who praised Mum as the ideal Catholic wife. St Hypocrite, I call him. I lost my faith in the trenches. They say there are no atheists in foxholes. There are no true believers, either. So, no sham church career.

"Paris was more forgiving. I began going to a pub called Liberty Bar. I wanted a relationship. The Liberty catered to straight men and women as well as homos and lezzies, and advertised what English Parisians called *fairy-nice-gentlemen*. If you say it fast, it's genteel. The ladies always came onto me, so that didn't work. I heard of a small place in the Pigalle just for men. Military types went there, and cops stayed away. Influence, obviously. I went home with different fellows. Some put money in my pocket afterwards. Money helped. My army pay just covered the rent. There's more to me than my cock and ass..."

"Of course." Jake pulled his chair close to Wip. "You're a complex, subtle soul."

"Drum roll. Ta-di-da. Ta, love, but subtlety's stretching it. Anyway, I was gob-struck by the new art and went to galleries, ballet, and films. I studied physics. Foreigners couldn't get jobs; returning French soldiers got them, which was only fair."

"Wasn't it dangerous, all this casual sex? I'm terrified for you. Don't get me wrong. I'm grateful you're telling me. Truth is the best aphrodisiac. It only makes me love you more."

"Your stud survived," Wip said drily.

Jake stood behind Wip and nuzzled his hair. Wip reached up and clasped Jake's wrists. "Haven't you had enough? You get the idea."

"You're still hiding." He continued unknotting Wip's muscles. "On Zealandia, you said to call you 'Wip without the h', a joke about a world I don't know, but you've lived. Let's get dressed and have a beer in the kitchen."

The flypaper now claimed seven victims. Seated at the kitchen table, Jake persisted. "Wasn't it dangerous? I saw horrible injuries in boys and girls who'd been anally raped. The anus is stubborn when it wants to stay closed."

"I've got a good nose for danger. Look, that old bloke in the Botanical Gardens—I told you he was my first blow job—he paid me. I couldn't believe the pound notes he put in my pocket. There was nothing about dancing—sorry, love. He told me to protect my nose and cheek bones; they were like a Greek statue. I didn't know Greek statues, but I looked them up in the library. I got his point; sellable asset."

"I wondered. Paris?" Jake pressed.

"One of my dates asked me to be, um, rough on him…"

"Wip without the h?"

Wip winced and nodded.

He's crossed his Rubicon. Jake was relieved.

"This kind of thing was never part of my wank-off fantasies. But after my initial disgust, it became logical and familiar, a metaphorical kill-or-be-killed of war. Pure. X force needed to subdue Y resistance. Normal people say, 'Pity the masochist', the supposed victim. I tell you, that's all wrong. The sadist manipulated into soul-shrinking antics needs the most pity. There's no smugger face than the married banker with bought welts on his ass and clip cuts on his nipples. Rawness was everywhere then. Art, poetry, everything broken up. The mental revolutions came before the war, which makes you ask: chicken? Egg? Three empires fell. All the order we'd ever known as kids was gone."

"You're trying to say something cosmic, love." Jake put up his hand. "Slow down. Your thoughts are running over each other. I want to understand every element. Start with art."

"I met Pierre at a gallery. I was the trick who never left, for four years. Pierre…"

"Hold on, art first, before Pierre. All I know are the French Impressionists. My sister's crazy about Monet. How do you connect all this?"

"Everything fits, if I could only find the words." Wip got up and paced, his shoes slapping tiles.

"Your terror of an atom bomb?"

"Closes the circle," Wip muttered. He paced the length of the kitchen again, then sat, leaning toward Jake, his brandy-tobacco-hibiscus breath tickling Jake's nostrils. "In the trenches, the bloke who made you tea, or you made him tea at 6 a.m., he's got this kind of nose, that colour eyes, he has an infectious grin or is a mean bastard. He's a solid human. You are, too. Whistles blow, over the top you go; one of you will be pulped meat." Wip shook his head. "There were ceasefires to collect casualties.

"So, picture this: Jerry and I look at each other in No Man's Land. We smoke. Let's call him Siegfried. Siggy holds up a photo. I squint and see two little girls on curled, shiny paper. I see tears dribble down a fresh-shaved face under the evil Kaiser helmet. Siggy has brown eyes; he's not Aryan. We look at our watches. Bye-bye, Siggy, time to kill. Siggy haunted my nightmares because the battle after we smoked was one of the worst. Smashing artillery, screaming next to me, the grey paste of brain on filthy red flesh, green-yellow smoke, semi-solid, rolling in. I'm untouched. The mind can't hold these polarities, love, it splits. You can mask against gas. Right now, someone's making a humanity-annihilating bomb that no mask could block."

Jake sensed he needed to not be touched. They smoked quietly. "I don't know how any of you came through it."

"We didn't. For months, I had re-enactment nightmares of the battle after Siggy, waking up shrieking, thrashing the sheets around and shaking. It felt worse than the actual action; shock dulled us at the time. Eventually, the re-enactment became a recurring jackhammer clattering through my skull into my brain. This abated with Pierre...but not for the best of reasons."

Jake reached for Wip's hands and kissed his wrists, palms and slender fingers. Exhaling, he asked, "You linked war, art and sex?"

"Yes." Wip sighed. "That felt good. Collins doesn't have art books; he's not the type. Let me draw from memory." He rummaged through a kitchen drawer and pulled out a pad and pencil. Jake watched him scrawl the outline of a descending widening drape, filling in irregular sharp cubes and half circles in his neat engineering script. 'Shades of brown', Wip wrote, turning it to Jake. "See the deconstructed stairs, the hint of an angular face, stringy arms? Braque's *Nude Woman*. Who knows what it means? All broken up. But it's gob-thwacking *true*, truer than your old landscapes and portraits. After the war, I needed to touch the …rawness of things, the brokenness. Nothing else was real. I didn't meet Pierre at a Braque showing, but at Picasso's clown."

He paused, gnawed a thumb cuticle, then lit another cigarette. "Pierre was, is, sophisticated, much older than me. Rich. He wanted the same...rawness. He'd fought in the Madagascar war of 1895, had a dreadful time, and knew the ghastly price of winning. Winning's as bad as losing; you just get more medals. We went for coffee. It turned out he had a recurring nightmare of a drill boring into his skull. His was a nineteenth-century model, a percussion drill powered by steam. We bonded. Many artists painted clowns then, life as a clown show. Clowns can't change things; they're helpless little creatures. All they can do is make everything else small and misshapen enough to mock. Pierre's sex rituals were to make him feel bigger than a clown, to dominate. Only then could he come."

"You weren't dominant?"

"Until Pierre, I played the abuser role. He needed to get to another's shock and fear. We had a contract: no injuries. He had a mansion outside Paris. In his wine cellar, he had handcuffs, chains, whips, and cords. A chandelier hung above a wall harness. The bed was the biggest I've ever seen, with silk sheets and a feather mattress, a mirror above. One of his friends was a radio sound-effects man. He'd installed a sound system, so, well, I thought I'd just laugh, it was so theatrical. But the amplified sound of wood on flesh and whips snapping. I did get to pure helplessness and fear. It was satisfying." He got up. "Isn't that enough?"

"You're still hiding."

"Yes, there's more. Unfortunately." Wip sat, and they each drank a bottle of beer. "Pierre liked to give orders. 'Undress. Close your eyes.' Then he'd tap my hip to turn around for the handcuffs."

"No blindfolds?"

"No. That's coercive. The whole point was submission. He liked me to be in the wall harness, arms cuffed behind me; me, a boxer who could easily have stopped it. He'd walk toward me and away. I could feel his breath closing on me and retreating, smell his woody-earthy cigar and pear brandy breath. He'd go away for what could be minutes, unpredictable. Waiting in restraints is unbelievably arousing. Then suddenly, he'd spit. I was supposed to sense his move, open my mouth and swallow. If I didn't, he'd slap my face, with the sound effects. Most of all, he liked to put a greased metal chain up my arse. If I blinked, I could see the mirror highlighting my muscles. When he was hard, he'd ease the chain out, unstrap the harness and mount me on the bed…" Wip stared at Jake, who met his gaze.

"I can't imagine wanting this myself but I'm with you," Jake urged.

"Over time, Pierre was less…capable," Wip concluded. "One night, when I was straight out hard, nothing happened for longer than usual. I could hear his quick breathing but didn't feel the heat of him near me. I opened my eyes. His erection sloped up and then drooped, but he still tried. In a hurry, he pulled the chain out, got me on the bed and rubbed himself to climax on my butt, the hardest things on that bed. I couldn't help it, love, I laughed. Afterwards, I discovered I was bleeding from the quick chain pull. That must be when I got the scar. Pierre wept, for himself, not me. I cried, too. It was over. I wanted to help him, but I failed. He was generous.

"I used the money to get a certificate in engineering and buy into the coffee plantation. Since then, I've had discreet one-nighters. Some of the goldfield blokes preferred men. My dominance/submission need went away, but the jackhammer returned. Until you…then the jackhammer would start clattering, but the blade would shiver into dancing crystals and never get near head. I thought *Nirvana*. Then Esther ruined everything."

Wip's voice tailed off. He sat with his hands on the table, fingers splayed out. He began to shake, a little at first, then violently.

Jake was silent, frowning as he stared at an impenetrable stand of bamboo outside the window. Rain tip-tap-plopped the stalks.

"Can't you even look at me?" Wip asked, his voice hoarse and trembling.

"Will you get bored with me? That's what terrifies me. I'm …ordinary. If I'm pure anything, it's bourgeois. What we have—had upstairs—that's the world for me, enough."

"Ohhh…." Wip stood, still wobbly, then sank to the

floor, rocking, arms hugging himself and sobbing convulsively. Jake sat down and cradled him. "Broken bits," Wip kept snuffling, the tears ran down his nose, over his neck and hands, wetting his belt buckle. It was a long time before he was sobbed out. Jake clutched him close the whole time.

When Wip quieted at last, Jake observed in a neutral tone, "It's still raining."

"Downpour," Wip corrected him with a crooked smile. "Sorry to blubber. You put Humpty Dumpty together again."

"No shame. That's over," Jake assured him.

"I'm sweating." Wip seemed surprised to find them on the floor.

"Me too. Let's mentally change environments. We're in drought-parched Aussie bush, bushfire smoke, fields smouldering. We're racing flames leaping treetops. The car windows crack, you scream when your hands sear on the broiling steering wheel. Still sweating?"

Wip rubbed his arm pits. "It's stopped. That's some trick."

Jake helped him up. "Mind over body. I'm so relieved you didn't get hurt. I've won the lottery. I don't care about this. We're together. You made me this adorable ring..."

Wip snorted. "Caveman crude."

"What I want. Partholonian, in every way."

"You remember that extinct tribe's name I yelled at you when we quarrelled?"

"I keep your words in my locked box of valuables."

CHAPTER 24

Sunday 31 October,
Malaguna Camp.

AFTER PINNING ON his yarmulke, Jake left his hut and strolled towards the shade of the trees at the new camp's perimeter. He'd taken to wearing his Jewish head covering on Sundays to avoid church. Wip had no such excuse; he'd soon be sitting on a hard chair under a sweltering sun bellowing hymns. Wip's friend Collins was still away, so they planned to meet at his house later, as they'd been doing for a month.

Jake's skin tingled, not only for the anticipated physical passion, but for the nestling and talking afterwards. Wip had described an inconceivable world of artistic revolution, erotic extremes and nihilistic politics in post-war Paris. For his part, Jake recounted outback medicine sagas: single-engine planes landing on farmers' runways marked by bonfires for just-in-time surgeries. Wip draped him with more admiration than Jake felt he deserved.

All the battalion's men were relieved to be in the new camp in northwest Rabaul. The huts were wooden, with solid siding and wooden floors. Goodbye, tents! They were further from Tavurvur, so it was breezier and drier. Goodbye, floods! The messes had plenty of beer at night, and the shower building was comfortable. A square of flat ground was roped off for competitive wrestling and boxing matches. Now, troops grumbled at being stuck in a backwater when they should be fighting in the Middle East. Jake disagreed; he was delighted with Rabaul.

Life wasn't lax, however. With new digs came a new commandant. Colonel John Scanlan was a decorated World War I veteran whose past courageous actions inspired awe. Clean-shaven, he had a distant manner, his thin-lipped stare giving him a supercilious air—Jake thought with indignation—of not quite believing that these unblooded men were *his* command. He drove tough drills and compulsory sports to harden them. Jake had chosen tennis. Yesterday, he'd narrowly lost a five-set match.

It was already hot when he reached the nearest tree. He stood, relishing the fragrant leaves above him as he massaged his calves, all the while visualising Wip's dimple and muscled chest, his myriad freckles and springy blond hair. He straightened and leant against the tree trunk, extending his hands to pat the air where his pre-war belly had reached. *Oh, for Talia's trifle.* His salivary glands burst forth at the memory of her passion fruit, cream, brandy-infused cake and custard combination.

Male voices boomed hymns while bells tolled from town. Organised religion, Jake mused. In the boxing field, Jake saw four other Jewish soldiers skipping church. *What's Danglow up to,* he wondered. His rabbi would be shipping out to New Guinea as an army chaplain again in a few months. Tonight would be All Saints' Day eve, Halloween, the time when the barriers between the world of the dead and living could be breached. Jake recalled the priest at Cohen's ball explaining that for the Tolai, every day could be Halloween.

While he wondered if such myths made life easier or harder, he saw an infantryman running toward him, waving a piece of paper, calling "Message for Captain Friedman!" Jake ran to meet him. *Don't let it be bad news from home.* Worry about Miriam's mental stability never left him.

"Sir, native boy at the gate askin' for you. I tried to shoo him away, but he rattled in Pidgin that you know him from the Cosmopolitan Hotel. Wrote these letters, says it's his name." Mystified, Jake took the paper: TOSAINA, in childlike block letters. He scratched his head. Not the boy who walked him from Zealandia to Rabaul Hotel or the boys who served in the hospital facilities. Jake had only been at the Cosmopolitan Hotel once, for Cohen's ball.

"Should I send him off, call the constable, Captain?"

"No, wait."

Jake tensed; he recalled his drunken challenge to Dr Blackwell over treating Tolai patients suffering from polio, and their mock duel of shimmying up the palm tree. A Tolai hotel boy had watched the contest. After Jake had won, the boy had climbed the tree, given Jake a coconut and named himself. *That's the boy? Why does he want to see me?* Father Rowland's caution rushed back to him. 'Tolai gift giving can imply obligation.' Jake had dismissed the idea as fantastical. *Oh, shit.*

Nervous, curious and angry, Jake pocketed his yarmulke and strode to the gate. Outside was a lanky teenager dressed in immaculate white shorts and a shirt with a correctly knotted black tie. His bleach hair streak was neatly barbered.

"I'm Captain Friedman. What's this about?" he said irritably.

"Dokta bigpela, o plis, plis, plis, imap yu helpim susa sik bilong mi!" ToSaina began. Jake mentally translated: 'Big fellow doctor, oh please, please, please, help my sick sister!'

"Take her to the Native Hospital. My job is treating soldiers here."

ToSaina wouldn't budge. He showed Jake another paper. Now Jake understood. His mouth went sour with bile as he looked at a crude drawing of leg splints, a pelvic calliper and heavy boots. ToSaina's sister had polio and had been splinted at the Native Hospital, perhaps by Blackwell. Splinted for how long? She was a cripple now who might not have to be. ToSaina *was* hoping to collect on Jake's obligation for accepting a perfect coconut. Jake stared at him, astonished. He must have understood what the quarrel with Blackwell was about. Perhaps his sister was in the Native Hospital at the time. Maybe he understood the talk about the worker strike.

The boy pointed at the street corner, where a large truck was parked. Trapped by his own arrogance, Jake felt compelled to walk to the truck.

Another surprise: Henry Lee leant out of the driver's seat. "Captain Friedman, Doctor Friedman, please forgive us. I promise to make this up to you. ToSaina's my brother-in-law. He told me about your disagreement with Dr Blackwell. I married IaKumu, his sister. Their little sister is sick. She's in the truck bed. We took her from the Native Hospital."

Jake sighed. As a ship-jumper, Lee would have been too ashamed to come to the camp gate. That made sense. In the truck's passenger seat, he saw the proud, bare-breasted Tolai maiden he'd photographed outside Hotel Pacifica. *Small world!* Her stomach bulged, probably pregnant. Jake looked intently at Lee, who wasn't crowding his wife—no arm around her shoulders or hand on her lap—but the hot scent of his protectiveness filled Jake's nostrils. Mind spinning, Jake walked with ToSaina to the truck bed.

A child of about eight was lying on a pile of blankets. ToSaina rattled strings of strange words at her, let down the truck back, climbed in and helped her to stand, her back against the side of the truck. She bent her little body over a steel cane, her pelvis bulging inward horribly, one leg shorter than the other, legs splinted, and feet in boots. Her eyes were that of an old person: flat with pain and defeat.

Jake was swamped by pity. No way could this little native child understand what was happening to her. "How long?" he asked ToSaina.

"Four moons."

What's her name?"

"IaLasliklik"

Jake nodded and climbed into the truck bed. "IaLasliklik," he said gently. "Plis."

ToSaina rattled off more soothing words.

Jake probed her abdominals, which felt unresponsive, probably a result of spasms elsewhere, causing her pelvic tilt and leg shortening. Behind the splints, some muscles were flaccid, others contracted. There was abraded skin at her ankles where the steel touched it. In this climate, they'd quickly ulcerate. She let out a howl, shrill, almost feral, to the heavens. "Lalala... Whooieee! Wat wat wat. Ohhhhhh!"

She would have gone on forever if ToSaina hadn't hushed her. "Lalala masalai, gut spirit," he explained.

"Well, she's got lusty lungs. At least she didn't need a respirator," Jake remarked. He knew he could help her. From the bottom of his heart, he yearned for them to go away. To treat her broke the rules of medical etiquette to another doctor and violated the government's policy of providing separate hospitals for white, Asian and black patients. But if he could be the answer to that prayer, he must try. *So, break the rules,* he decided.

Back at the driver's seat, he said, "Lee, listen to me. If I help, it must be kept secret. No more sorry cases. Do you understand? Or I'll report you for desertion. Deal?" To Lee's nod, Jake added, "Then wait here. I have to telephone someone."

He ran to his hut, got Father Thomas Rowland's card, and entered the communications building. Fortunately, it was empty; everyone was still at the church service. He dialled the number on the card and waited impatiently through multiple rings.

Finally, someone picked the phone up. "Hello?" A scratchy male voice.

"Father, not at Mass? I'm shocked!" Jake heard a startled, indrawn breath. Had he tried for a stupid joke? That's how nervous he was. "It's Dr Jake Friedman, Captain, 2/22 battalion."

Rowland let his breath out, half laughing. "You're the rude fellow from Cohen's ball, the tree-climbing doctor. I went to Mass at 6. I hope that satisfies you. What's up?"

Jake's explanation tumbled out. "I can help her using Kenny's methods if I can communicate with her. It's not too late for her to recover mobility, but it will be if she's left as she is."

"Son, you're taking a terrible risk."

"Father, I don't have a choice. ToSaina heard the quarrel with Blackwell and understood the whole thing. Hippocratic oath."

A long silence. "Father?" Jake waited.

A smoker's cough. "That lad's one of the smartest boys I've met here of any race."

"You know him?"

"I baptised him John and his older sister IaKumu, Anne. My successor baptised the young one, Mary. Her birth name, IaLasliklik, means *little last one* because she was premature, and their mother died soon after. She isn't old enough to have earned a tribal nickname. They're good Christians but keep their tribal names and old customs. Let me warn you, if your treatments don't improve her condition, the tribe will be angry, and your superior officers will be furious that you're breaking the rules." A sigh. "Oh, very well. I'll help you. That's what you want, right? Oh dear, it could go horribly wrong. Tell Lee to get a suite with a bathroom at Hotel Pacifica and any medical supplies you need from the Chinese hospital. He's well connected here, as you must have realised. Bring your helmet."

Jake was so discombobulated that he didn't think to ask why he should bring a tin helmet meant to protect against bombs, to treat a sick girl in a hotel room. He picked up paper and pen and ran back to the truck, watched by the intensely curious sentry. "Fair sex gets you every time," he flung at him. The sentry leered conspiratorial approval.

Jake scribbled a list of what he needed. He explained it to Lee: a hospital fracture bed, a massage table, a wooden board four feet long and three feet high, clamps to attach it to the bed, linen, waterproof cloth, wax, and towels. "And hire a licensed nurse and two masseurs, medical masseurs not...um..."

"Pleasure ladies." Lee finished.

Jake nodded. "The suite must be near the kitchen so hot water can be brought instantly. You all must shower or have a bath before I arrive."

Tears ran down Lee's face. His nose still had a bump from the beating by Bruiser on Zealandia. "We're so grateful, even if it doesn't work." He paused. "Matrilinear descent, sir. She has land. It would be marvellous if she could eventually have children to pass it on to."

"Oh?" Jake felt dirtied by a property motive. Lee had quickly adopted the customs of his wife's tribe. But he was committed. The girl's uncomprehending despair bound him to her with every morsel of knowledge he'd acquired on polio.

Lee drove off, leaving Jake feeling alone and bleak with self-doubts. *Am I good enough to get her walking?* He left Wip a note begging him to meet at 'hot pac', hoping desperately that Wip would understand his code.

An hour later, Jake walked into the Hotel Pacifica carrying his medical kit and white coat, his helmet dangling from his wrist. Kenny's book and his notes from watching her in Brisbane were in his pocket. Father Rowland met him in the lobby. The priest had a bucket of something white, a priest's robe and collar with black and red circles painted on it.

"What's this?" Jake asked.

"You can't wear your white coat if you want her trust.

Think of what she's been through in the last few months. We'll do better with a hint of sorcery."

He said we. Jake was grateful to have an informed liaison. In a bathroom, Father Rowland daubed Jake's face with lime paint, then taped the bright bird feathers on his helmet.

The suite was crowded. IaKumu was singing to her sister, who rocked on her splints, crying. Lee and ToSaina stood by a hospital fracture bed covered by linen. A wizened old woman huddled in the corner with a wrapped package mumbling what Jake assumed were invocations to the appropriate spirit; she must be the tribe's healer. Around her, the air smelled of sweat, grit and plant matter. She rolled her eyes at his greeting, then resumed her chants. She hadn't bathed, but he didn't think he could evict her.

He'd never worked in an environment like this. He felt ridiculous in his priest's robe and painted face. But the girl looked at him in fright and awe; she didn't recognise him. After ToSaina spoke for a long time, Jake removed the callipers, undid the splints, and then eased off both boots and splints. Together, he and ToSaina lifted her onto the bed on her back. He attached the baseboard to the bed's end. One foot had a bad drop. He dragged the tip of a spoon along the sole of her feet, hoping, even praying, for the hint of a reflex. One foot was unresponsive; the other gave a slight flinch. Marvellous! Had she just felt what he did? There was hope. She stared at him with intense, wide eyes despite IaKumu's constant soothing song. He asked Rowland to hold her, not allowing her to wriggle. He pressed the board against her feet to simulate a body in its natural standing position.

The old woman approached the table. Rowland whispered to Jake, "Let her give the girl bush medicine; it's harmless. She's not Christian, but IaKumu's father asked her to give you a chance."

Jake stepped back. The old woman unwrapped the package and took out a piece of coconut shell with a steaming viscous fluid in it. Gently, she dribbled the fluid into the girl's willing mouth, singing with an unexpectedly low vibrato. A powerful spicy burnt sugar scent: *tree sap,* Jake decided. The old woman shot him another sceptical glare and went to the door. Before she left the suite, she chewed something in her mouth and spat out the juice in their direction, singing again. "Evicting bad spirits," Rowland interpreted. "She's cooperating." He looked relieved.

The sap's vapours seeped into Jake's brain. It was mildly intoxicating. He sneezed to clear his head. "This session will ease the spasms," he explained. He'd decided that IaLasliklik's foot drop originated in spasms in the muscles in her knees and calves, the gastrocnemius group. Spasms in her hamstrings were causing seemingly paralysed quads and near-nil response in her right abdominals. He treated the spasms one by one. He wrapped a piece of wool blanket soaked in near-boiling water and wrung dry around the spasming area, covered it with cotton wool lengths on waterproof fabric, and tied the three layers of cloth together with a towel. It took hours. IaKumu held her sister's hand throughout. Jake tried to establish eye contact with his patient, but they had no common language. He could smell her terror. He heard her thudding heart, then saw wonder in her eyes when he unwrapped the towel and her body sagged, suggesting that the pain had eased. Her wonder wasn't trust, he decided. It contained awe, perhaps even hatred.

When he stood stiff and exhausted, around 4 p.m., he looked at her foot and leg. Both deformities seemed reduced. He let her rest for a while, then applied hot wax to her stomach to close the pores and stimulate circulation. After half an hour, he removed it. Her abdominals were looser.

He didn't want to test this progress, but he was exhilarated. The others in the room had seen improvements, too. Mouths were opening, but Jake put a finger to his lips. The situation was delicate; he had to keep the atmosphere calm.

There was a knock on the door. Wip walked in, trailed

by a Chinese woman and man wearing hospital scrubs. They were both stocky, with pockmarked faces. Bowing, they greeted him in English. Jake grinned; Lee had understood who to hire. As he nodded approvingly to Lee, he registered Lee looking at Wip, puzzled. *Why is Whipple here in this secret treatment room? A gunner and the doctor? What's the connection?* Jake sensed Lee's mind clicking.

"Enough for today," Jake said, making for the chair the old woman had vacated. While Jake wrote up the chart, IaKumu fed her sister taro with chicken and spices, then emptied her bedpan and washed her. IaLasliklik was soon asleep.

"I need about four weeks," Jake said, finger on the chart. "Please all leave, except for Lieutenant Whipple. I'll stay tonight; I'm off duty until inspection tomorrow." He gave Kenny's book and his notes to Lee. "Get the masseurs to study them for a test in two days."

Lee didn't speak. Staring from Jake to Wip, he went pale; his mouth dropped open.

"So your favourite officers are that way," Wip snapped. "Get over it."

With an unreadable expression on his face, Rowland put an arm around Lee and led him away. Jake scratched his forehead and then pulled Wip into the bathroom. "Thank you. I couldn't have done that. Hope there's no trouble.'

"There won't be. Lee's a ship-jumper, remember? At heart, he's a good bloke. My God! What, why, how, when? I waited at Collins' house for hours, sure you'd left me. When I gave up and returned to camp, I found your note. You damn fool! It could go terribly wrong! If she gets worse, the tribe could come after you with clubs. And you'll be in trouble with the army and the town magistrate." Wip was echoing Father Rowland.

"I can do it. You don't understand."

"Don't understand what?"

"Grace, a nurse, is dead because of me, and two children got the wrong treatment for polio. The car crash in Colac, when

I got a concussion." He sobbed against Wip's shoulder. The full story tumbled out: the suspected polio case, Jake not reaching them because he didn't see spilt gravel and broken glass on the road, the car skidding and overturning, and Grace dying of internal injuries. "I can't fail another child. A few days treating spasms is easy. Then three weeks or so, reviving the disused muscles. That's the hard part. How do I communicate with her? It's wracking my brain. I'll spend every hour here that I'm not on duty. Sorry, love." His face felt hot and sweaty.

"Am I looking at a saint or a zealot?" Wip hugged Jake hard and long.

"A bumbler who wants to do better," Jake replied simply.

"I thought I was the rebel," Wip continued, "boxing Bruiser in an unsanctioned fight. You told me, 'Less Lancelot.' Here you are, breaking every damn rule of racial separation and taking another doctor's patient." He pulled away, laughed, and drew Jake close. "How magnificent. I'm your partner. I'll be with you every hour I'm free, drive you back to camp, buy whatever you need."

Jake fingered the ring against his chest. "Our rings. Oh, I'm so grateful you're with me. I'm so alone and scared." He started shaking.

"Malaria?" Wip asked, alarmed.

"Self-doubt."

"You'll do it."

They stayed entwined on the massage table. The girl cried out once in pain. Jake leapt off the table. He sent Wip to the kitchen for hot water, then treated her for spasms in her hamstrings. When she'd fallen asleep, he changed her bedpan. Wip watched, his face softening. "You've helped already."

"Anything could happen," Jake said wearily. "I'm so relieved you're here."

Before dawn, Lee returned with a nurse, IaKumu and ToSaina. Jake washed up in the bathroom and then gave the nurse his chart.

Lee bowed low to Jake, his lips brushing Jake's trousers. "Forgive my reaction yesterday. I'm grateful for the help you and Lieutenant Whipple are giving me, us, beyond thanks."

"Oh, this is a bit excessive." A blushing Jake pulled Lee up. They stood face to face, Jake maintaining distance.

"My high-school science teacher said, 'sex exists on a continuum, with much variety'," Lee gulped out.

"Well," Jake acknowledged, unsure what to say next. After a moment, he offered his hand. They shook hands formally. "Alright. I've got work to do and need your help." Walking into the corridor, he resumed, "What's IaLasliklik's favourite insect or little bird? For the next stage, I need to evoke something with a light touch on her skin for her to feel her nerves again."

Lee thought, then smiled. "She adores red-breasted kingfishers…" His voice caught. "And there's a yellow and red butterfly she used to run after."

"Can you ask your wife if the Lalala spirit can enter wildlife?"

Lee huddled with IaKumu. "Yes," he reported. "Also, visitation by an ancestor's shadow soul. The old healer could help to convince her."

Jake nodded. "Alright, when I say she's ready."

He slept against Wip's shoulder while Wip drove them to camp for morning inspection and the routine quinine dosing of a modern battalion.

On the third day of coming and going, Lee asked Jake for a private talk. "Sir, I have something to give you. Confidential. Please?" Jake saw IaKumu nod approvingly at her husband. Wip got the hint and left the hotel to do errands for Jake.

Jake led Lee to the suite's front closet. They stood close, heads bent together, Jake smelling of lime and tobacco, Lee of sweat. Jake had entered a zone of floating relaxation; he'd rediscovered the coping skills of his student rotations: dozing minutes sitting, slumped against a wall, bed rest a luxury. He'd tested the masseurs' understanding of Kenny's protocols. They were watching him to learn about this patient.

He nearly toppled against Lee; he was so tired. To his surprise, Lee thrust two pound-notes at him. "Patient confidentiality, please, sir."

"You look well. Consultation's over." Jake handed back the money. "What's this about?" Lee pushed the coloured notes back. King George VI gazed placidly at Jake. "For confidentiality, sir. I want to give you some valuable information to reciprocate for all you've done for me and for us. I always said I'd repay your kindness." He pulled out a piece of tree bark.

Jake broke out in manic laughter. "Oh, thank you. A beautiful gift!"

"Sir, please smell it." Lee was urgent.

Jake sighed. He sniffed and felt fresh, congealed sap. He was no botanist. "Cut recently," he said authoritatively. "Why should I care about this bark?"

"Sir, it's mature cinchona bark, ready to be processed into quinine. My wife's tribe owns several acres of the trees. It was originally bush land that my cousin Ah Kuan Ho bought from the tribe in 1931. He grew the trees. He returned the land back to the tribe as part of my bride price."

Jake felt confused. "Bride price? But the trees are worthless. There's plenty of quinine."

"That's true now, sir." Lee whispered. "But there won't be when the Japanese invade."

Jake straightened, his tiredness gone. Toshio's nasty plot to see the Praed Point guns and John Smith's warning to Jake on Zealandia about Japanese spies rushed back. "You know something, or are you speculating?"

"Both, sir. Ho believed enough in the Japanese threat to invest in the land and plant the seeds he got from Java. The

Dutch grow forests of them. At his shop, you saw newspaper reports of Japanese atrocities."

Jake nodded—the massacre in Nanking. "I have to get a chemical analysis, but I'm listening. What made your cousin willing to invest in growing the trees? There's no foreseeable return-on-investment. He struck me as a hard-nosed pragmatist."

"He has a nephew with the Chinese Communists, sir. That boy's group killed a Japanese Kempeitai officer. They found Japan's plan for conquering Pacific islands south of the equator. He knew enough Japanese to translate it. Rabaul is the number one strategic target. This boy got word to his uncle. I only learnt this when he traded the land for me to wed IaKumu. We had to pay off her intended husband, who was negotiating with her relatives. But she wanted me."

Jake laughed. "I see why. You're a piece of work, former Seaman Lee, full of surprises." Lee was transformed from the victim he'd stitched up after vicious racist beatings on the ship to a young man comfortable manoeuvring between his Chinese entrepreneur relatives and the Tolai tribe he'd married into.

Jake pocketed the bark. "I'll get it tested in Australia." He scratched his face. *Is this "Through the Looking Glass", or a portent?*

Lee left, his sandals receding slaps along the corridor's wooden floor. Jake hoped the bark wasn't cinchona, or that it was bad quality. If it was viable, he had a new moral problem in keeping Lee's confidence. The pound notes rustled in his pocket.

Three days later, Wip picked Jake up at Hotel Pacifica to take him to what Jake assumed was the morning inspection at camp. IaLasliklik's spams had eased enough for him to plan the tricky series of exercises to restore awareness and coordination in the disused muscle groups. A part of him was supremely confident he'd succeed; mostly, he was a shaky wreck. He blubbered to Wip every day, terrified of making a mistake. Wip had become his rock of stability. But they hadn't made love in a while. Jake assumed Wip was waiting for a decent time to break it off; could anyone really be as patient as Wip?

Half-asleep, half-visualising the first exercise, he opened an eye when Wip turned the truck engine on and drove left instead of right. "What's up? Malaguna's the other way."

"Love, I told you ten times. You're in the army. Remember? Inspection's at Praed Point today. Visiting colonel poohbahs from Melbourne HQ touring our battery. Heavy Battery Unit inspection on site, plus a civvie cove from Public Works. I've got your spare uniform. When we're out of town, I'll pull off the road, and you'll shave and change. I've got water."

Jake looked at a glowingly neat Wip. How could he have forgotten? "On the first day of Christmas, my true love sent to me a partridge in a pear tree," he sang. "How am I so lucky?"

Wip sang the second line. They laughed, alternating verses. Then, they made up twelve verses of new words: "On the first day of Christmas, the captain sent to me a gun cartridge in a pear tree."

The unit of 130 men stood in small groups according to their duties. Praed's slope was too narrow and steep for a single straight line. The gunners were at their respective guns, which were run out. Jake, Wip and the other mechanics in front of the supply hut. Two cooks were down at the two-level dugout. Well-groomed, they all stood to attention as their unit commander, Major Edward Clarke, led the visiting colonel and a stooped civilian in tropical whites around. The men were expecting praise, even free beers, for the neat grounds, solid huts, and the strength of the netted stone blast wall beside each gun.

Major Clarke told them that the colonel, whose name was Nurse, had designed the battery. Frowning, Nurse stalked around the guns, then strode up and down the gravelled tracks between the buildings. His face finally relaxed with an explosive sigh. "What bloody fool ordered ripping up all the bushes, palm trees and roots? Every damn one? Clear the pine trees—that's all I ordered!" he bellowed.

Men stood shocked and silent. The jungle clearing had been organised by the fastidious commander, Lieutenant Colonel Carr, along with Public Works, whose mission was digging up trees to make permanent roads.

Nurse continued. "The guns can be seen in detail by any reconnaissance plane. Growing proper concealment will take years. You fools! I flew over in a Catalina seaplane. Didn't want to believe my eyes."

At the supply hut, Wip was in Jake's eyeshot. They exchanged glances. They'd seen the guns just by hiking the Mother. Nurse was right; Major Clarke was beet red.

"Plant creepers," Nurse roared. "It's the only ground cover that'll spread quickly. A mockery of concealment, but better than dirt around cannon on steel platforms. Get creepers. Oh, my Lord!"

Jake and Wip had jobs at Malaguna Camp, so they were excused from the rush to plant creepers. They drove back to Rabaul in silence. Jake's mind was on Lee's bark. The envelope from Australia had arrived last night, but he hadn't opened it yet. Wip was glowering, perhaps reliving the last war.

*
**

From the first time Jake wrapped hot wet wool around IaLasliklik's hamstrings, he'd worried about re-connecting her mind with her disused muscles. The exercises required the patient's ability to distinguish contraction from relaxation of specific muscles and obedience to his instructions. He'd settled on getting IaKumu to verbally invoke the sensation of a red-breasted kingfisher treading lightly on her abdominal and hip muscles, and her favourite yellow and red butterfly for her leg muscles. Looking at his patient, he didn't know who was more scared.

The dreaded moment was here. The old woman put a new packet of pungent herbs behind the girl's head, sang an invocation, and then sat on the chair by the door, glaring at Jake. At least, Jake felt it was a glare.

In preparation, Jake had IaKumu lie on the fracture bed. He raised IaKumu's head a few inches, cradling it gently. He stroked her throat to indicate that she should let her neck relax so that her head could rest on his palms. She got it on the second try. For the first exercise, IaKumu would hold her sister's head while he lifted his patient's leg. IaKumu got off the bed and coached her sister with the story Jake had prepared with Father Rowland's help: the good spirit LaLala had entered a glorious, red-breasted kingfisher spirit, which was walking on her abdominals—Jake touched her right abdominal muscles. All other muscles—he touched her trunk and quads—were to be deep in sleep to receive a healing vision. The patient looked confused and unwilling.

Then IaKumu had an inspiration. Before lifting her sister's head, she took IaLasliklik's hand and put it on her own bulging belly. IaLasliklik opened her eyes wide, stroking the lap-lap over the tight skin. The baby growing in IaKumu's womb must have kicked. IaKumu wriggled her own fingers on her sister's abdominals. Movement beneath the skin suddenly made sense to the girl.

IaKumu now cradled her sister's head. Jake gently raised her right leg and then smoothly lowered it, motioning her to rest it. He was alert for a spasm in the abdominals, massaging the spot when it occurred. They repeated this movement several times. Gradually, he felt the beginning of her mind connecting to her right abdominals, allowing them to work so that the leg movement was more effortless. He did the exercise once with her left leg. Her left abdominals weren't as contracted as the right ones had been, and worked better. He then repeated the exercise with her right leg, hoping she understood that the abdominals on each side should feel similar.

After she slept for an hour, he repeated the exercises. Then he cradled her head. IaKumu repeated her instructions about the spirit walking on her abdominals as Jake touched the areas that should stay asleep. He directed her to lift her right leg by herself. The girl's eyes opened in fear, then shut. He felt her tense concentration. The masseurs watched impassively. *Waiting for results,* Jake realised. He needed them; he couldn't always be here. She managed one small lift by herself. The masseurs looked at each other and nodded; Jake sighed with relief.

The next day, these initial exercises went faster. Jake began the next stage: she was to lift her head and both legs simultaneously, then lower them. As he cradled her head and lifted her legs, he felt her becoming more compliant to his touch.

After several days of this exercise, they'd achieved a rhythmic sequence. With a new song from IaKumu, as she touched which muscles were asleep, and which the bird was walking on, Jake ordered IaLasliklik to make the movement herself. She managed a quarter-inch simultaneous lift of her head and both legs. Jake was beginning to believe that Kenny's protocols were helping regenerate the affected nerves, allowing the patient's muscles to function. And why not? He'd seen them work in her clinic in Brisbane.

He sighed happily. It was a small triumph, but dazzling. The room—IaKumu, Lee, and the nurse—burst into song. The masseurs clapped, and the old woman in the chair muttered a prayer. IaLasliklik realised she'd done something spectacular. For the first time since he'd met her, she laughed. He had her now. He wished Wip was here to share the thrilling moment, but Wip was repairing the sighting gearless telescope of the upper gun at Praed. The guns were to be fired tomorrow in the presence of the anti-aircraft battery soldiers, all inexperienced, to accustom them to artillery noise and recoil. To Jake, the army felt far away.

A few days later, Jake was supervising one of the masseurs working on IaLasliklik's hip muscles. He clutched the envelope with the analysis of Lee's bark in his pocket. He'd mailed the bark to a school friend at the elite research institution, Commonwealth Scientific and Industrial Research Organisation, in Canberra. All these days, he'd been too busy to open it. Finally, he read it. The bark was from a mature cinchona tree. Lee had been truthful.

"Try passive movement," he directed the masseur, pondering his new dilemma of keeping the cinchona trees secret.

The female masseur was at the foot of the massage table, the patient on her back. The masseur grasped IaLasliklik's right leg below the knee with one hand, while the other held the sole of her foot. IaKumu sang of Lalala, now a yellow butterfly, fluttering where the male masseur touched, where the hip muscle attached to the femur. The masseur gently moved the thigh up and down. Rest. Several times. Then, one movement by the patient. They turned IaLasliklik on her stomach and repeated the exercise.

Jake and Lee went outside. "So you have usable cinchona trees. Your gift to me is?"

Lee paused a long time, as if delivering the promised gift was too much for him, after all. Finally: "These trees are located a mile from Mandres Sawmill off Ataliklikum Bay, up a steep animal track. Secret, please."

"The information's worthless now," Jake said. "But I can't promise anything if the situation changes. Higher duty may require me to say what I've heard."

"Sir, I expect that. I want you to know where to look if the need arises." They shook hands.

When they returned, Wip had arrived. He was smiling as the girl made two moves of the thigh on her own. "You can't imagine how stunned I am; how I revere what you're doing," he whispered.

"We're not out of danger," Jake sighed. "But my instinct was right. Tolai have amazing motor skills."

The next week went in a blur. IaLasliklik regressed a few times. Jake worked for hours on old spasms, but the trend was toward progress. The masseurs worked down her body, restoring coordination in her glutei, hamstrings, and flexors in the feet. Five weeks after he had met her, the pelvic tilt, leg shortening, and foot drop were almost gone.

"Tomorrow," he announced, no longer terrified of jinxing his work, "tomorrow, she walks!" He marked the chart: December 7, 1941.

BOOK THREE
WAR, BETRAYAL. MEETING THE MOMENT, DECEMBER 1941 – MARCH 1942

CHAPTER 25

· · · · · · · ·

8 December, 1941

J UST AFTER MIDNIGHT, a weary Jake stood and rolled his shoulders. On the massage table, IaLasliklik looked at him with huge black eyes. She lifted her left leg. Jake pointed his finger, and she lifted her right leg, then both together. Three moves without his help. He nodded to a masseur on the other side of the table. They helped her off the table to stand. Jake nudged her with his foot to walk. Tentatively, she moved one leg forward and then the other. Astonished, she gazed at the hated calliper, splints and boots in the corner. Raising her arms, she whooped, "Wooeeeiii!"

"Enough," Jake said, helping her into the hospital bed. He regarded her tenderly, feeling a little in love with the patient whose efforts had been nothing short of heroic.

Behind Jake, Wip's brilliant blue eyes peered anxiously. Then his breath exploded out. "Mate, you did it," he boomed. "You magnificent sorcerer! She walked!"

ToSaina and Father Rowland cheered.

IaKumu climbed onto the bed and folded her pregnant body around her sister's. She wept loudly, then crooned in

Pidgin, which Jake now understood. "You are healthy, my good sister. I am happy, happy. Oh, my sister, you came back to me! Oh, oh, you kicker, little sister full of life, you are back. I am happy." Her new song, made up for the occasion, used just five pitches but erupted with joy and passion.

Jake slumped onto a chair, beyond exhaustion. Between him, the nurse, the two masseurs and her family, she hadn't been alone for an hour. He smiled with contentment. *As sweet as sex,* was his seraphic thought before he tumbled into sleep.

He woke to Wip shaking his shoulders roughly, pulling him upright. Jake registered voices in the corridor: female shrilling, male shouting, footsteps running, radios blaring Chinese, followed by accented English they couldn't decipher.

"Something's up!" Wip shouted. "Back to camp."

"Our face paint?" Jake murmured drowsily. Looking at his watch, Jake realised he'd slept only minutes.

"Kitchen," Wipe snapped. "Let's go."

Cleaned up, they ran for the truck and hurtled west along Chinatown's main street, which was filled with people clutching each other, wailing and waving their arms. Jake looked in Tavurvur's direction. No skyward spews: their usual tormenter wasn't the culprit. They didn't see any sign of upset Tolai gathering, so whatever the event was, it hadn't disturbed them. North of town, they drove up the hill road to camp. Once through the sentry's name check, friends mobbed them.

"Where were you?"

"What's the white flake on your eyebrow? You didn't have town leave."

"We're here now. Wassup? You fellas are as excited as cats that overturned a milk jug. Calm down, kitties," Wip deflected. A grateful Jake grinned.

Egan had never seen them together. Jake saw suspicion, even disapproval, creep into his hut-mate's eyes, but the news was apparently too urgent for distractions. Egan pulled them into a crowded officers' mess, clapping them both on the shoulders. "Glad you're here."

A few men were poring over a map hastily marked with Japan's Pacific islands and those of the Allies, the configurations Robinson had explained last June. An officer cranked up the radio, cursing the static. "News, you bloody bastard."

On the hour, it came. "The Japanese War Government just bombed the American base at Pearl Harbour and British bases and airfields in Hong Kong. There are reports of attacks on Malaya..."

Over gasps, Egan shouted details. "Surprise attack, massive casualties, ships and planes destroyed. We're in it, cobbers. No more longing for Libya."

"Hush up!" an officer called, his ear to the hut's telephone. "PM reaction."

The radio host's terse summary followed: the unprovoked air assault by Japan on British and United States territories meant that Australia's vital interests were imperilled. Consequently, Prime Minister John Curtin had, within an hour of the bombing of Pearl Harbour, proclaimed that Australia was in a state of war against Japan. He would address the nation tomorrow at 11.15 a.m., at which time he would announce formalising the legal declaration of war against Japan.

They broke into groups and speculated all night. Egan took two helpers to clean the telephone cables and radio antennae, and Tavurvur cooperated by staying quiet.

Bleary with exhaustion, Jake went to the communications building. After waiting two hours for his turn, he telephoned Father Rowland. "You heard?"

"Yes, son, terrible news. I pray for peace." The priest's quick pickup of the receiver showed he hadn't slept.

"Father, I need more than your prayers. The girl is nearly functional. Can you pick up my Kenny book, chart and notes? Work with the masseurs if she regresses. I can't get away now, and IaKumu's husband can't come here and collect it."

"Yes, dear boy..." Jake thought the old priest was stifling a chuckle. "I know...um..." Jake tapped a foot impatiently through Rowland's pacing. "...about Lee's indiscretion. Friedman, I don't know if we'll meet again, but you were right to treat the girl. I was sure you'd fail, that there'd be violence from her tribe and legal repercussions. But you succeeded brilliantly. As long as I draw breath, I'll help. God loves you, son. I do, too. Be safe."

Disconnecting, Jake exhaled. Oddly, approval from this Catholic priest meant a lot to him. Despite the impending catastrophe, he was happy. The girl would recover; she could birth a child when she grew up. He'd expiated his guilt over the polio cases he'd never reached in Australia and gone a tiny way toward giving Grace's death meaning. And throughout the treatments, Wip couldn't have been a more devoted partner. He returned to the mess, sat on a bench, put his head on his arms, and slept through the drinking and talking. Wip went to a different bench and slept, too.

As 11.00 approached, the main mess filled with sweating bodies crowding together. At 11.15, the radio host began in an Anglicised voice: "Ladies and gentlemen, the Prime Minister."

Prime Minister John Curtin spoke. His voice wasn't yet familiar to the country because he'd been elevated from Labor Party Leader to Prime Minister just nine weeks ago. With little inflexion and entirely Australian intonation, he declared, "Men and women of Australia. We are at war with Japan. This has happened because, in the first instance, Japanese naval and air forces launched an unprovoked attack on British and United States territory, because our vital interests are imperilled, and because the rights of free people in the whole Pacific are assailed. As a result, the Australian Government this afternoon took the necessary steps, which will mean that a state of war exists between Australia and Japan. Tomorrow, in common with the United Kingdom, the United States of America and the Netherlands East Indies government, the Australian

Government will formally and solemnly formalise the state of war it has striven so sincerely and strenuously to avoid..."

There was the required recapitulation of all the efforts at diplomacy that Japan had rebuffed. Lieutenant Colonel Carr turned the radio off and strode to the microphone, papers in hand. His cheeks were pink with excitement, hollow eyes showing the burden of leadership. "Well, men of the 2/22 Battalion, that's the situation."

Breaking a momentary silence, a voice cried, "Crikey, is Curtin up to it?"

"He's what we've got, mates."

The room rumbled.

"They'll send reinforcements."

"Dunno 'bout that. We're in the Middle East, the Med, and Singapore. Who's left?"

"Won't Civvies be evacuated?"

"Women and kids. Civvie men gotta run the town."

"Nips'll flame out."

"Maybe Yanks flamed out."

Carr rapped the microphones to quiet the room. He ordered the Anti-Aircraft Battery unit to sleep at their battery on Frisbee Ridge from now on instead of returning to camp at night; likewise for the Heavy Battery Unit at Praed Point. "Some of you Royal Australian Artillery men will help Public Works upgrade the two aerodromes for our air force brothers: we're getting a few Wirraway fighters and Hudson bombers. Infantry and the 150 local New Guinea Volunteer Rifles will drill and prepare beach defences. Alright, dismissed."

Jake realised he'd be at Praed, while Wip would shuffle between gun and vehicle maintenance at Praed Point and aerodrome upgrades.

That evening, their first at Praed Point, Jake and Wip joined three sergeants from the Signal Fortress unit in their hut. They had a radio. Scouring channels, Wip held up his finger at a husky female voice with Asian clipped consonants and American drawled vowels. The voice welcomed listeners to the daily *Zero Hour* show.

"Yesterday, the Imperial forces of Japan dealt mortal blows to their British and American enemies. Bombing at Hong Kong and Pearl Harbour destroyed most of Britain's planes parked on runways, their pilots slumbering like the decadent colonials they are. Most of the American fleet and planes at Pearl Harbour were destroyed in a similar manner. The brilliance and spirit of modern Japan's armed forces cannot be denied or resisted.

'Men and women of Australia, our hearts are heavy with grief that your stupid, deluded Prime Minister declared war on Japan. We are peace-loving, forced to defend ourselves from strangulation by British and American embargoes. Men and women of Australia, you are the orphans of the Pacific. Your Australia is an Asian country, not European or American. Wake up from your confusion. Cooperate with us for greater prosperity. Let me remind you: where are your beloved men bleeding and dying? In Egypt. Where is your navy? In the Mediterranean. Where is your 8th Division? In Singapore, which we will soon conquer. Our forces are already in Malaya, forcing the British to retreat. Our victory is inevitable. Will Britain rush to save you, Australia? No. You are fodder for their interests in the northern hemisphere. You are the orphan continent. Lay down your arms. Think about untroubled sleep, plentiful food and a happy life in cooperation with Japan. Only on *Zero Hour* will you hear the truth. Tune in tomorrow. Goodnight.'

Wip wrenched the dial to white noise, then turned the radio off. "My God, that's Radio Tokyo, clear as a church bell. Where did they get that sultry Medusa?"

"We shouldn't listen to such rot!" Jake exclaimed.

"But very clever," another officer said, "using our Prime Minister's 'Men and women of Australia'. They must have been developing their propaganda for years. Who *is* going to reinforce us?" He ground a cigarette butt into the earthen floor.

A distant owl screeched.

"Ten bob Scanlan forbids us to listen to RT in, say, a week," Wip began. "Twenty days," the other officer countered. They shook hands on the bet.

"Well," Jake said, yawning. "Look on the bright side. You've agreed the Japs won't overrun us in less than twenty days. Little Hell, here we come! Bedtime, all. Quinine at dawn."

*
**

The first night at Praed, Jake and Wip met with binoculars outside Jake's medical tent to watch the dawn. They focused first northwest across little Matupit Harbour, the site of their fetid first camp, beyond Simpson Harbour, on pinprick lights of Malaguna Camp. Rabaul, out of range, was a hint of orange-yellow smears.

"I wrote to Esther last night, releasing her from our engagement," Jake whispered.

He felt Wip recoil. "I thought you didn't know her address. Did you lie to me?" Wip's voice was flat. He moved away.

"No, love. I sent my last letter to the address I had, warning her that my, um, attraction to a man had returned, obliquely, to get past the censor. Now we're in for a real war. I owe it to her to free her completely."

Wip sighed through the darkness. "If she doesn't get the letters, you're still engaged in the eyes of God." He paused. "Ah, what the hell; we're together. We're both mixtures of dross and gold. She'll ditch you if she has any sense. Anyway, life's a loan."

They held hands through the first hints of day, shivering as a breeze licked their bare arms and legs. It was a fairly clear night, a bright quarter-moon sitting squat over the jungle ridge south of Rabaul. Venus was pale, near setting, while the Southern Cross constellation winked, struggling to define itself as thin clouds passed under one of its stars and then another.

Looking east across the endless ocean, they felt, rather than saw, a lessening intensity of night, as if the vista enclosing them had a flutter of uncertainty. The waters stayed broodingly black, except for silvery wave caps that seemed to get bigger and more rhythmical. Their nearest landmark was accursed Tavurvur. This first intimation of change imbued its rising smoke with a grey-pink hue. It was night and day at the same time. Lights still split the dark at the camp, the coast invisible. Rabaul, snug in the armpit of Simpson Harbour, was beyond their range; its existence was signified by an orange-yellow smear. Jake and Wip risked a long, arousing kiss.

"Sweet," Jake purred. "How am I so lucky?"

With delicate majesty, purple rays tinged the eastern horizon, gradually paling the moon and stars to insipidity. Palm trees and jungle vegetation defined themselves, as did hill, high-grass, beach and coral, but still dark. Purple clouds morphed into a spread of tomato-scarlet, reflected by the waters into incandescent glory. Then a blatant burst into yellow, blue, white and green shouted it was day.

"Let's make this our daily ritual," Wip declared. They pressed hands and separated.

*
**

A string of strangely happy days followed, the happiest Jake could ever have imagined. Sunset could be a miracle in reverse of dawn, with orange-red vistas fading lilac to grey in the west, draping native fishing canoes in Simpson Harbour in a magical pale mist.

Predictable tasks filled their days. Adrenalin pumped at high-flying Japanese reconnaissance planes, but, as yet, there was no fighting. In remote Praed Point, if Jake looked away from the creeper-covered gun emplacements he could pretend he was working in a tropical resort.

Mornings began with a single Catalina seaplane revving up and lumbering into the air on patrol. The weekly mail plane from Australia landed at nearby Lakunai aerodrome. Whenever Jake and Wip had free time, they hiked to their cave and made love. Father Rowland left a note for Jake at the checkpoint, saying the patient was walking. The news thrilled Jake. Time flowed with surreal tranquillity.

"Europe had a 'phony' war," Wip remarked one morning. "War-footing when Hitler invaded Poland in September '39. Conquered in a month, then nothing 'til May '40."

"Don't spoil my sunrise," Jake murmured after their morning kiss.

One afternoon, shouts brought Jake running out of his medical tent, hands dusty with sulfamate powder. He met Wip emerging from the upper gun emplacement, his arms slick with oil. They followed their mates' pointing fingers. Two float planes were circling Rabual's inlets. Red circles under their wings showed they were Japanese. Two Australian Wirraway fighters were climbing to attack them.

"Hope the AA boys have the sense to shut up," Wip muttered.

"Why not fire?" a private asked.

"Because our shells can't reach'em, and it'll give the position away," Wip snapped. The AA battery stayed quiet. Wip watched the Wirraways intently. "How do you interpret what you're seeing?" he asked Jake.

"I see those Jap planes in a helluva hurry to get away from us."

Wip laughed. "You're a surrealist, optimist, Doc, turning one thing into a different reality. What's actually happening is our fastest planes are outrun by their slowest. May God or Kaia, the volcano's spirit, protect us."

He and Jake walked to the showers to clean up. "I wonder…" Wip began.

"If the Japs were searching for coastal guns, apart from Praed." Jake finished Wip's thought.

"Yup. That bastard Toshio. I stupidly hinted at more access roads to artillery batteries."

Persistent reconnaissance flights indicated high Japanese interest in Rabaul. The Australian government announced that civilian women and children would be evacuated by ship, meaning whites. Chinese and Tolai civilians weren't mentioned. Rabaul was to become a town of men with servants and a few soldiers. There was no word on reinforcements. Although the battalion had two years of supplies, Colonel Scanlan rebuffed any suggestion that prudence required pre-positioning food, clothes, weapons and medicine, along escape routes with "There will be no withdrawal." Defeatist talk would be punished. Scanlan didn't add jungle drills to their training.

"Little Hell, here *they* come," Wip snorted in disgust. Colonel bloody *Ostrich!*"

Jake remembered Lee's cinchona trees near Ataliklikum Bay, but with the order "No withdrawal," a potential supply of quinine was irrelevant. He kept Lee's secret, even from Wip.

The next Radio Tokyo broadcast on December 11 was ominous. "Men and women of Australia, welcome to *Zero Hour,* the only news broadcast that tells you the truth," came a new female voice. "Yesterday was another glorious day of victory for the armed forces of Japan. Units landed on North Borneo, while the American base in Guam fell to our brave soldiers. You, Australia, are truly the orphan of the Pacific. You may think the arrogant Americans will save you. Wake up! They are falling to our forces. Their only interest in you is to have a naval base in Darwin…"

"If the Yanks want a base in Darwin," Jake jeered, determined to find a bright side in the news, "then Japs didn't wipe out their fleet at Pearl."

"Hear, hear," Egan agreed.

"Let's hear the tease," Wip urged, turning up the volume.

"Make peace with us. We promise you benefits in our Greater East Asia Co-Prosperity Sphere and independence from Britain. Do you know the British have withdrawn from Libya, leaving you Australians to fight the Germans alone? Why endure such indifference…"

Still no order came from Scanlan banning Radio Tokyo.

A week later, there was a break in routine. Mid-morning, Jake was outside his tent studying a patient's arm fungus when the soldier jerked his arm away and pointed. "Look, sir!"

Jake looked up. A single Australian Hudson bomber was climbing over New Ireland, the nearest island northeast of New Britain. Through his binoculars, Jake saw the speck turn north. All day, the men kept glancing at the sky, but the plane didn't return. With dread, they silently prepared for the news it had been shot down, an expectation expressed by clenched lips. When a Hudson appeared around 5 pm, the men cheered deliriously, hoping it was the same plane. It wagged-wagged its wings and landed at the upper aerodrome Vunakanau in Rabaul. Speculation was fever hot.

Egan made for the telephone cable to check communications. He came running out a half-hour later. "We fired the first shot, mates!" he shouted. He had a map. Work stopped as men crowded around him. He pointed to a group of dots in Micronesia. "Kapingamarangi, Jap. fortified atoll, 350 miles from us. Heard Cap. Lerew report they dived through ack-ack, circled and photographed as ordered, then fired at and hit Jap float planes trying to take off after'em, dropped two bombs on slipways. A thousand Japs runnin' around like scared as rabbits. No damage to the Hudson. love me for gettin' the skinny?" He earned as much free beer as he could drink.

Official confirmation came that night. Carr circulated

a memo congratulating the crew on the daring long-haul attack. Officers were invited to a party the next evening at the Cosmopolitan Hotel.

Jake, Wip and Egan went. The party was low-key compared to earlier balls. Dance music was ad hoc, dependent on which amateur pianist, violinist, accordionist or saxophone player wasn't on duty. Recorded tracks filled the gap. Still, the room rocked with pride and good spirits.

Egan saw his ex-girlfriend, Betty, walk into the room alone. He went white momentarily, then rushed up to her, shouting for all the world to hear, "Why didn't ya go? Fool, fool, fool!" They had a long, whispered conversation, then danced together for the entire event.

Jake jitterbugged with Priscilla. After a few sets, they walked into the beer garden and sat on a bench near the palm tree Jake had shimmied up last August. Jake gave a happy sigh. What an amazing time he'd lived since then: his grief at the break-up with Wip, then their reconciliation, his insane decision to treat IaLasliklik and his improbable success in recovering her mobility. He laughed.

"You're happy?" Priscilla asked, incredulous, after he bent to light her cigarette. He lit his pipe.

"S...surprisingly, yes. But a private happiness. On a different subject, isn't it ironic that Palmer will be in the fixed hospital building with you nurses while I'll be the only doctor in a Regimental Aid Tent at a battle front? I've stolen his risk! I never meant to."

Priscilla giggled. "Oh, is he pissed! Not at you, at the world in general. Black frowns and snapping at everything. We must grab laughs where we can, I suppose."

"But you're evacuating! Home for Xmas. You're sailing on the ship leaving on the 22nd."

"Oh no. We all refused, together and individually, many times. We're army nurses. Our place is with the troops."

"What? Bad decision, Sister. You must reconsider. We're

not allowed to express doubts, but Guam fell last week. 'Little Hell, here we come' is a chant, not guns, bombers or troops."

Priscilla brooked no argument, her green pupils obdurate. Her florid Celtic complexion was less sweaty than he remembered; her body had adjusted to humidity. Still, she should leave. Jake suspected her stubbornness covered fear as their own bravado did. On the veranda, he hugged her. "Please reconsider," he said as he went to find Wip.

*
**

To celebrate Christmas, Wip and another officer hired a Toali hunter and killed a boar. Egan also went to town and bought a few ducks. Praed was given a half-day to party, open gifts sent from home, and answer mail. High spirits fuelled a gorging feast and multiple toasts to King George VI. But the pleasure was dashed when they tuned in to Radio Tokyo.

"Today, we can talk of nothing else on *Zero Hour* but hoisting the Rising Sun flag over Hong Kong," a female voice enthused. "The British colony surrendered. The immoral, soft colonists suffered the same fate as the Americans in Guam. Men and women of Australia, orphans of the Pacific, Japan will annihilate all who oppose it. It is time to cooperate with us." The broadcast made no mention of the single Australian plane that bombed Kapingamarangi a few days earlier, but the threat was clear.

"They don't *really* love us orphans," Jake snorted, remembering how Toshio had struggled to hide his rage when Jake and Wip kept him from seeing the Praed Point guns.

"Despite our irresistible charm," Wip quipped.

"Manila and Singapore are in the way," Egan remarked hopefully. They fell silent. Thus ended Christmas Day.

At last, long after anyone had wagered, Colonel Ostrich banned Radio Tokyo. Wip and his counter-bettor had no debts to settle by drinking. For days, there was no war news. In the vacuum, wild rumours of an approaching invasion fleet filled men's mouths at widely separated units. Finally, a newsletter was dropped at Praed's checkpoint. Titled *AA News Bulletin*, it announced it was produced by the AA Battery on Frisbee Ridge. It would be a daily compilation of radio news. It updated football and cricket scores and horse races and summarised international war news. The *AA News Bulletin* and weekly mail plane became everyone's anchors.

CHAPTER 26

S UNDAY, 4 JANUARY, began as the sun-kissed mountain foliage and birds awoke, and the ocean rippled with whitecaps. Tavurvur's smoke was blowing out to sea, leaving the air free of sulphur. Jake and Wip watched the daily dawn air patrols take off. They were at work when the patrols returned with nothing to report.

Just before 11.00 a.m., Jake was stretching his arms outside after a tedious hour of taking inventory. He'd written a formal request for an orderly. Knowing that the OC, Major Palmer, would never let one of his licensed assistants go, Jake specified that a good attitude and a high school education were required; he'd train the recruit. He was considering when there might be more injuries than he could handle. He hoped his assistant wouldn't intrude on his snatched moments with Wip. Still, medicine came first.

Mechanical droning drowned out bird calls and men at work. The thrumming grew to a roar. Air raid sirens were silent. Men came running to look at a V formation of large planes.

"Ours?"

"Don't recognise 'em. Reinforcements from Moresby?"

"Dream on. They're bombers, not fighters. Must be the Yanks. Stars 'n Stripes still flying over Manila."

Several men jumped and waved at the planes. Then, they opened their mouths in shock as the planes' bellies opened and cylindrical shapes fell in graceful arcs. Clouds of smoke and loud explosions from nearby Lakunai aerodrome shattered their fantasy of reinforcements.

"Fuck! Japs!"

A rush for helmets and to the slit trench. CO Major Clarke bellowed through his megaphone, "Battle stations, gunners, the rest take cover!", long after the men had done it.

Wip sprinted to the upper gun while Jake dived into the trench. When it was clear the planes weren't heading for Praed, men poked up their heads. There was no challenge from Australian planes.

"Shit, surprise. Pearl and Hong Kong again," Egan groaned to Jake. The anti-aircraft guns were firing manically, but the smoke of their shells was visibly short of the targets. "First world war ammo," Egan cursed. Eventually, the planes droned away. Officers clustered by the telephone for after-action reports.

The first to come in was Major Palmer: "No casualties." Wip and Jake, among the other officers, cheered. Lakunai aerodrome reported a damaged runway, already working on repair: "Bombs missed the planes." The small naval squadron reported bombs hitting the harbour: "Killed a lot of fish."

"Not Pearl or Hong Kong, after all," Jake said to Egan. They laughed with nervous relief.

The unit went back to work. At dusk, a second raid came with no sirens. This time, the men counted nine flyboats bombed heading toward the upper aerodrome at Vunakanau. The after-action call was that forty bombs missed critical targets.

Ebullience was in the air for the nightly news. "'Little Hell, here we come' is our motto," Egan insisted as they clustered around the radio. "We're the 2/22 battalion. A three-two's hand can win at poker, our commander says, and he'd know 'cos he's a poker addict."

Perhaps we can withstand a Jap attack. Jake thought, admiring his mates' confidence. Then the news began: "In the raid this morning, the reports that there were no casualties have turned out to be wrong. Fifteen native workers were killed and fifteen were injured at the labour compound of Rapinduk Native Hospital near Lakunai aerodrome. Experts say the bombs were daisy cutters, which spray shrapnel in all directions. They are anti-vehicle weapons and particularly vicious anti-personnel weapons. The Native Hospital has no military value. The workers were contract labourers from other islands, not Rabaul. Medical staff are treating the injured."

Wip punched Jake's arm. "You saved IaLasliklik a second time. She's no longer a patient there."

"Palmer said no casualties." Jake was puzzled.

"He meant army. Someone else's workers aren't his concern," Egan snorted.

That night, an excited Egan woke Jake in his tent. Wip had bedded down in the supply hut near his upper gun. "Listen, Doc, I was wipin' ash off the phone line. You gotta hear this."

Reluctantly, Jake decided he was awake. "I hope you're going to explain why we got no sirens. Were the plantation coastwatchers asleep?"

"No, screw-up was in town. Coastwatchers phoned in both raids to the central switchboard, where we've got a bloke, but the alert didn't reach the Air Raid Warden. Switchboard sent a Tolai runner in case the line went down. Seems Warden didn't understand the message. Promises to do better."

"Shit. Those poor native workers didn't have to die."

"Right. And there's more. There's one pissed-off surgeon at the Native Hospital," Egan continued. "Reported Jap shrapnel he dug out of his mashed patients and corpses was stamped VR."

"Egan, that's my hometown's railway material," Jake exclaimed. "Victorian Railways. VR is stamped on its steel. What the hell? Bombed by our own stuff?"

"Yes, civvie friend. Our last Prime Minister, "Scrap Iron" Bob, incentivised businesses to sell scrap iron to the Japs. Grow the economy. Colonel Scanlan tried to stop the fuming doc from making a fuss, but he's gone home to kick up a stink in parliament and the papers."

"Is it Blackwell, the bloke I challenged to climb a palm tree?"

"Yes, I think that was the name."

"Then he's a great bloke. Just wrong about polio. Bombed by our own iron." Jake could imagine Wip's bitter sneer.

"One good thing, though, but keep it to yourself. Our Hudson bombers made a top-secret flight 650 miles to Jap stronghold at Truk, never been photographed, all got back. Our boys are the best pilots ever. They saw massive fortifications, but no fleet."

"What use is that?" Jake snapped, wanting to sleep. "Those planes came from less than 650 miles. Aircraft carriers are on the way." He felt momentarily sophisticated about war tactics.

Over the next few days, men wrote letters home for Wednesday's mail plane, knowing their families would be worried. Who knew how long the mail planes could fly?

Dear Tal, Mirrie, Simon, Jake wrote, *don't worry about me. We are managing well. It's not as bad as the newspapers may say. They sensationalise everything. All in high spirits, Love, Jake.*

Wip wrote, re-introducing himself to his niece and nephew, Tommy being Jake's sister's piano student.

Dear Sally and Tommy, There's no way you could remember me because I haven't been in Melbourne since your baptisms. I am your uncle. I am embarrassed about the years of no contact. Fate kept me away. Now, a kind fellow officer has connected us through Tommy's piano teacher. You know who I mean. We don't name names. After the war, I will visit you, and we will have grand adventures. A promise. Your reprobate, regretful uncle, John

Alexander Whipple. He addressed it to their parish church, as he wasn't sure where they lived now.

The glitch in communications between the coastwatchers and the air raid wardens was fixed. Long before any enemy planes appeared, sirens wailed, and Wirrie fighter planes were in the air. But try as they might, they weren't fast enough to damage the attackers. Anti-aircraft shells fell short.

Enemy bomber pilots began to aim better. A cycle of damaged runways, navigation and communication towers, frantically repaired, were damaged in the next raid and repaired again with increasing improvisation. Maintenance crews were exhausted but in manic high spirits; there had been almost no casualties. Jokes grew dark. When the roof of the one-room quarters for pilots and mechanics at the upper drome was destroyed, Wing Commander Lerew said their accommodation was now "well-ventilated".

"Amazing, in an awful way, how being bombed has become normal," Jake said to Wip after one of their pre-dawn kisses. "Cargo ships and the mail plane still come. I'll write home."

"And no reinforcements. We're lucky we don't have more casualties."

Spirits stayed high until the Herstein affair. On 14 January, the Norwegian cargo ship steamed across Simpson Harbour between bombing raids, untroubled, and docked at the main wharf. Men at Praed watched its progress through binoculars in astonishment and terror for it. They decided it was charmed. Many of them had civilian friends, even one or two girlfriends, still in Rabaul and desperate to be evacuated. Hopes rose to a screech level that salvation had arrived.

Day after day, the ship squatted at the dock, pudgy, large, empty, an easy target but still charmed. Soldiers waited to hear who of their friends had permission to leave on the ship, which really ought to get going. Hour after hour, civilians and soldiers heard the dreaded words 'Embarkation refused'. The only cargo to be loaded was copra, Melbourne military HQ decreed. Copra was valuable. Rabaul's governor appealed to the Prime Minister. The War Cabinet in the capital, Canberra, agreed with Melbourne.

"There's your Lord Acton democracy," Wip shot at Jake. "I told you that democracy doesn't give a fig about you or me. We're army. We expect to stay. But civvies? It's criminal!"

"Don't snap," Jake protested. "I'm not doing the refusing." He paused. "But no reinforcements? It's like we don't exist."

"I doubt our commander's stomach."

"Scanlan's a decorated war hero."

"I've met many medalled blokes. A monument of valour in one era, that moment passes, and it's all crumbly inside."

"Paris bed-mates?" Jake prompted.

Wip nodded with a crooked grin.

Dawning awareness of the soldiers' unimportance to their own government nibbled the men's psyches, but was instantly brushed away. Abandonment was inconceivable.

CHAPTER 27

20 January 1942

"WHERE'S THE MONSOON RAIN? AWL three weeks." Jake tried a joke on his new orderly.

Four days earlier, Danny Kelly had saluted him and started work. A trombonist in the 2/22 band and a Salvation Army volunteer from Melbourne, Kelly had been promoted from private to corporal and sent to Jake. He was twenty years of age, with a snub nose, curly auburn hair, and freckles. He turned out to be a quick learner, hardworking and religious. Fortunately for Jake and Wip, he slept as late as he could, and when the day's work was done, he ran to the Q Store at camp, where he stored his trombone, walked behind the bushes and played. Jake had heard jazz, scales, and a discordant modern piece whose sections Kelly went over and over. He never intruded on Jake's pre-dawn intimacies with Wip.

"Dream day for bombers," Kelly proclaimed with faux wisdom.

Jake shaded his eyes. A small bank of clouds around 9,000 feet, a thick one much higher up; otherwise, the sky was clear. "Weather's no right to be this good," Jake agreed. He and

Kelly knew nothing about aerial warfare but assumed the air of experts.

So far, the bombing hadn't devastated the town or battalion's resources, but the Japanese just had so much of everything. The men had grown used to reports of damaged aerodromes, wharves, and infrastructure, calls for all-hands-on-deck repairs, and duds slamming into the earth that had to be defused. Wip had done several bomb defusals. After one marathon effort, he came back shaking.

They went to Jake's medical tent. "Hell, love, I felt like a three-month-old, all clutz. What a lesson in Einsteinian physics. I was sure three hours passed, but it was two minutes thirty-six seconds. Yet I aged ten years. Look! White!" Still shaking, he pulled out a hair and thrust it at Jake.

"Silly, it's dirty," Jake consoled him, giving him a drop of brandy. Jake was treating anti-aircraft gunners for colitis, which he put down to stress. Most of the ailments or accidents came from exhaustion.

Wip wasn't there that morning; he'd stayed in town for a night of relaxation after weaselling supplies from Army HQ near the main wharf. Jake expected to see him that afternoon. Staring at the sky in its glorious clarity, he licked his lips, achingly conscious of Wip's absence. Town buildings, harbour, and docked ships would be etched, repaired runways glinting black against green. Jake hoped the Red Cross on his medical tent shone as brilliantly as everything else.

Air raid sirens wailed. Jake walked to the slit trench, helmet on, ready to scramble for cover. He wrinkled his nose at the foul, squelchy bottom. Sheltering there was rotting their uniforms. Most Chinese businesses had closed, their owners and employees fleeing to the bush. Lee's family was long gone. With the laundries closed, soldiers did the cleaning. Spit-and-polish Carr finally bowed to reality and stopped demanding knife-sharp pants creases at inspections.

The Japanese hadn't attacked Rabaul's major buildings.

Everyone understood the ominous meaning of the omission: an invasion was imminent, and the Japs planned to use them. The coastal guns hadn't been attacked, either. Jake wondered what Toshio had reported. Was today Praed's turn? Japanese reconnaissance planes had flown over in December. After Colonel Nurse's enraged protests, tropical creepers had done their best to spread. The base was streaks of green on grey, with naked soil borders, as easy to spot as before.

There were no enemy planes in sight. Two Wirries patrolled Blanche Bay, soaring and weaving. It had come as a sucker-punch to the troops when they saw how outmatched their planes were by Zero fighters and Nell or Mavis bombers. There were no better pilots than RAAF fellows; it was the planes. The Wirraway was a trainer with Vickers World War I machine guns and a rack for a little bomb. They looked elegant and fast until they met a Zero. The poor Wirries, of which only ten were defending Rabaul, could never get close enough to destroy a Zero, although the pilots always tried. So far, they'd faced formations of 16 to 19 attackers. Despite the odds, miraculously, eight Wirries could still fly. They couldn't save Rabaul, but they'd survived. The crews kept their spirits high.

Jake knew the AA gunners on Frisbee Ridge would be itching to fire, even knowing their World War I shells fell short. Wip had told him about a talk over drinks he had with one gunner after they met at HQ. "Love, he told me that during training, an intelligence bloke said the Japs had a new fighter plane—military calls it a Zero—that can fly 100 mph. At Frisbee Ridge, they can adjust their range for 80 mph. Lads were sure they could save us. Then they met real Zeros, flying 300 mph! Still, they'll try to their last shell. We drank five whiskies apiece." Praed's gunners at the coastal guns and AA battery were also ready, but there were no enemy ships or planes in sight.

A minute passed. "Is it a drill?" Kelly asked. Affecting indifference, he waved the soldiers' newsletter. He read an item about German troops being pushed back from Moscow.

"What Egan said is turning out, Doc, Jerry eaten up by Russian ice. Good onya, ice. Oh, listen!" He chuckled. "A new three-year-old mare just broke the five-furlong record at Flemington racecourse. Trust the fair sex, I say."

Jake glanced at the paper, then looked up. Five Wirries were climbing to join the two on patrol. There was a crack and a puff of smoke rose from Lakunai aerodrome near Praed. "Look! Did it crash on take-off?"

Kelly crossed himself and prayed for the crew. Jake did the same. He found the Christian gesture a convenient form of togetherness; he'd decided it didn't compromise his Judaism. The five Wirries flew over Blanche Bay, darted in one direction, then another, climbing, diving, darting. Still no enemy planes. Perhaps it was a drill.

Finally, the complex drones of multiple planes became audible, and grew louder and louder. Above the relentless thrum of bombers, Jake heard the variable whine of Zeros. The bobbing and weaving Wirries weren't practising.

More men joined Jake and Kelly at the trench rim. "Fuck, loudest ever. How many buggers?" one man yelped.

Today wasn't like the other days. The sky blackened as three huge formations came from different directions, one hundred planes at least. To Jake, the Wirries, which had looked so fleet, now seemed to be suspended on wires from above that twisted them with excruciating slowness as enemy fighters and bombers swarmed around and above them. The Wirries' weaving had been because there were so many targets to try and fail to reach that the pilots couldn't choose. Praed Point offered a close, ghastly view of the action. Jake's heart pounded. *Where's Wip?*

He saw one Wirrie emerge from high cloud cover behind a formation of about twelve bombers attacking Rabaul's docks and move close to fire. Several Zeroes above dived. The Wirrie scrambled to climb, oafishly slow. The men at Praed's trench groaned when the Wirrie stalled—a stationary hunk. It seemed to disintegrate. Through binoculars, Jake saw bits of metal flying as the plane spun down.

Kelly grabbed Jake's arm and pointed. Was it? Not possible! A man was outside the spinning plane, hanging on. A second later his parachute opened. Man and fabric drifted slowly over the water into the jungle. Somehow the Wirrie pilot pulled his wounded plane out of its spin at about 2,000 feet and was soon disappearing into cloud near Vunakanau aerodrome, dodging the chasing Zeros. "My God," Jake shouted. "Maybe it can crash land!"

A second Wirrie tried to escape three Zeroes on its tail, another three astern. Every manoeuvre the Wirrie made, the enemy outpaced. The Wirrie came down in flames, plunging into the ocean near Praed. A stink of petrol-infused smoke and burning flesh wafted into the men's nostrils. No survivors possible. A third Wirrie, much of its tail gone and billowing smoke, crashed at nearby Lakunai aerodrome. The men saw Zeros above it firing to destroy it on the runway. In a few short minutes, three Wirries had been shot down. Perhaps Rabaul had one Wirrie and two Hudson bombers left able to fly.

It seemed that Praed wasn't on today's menu. Jake shuddered at the butcher's bill: shattered limbs, burned flesh, excruciating pain. Wip had told him on Zealandia that the guns and planes being sent to Rabaul were a farce. He'd never believed it until now. It wasn't a surprise attack like Pearl Harbour. Seven heroic slowcoaches flung themselves at a hundred racing fighters and bombers. They had to have known the outcome.

An old newspaper picture flashed before Jake's eyes: September 1939, Polish cavalry trying to hold a crossroad against Nazi dive bombers and armoured trucks. Poor horses, poor Wirries. Jake squatted and wept huge, nauseated sobs. He wasn't alone. As the bombers droned on toward the aerodrome, the men at Praed were immobile with shock, or throwing up, weeping or cursing.

He dried his eyes at Kelly's shout "Testament to the

human spirit!" Looking up, he saw that a fourth solitary Wirrie, very high up, was darting in and out of clouds to evade a dozen Zeros. The Wirrie moved out of the cloud to attack a bomber. The Zeros separated.

"Why separate? They had him," Jake asked the soldier next to him.

"Ego. Each bastard wants to claim the kill for himself." The soldier's insignia identified him as a sergeant in the Royal Australian Engineers. "Got quotas, like cops and salesmen."

"Then our bloke's taking advantage of their pride," Jake shouted. The Wirrie pilot had slipped back into the clouds and stayed. The Zeros flew around the cloud bank. And around.

The bombers concentrated on the aerodromes then wheeled and flew low over the anti-aircraft battery, as if mocking it. "It's not our day today," Jake murmured to Kelly. The bombers turned toward Rabaul's harbour, beyond their vision. Jake's heart thudded against his ribs. *Why did Wip have to stay over?* There was a mighty explosion, smoke pouring into the sky. Whatever had been hit was major. Then the bombers and Zeros droned away. *Oh Wip, where are you?* All Jake could think of was Wip at army HQ near the wharf. *No, selfish,* he tried to check himself. *Those poor pilots. Wip,* his heart screeched.

"Wait! That one's not ours," a soldier cried, looking through binoculars. He pointed at Mother, the extinct volcano. A large plane was spiralling down in flames. It crashed on the slope. "Bloody red sun on it wing." Manic cheers erupted. "Lads got one." The excitement faded as fast as it erupted. One Jap downed.

The fourth intrepid Wirrie was still hidden by clouds. When the Zeros left to escort their bombers back to what must be an aircraft carrier, the Wirrie emerged and headed for the upper drome.

Jake's instinct whispered that Wip was safe, somewhere. His immediate panic stabilised, but other emotions swept over him. He yearned to go to the dugout and drift into oblivion, waking in an earlier era, before this mechanical carnage. Nothing made sense. Simonides' epitaph for the Spartan 300 pounded his mind:

When You go Home
Tell Them of Us and Say
For Their Tomorrow
We Gave Our Today.

Am I the *you* or *us*, he was wondering, when distant voices shrieked, "Jap planes here."

Jake didn't move. His body was congealed molasses, he couldn't form an intention until a punch in his back got him scrambling into the trench with everyone else. "Can't lose, Doc," came a voice he didn't know behind him. There was a deafening explosion a half-mile away, clouds of smoke and dirt, and the clatter of the unit's anti-aircraft guns. *Huts near the beach,* Jake's rational thought returned. *Please, God, no casualties.* They waited. No more explosions. When the All-Clear sounded, Jake ran in the direction of the explosion. Now he felt calm. The men running with him stopped suddenly, taking in the damage: a big crater breaking the road; one of the two searchlights a mangled wreck; the signalmen's hut and other sleeping quarters demolished; the Q Store damaged. Work crews were already clearing the road.

"Road's essential. Leave the huts. It's tents and the dugout tonight," a lieutenant cajoled.

Kelly cried with rage when he reached the damaged Q Store. His trombone, hurtled over a smoking bush, was partly melted. "Sorry, Kelly, you're really good," Jake consoled him, putting an arm around his shoulder.

They saw Major Clarke head for the communications hut. Jake followed, joining Egan and two other captains. The phone was silent. Why report? Everyone saw the rout. Loud irregular jangling sounded. Clarke grabbed the receiver and held it up, his mouth dropping open: a roaring crowd, 'Carlton' or 'Richmond' as an announcer called 'Bounced off and through the uprights! A beauty!'. "Bloody crossed line. Footie game in Melbourne. What can you do but laugh and cry," Clarke asked, slamming the receiver back on its stand. Nothing from Rabaul.

Jake and Kelly ran to the medical tent, fortunately untouched. Four men were waiting, too shocked to speak. Three had bleeding arms and faces; the fourth man clutched his ears, opening and shutting his mouth without a sound. None of the wounds was serious. Jake treated the skin wounds first, then gave the deaf man brandy. Pointing at a chair, he bent over the patient so he could lip-read, and said, "Sit here until your hearing returns. I'm sure it will." Work on the road continued.

*
**

Late that night, Wip strolled into the dugout where several men were snoring. Jake hadn't closed his eyes. After Jake gasped with relief, they went outside, climbed the steep path and stood by the upper gun, smoking. Wip insisted on naming the stars through Tavurvur's gauzy smoke before they talked.

"Are you alright? Thank God, we had no serious injuries."

"I saw the damage here. I'm perfect, feel guilty to be untouched. After I left HQ, I slept at the Collins' house. Their garden boy banged on the door, before the sirens. 'Balus i kam, hairiap hariap, bombom. Hairiap.' They call planes balus, don't know why. Did he smell something? Feel vibrations? Hear sounds we don't? When the sirens blared, I sheltered at the civvie hospital on Nanamula Road, near the Collins' place. Didn't think Japs'd bomb it; they'll want to use it." He stopped to spit out a flake of tobacco.

"I was terrified for you," Jake prompted. "You know about the Wirries? We saw the whole thing. Cried and threw up. What happened in town?"

"As bad. I had an opera box view. That ship, the Herstein, was bombed to smithereens. The copra burned. No escape for civvies now, no copra, no ship, dead and injured Norwegian sailors. Some were brought to the civvie hospital. Our government's finest hour."

"ToSaina, John, was hanging around the hospital. He asked, 'Japan i kam?' I said maybe. He wanted to know what Jap soldiers look like. I gave him a jolly frightening description. He said he'll try to help us. I told him to scram and keep his family safe; this was a fight between colonists with guns. He gave me a pitying look. They're reassessing the white man's power and intelligence. Don't blame 'em. Let's grab some shut eye."

As they started back, Jake pressed Wip's hand. "We're good?" he murmured.

"Good, oh yes," Wip replied.

"Take this." Jake stopped. He pulled Sally's painting in its waterproof cover from his pocket and handed it to Wip.

Wip looked at his niece's image. The fold in the paper had flaked the paint at Jake's chest, and the edges curled. But it was still vivid, Jake's face and Wip's brother's face unmistakable. "She gave it to you, a talisman to keep you safe," Wip protested. "So far you have been. I can't take it."

"She's your blood. She'd paint an even better one for you if she knew you. She'll want you to have it."

"Well, it does mean, well, so much, to me. I'll raid the communications hut for a waterproof envelope to protect it. We shouldn't be superstitious just because we're in this spirit-filled land, me. Thank you, love. I'm stunned."

CHAPTER 28

· · · · · · · ·

21-22 January 1942.

T HE 21ˢᵀ WAS QUIET at Praed. Egan got the lines untangled and the phone rang early. A grim-faced Clarke called the men to order. He told them that the army would begin demolition in the town the next day. Stores would be opened to all takers. Civilians were evacuating to Refuge Gully, outside Rabaul. Military orders were 'No withdrawal;' pre-arranged deployments would be activated.

"Shindig'll go down," Egan muttered. His face was sickly green. He bolted to the latrine building.

"Derek," Jake said gently, when he came back. "You've wanted a chance to shoot these bastards. What's wrong?"

"Plenty. Betty called me frantic, before Clarke's news. She hasn't left. I screamed not to go to Refuge Gully, too bloody close. Drive to Vunapope or south to Put Put Plantation, and get a boat and off the island while there's time. I'm helpless. She was waitin', sure husby in Singapore would be posted back. Nuts. They're in it, deep doodoo. Can't stand each other, but still married..."

"Awful. No wonder you're upset." Jake said. At least he

and Wip could protect each other. "But you must take care of yourself. If she does what you said, she might be alright."

"That's not the worst…" Egan grabbed his belly and made for the latrines again. When Jake joined him, he muttered. "Can't believe it. Must be wrong. Won't burden you." He tromped heavily to the lower gun.

Jake thrust away Egan's misery and sent Kelly to town with a list of medical supplies: quinine tablets, bandages, disinfectant, powder and mercury for fungi and ulcers, morphine, and more.

Late afternoon, they heard muffled, distant booms. When Kelly returned, he reported seeing natives making for the bush, loaded with goods; Chinese stores and houses were boarded up; the European department stores were rapidly being emptied. The pubs were closed, but a few people who hadn't evacuated were drinking liquor and roaming the streets like zombies.

The next morning, soldiers were shaving when lookouts yelled, "Planes coming!"

"Earliest raid ever. Carriers closing in. Six bloody thirty," Wip grumbled. "No sirens."

"HQ doesn't have anyone as good as Egan to fix town lines," Jake replied. He punched Egan's shoulder. They all felt close. Egan's discomfort with Jake and Wip's connection counted for nothing now. They were sitting in the dugout, below the guns and blast walls. Hastily, they packed razors and towels and joined others outside. Grey radiance penetrated sparse clouds, defining the curving coastlines. Rain was coming, but not yet.

Everyone went to battle stations. Wip and his group were at the upper gun, while Jake walked up the precipitous track to the slit trench on a flat ridge behind two wooden buildings. It was near his medical tent, which was near the tree line. When Kelly arrived, they felt the heat building.

Then, the hum of bombers and whining Zeros. About forty planes appeared over the coast of New Ireland and turned toward Vunakanau, the upper drome. The birds had stopped singing, and they heard faint ack-ack from Rabaul's invisible waterfront. The formation continued, untouched.

No Wirries rose. Jake exchanged glances with Kelly. "Thank God," Jake exclaimed spontaneously. He'd heard there was only one Wirrie and one Hudson bomber able to fly. Human casualties were unsustainable: half of Australia's pilots or mechanics were dead or wounded. The rumour was that Wing Commander Lerew would use the planes to extricate his pilots and mechanics, leaving the infantry and local militia to face the invaders. The AA battery on Frisbee Ridge was quiet. These planes were above even the most fabulist gunner. Jake knew they'd be watching with the same sullen helplessness as he and his mates were.

Bombs fell over the distant aerodrome, and Zeros dived to strafe. Through binoculars, Jake thought he saw red pricks rising, trying for a lucky hit. For the moment, the Japanese showed no interest in Praed. They wheeled in the direction of the town, invisible from Praed. Now, there was silence from the ground. Had they neutralised the waterfront machine gunners?

The formation must have turned again because now they were heading for Praed.

Clarke blew a whistle. "Helmets. Cover!" He followed some men into the slit trench while others made for the dugout. The planes made another wide high wheel around the AA battery.

"Scaredy cats remember we bagged one," Kelly said. Jake nodded. They were at the trench rim, watching seventeen bombers circle. As the first bombs began the terrible grace of their tumble, Kelly dived into the foul trench, bumping his cursing mates. Jake looked for Wip at the upper gun. Wip waved. Jake decided to stay near his tent and tree line.

At first, the men sang or hooted over the whines and crashes as trees and the cleared earth sent up burning foliage, swirling brown dust and cloddish roots. Voices spasmed with coughs. Someone prayed loudly. Was it Kelly? Someone else shouted, "Shut ya gob. He ain't helpin'!'"

Jake stood, rooted to the ground, coughing. He didn't know whether he'd made a fatal or life-saving decision to be outside. The bombers made turn after turn, aiming at the creepers covering the guns. "Here are the emplacements!", the creepers screamed visually, but they were untouched.

Planes dived; bombs fell. During a lull when they were circling higher to assess what they'd achieved, there was a moment of miraculous nothingness. Jake felt his way through smoke to his tent for wet rags and a mask.

He tripped on a tent peg. A shrieking missile hit the upper gun emplacement. Smoke covered the entire construction. Jake couldn't see anything. Wip had disappeared. At the same time, a bomb hit the building next to the medical tent. Fire spewed, and Jake heard screams. *Surely no one hid there!* He started toward it. The humming sound decreased. *Are the bombers leaving?* A deeper roar pulled his eyes up, away from two men crawling out of the burning hut, their shirts on fire. *Bombers haven't left.* He threw handfuls of earth on the two men and rolled one over, then the other, to smother the fire.

He was sitting on one of the men when there was a deep new sound, like the universe clearing its throat: clicks and rustlings coalescing into a mighty whoosh, swarms of birds beating the air. Jake leapt upright, opening his mouth in a hoarse cry. The burned men half-crawled to the trench. Half the mountainside, it looked like, was coming down on them. Earth, mud, rocks, sharp pumice, and bushes were hurtling down Praed's slopes, a cathedral of nature's innards. The planes whirled and whined. Jake's brain stopped. His body clawed him up a palm tree at the clearing's edge and cleaved him to it. The last thing he could see was a stinking sludge and a wrenching of roots under his feet, and he floated, propelling on and on.

*
**

Hands were prying his fingers off the tree trunk. Lying flat, something pressed his chest, in, out, in, out. He sat up and vomited gravel, blood, mud, and phlegm, and heard cheers. "Doc, we got ya, Noooo... worries." A voice that wasn't Wip, Kelly or Egan. But he glimpsed Wip's familiar back with a group of men trying to clear the trench. Jake was vaguely aware of a bumpy truck ride a long way to town.

When he woke, he was on a cot. He smelled bleach, varnish, disinfectant and lemon, a tropical citrusy oily scent. He touched his collar—cotton pyjamas. He was in a ward full of cots, groans swimming in his ears. Ceiling fans whirred. A strange kind of hospital: solid, opulent. It was noisy and getting noisier, with incessant phones jangles, mixed uniforms coming together in groups then jerking apart, and stuff being shoved in boxes. The hubbub split his temples. He put his hands over his ears. Suddenly, he knew where he was.

"Ah, you're with us. I'm so relieved." A soft, familiar brogue. Priscilla.

"Oh, a friend. What day is it?" *How much time have I lost? Where's Wip? Are the Japs here?*

"Same day, Doctor. It's..." she looked at her watch... "10.24 a.m. You're one of the lucky ones."

Jake coughed. Priscilla held a bowl to his mouth. He leaned over and spat out black mucous, gravel and blood. "Vintage jungle dessert," he attempted a joke. "God, my throat hurts. And my back." He felt under the pyjama top—a bandage. "Who did the chest compression?"

"I don't know. Someone quick-thinking."

"I'm blessed...."

She turned away, then back, sobbing.

"Casualties? Tell me everything."

"Animals, those Nips. The dugout collapsed, burying

some of our boys under the landslide." she gulped. When she could speak again: "Others are in the trench; the lads are trying to dig out. You escaped because you were at the tree line. Some of your mates have broken bones and gashes that will get infected if they're not in a place with good sanitation. You apparently saved two burn cases, second-degree. They need good care. We'll have a couple of amputations." She took a breath. "Officer Commander Major Clarke?"

Jake nodded.

"Severe shock. Under trench dirt too long for his liking. He was pulled out, gave strange orders; hasn't retrieved his wits. A truck is bringing him here. His aide took over. An artillery officer from the upper gun was sheltered by the blast wall. He's now directing the digging; lads say he deserves a medal."

That sounded like Wip. Jake smiled with relief. Maybe Sally's drawing saved him from going to the dugout. *Absurd.* He looked around, feeling more alert. Amputations. This wasn't the kind of place with an operating theatre. It had a residential feel. "We're in Government House, right? Town gave it to the army a few months ago. Amputees went to the civvie hospital…" He reached for the name. It didn't come.

"Namanula Hospital," Priscilla said.

"I suppose Palmer and your unit are there."

"Coming and going. A lot's happening. Drink this." She gave him a glass of water, which felt sweet on his raw throat.

"Where's my uniform? I've got to go back and help."

Priscilla smiled as she upended a pillowcase. She held up filthy pants and a shirt, the Red Cross band in tatters. They both laughed. "Your spares are under tons of muck, and you're not fit to be discharged. You have a concussion. No doctor will sign your release. Listen, there's a plan. The invasion hasn't begun. You're going to Vunapope with the rest of us. Our wounded will be treated there. Convoy's assembling now. That's what the phone calls are about." She checked his identity disks and then went to answer a call from another patient.

Jake lay back. *What's Vunapope?* Phones jangled.

When Priscilla returned, she had Jake's transfer paper to Vunapope. He waved it away. "Don't you remember our talk at the dance? You nurses could have gone home. I urged you to go. You, in particular, don't do well in the humidity. You rejected my medical opinion and insisted on staying with the troops. I admired your stubborn integrity. Why should I give your medical opinion any more weight than you gave mine?"

"It's different. Much worse. Maybe we were wrong." When she chewed her lip, he saw her fear. Leaving the transfer paper on the cot, she bustled off. Some soldiers limped or were carried outside, while two others were brought in on litters. Trucks honked and roared off.

"What's Vunapope?" he asked when Priscilla returned. He should remember, but the local names merged: *Vunakanau, Vunapope, Malaguna, Matupit.*

"It's the biggest Catholic Mission. Many buildings, good land, missionary priests and nursing nuns. The nuns say there are plenty of beds and food. The best thing is that the bishop, who arrived just before the war, is German. The Nazis' good relations with the Japs will keep us safe. If the Japs get brutal, the bishop will trot out his "Heil Hitler," and tell the little monkeys not to anger the Fuhrer. They won't know he doesn't like old Adolf." She giggled nervously.

Jake closed his eyes, feeling almost betrayed. Heil Hitler. Some Lutheran missionaries wore swastika armbands. Even as a tactic, he couldn't take German or Catholic charity. Didn't Priscilla know what Germans were doing to Jews? Had she forgotten that her ancestors burned Jews at the stake for centuries?

She misinterpreted his reserve. "Feeling sick? Don't worry. We'll soon be under the bishop's protection. I'll be back in a jiff."

He'd conflated her concern for her own worries with understanding of others. Jake bit down disappointment. Vunapope? No.

After tearing up the transfer paper, he walked through the improvised ward, passing screened cots and hearing moans, snores or soft chatter. A table near the double doors was piled with papers. He found his chart, signed his discharge and slipped it under the pile.

On the veranda, he stared down at soldiers and nurses milling between Government House and its vine-covered white picket trellis gate. Cars and trucks stood on the road. A soldier with a megaphone was calling for able-bodied men to help evacuate Praed Point. The guns were destroyed; everything had to be removed or blown up. Jake ran down the steps and through the gate. Priscilla saw him. She opened her mouth to protest, but she was too slow.

He'd seen a large idling motorcycle—a dispatch rider's? He hauled himself onto it, kicked off the brake, and tossed the dispatch bag to the ground. As the engine roared, he put his foot to the pedal.

He drove north to Malaguna Road, passing the recreation fields, and sped right through town to the steep, winding road to Malaguna Camp. It was deserted. He parked and wandered down huts and barracks. He needed a uniform, boots and medical supplies. The soldiers had left plenty of spares under their bunks. Why? After several tries, he found a uniform and boots that fit. He left a note for the owner and then put on the socks and boots. He picked up Wip's spare uniform and folded both uniforms into a bag so they'd fit on the motorcycle's back seat.

By contrast with the barracks, where the soldiers had left belongings as if they expected to return momentarily, the medical cabinets and refrigerator had been stripped almost bare. He stood, scratching his head. What did the three other doctors in the battalions know that the soldiers didn't? There was also ample food, but he could only carry a few tins of bully beef and beans.

There was petrol in the drums. Jake assumed the

plane circling overhead was Japanese. Hastily, he refilled the motorcycle's tank. He stayed in the pyjamas, hoping the silly stripes would be less tempting to strafers than army khakis. Still needing medical supplies, he rode back through town to Government House. Crowds pressed the other way. A few shot odd glances at him, but they were too preoccupied to care. A plane dived and fired at a car, but missed.

At Government House, he reconnoitred the lush gardens. The soldiers and trucks were gone. A few Tolai had bikes with crammed baskets, talking excitedly. Jake couldn't understand them—it wasn't Pidgin. But they'd be speculating on life under the Japanese. Would they be liberators or oppressors? Would the newcomers be like the Chinese entrepreneurs they knew well, or different? When they saw him, they turned away, indifferent. *Looking **past** Australian rule,* Jake concluded.

He strode inside, boots rapping the polished floors. Thwack, thwack. With an exclamation of relief, he found rubbing alcohol, a few bottles of expired quinine tablets— anything was better than nothing—needles, a blunt scalpel he could sharpen, and coarse bandages. No safety pins. Everything else had been taken. He began the eight-mile ride to Praed Point. Ears cocked for planes, he navigated craters and a couple of broken-down trucks on Battery Road. Whatever happened, he was happier in his current predicament than if he'd stayed in Melbourne. He felt his usefulness was more significant here.

When the put-put of the motorcycle reached ears at Praed, men raised aching backs from digging up earth or fallen pine trees for signs of life. They stopped digging and wrapping dead mates in blankets to embrace him. "Doc's back! He's the best."

Wip, his body a coiled spring, started to charge at him, arms open. Collecting himself, he jerked to a stop and saluted. To Jake's surprise, he was wearing sunglasses.

"Jammies suit you," Egan snorted.

Oh God, why spare me? Jake thought as he took in the

destruction of the site and piled bodies. He changed into his borrowed uniform, gave Wip his spare uniform, and then put his supplies on a blanket. He started digging where his tent had been, hoping to find his case—would anything be usable?—and strips of red cloth he could sew on his new shirt. The others continued work at the dugout. He felt surprisingly well. It was 11.30.

Wip brought him up to date. "Orders are to find the dead for burial. Listen love, we aren't blessed with a good commander. Clarke got confused. Went a bit balmy covered with dirt in the trench. Two rookie gunners from the lower gun told him the upper gun crashed on the lower gun, destroying both. You know they were built roughly vertical because of the slope?"

"Yes, Egan explained it to me. 10% chance a bomb could cause the upper to fall on the lower. See, my concussion isn't bad. I remembered that." He pressed Wip's hand.

"Right. 10% was enough for Clarke. He didn't check, just reported both guns out of commission to Ostrich, who said to get the dead, blow the magazines and join the infantry at beach defences. Clarke walked around, white and shaking, and then collapsed. They're taking him to hospital. But the order stands. Thing is, I did check. The upper gun's my gun! It's knocked askew, missile hole, but both guns could be repaired in a few hours. Keep that to yourself." With a disgusted "hmmph" he went back to digging.

Jake scrabbled though a bush and gravel and pulled out his case. It was filthy; he'd go through it later. A minute more, and he found a piece of red cloth. In the distance, they heard an explosion. Jumping up, they stared at the sky. No planes.

"AA boys. They have to blow their guns. We'll see 'em on the beach," Egan shouted.

At 12.00, Clarke's aide blew a whistle. "Righto, men. Stop digging. The rest are too deep. Sorry. Very sorry. Time to go. Load the trucks."

Wip, filthy and trailing creepers, wriggled out of a tangle where the upper gun was. To Jake's surprise, he still had his sunglasses on, even though they were mud-spattered.

"Got locks and slide boxes, sir," Wip shouted triumphantly, waving a sack. "Both guns," he said emphatically. Jake assumed he was hinting at his disapproval of Clarke's report.

The officer gave him a meaningful look. "Approved. Well done, Whipple. Into the truck."

There was a rushing blur as corpses were loaded on a truck to be driven to the civilian hospital for burial. Weapons, ammunition or equipment useful in repelling a ground assault were collected. Clarke's aide gave Jake a pistol. "Good man, Friedman, coming back and finding the case. Be sure to sew on the red patch."

On Battery Road, they gazed at smoke curling into the sky. From time to time, there was a loud crump and fresh fire: army demolition. As the trucks drove into Rabaul and entered York Street, men reminisced about their favourite haunts: parties at the Yacht Club, the saltwater swimming pool, holding hands with girlfriends at the Regent Theatre, the Cosmopolitan's beer garden and gambling dens in Chinatown.

"Wip, let's get out and walk up there." Jake pointed at a residential side street. "I want you to take off your sunglasses; I have to look at your eyes. We'll catch up in plenty of time."

"No need."

"Doctor's orders. I'm a captain. You're a lieutenant." The truck slowed, and they got out. Wip gave him a mocking salute with a trembling hand. His crooked smile was like a child trying to charm his way out of trouble.

The red-roofed bungalows were empty of people. Some asphalt was pitted from volcanic ash. One house had been bombed, the garden full of upturned and crushed plants.

Jake felt happy with Wip at his side, walking in the open. Wip seemed to be energy incarnate, heightened senses of smell and sight making him an excited commentator on the flowers and trees. Or perhaps it was adrenaline for the coming battle. Still, Jake sensed the energy coming at him was willed and dangerously depleting.

They leant against a white picket fence. Wip took off his sunglasses. There was a red patch in one eye. Jake wiped the sweat off Wip's face. "Retinal bleed. Malaria. You've had it before. You know how it goes. Why did you hide it?"

"Shindig's about to blow. You're one to talk. Bet the docs didn't discharge you. Discharged yourself in pyjamas." He laughed.

Jake took his temperature. 103 degrees. He dosed Wip with a quinine tablet. They sat on the lawn as a flock of emerald-green, red and yellow-throated parrots squealed and flew from lush branches. Wip's flushes turned to chills. Jake took his own shirt off and covered him. "Rest. We have time." After a violent shaking, Wip lay down and closed his eyes.

Jake leant back, closing his eyes, hands cradling his head, stillness amidst crises. He breathed in the orange-like smell from wide-veined croton leaves. Other plants had fallen from the veranda, their crushed stems smelling like cat piss. But the dominant scents were sweet frangipani and, oddly, roses. Sulphur, a tang of sea air and smoke from the city fires completed an intoxicating stew for the nose. *Smell's subjective,* he mused. *Rename skunk squirt truffle sauce, and you'd have a delicacy. Rename Pâté de Foie Gras Leper's Poop, and the geese would have a decent, if short, life.*

Who owned this house? He saw a twisted child's tricycle on a gravel path and a locked wooden garden shed. Two scrawny dogs scrounged under the veranda while a few hens in a wire cage pecked at seeds. How many lives would be expended to allow them to return? The dogs turned to the hens' cage and tried to jump in, but the wire held. The hens cowered. The dogs barked.

"Do hens have heart attacks?" Wip's voice was loud.

Jake grinned. "Vets say they do. But you won't right now. You look better. Let's go."

When they got back to York Street, they were amazed to find a cruising taxi—there were still a few hustling for last business—and were driven to Four Ways, an intersection of four main roads above Rabaul, where Colonel Scanlan had established his headquarters. There, they found hundreds of soldiers. To their joy, Egan, Kelly and others from Praed Point, along with Robinson from Malaguna Camp, were awaiting deployment.

"Where's everybody?" Jake asked. There weren't fourteen hundred men.

"Some at the beach already. Flyboys said the invasion had already happened. That got some of our boys retreating south, hoping to commandeer a boat and get to our headquarters on mainland New Guinea."

"It hasn't begun!" Jake protested. Senior officers quickly formed new companies. Jake, Egan, Robinson and Wip were initially assigned to R Company to defend Four Ways. But within an hour, they were reassigned to A Company, the largest unit, commanded by Major William Owen and set up at Vulcan Beach. Jake took a large truck, and they drove back toward Rabaul, then turned right, down the steep, winding unmarked road called Big Dipper to the beach.

"A Company must be good," Jake remarked, feeling both insubstantial and pulsing with fear.

"A, right," Egan agreed. "Hey, there's the local New Guinea Volunteer Rifles." He pointed behind him to about eighty men marching with rifles over their shoulders.

"We'll be the best!" Wip boasted. He was in high-energy mode again.

"Owen's supposed to be solid," Egan said, unsure if Wip was being sarcastic.

"What, a real commander at last?" Wip pressed his lips shut.

CHAPTER 29
• • • • • • •

"**Y**OU'RE A PERSISTENT BLOKE, Captain Friedman. I'm relieved you're here," Major Bill Owen shouted above masses of moving men and machines. Carrying his medical case, Jake had just saluted Owen. "You could have stayed in hospital—yep, I heard about the pyjama discharge—but you didn't. You're the only doctor at the front. You and your orderly are *it* for medicine. Field Ambulance blokes are at Vunapope, installing the nurses and wounded. Haven't heard from them."

Egan saluted Owen. "Sir, communications down. Army engineers blew town's transmitter when they bombed the ammo dump, accident, like. Amalgamated Wireless building's near the ammo, sir."

"So OC Major Palmer couldn't contact you, sir," Jake offered, feeling a need to defend another doctor.

Owen sighed. "Our bang-bang boys were over-excited. A tad imprecise? Why am I not surprised? We've got a working telephone to Colonel Scanlan for the time being." He pointed at trampled grass near his tent, between trees. "Set your Regimental Aid Post here, the truck off the road, and put signs on a few trees. If the Japs land, we'll give'em a warm welcome, metal complimentary." He chuckled. "Here's a map. Look for laughs, Doc. Only way to cope."

"Sir, the aid post's triage and first aid. Where do I evacuate the badly wounded who could survive?"

"Mystery. Rabaul hospitals are closed. I'll get you some stretcher-bearers, but no nurses of course. Drive the worst cases up Big Dipper to the plateau observation point. Hopefully, someone can take them to our Field Ambulance unit at Vunapope. It's ten miles. Do your best."

Owen had an unusually long face, short hair on a low forehead and very kind eyes. Jake liked him instantly.

"Yes, sir."

Jake and Kelly found a tent in a truck with a Red Cross on its canvas that could be erected to accommodate a few stretchers. As Jake hammered in pegs, he couldn't get over the irony that he was the doctor at the front while Major Palmer, who'd done everything he could to avoid being consigned to the rear, was shepherding nurses and wounded servicemen to refuge with the nuns. He was laughing when he walked into the erected tent to sort through his case and the other supplies. Owen was right: cherish the funny side.

Kelly looked up from sterilising instruments.

"Irony," Jake said. "We're medicine at the front, not OC Palmer, the senior doctor of A Company 2/10 Field Ambulance Unit."

For Kelly, former Salvation Army bandsman, nuance had evidently been new. At the beginning, he'd laughed at the swear words with religious origins that tripped off his mates' lips. But he hadn't laughed since the Wirries went down. Now uncertain, he murmured, perhaps in deference to Jake's rank, "Yes, sir. We did irony in fifth-form English, I think." He waved a mosquito away and continued sterilising. Jake smiled.

A lookout on North Daughter that afternoon had reported a fleet of ships approaching Blanche Bay. Action was imminent unless the weather helped.

Soldiers from infantry and artillery units, along with eighty local New Guinea Volunteer Riflemen, had been cobbled into a force of 280 defending a beach a mile north of the dormant volcano, Mt. Vulcan. Jake unrolled Owen's pen-drawn map. He and Kelly studied it.

"Some task to hold," Kelly remarked.

"Let's have a smoke and memorise the terrain," Jake suggested. "Nothing happening at the moment."

The beach proper, sand and coral, was narrow, with ferns, calf-high grasses and palm trees encroaching. Unlike Praed Point, it hadn't been cleared. It looked congested, with natural cover. The defence line ran in the shape of a squashed sphere running two miles long and a half mile deep. Mt. Vulcan dictated the contours, its densely forested slope cut by ravines. The New Guinea Volunteers were to hold the left flank, covering Big Dipper, the one access road to the rest of the peninsula, a position of trust. The unpaved Big Dipper wound up about three miles to Kokopo Road, the throughway that led to the intersection hosting battalion headquarters.

Small companies defended key intersections on Kokopo Road, including two pre-planned meeting points, Four Ways, where Jake had come from, and Three Ways. Y Company was to defend a beach ten miles south of A Company. Thirteen hundred men would defend landing sites encompassing three hundred miles. Chance would determine whether invaders would meet defenders. But the invaders would vastly outnumber the defenders, as the past weeks had tragically shown.

It was a purple-grey dusk, the clouds promising rain. Jake felt intensely alive. Adrenalin, maybe. Over-exercised from erecting the tent and slightly concussed from the bombing at Praed, he should be comatose, but he'd never felt better.

Leaving Kelly to deal with minor injuries, he wandered down to the beach with Wip and Egan to taste, smell and feel the map. New Guinea Volunteers were placing rolls of barbed wire along A Company's position. They'd cleared about forty yards of vegetation to give the defenders room for weapons and mobility behind the wire.

The view was extraordinary. Jake could see right across Simpson Harbour to Tavurvur, the live volcano, and its extinct companions, Mother and South Daughter. Domineering, they framed the coast. He took it in, then skipped back a few yards to let the wire rollers finish their work.

Behind him, soldiers were piling coconut tree logs as cover while gunners placed mortars, Vickers machine guns, and two anti-tank guns. The environment was as fecund and congested as the black lines on white paper suggested. Groups of five to eight men cleaned and oiled their Enfield rifles or Thomson sub-machine guns with the skill honed by months of Tavurvur's corroding ash.

Owen went from mortar to mortar, checking that the shells would land beyond the wire. "Wait until they're out of their boats, lads, calf-deep in waves and crunching coral." Deprived of a fair fight for far too long, the men cheered him exuberantly. Wip and Egan manned mortars.

With the beach organised, Owen checked the flanks and rear. Jake could see snipers positioned to counter encirclement by Japanese who landed beyond their flanks. It looked awfully fragile, but Owen had done his best. Jake was honoured to serve him.

Back in his medical tent, he and Kelly had just taken everything out of his grimy case when the skies opened. For a moment, they listened to rain pounding their tent. Then they grabbed buckets and ran outside to catch fresh water. They washed and dried the usable instruments and drug bottles in the case.

"Listen, Dan," Jake said. "We should divide what we have into portable kits for each of us. We might have to go jungle with little notice. The men will need all the medicine and bandages we can carry."

When they were done, it was still raining. No patients had reported. Jake sewed a scrap of red cloth onto his shirt sleeve. They settled into a poker game.

Outside, lookouts sheltered under palm trees, every so often wiping their binoculars and patrolling. Soldiers in the front row kept their weapons under the logs, making the best of things in their digger slouch hats. There was no moon. Around midnight, the rain eased and then stopped. Jake ran outside to find Owen. Along the line, men stretched and shook themselves off.

"Good landing conditions, Doc," Owen pointed at three planets. "Mars in the east, Jupiter and Saturn in the west. Enough light for barges." He lit a cigarette, cupping his hand over the glowing tip. He sucked the tobacco in quickly, then stubbed out the cigarette. "Don't do what I did," he muttered, embarrassed. "Irresponsible."

They gazed at the sky. Clouds parted under a nudging breeze, allowing stars to wink, disappear, and wink again. The air was sweet with crushed grass, rotting crabs, and excited male sweat. An eerie red glow from the demolition fires in Rabaul gave a hint of visibility. Word passed to be ready, which generated a bustle of gun-cleaning, then expectant quiet. Jake and Kelly brought stretchers to the front line and stood behind a palm tree.

An eternity of time passed. The tension was too high for Jake's brain to get around concepts like minutes. The past disappeared; the future was inconceivable; the present smothering.

A rasping whisper: "Buggers are here."

Owen held up a cautionary hand. They heard the sounds of metal cracking coral en masse. To the Australians' amazement, foreign chatter and hawking titters amplified the thwack and suck of boots in sand and legs splashing through waves. What sounded like a curse was met by laughter. Helpfully, one of the invaders waved a flashlight to help his comrade. 2.30 a.m., Jake noted, peering at his watch.

Owen and the other officers shot up flares. The beach lit up. Throngs of assault troops flailed toward the sand, the barges bobbing far behind them.

Coconut logs leapt to red-hot life as barrages of bullets and whooshing mortar shells hit the first attackers. The Japanese fell back, leaving bodies on the sand. Warships shelled the beach, lighting the sky with bright white pricks. The first shells landed harmlessly behind the line. A Japanese plane dropped flares. "Hold your fire," Owen ordered. The order was relayed down the line.

Japanese shelling intensified. The smell of oil, sulphur and, from beyond the barbed wire, burning flesh, swirled. A soldier by one of the mortars started screaming. Kelly ran to him, Jake following. Kelly started to prod the soldier for the wound.

"Not the screamer. His mate! Screamer's OK!" Jake shouted, arm around a man stuck in a half crouch, hands cupping his belly, his mouth agape. Red mush was running over his arms. Stretcher-bearers loaded him on the stretcher, the wounded man half sitting with his hands on his belly. As gently as they could, they carried him to the tent.

Jake thought about a pressure bandage, a careening drive up unpaved Big Dipper, a rush to Vunapope. More bumps, shells from Japanese ships. It wouldn't do. He had to try to stabilise his patient first. With Kelly watching wide-eyed, he injected the patient with morphine.

"I'm sorry this is your first emergency," Jake said to Kelly as the man slid lower on his back. Jake pressed on the stomach gash and protruding intestines as the patient slipped out of consciousness. "You clean, I hold."

When the dirt was off, Jake said, "You hold, I'll inject Thiopental." He rushed to set up an intravenous drip and emptied a vial of the barbiturate into the patient. In ten seconds, he was fully out. This was a short-term anaesthesia. Working fast, Jake took out the steaming pink-grey loops. Holding them between fingers, he eased them back in the correct position. "It's only small intestines," Jake chided the shocked Kelly. "You've got them, too. Bully beef filling yours just like his, I bet." Kelly then held the stomach skin together while Jake stitched. Sitting back, exhausted and nervous, Jake watched Kelly bandage the patient and sterilise the instruments.

The soldier stirred. He whispered, "Deb, I love you. Take care of the kid."

"You're not done yet, mate. Courage," Jake said.

"I'll pray for you," Kelly added. His face shone with shy pride.

They moved the man to a palette in the corner and gave him more morphine. He fell asleep.

When Jake and Kelly returned to the coconut logs, shelling from the warships had stopped. There was a lull. Owen shouted. "Cease fire! Save ammo. We pushed them back."

Foreign voices rang out, but not with laughter. The intonation sounded like orders, threats, exhortation. There were moans and a lot of wriggling at the wire.

Owen risked a flashlight. "Mates, they're reforming and piling their wounded and dead at the wire to walk over them." He jumped back as a bullet whizzed by his head. "Fire, mortars, anti-tanks."

A Company's second barrage met the yowling rush. Enemy boots slithered on their own casualties, hurling them backwards again and blocking the rank behind. Tripping, climbing men made easy targets for rifles and machine guns. Mortars whooshed, and the two anti-tank guns cracked, seeking the barges. A second retreat earned jeers from the Australians. There were more furious foreign yells, presumably from frustrated officers.

"Cease fire!" Owen yelled. He went to his tent, emerging a minute later, cursing. "Bloody telephone line's broken. Can't call up reserve ammo. Fuck! Reckon we downed hundreds, but more coming."

Jake offered, "Sir, I can drive the truck up Big Dipper to the observation post. We've had one surgery. He's asleep, but bad. I can take him, too, get him on the way to Vunapope.

Kelly can treat minor injuries while I'm gone. I can collect what you need. It will only take a half hour."

He saw Owen consider. "No. Our one ambulance truck, headlights off, on an unpaved unmarked winding road? Too dangerous. Can't risk the truck or you. Now I think about it, repark the truck to the left of your tent, not in front. I expect flanking attacks from the mountain slope on the right sooner than our left."

He called for volunteers to climb up the escarpment and bring back the pre-placed reserve ammunition. Wip and Egan leapt to go. "We know what you need, sir."

Jake opened his mouth to protest Wip's malaria, but Owen cut him off. He rattled off acronyms Jake couldn't follow. Robinson took over Wip's and Egan's mortar while a guide from the New Guinea Volunteers showed Wip and Egan the animal track. Two snipers covered their ascent. Two soldiers drove a small truck up Big Dipper Road to meet Wip and Egan on the plateau.

The rest of A Company watched the Japanese flounder to their barges, carrying some of their wounded. They were beyond rifle range. "Oh, for a Wirrie," Owen groaned. "Strafing those blokes is something they could manage."

Jake looked in the direction of Rabaul. He blinked. Was there a smear of light? *Where's Wip? Please, come back now.* This new light was sharper than the purple embers of the demolitions. He pointed to the hints of yellow, then checked his watch. It was 3.15 a.m. He was amazed at how energised he felt after his hard work on the stomach wound. "Do you see that?"

Many men trained their binoculars in Rabaul's direction. In the quiet, they heard a dull crump of shelling to their south.

"Too far. We need a naval telescope," Owen said. But there was no need for a naval telescope when the bright green flare everyone could identify soared up from the town. "Japs've taken Rabaul. Fuckers we bloodied'll flank us on the right. We have to watch the slope. Plenty of darkness left." He listened—more crumps from the south. "Our buddies at Raluama Point sound like they're coping for the moment. We'll be encircled eventually, but I won't let then close the pincer." While he re-deployed artillery, Jake returned to the tent.

After about twenty minutes, he heard whoops outside. He pushed through the flaps. Wip and Egan had brought all the ammunition they could carry and slither down. Wip's eyes glittered. "Did my bit," he said happily. The two soldiers who'd driven to the plateau brought the truck back undamaged, crammed with ammunition.

Jake and Kelly were busy in the tent for the next few hours. All they could do was glean what they could from sounds outside and patient accounts. Episodes of intense gunfire from shifting locations on the mountain erupted amid continuous shelling from the ships. There was a lot of yelling, some distant and foreign, some close, from the right flank. Every time they heard a shell whoosh overhead, the injured men in the tent jerked their heads up, but their luck held; no shells exploded near them. Jake was vaguely aware of Wip exulting over a truck run up Big Dipper again for more ammunition.

"Talk to me," Jake said to one patient. "Take your mind off me getting the bullet out of your shoulder. Pain?"

The soldier shook his head, "Not much." Trembling but excited, he babbled, "Jap signal flags..." He gasped at a stab of pain and then steadied his breathing. "On the slope. Buggers yell to rally at the flag. Nice white flags. We shoot the cloth or the buggers holding them. A hoot." Kelly gave him a pain killer. The man rested for a minute, then left, eager to get back to his platoon.

A soldier with burns on his arm from a gun that misfired told them that one of his mates had wriggled beyond the deployment's perimeter and killed an entire enemy machine gun nest.

Sometime later, a soldier limped in. He showed Jake two

reddening punctures on his leg and swelling around the site: snake bite. He was a sniper. "Hunted possum before the war, Doc. Got bit when I crawled near a ravine and shot a Jap flag. Reckon it's poisonous?"

The battle seemed to be stalemated. Bursts of fire, quiet, foreign cries, close Australian voices reassuring each other, more bursts of fire, quiet. Nothing had dislodged A Company.

"Venomous, yes. Have to do it the old-fashioned way," Jake answered. "Army didn't give us anti-venom. Cut, suck, boy scout stuff. Then go to Noah's Mission and see a medic there. I'll square it with Owen. I don't know local snakes."

While Kelly tied the tourniquet, Jake noticed the tent flap. It looked paler, the lamplight duller. Dawn was close. Outside, the sputtering rhythm of firefights continued. It took Jake ten minutes of sucking and spitting before he judged the flesh clean. He disinfected the puncture and bandaged the leg. He'd just finished when a mighty crack came from a new direction. Left? Cries of fear came from nearby. He stiffened.

Owen strode in, grim-faced. Stretcher-bearers carried in four soldiers, blown apart, obviously dead. But Jake had to make the formal pronouncement. Owen closed one man's eyes. "My batman. Goodbye, you loyal, beloved friend."

While Jake removed one of the paired identity discs from each dead man, Owen listened to another crack. He sighed. "Howitzer from Rabaul. Jig's up, fellas. Low on ammo and cut off." More pounding cracks came from the howitzers.

Dawn glowed golden. The gunfire seemed to be waning. Jake heard shouts and gasps. He walked to the coconut logs. At least thirty warships were in various harbours. The New Guinea Volunteers still held Big Dipper. Probing attacks were coming from many places on the mountain slope and ravines. Enemy bodies sprawled on the sand beyond the wire and others floated in the water, eddying to the sand, snagging on coral, or pulled back by receding waves. Not one Japanese attacker had made it over the wire, which was bloodstained and snagged with scraps of uniforms. Wip ran to the wire and pulled off a bit of a sleeve while Egan used a palm branch to lever up a helmet. The ships were shelling, but aiming beyond the beach.

"Wire's the safest place now," a soldier grunted. "Fancy a swim with the sharks, sir?" he joked.

Whistles blew. Owen and the platoon leaders gave the order to execute an orderly retreat. "A Company," Owen roared," we're cut off. Jap planes will come soon, and we need to keep the road open. Platoons, make a leapfrogging retreat up Big Dipper and provide covering fire as you go. Others, hike the track. Up you go, take the ambulatory wounded, and watch for snipers and strafing planes."

Jake ordered Kelly and a litter bearer to stack the corpses in the ambulance truck and help him with the surgery patient, then leave immediately. "Take the drugs and small instruments, Dan, and hike the track. I'll finish up here and drive."

Tenderly, they carried the drowsy stomach wound into the back, strapped him onto a litter, and packed cloth around the litter to hopefully keep it from sliding. "Courage, mate," Jake said as he gave him a morphine shot.

A Zero whined, and another Zero joined it. Japanese signal flags fluttered on the mountain slope. The planes took turns diving and strafing men scrambling up the track Wip and Egan had used hours earlier. At first, the Australians took cover and fired furiously at the planes, but the track was tough. Soon, packs and rifles littered the slope as men hauled themselves higher, into cover, out again, slowly achieving the defended plateau where they expected to find their commandant, Colonel Scanlan.

Jake started the engine idling, with the brake on, then went back to dismantle the tent and pick up his case. Suddenly, the engine roared to life. Jake stood, open-mouthed. Owen was at the wheel. There were no other soldiers anywhere. The truck rolled toward Big Dipper, gathering speed. Jake ran. He yelled, banged on a window, grabbed the door handle and was dragged a few feet. He dropped the canvas but held onto his case. Owen slowed. Jake climbed into the driver's cabin, heaving.

"I thought I was last!" Owen shouted over the engine. "Commander leaves last. You're a persistent bugger, Friedman, a sight for sore eyes."

Owen zig-zagged as shells burst around them. Jake put his hand out of the open window and thrust his middle finger at a Zero that couldn't find a good angle on them. Sally's drawing flashed before his eyes. He'd given it to Wip, but maybe the spirit of the image was protecting them both.

"It's after 7.30 a.m.," Owen said, when they were out of shell range from the warships. "We held them off for five hours. Less than three hundred of us. Most of our boys are volunteers, not veterans. They were better than the old Spartan 300. Japs aren't invincible; the myth's balderdash. I reckon we sent hundreds, maybe a thousand, to Nip Valhalla. We needed modern artillery to counter their flanking us, and, oh God, an air force more than trainer planes. Our poor bloody pilots!" He stopped as the truck lurched, then righted itself. "Doc, when we reach Four Ways, we'll have a good smoke and a drink if we can scrounge one. Get ready for mayhem ahead."

CHAPTER 30

· · · · · · · ·

23 January 1942

AT FOUR WAYS INTERSECTION, they found a small company led by a Lieutenant Tolmer untouched by the fighting. But no Colonel Scanlan or his aides, and no Lieutenant Colonel Carr or his aides. The observation post overlooked Vulcan and the southern beaches. Men groaned at the sight of Japanese landing parties pouring ashore at many beaches. Apart from four destroyers, a myriad of barges, and troop transports in the harbours, an aircraft carrier was launching Zeros. Sporadic gunfire clattered from the mountain slopes and ravines.

"Colonel Scanlan moved around 3.00 a.m. to Tallilgap Mission near Vunukanau aerodrome. Captain Appel's defending the position with a company plus strays," Tolmer explained to Owen and Jake. "Less exposed. He took the communications truck, so we're temporarily out of contact." Jake thought Scanlan must have moved just before Wip and Egan made their daring climb for ammunition. "Then Lieutenant Colonel Carr moved from Noah's Mission to Three Ways," Tolmer added.

"Battalion's rudderless," Owen muttered audibly, scratching his hair.

Several men walked to the edge of the road and looked down at Vulcan Beach and its surroundings. One soldier shouted, pointing. Owen and Jake joined him. They could pick out an overgrown winding track linking the shore and plateau.

"Tawlin Mission," the soldier growled. He pointed at buildings near the track. Jake noted the local NGVR badge on his sleeve. "German. Sir, guests! The wrong kind!"

Two native boys were leading a large group of Japanese soldiers up the track, followed by a missionary. "Japs could never find this track without help," he cried, furious.

"Right, snipers," Tolmer called.

"We were too kind to Kraut clergy," Owen snorted.

"I heard some Lutherans wear swastika armbands," Jake exclaimed.

"Some Tolai will help us, others won't," Wip said, joining them. "Those two suckers can't tell Aussies from Germans from Japs, from a moral perspective. Natives don't know the Japs yet. We just have to be careful."

Gunfire clattered down the track. Then boots crunching undergrowth. "Threat gone," a skinny rifleman reported. "Them two poor fools and ten Japs. No casualties to us."

While more men gathered at Four Ways waiting for orders, Jake and Kelly drove the ambulance truck to Noah's Mission. They entered a bucolic oasis of palm trees and orchards amidst bombing and dust. A distressed-looking, grey-haired, thin reverend hurried out to meet them. "Lieutenant Colonel Carr and his aides have left. We don't want to be involved. No more army."

Jake snapped, "I have a patched-up stomach wound who can make it, and four deceased. Rabaul's fallen, and I have no leave to go to Vunapope. Take my cases and get them to Vunapope yourself, if you're so indifferent to human suffering. Our Field Ambulance unit, the 2/10, is there. That Mission is fulfilling its pastoral duty."

Never in his life had Jake thought praise for a Catholic

institution would trip off his lips. But Father Rowland had been terrific, and the nuns at Vunapope had offered to be all in for wounded Australians.

Kelly watched, shocked. Jake prevailed for one case, the stomach wound.

As they backed out of the driveway with the four corpses five minutes later, a young missionary ran after them. "Sir, I think your man died. Can you please come back?"

Indeed, he was dead. Jake made the formal certification and removed one of his identity discs, pondering clinically at the deteriorated fibre material with blurred script. *Like everything else our superiors have done, unfitted for the tropics.* The reverend was unctuously helpful. "We'll take care of all your burials, keep the appropriate records, no need for the army to pay." He was unable to hide his relief.

"Boy, that clergyman just dodged a moral test," Kelly exclaimed as they headed back to Four Ways. A Zero circled. At the wheel, Kelly accelerated, cheeks flushing with excitement.

"He faced it and failed," Jake retorted. "You're too charitable. You need some Old Testament severity. Get used to mixed receptions from missions. They're just scared humans like everyone else." He slammed the glove compartment with his left hand.

"You did all you could for Stomach Wound, sir," Kelly declared, following the custom of naming patients by their ailments.

"With an anaesthetic that lasts more than fifteen minutes, I could have cleaned and sutured better. He would have made it in a hospital. No yellow telegram to his wife, Deb."

At Four Ways, Jake gave the identity discs to Tolmer. Carr had met Scanlan at his third headquarters, a plantation two miles southeast. Communications weren't re-established, so Carr sent a dispatch rider. To the hundreds of milling men, some with trucks or motorbikes, Carr's aide read: "Retreat to Three Ways intersection for more orders." Jake and Kelly started the drive, the vehicle's back full of soldiers. Trucks hurtled past them beneath strafing Zeros. Jake stopped at the roadside, everyone jumping for ditches, emerging to do the same again and again. When they reached Three Ways, many trucks roared on.

"Stop, fellas. This is the place!" Owen yelled.

"No, sir. We're going to find Commandant Scanlan." Anxiety was manic.

At Three Ways, there was more waiting, between dodging strafing Zeros. Finally, as enemy planes began strafing, another of Carr's dispatch riders brought fresh orders. Everyone moved off the road. "We're almost overwhelmed. Your commander, Colonel Scanlan, instructs, 'Go bush. It's every man for himself.'"

Senior officers shouted over yowls of: "What the fuck does that mean?".

"Men, there's a plan," the dispatch rider reported. "You're to assemble at either of two rivers: Warangoi, southeast of here, or Keravat, northwest of here, whichever is closer to defended positions.... "

"Are there defended positions?" Jake heard Robinson ask.

"Communications are down. The message says naval officers with the one functioning radio, a giant contraption, are waiting for native porters to haul it into the mountains."

"Good luck with that!" Wip snorted.

"Both rivers meet coastal roads," the dispatch rider shouted, flushing. "Make for plantations and call for air rescue from a RAAF Catalina seaplane, or find a boat and get off the island." A few minutes later, coded signals from the communications truck confirmed the orders.

"Whaaat!?" Robinson shouted. "For weeks 'no withdrawal, no pre-positioning supplies for a retreat'. Now it's 'good luck, boys, enjoy the hike!' I came from Malaguna Camp. We were told to pack for a short deployment exercise..."

Jake realised now why the soldiers had left so much

equipment at camp yesterday. Hadn't Scanlan levelled with his men, even then, that the invasion was real? His temple began to throb, then hammered. Betrayal. Hard to get his mind around the concept, but it was the right word.

Robinson was ranting. "...treks'll take weeks. Japs'll be everywhere open. We don't have jungle gear. Some of you boys went into battle in shorts!" He was apoplectic with rage, and very scared.

"Is there an evacuation plan from Moresby or Townsville?" Jake asked Owen. Port Moresby was Australia's base on the southern coast of mainland New Guinea, Townsville, the closest base in Australia.

"If there is, it's the secret of the century. Sorry, Doc, it's improv from now on."

Men clustered over maps, deciding which route to try. There were no maps of the island's mountainous interior, which Europeans had never fully explored. Some chose to stay, while a few decided to walk back into Rabaul and surrender. All seemed stunned. A couple took out photos of loved ones and kissed them. Others stared down, digging for resolve. Some looked straight ahead at nothing, glowering with rage.

Jake said to Owen, "We grunts fought off the Japs, got reserve ammunition, and retreated in good order. No contingency plans? It's been seven weeks since Pearl!"

Owen shifted from boot to boot. "Have to make the best of it. Pre-planned deployments were by the book. The best they could have been, given our resources. I can't explain."

Jake and Owen, with ten men from different units, opted for a jungle track parallel to Kokopo Ridge Road. They'd walk to Tallilgap Mission, Scanlan's prior headquarters, and stay the night there or in the bush. Then cross the Warangoi River and try the southeast coast. Visions of Catalina seaplane rescues lit up their brains; abandonment was still inconceivable. They started, willing optimism.

After some time, Owen raised his arm. "Hush up." They

were preparing to leave the jungle for Tallilgap Mission. "Heard something." The sun was setting, though they only knew this from their watches and a shifting shine on dark leaves that dribbled moisture down their backs. He and Jake wriggled through stands of bamboo to the road.

"Shiiit," Owen cursed. "They outran us. Nearly got caught. Praise the Lord, they're noisy buggers. Never stop chattering." They stared at hostile uniforms setting up a battery, then wriggled back. The men plunged deeper into the bush, looking for flattish ground to camp. There was none, so they separated into groups of three to five.

The Praed men with Robinson stuck together. Egan tried to fashion partial cover by stripping leaves off a tree. They slumped against the tree trunk under their slouch infantry hats or helmets, then pulled cans of bully beef from their packs.

Jake watched Wip try to open his can. Wip's hand shook on the can twister. The half-open can sprang free, flew into the air, hit a branch and fell. Wip crawled after it. The exposed red meat had a leaf and dirt on it. Wip grabbed the twister and held his wrist with his other hand—hard, the knuckles white, hunched with concentration—and wrenched. Both hands shook. He collapsed back, weak. The blackened red meat lay beyond his reach, a grotesquely grinning mockery.

Jake saw deep sadness in Wip's eyes. He felt Wip's forehead. Burning. He gave him a quinine tablet and then fed him his own meat. *My quinine isn't infinite. Still, Kelly had plenty.* He felt the others' foreheads. Egan and Kelly were normal, but Robinson was a little hot.

They slept fitfully through the jungle symphony of crickets thrumming, an occasional owl hoot and distant frog song. Dawn bird song woke them. They stretched. There was no gunfire, no droning planes. Gradually, the ten men found each other. But no Owen.

Wip seemed better. "I'm a lieutenant, busted from

captain for breaking rules," he said. "Egan and you are captains, Doc. Who's in charge?"

"Egan," Jake answered quickly. "He's army, and I'm a non-combatant officer."

"Right," Egan said, enunciating clearly, with sudden authority. "It's 6 a.m. Clean weapons 'n bury signs we've bin here, includin' um, piss and shit. Catlike. We look for Major Owen in pairs: one hour. If you speak, cuckoo call. Meet here for breakfast. Don't get lost."

Wip, who looked viable, led Jake along what looked like a deer path. After twenty minutes, they found an abandoned native hut, empty except for some mouldy sweet potato. There was no sign of recent use. Jake cocked his ears, hyper-alert. "Cry? Fake cuckoo?"

Wip strained, hit his head. "Sorry," he mumbled, almost stumbling. "Bad ears all of a sudden."

Jake heard another call and running water. "Let me lead," Jake said. "I'll dose you later." When they reached the water, a dripping Kelly was sobbing, "I let you down." He banged his forehead against a tree trunk. Bang, bang, bang. "Unforgivable," Kelly moaned.

"Stop. You slipped," Egan consoled him. Both of their legs were a mass of leeches.

"No guilt, Dan," Jake confirmed. "We've been through too much. I'll get the bloodsuckers off."

Egan filled them in while Jake worked fingernail by fingernail to dislodge their leeches. Kelly gulped and began to dry patches of himself with leaves. "We were wadin' across this damn calf-deep runnin' wild stream. Thought we saw khaki the other side. Kelly tripped on stones, strap on his medical kit snapped. Him and the bouncing kit washed downriver. I powered back to the bank, found Kelly clingin' to a stone midstream a few hundred yards down. I hauled him out t'other side, but the kit was gone. We trekked back to the khaki. A rottin' pig corpse even natives wouldn't eat. Better find the mates now."

Over breakfast, the rest of the men dribbled in. No one had seen a hint of Owen.

"What else can go wrong?" Jake groaned.

Egan jumped up, finger on his lip for quiet. "Jap patrol? Sound's a knife on me nerves." No one else detected human sounds, but a minute later, boots squelching mud approached. The men slipped behind trees, dragging their kits, guns cocked. A lone Australian soldier sat on a fallen log. He sighed heavily and ate a biscuit.

When he got over his terror at the unshaven men pouncing on him, he was ecstatic. "I'm Private Ben Williams, sir, dispatch rider. Just back from Vunapope, where the wounded blokes and nurses are. My unit's gone. Jap machine gun battery's at Three Ways. Damn lucky I wasn't caught. Lucky twice today. Someone up there looking out for me, I swear. Japs were anchoring at Vunapope's dock. I scarpered before they reached the grounds."

He was hugged, given a can of beef, and hounded for everything he knew. "Dr Palmer and all his doctors and orderlies left last night. Didn't tell anyone. Took the unit's medicine, too. I mean, mates, they didn't tell their own employees and charges, the six army nurses, what they planned to do. Gone jungle after the men hiking south, I reckon. Nurses are hysterical. Dependent now on a buncha nuns and a Kraut bishop."

The men looked at one another. None spoke. Jake felt the helpless fury seeping out from their pores. Many of them were friends with the nurses. Jake sent up an agnostic's prayer for their safety, especially Priscilla.

After a moment, he proposed, "I'm thinking Keravat River and the northwest coast. Helluva hike, but we know here's a hornets' nest of Japs. We don't know about the other coast." The loss of Kelly's quinine was beginning to worry him. For the first time, he remembered Lee's cinchona trees. "Is there a sound military reason for the Keravat route?"

Robinson pulled out a map. "About six miles to

Warangoi, two more to Put Put Plantation. Bet a lot of our boys are on the way there and will continue along the coast. About eight to the bridge on Keravat, twelve more to Harvey's Plantation. But there'll be native villages around Ataliklikum Bay; it looks settled. Less steep climbs if we have to avoid roads and go inland."

"I'm good for climbing Mt. Kosiusko, no worries," Wip declared.

Bullshit, Jake thought.

A soldier from the quartermaster's office said, "There's a locked sawmill off Ataliklikun Bay. The owner fled the day after the Japs bombed Pearl. Three miles past Keravat. I know two blokes disobeyed Scanlan's orders against pre-positioning supplies and hid guns, ammo, boots and food there. I helped them."

"Medicine?" Jake asked.

"Dunno, sir. Kept separate. Harder to filch." He grinned, and everyone laughed.

"Assume no," Jake concluded. The name Ataliklikun Bay sounded familiar. The sawmill seemed to be near Lee's trees.

The men voted for Keravat. Egan assigned Jake to lead the party with Robinson as scout— "You're *it* for medicine now, Doc."—echoing Owen's remark last night. *Has it only been a night?* Jake felt Owen's absence acutely.

They set a cautious pace. It was dark, the dense green oppressive. The track curved beside Bamboo Road, which linked Vunakanau aerodrome to Kokopo Ridge Road. From time to time, they stopped to listen. The ground was uneven, with thick roots under leaves or mud, deep pools of water, stones and tangled vines. Their boots were scraped and sodden, mud working through the seams. Robinson rasped, "Root 2 o'clock, puddle six inches deep."

They sweated, a feast of bare arms and necks for delighted sandflies and mosquitoes. Two men wore shorts, their calves a prime location for the insects, further from the prey's slapping hands. Having to resist loud slapping was almost as bad as the bites. Jake thought he glimpsed a black figure flitting between trees. The native, whoever they were, disappeared when he trained his binoculars in the direction of the movement.

After an hour, Jake and Robinson wriggled through bamboo to the road. They were only halfway to the intersection of Bamboo and Kokopo Ridge Roads, less than a mile's progress. Jake was depressed. He was mentally hunting for options as they wriggled back. He had eight quinine tablets left and suspected they had little food.

Planes suddenly whined and roared, gunfire from above chattered, a bomb exploded nearby, and the stench of smoke and oil broke the fragrant morning.

"We'll have to slash our own trail to give Three Ways and Four Ways a wide berth," Wip advised when they conferred.

Robinson agreed. "Might be less Japs on the other side of Kokopo Ridge Road, if we can cross," he suggested. "Good forest cover. They've secured the beaches, so they're less likely to look for Aussies there."

Egan decided. "We're not far enough, hafta cross at night. I say, stay this side, get past Four Ways, then stop for the night."

They followed the current track until they reached Kokopo Ridge Road. Then began an arduous hack through bushes, vines and tall grass. One hard pull on a parasitic vine dislodged a coconut, which they picked up.

They stopped at a small brook around midday. "I need to see our supplies," Jake advised Egan, who agreed.

The men upended their kits: a sorry tale of little. Three men, including Wip, had no rifle ammunition, having unloaded it on the enemy. Men from Malaguna Camp had no quinine—Scanlan had told them they were on an *exercise*. Everyone had bandages, safety pins, scissors and matches. But the matchboxes were sodden, making it doubtful the matches would strike. Food was down to a can of tuna or beef and green beans each. Some had biscuits; everyone had Rolaids. None had spare socks, pants or boots. The group's money totalled ten pounds.

"Safety pins, excellent," Jake joked. Egan placed men with ammunition into lead, rear or watch. By mid-afternoon, they'd skirted Three Ways and Four Ways, and returned to the native track. Once, Jake thought he saw a black form following them, this time a fat one.

They finished their canned food then, holding back the biscuits. While Robinson was burying the cans, they heard a low guttural rattle. There was no time to hide. They stood, their guns pointed. A dwarf cassowary darted at a can, shook it, and then pecked up a blob of dirty bully beef a soldier had overlooked. Ben Williams's finger tightened on the trigger of his pistol. Robinson pushed the barrel down. "Can't risk sound, mate." The bird got away. Deeper in the jungle, they heard a human voice call in a native language. Then, the sounds receded.

"Some natives following us," Robinson said, hand on his pistol.

"I know," Jake replied. "They're not hostile. If they were, the Japs would already have us."

Rain soaked them, slithering down their shirts, into boots and between toes. Around 6 p.m., ravenously hungry, they sheltered under broad-leafed trees. Egan made another bolt through bushes to void his bowels and returned looking better. Robinson shook Jake's shoulder and turned him to a low bush with twisted limbs.

"Look, a little cross with an arrow tip fresh carved, sap's still seeping."

Jake stooped, following the arrow's point and saw trodden grass. "Share the coconut," he ordered, "while I check this out with Egan and Robinson. If we're not back in fifteen minutes, move on." He gave his medical kit to Kelly, then the three officers followed the trodden grass.

Egan and Robinson kept a hand on their loaded rifles

while Jake led, cutting branch ends. After a couple of minutes, Egan said, "I smell smoke." Another scramble through bushes, and they emerged in a small clearing. Smoke eddied from an oval on the ground. "I'll be dammed. Native oven, old style," Robinson exclaimed.

"Improvised?" Jake suggested. "No hut." The oval was protected by a tarpaulin roped to stones, allowing steam to escape. "This is a gift for us." He was sure ToSaina and IaKumu were shadowing them. He wondered if she could have a pet dwarf cassowary.

"Doctor of mystery," Egan prompted, rubbing a rumbling belly. "If you reckon you know these natives, you lead."

"No questions, anyone." Jake had no intention of endangering the siblings by naming anyone. He moved the tarpaulin, and Robinsons kicked away the topsoil layer and levered up several hot stones with his bayonet. Two roasted hens lay on other stones, a smouldering wood fire beneath.

"You two take the food back and move on quickly. It's not safe to stick around," Jake said. "I'll cover the oven, hide the tarpaulin with some money and follow. Do you have any valuables to add? Aussie silver won't mean much now." Robinson pulled off his watch. "I've got a spare."

"Good man, Robinson. Thanks." When Jake got back to the track, the bush with the arrow had been torn up and tossed off the track. He caught up with his men a half mile on.

The food fortified them, but Wip and Robinson had a terrible night. It was Robinson's turn to shake as he tried to clean his bayonet blade, scummy with chicken. His hand shook, a little at first, then with wild gyrations, the rifle almost skewering his tree companion. "Cold," he muttered. "That's what's wrong. Bloody freezing. Gimme a blanket." Everyone else was sweating. Jake, a tree away, walked over and took his temperature. 105. Robinson vomited up the precious piece of roast chicken all over his own shirt. Jake took off the shirt. Kelly gave Robinson his shirt and washed the dirty one. Jake pushed a quinine tablet down Robinson's throat.

Next morning, while Egan went to check the road, Wip and Robinson, dosed into rationality, insisted in a chorus: "Leave us with a helper. Or without a helper. We'll slow you up. It's military protocol." Wip thrust Sally's drawing at Jake. Jake put the damp paper, which had acquired talisman stature, back in Wip's pocket. "We go at the speed of the slowest," Jake retorted. "Leave no one behind is also military doctrine." The others agreed; it could be them.

Jake walked back along the track, needing time alone. His pulse was racing. Fear closed his throat. He leaned his forehead against a tree trunk. *I'm* well. *They're* sick. I can get off the island by sheltering with IaKumu's tribe and using their trading connections down the coast. The tribe can shelter Wip too. *I. They.* His throat opened and he retched with disgust at his sudden yearning to be taken care of. A woman making him roast chicken had turned him into a near traitor to his men. The moment passed. When he returned, he was fully *We.*

They heard more than one pair of boots approaching. Jake turned; pistol raised. Egan was leading an Australian officer, a lieutenant by his two pips. Smiles split every face. They saluted then crowded him, as if he were a gourmet meal or a whole division to the rescue.

Lieutenant Lennox Henry had been on the southern beach. "I was the only professional soldier in Y Company. Good blokes, but all odds and sods. Position was nuts. Seven miles from Owen at Vulcan or the plateau companies. Bad roads and no working telephone."

"We were at Vulcan. Heard you Y Company boys firing up a storm," Egan said. "But not for long."

"Overrun in fifteen minutes. A few of my men were captured, but most got away. I've been army for years. Never imagined such a fuck-up. With the 'every man for himself', I started southeast with four others. They voted to surrender. I wouldn't. I came back and met Owen. He was upset at losing his group."

"That's us, that's us! Boy, do we miss him," Jake cried. "So he's alive."

"Hiking into the mountains to find OC Dr Palmer's group going south. Palmer's got medical supplies and is intent on saving as many of our men as possible. Major Owen said that the first night, he went to the upper drome and next morning couldn't find you."

"Ah," Jake sighed. "He crossed the main road. We spent the night on the other side and went bush from there. Too many Jap planes to approach the road the next day. Will you go south?"

"No. I'm trying Keravat."

"Lieutenant," Jake continued, excited now. "I'm one of your 'odds and sods'. I'm a doctor made captain because I was the sole medical officer at Praed Point. I've been in charge here today. Egan's an artillery captain, but he's not a veteran. I don't know about the others, but I want to pass leadership to an experienced soldier. We have two bad malarias, a diarrhoea, and everyone has bites and sores. The malarias urge us to leave them with a helper, so the rest of us can get off the island quicker. The rest of us have voted to go at the speed of the slowest."

Wip and Robinson renewed their plea to be left behind. "I'll stay with them," Kelly offered. Enemy planes droned above them, strafing treetops.

"Waste of ammo," Henry growled. "Chest-pounding idiots."

The men liked his attitude. They walked deeper into the jungle.

"Alright, I'll be your senior officer. First thing is a frank talk." He passed around a few leaflets. "Jap planes are tossing out bundles of them between strafing runs." The men clustered, looking over shoulders to read.

"To the Officers and Soldiers of the Island.
SURRENDER AT ONCE!
And we will guarantee you life, treating you as
prisoners. Those who RESIST US WILL
BE KILLED ONE AND ALL. Consider seriously,
you can find neither food nor way of escape
in this island and you will only die of hunger
unless you surrender.
23 January, 1942
Japanese Commander in Chief."

"Be honest," Henry continued. "There's no dishonour in surrender. The civil administration officially surrendered Rabaul to Admiral Horii, the Jap fleet commander."

Every man put his thumb down.

"I want to hear why from each of you," Henry persisted. "No group pressure. Surrender's a rational choice."

Egan began. "At Vulcan, they trampled their own wounded at the wire, made'em into ladders to get to us. Left hundreds on the sand and snagged on coral when they withdrew to hit us from the ravines. If that's how they treat their own, they'll do worse to us."

The verdict was unanimous: Don't trust the leaflet.

Robinson and Wip, shivering, renewed their plea to be left behind. "Save yourselves."

"We don't leave our sick to fend for themselves," Henry decided. "Thank you for keeping high morale. I'm honoured to lead you." He looked deeply moved.

Jake handed him their only compass. It was Robinson's, from his scout days, but in his fever, Robinson had trodden it into muddy stones.

"Broken," Henry laughed, after shaking it. He scratched an insect bite.

"With respect, sir, stop scratching. Bites suppurate."

Henry reddened, then laughed harder. "I stand corrected, Doc. All: no scratching. King's orders."

With renewed determination they continued on the track. As the day wore on, the skies quietened. They risked the road, which blessedly was clear. Four men, half-carrying Wip and Robinson, hustled them forward. As they approached the bridge over Keravat River, where all roads ended, there were accumulating signs of fleeing Australians: disabled trucks, emptied and fired petrol cans, axe-bashed heavy equipment, empty food cans. Shell casings littering the road and ditches told the tale of Japanese patrols exchanging gunfire with harried retreating units.

"Is it good or bad that we're a day or two behind?" Jake asked. No one had an opinion; too much mental effort.

The sun was setting when they crossed the bridge. Jake asked Henry to call a stop so he could examine his charges, All the men had infected bites, two had fungi on their backs from wet dirty shirts. Egan bolted into the bushes for the fourth time that day. Wip and Robinson were feverish again. While Kelly and Williams, the dispatch rider, held them, Jake ran to the river, soaked his own shirt in cool water, and mopped their faces and chests. He did it a second time. Wip moved his lips, but nothing came out. Robinson seemed to be hallucinating: "Rats at my skin," he rasped. Jake bit his lip, worried about their resilience, and aching at Wip's suffering. Henry looked on, concerned, as Jake pushed quinine and sleeping tablets down their throats, holding their jaws shut as if he were dosing a cat.

"I'm down to two quinine tablets," he told Henry. "I've been told there's cinchona bark nearby. Mandres Sawmill's supposed to have clothes, ammo and food. Got no proof though. Verbal report."

Henry clapped him on the shoulder. "I've got one bottle of quinine. We'll reach Mandres tomorrow. Can the boys last?"

"Oh yes, sir. Could the boys wash in the river before I treat the infected sores? Is there a safe way to handle it?"

"I'll find a way," Henry said. "Wait."

Wip and Robinson hardly stirred while two soldiers crept

to the river with their bayonets, keeping low. They returned ten minutes later, triumphant, with an eel, two fish Jake didn't recognise and a big frog.

"Where there's fish, there'll be a fisherman's hut," Henry predicted. He walked into the bush and returned shortly, beckoning them. The hut was small, the walls made of split logs tied with split cane, the roof thatched coconut leaves supported by sapling logs. The earth floor had space for six adults, if they crammed together. Pegs on the inside walls were bare. But it was paradise for the night. Blackened stones and kindling outside suggested a recent fire for smoking fish; the hut's owner must have fled the fighting. Henry organised a watch and approved Jake's suggestion that three by three, discreetly, the men should clean themselves in the river. Wip and Robinson dozed sitting, while Jake and Kelly disinfected the returning men's cuts and put powder on the fungi.

They risked a quick fire to sear the catch, then, skin to skin to use each other's warmth, the men sucked their meal down to the last spurting flake of flesh.

"You should have left us at the bridge, "Wip said suddenly. Awake, he was surprised to be on dry earth.

"That argument's old," Jake said.

"We have Christian decency," Kelly added.

"Judeo-Christian," Jake corrected.

"Buddhist, Muslim, Hindu, Rosicrucian, Zoroastrian and atheist," Henry said.

Everyone enjoyed the repartee.

"The AIF doesn't abandon its men," Henry affirmed, turning serious.

"Our government *has* abandoned us." Wip sat up. Jake offered him some eel, and he ate it ravenously. After swallowing, he continued, "Scanlan did diddly-squat to prepare a jungle retreat when there was time. Our flyboys got out. Spill your secret, Derek. I heard you mumbling crazy stuff, thought you were dreaming, or I was hallucinating."

Eyes bored into Egan, fixer of telephone cables and star eavesdropper.

Egan's unshaven face was a mass of bites, his green eyes bloodshot, pounds shed from his stocky frame by diarrhoea. Since the men had been told they were on their own, he seemed to be gripped by some inner misery beyond the hardship and danger of their predicament.

"Careful," Henry snapped. "Abandonment's a much heavier accusation than mistakes. We have to keep our morale high."

Egan gazed at the roof; the shadows garish in the one roving flashlight beam. He spoke slowly, finding his way through a thicket of thoughts. "You're the best mates. Gotta right to know. What if CO Scanlan isn't the main abandoner? What if he's a scapegoat for bloody toffs at Melbourne HQ?" His face gained colour. "Wip's right. I heard Melbourne tellin' Scanlan afore the shindig went down that invasion's comin': fleet, bombers, infantry, the whole lot. Heard headquarters confirm Scanlan's original orders..."

"No withdrawal?" Jake asked.

Ben Williams interrupted. "I was one of the blokes from camp ordered to prepare for an exercise. How does that make sense?"

Egan said wearily, "Get's worse, Benny boy. Not only 'no withdrawal'. We're to stay near Rabaul. No jungle survival trainin'. HQ's theory is: it's kinder—get this—*kinder*—for us to be abandoned in Rabaul—'hostages to fortune', the very words, no kiddin'—than equip us for resistance inland, where hostile natives might kill us, since there was no intention to extract us."

"What?" Jake gasped. "Some natives will help us, others won't. We can handle that if we're careful. Our men at Four Ways already did. Is that a reason to kneecap our chance to live?" He paused. "So we were expendable from the beginning?" Anger started in his toes, turned his torso to a vibrating husk and boiled up over his scalp. He'd never known such rage, mixed with astonishment so intense that it was as if he was seeing a miracle, but of the darkest kind. He had no words; his blood thrummed *it was the **plan***. He put an arm around Egan, who smiled wanly. Egan looked stronger. Sloughing off his secret was saving him.

"Last thing," Egan raised his voice. "Scanlan acknowledged he had no jungle experience, bein' a trench man. We have a code name: Lark Force."

After a stunned silence, Jake found words. "Lark as in bird or caper?"

Egan flapped his hands, "Chirp chirp."

"My God," Jake exclaimed, "what happened to our CO? He was decorated for valour in the last war."

Henry clapped his hands to regain control. "If you're right, Captain Egan—if you didn't misinterpret through static—then we must prove them wrong. They've underestimated larks."

No, Jake thought. *It's betrayal.* He was filled with love for every man in the hut.

"Leave us and save yourselves," Wip urged.

"Tomorrow's another day," Henry said firmly. "Not a word about this to anyone."

CHAPTER 31
• • • • • • • •

W IP WOKE AT DAWN and nudged Jake. He seemed a
little better. "Moment by the river?"

Jake nodded.

Quietly they followed an animal track to part of the bank
overlooking shallow water. As it got lighter, they could see the
riverbed clearly, water rippling over stones, wriggling tadpoles
and larger fish. A long eel weaved in and out of stones and
river grass.

"Serene," Jake murmured. War seemed a galaxy away.

"We haven't had private time, but I'm not up to much,"
Wip apologised. He touched Jake's hand lightly.

Jake touched his hand back. "Symbol of our everything.
'Place me like a seal on your arm', Songs of Solomon." The
hand presses turned into a prolonged kiss. They looked at each
other. No, their eyes acknowledged, they just didn't have time.

"You were asleep while the other blokes washed in
the river last night," Jake said with a loud sigh. "Get the grit
and sweat off your insect bites before we rejoin the others. I
won't allow infected cuts to add to your malaria. Sorry to be a
pragmatic bore."

"A mother, maybe, but never a bore." Wip laughed.

When they got back to the fisherman's hut, the men

began their hike with renewed determination. After a couple of miles, Henry motioned a rest stop. Wip's pre-dawn energy had faded, and he was weak again. Step by step, Jake and Kelly encouraged him and Robinson. "We're getting close," Henry assured his men. Visions of a Catalina seaplane swooping in to rescue them on Ataliklikun Bay kept them moving.

In the silence, they heard a new sound: distant uneven raps on wood. A native log drum. What was it saying? If the villagers were friendly, it could be a warning that Japs were in the area. If hostile, that Australians were ripe for the taking. It could be announcing an elder's death, or that hunters had killed a wild boar. Jake kicked himself for not learning more Tolai language. His sister Talia would love to know how to speak drum. As the drummer thrummed on, he tried to memorise the pattern. *Quixotic,* he decided. Abruptly the drum stopped.

A little more trudging, and they achieved the end of the native track they'd followed yesterday and today. It petered out at a large mangrove swamp on both sides and a clearing around Mandres Sawmill up ahead. *Is Mandres taken?* Jake wondered. Still, the swamp's tangled impenetrability offered cover. Mosquitoes swarmed them the moment they stood still.

Above the insects' whine came the crumps of naval guns. Henry knuckled his head in frustration. Japanese destroyers were apparently in Ataliklikun Bay. The men looked at each other and mouthed curses. Japs had outrun them again. The dream of rescue by their beloved Catalina flying boats shattered.

"Come on, fellas. Worry when the guns stop," Henry counselled. "Silence means a patrol's landing."

Jake, bringing up the rear, heard a rustle off the track. He turned. A bare-breasted native woman with a swollen belly half emerged from dense forest, held up a finger, then disappeared. He blinked. Nothing. No one else had noticed. Had he seen what his brain conjured up, a pregnant IaKumu?

"Into the swamp," Henry ordered.

They picked their way between mangroves and ferns,

sinking into ankle-deep muck. The ripeness of decomposing plant and animal matter was suffocating. Jake drew Wip and Robinson behind a gnarled mangrove with twisted branches and administered his last quinine tablets.

A few feet away, a soldier murmured, "Shellfish." For a couple of minutes, he dug at roots, pulling out black shells after black shell. Prying one open, he displayed a wriggling mollusc. "Cure ya diarrhoea, Egan," he joked. They collected a bag full.

They heard a click. Each man froze in place and held his breath. Silence. Clicks. A moment's quiet. Then, suddenly, rattling gunfire, bullets smashing branches above them.

"Shit." Henry waved the malarias, with Jake and Kelly, deeper into the swamp.

"Listen," Jake whispered urgently. "Stay here. There's help nearby. Medicine. Don't surrender. I'm a captain. I order you to stay hidden. I'm joining Henry."

"One of our outpost clinics?" Kelly demanded.

"No. Trust me. Wait." Jake pressed.

He added to Wip in a whisper, "Lee has cinchona trees. Saw Iakumu a while ago. Don't be specific to Kelly and Robinson. We can't risk exposing them. Just keep Kelly and Robinson here with you."

Wip raised his eyebrows. "My God…quinine? Yep. Love you."

When Jake reached Henry, he was saying, "Rifles, not machine guns. Rush the Mill. I don't think it's occupied yet."

"Draw them off our boys in the swamp?" Jake asked. Henry nodded. Before Henry could add that he would lead, Jake sprang to execute his order, squelching to the track end amidst sputtering gunfire. Fear gone, he jumped over a thin screen of bushes and burst into the open. There was a millisecond of quiet as he ran low, jumped and zig-zagged, then metal was flying all around him. He made it untouched to a storage shed and hid behind a corner. Henry and his eight soldiers fired at the ambushers and followed Jake, taking cover.

More than thirty Japanese soldiers were running from the road that led to the sawmill. Ten more at the swamp's edge joined them. They didn't seem to have heavy weapons or flame throwers. With the same curdling yells Jake had heard at Vulcan Beach, they fired at the storage shed, then took cover behind a huge pile of tarpaulin-covered tree trunks.

The two groups exchanged gunfire. Jake stayed behind the shed. Ben Williams, the dispatch rider, screamed and hobbled back to Jake with blood coursing from his leg. Jake concentrated on putting a tourniquet on the leg, feeling for the bullet and extracting it while the gunfire continued. Splinters were blown off the shed's wall and cut several men.

As Jake was bandaging Williams's wound, somewhat amazed by his own cool, the fire stopped. Jake raised his head and heard Henry's voice. "Sorry men. Jig's up. Damn, damn, damn." Henry dropped his rifle, walked into the open and raised his hands. His men followed, gathering in a half-circle behind him. Jake hadn't drawn his pistol; he was a doctor.

A plump Japanese officer in a khaki cloth cap with a gold star, khaki tunic and breeches approached Henry, shouting Japanese. Henry towered over him. A rifle butt slammed Henry's kidney—the officer's aide—and Henry bowed. The captors began a leisurely search. They confiscated weapons, money, food, first aid supplies, and the better watches. Christian crosses and photos were passed around, discussed, and returned. Jake's precious ring, the wild pig tusk set in gold that Wip made him, was returned. Jake assumed they thought it was a barbarian's religious icon. One by one, the Australians' hands were tied behind their backs, they were roped together then a long vertical stick was placed behind each back, making movement difficult.

Jake stared at a vaguely familiar round face. Slender, with thick lips and glasses, this officer's long khaki tunic had red highlights on a high collar and a white armband with red characters on it. His red cap had a khaki peak. Jake gulped.

Toshio Iijima, the man who'd crashed a car near Praed Point in an effort to see the coastal guns. Toshio's tall driver wasn't with him. Jake's blood thrummed. Was this good, or terrible? He looked Toshio eye to eye, and then stared meaningfully at Toshio's sleeved arm. "I'm a doctor. Didn't fire my pistol. Red Cross patch."

The ambushers' commander called Toshio, who ran to the front, sank into a deep bow and spoke fast. The commander nodded. Toshio walked up to Jake, and cut off his improvised red sleeve patch. "Not Red Cross Band," he said in Japanese, then English.

"Check my pistol," Jake persisted. "You know I'm a doctor. I stitched your arm." The Australians looked at Jake, puzzled.

The commander waved at the pile of weapons. Toshio examined Jake's pistol, grinned and fired it. Then he stepped back. Jake saw satisfaction on his face. Toshio's body seemed to relax.

Henry protested. "We surrendered. The Geneva Conventions apply."

"Lieutenant Toshio Hisanda, Kempeitai military police," Toshio said in miraculously improved English. "You obstructed our work for the emperor and made a barbaric tea ceremony." Jake's blood sank to his toes.

"Atta boy, proud to know ya," Egan yelled. He hip-bumped Jake. "Whatever ya did."

Toshio interpreted the commander's next orders. "Name, rank and serial number. You're all guilty of a terrible shame by surrendering. A Japanese soldier with honour would take his own life. You are scum." Opening a notebook, he wrote down each prisoners' basic information, his contempt for them clear with each notation.

Jake felt his insides turn to concrete blocks of dread. He stopped himself from glancing in the swamp's direction, hoping that Wip, Kelly and Robinson had the sense to stay hidden.

The log drum and IaKumu's courageous appearance had been warning him of the danger.

The Japanese commander screamed an out-of-tune violin glissando. "It's time," Toshio translated. The Japanese soldiers formed a line, prodding the Australians to form up in front. Three Japanese soldiers grabbed Henry, cut the rope tying him to the next prisoner, removed the stick from his back, and led him to a flat patch of earth.

"Dig," Toshio ordered, handing him a shovel.

The brutal illegal plan was clear. "Australian officers never dig their own graves," Henry snapped contemptuously. "It's against the King's rules." There was no such rule. But it got the Japanese conferring. A Japanese private took the shovel and dug.

"Geneva Convention," the Australians chanted when two soldiers forced Henry to his knees, removed his cap and blindfolded him.

"I love you, mates. Good luck," Henry called. "You'll regret this," he told the commander. Toshio translated. The commander stood behind Henry. His stance relaxed, he studied Henry's scrawny neck as if it was a half-finished sculpture of his own creation. Face angled, he looked at one side, then the other. Gently, he touched a spot above the last vertebra.

Jake closed his eyes. *God, if you exist, please no.*

Toshio screamed. "Watch. All watch."

Jake kept his eyes closed. He was at his bar mitzvah, his father's man-to-man talk. "You're a man now. Life is hard, but there are usually options." *Dad, what's the option here?* They wanted him to watch. Every second of delay gave Wip, Robinson and Kelly time to get deeper into the swamp.

Nothing happened immediately. There was more talk, but softer, a rasp of wood. Curiosity forced Jake's lids apart. The commander had a dishevelled soldier in tow, bowing so low he almost fell over. The commander was standing over a plank of wood the thickness of a man's neck. The commander stroked the wood and pointed at a spot. He sprinkled water on his sword from a bucket, then raised it and split the wood. The soldier bowed again. He was shaking. He drew his own sword and dipped it in water. He seemed to be muttering an invocation.

Henry was craning his neck to one side and then the other. Jake could smell his rancid sweat. The soldier stood behind Henry and looked to his commander, who nodded.

Jake closed his eyes. He was risking putting the soldier off his aim, botching the execution. But he was sure Henry would approve. Every second helped the others.

"Watch!" Toshio screamed—a hard slap on Jake's face. The violation rocked him more than the blow hurt. While his brain was trying to name what had just happened, his body opened his eyes. The trembling executioner dipped the sword in water again and repositioned himself behind Henry. Jake let his eyelids drop, sensed the blow coming and swayed with it. Not too bad. He moved with the second slap. Then he felt something hard smash his lower back. His eyes jerked open, and he stumbled. He couldn't do it again or he'd get a bayonet in the eye.

"All watch!" Toshio yelled again.

The soldier crashed his sword through Henry's neck. The head flew. Blood gushed. Several Australians vomited. They were herded into a truck, their boots slopping through Henry's blood. Three Japanese soldiers tipped Henry's corpse into the shallow grave and covered it with leaves and topsoil, an invitation to wildlife. The graduating executioner bowed to his commander, then washed his sword. He seemed in an altered state as he rejoined his comrades. He wasn't strutting. *It's worse,* Jake realised. *He's spiritually complete.*

In the truck, a Japanese soldier stuck twists of cigarettes between the prisoners' lips and lit the smokes. The truck rolled to the coastal road and back toward Rabaul.

*
**

Wip, Kelly and Robinson spent a miserable night in the swamp. They ate a few of the molluscs and promptly threw them up. They had to settle for a biscuit each. For water, they dribbled rainwater from leaves down their throats. The hours went in circles with slapping mosquitoes, periodically probing the mud for snakes, or finger-nailing leeches off each other's legs. At dawn, they heard mud-sucking sounds. Boots? They struggled upright, Wip and Robinson pointing their rifles, Kelly pointing a pistol. Only Robinson had bullets.

"Friend," softly came the English words. Two masked figures emerged, unarmed. The Australians relaxed, lowering their weapons. Wip recognised a booted Henry Lee and a pregnant IaKumu in bare feet. "We'll save you," Lee said. "Wife's brother's following the truck. No names."

Wip shook Lee's hand. "They're good people, promise," he told Kelly and Robinson.

Kelly looked dubious. "Is there an outpost clinic here?"

"No, but they have medicine. Jake said to trust him and stay. I certainly will. You must."

"Hurry," Lee urged, kicking a crab off his boot. "Can't waste time."

Kelly and Robinson conferred. "We've decided," Kelly declared. "You go with them. The lady's about to deliver. They need us more than they could help us. Robinson wants a modern hospital. We'll clean up in that fisherman's hut, then surrender to the next patrol."

Wip tried to change their minds. "Robinson, you've got wilderness training. You can handle more jungle life with a little help." He tried three times, futilely, while Lee shifted his squelching feet nervously. Hampered by the need to protect Lee's and IaKumu's names and the nearby source of quinine, Wip could only repeat Jake's advice never to surrender.

"Goodbye and good luck, then, you sweet-ponged blokes," Wip said sadly, embracing them. He followed Lee and IaKumu. His last glimpse of his mates was Kelly sitting Robinson on a branch and mopping his face.

CHAPTER 32
• • • • • • • •

T HE TRUCK STOPPED at a residential compound in Chinatown. Jake was hustled out. His stomach went sour with fear as he watched the vehicle belch off towards Malaguna Camp with his mates.

Toshio stalked inside. Jake was pushed to the veranda floor, hands still tied behind him, but a guard removed the stick. The guard stood over him, bayonet touching Jake's shoulder. The boy with a first-fuzz moustache was sweating and began to shake. Jake wriggled away from the bayonet's gyrating blade. The boy didn't follow, just stared blankly at the air. *Malaria,* Jake assumed. He looked around for exits, planning an escape.

But the front door opened. Three soldiers pulled Jake upright and marched him into a wood-panelled room. Tapestries and books with broken spines were piled in a corner, the bookshelves crammed with new-looking files. *Are the owners dead or hiding? Are they Lee's relatives?* Toshio was toying with a pen, a stack of paper by him. The soldiers who'd brought Jake stood behind him some feet away.

Jake took the initiative. "Your guard outside needs quinine before he's too sick to work." He met Toshio's astonished stare. Toshio came out from behind the desk and whacked Jake on both sides of his face with his sword hilt. Jake gasped and swayed with the blows.

"Nippon strong, not weak like whites. Bow, you shameful coward!" Toshio yelled. Jake remembered how Toshio and his driver had given him and Wip a slight inclination of the head at the Praed Point checkpoint. He dipped his head like they had. With guttural grunts, two soldiers pushed his neck down until his nose nearly hit his thigh. "Proper bow," Toshio howled. "Little bow, big insult!" *So they were mocking us at Praed.* Jake held his pose, smelling his filthy pants. *Bet Wip's pong is worse...* Jake was prodded to rise. Ignoring the ringing in his ears, he looked pointedly at the neat stitches on Toshio's forearm, his stitches.

Toshio looked away, then back. "Where is the blond officer from Praed Point?"

"I am Captain Jake Friedman, V...", giving his number. He tried to still his racing mind. After Henry's decapitation, he knew his head was still attached only because they thought he knew something. Toshio walked behind him. Jake heard the swish of a drawn sword and felt metal tap the back of his neck. Jake tried to stifle his frantic bowels. Silently, he gabbled out sin after sin to a nebulous administrator up there of forgiveness.

The tapping stopped. "We understand each other," Toshio said. "You and the blond thug caused me to lose face. You caused inconvenience to the emperor's soldiers." Jake had no idea what he was talking about. "I have important things to do now. You have a night to think."

It was dusk when he was bundled into a car, hands tied and in ankle irons. The sky was a grey-green roiling thickness as a downpour fought to expel the last splendour of the setting sun. Rabaul's streets swarmed with Japanese soldiers, trucks and tanks. Rising Sun flags fluttered from the major buildings. Smoke from dying fires eddied from the wharves, its smell mingling with the familiar sulphur. Through the window, he saw masts from anchored warships. Under Japanese supervision,

Tolai labourers, their body language radiating unease, were clearing rubble hours past the end of the normal workday. There were no white or Chinese people in sight.

Jake's destination was the town jail. His cell was small, with a concrete floor, a thin mattress and a bucket. Alone, he sat against the wall. His face was hot, skin probably reddening from the blows. The ringing in his ears had gone, but his temples throbbed. *Hear my thoughts, love. Wip, stay safe in the swamp.* He murmured it again and again.

After a while, he needed to piss. It was an athletic feat, wriggling his pants down part way, bouncing backwards on his buttocks to the wall and using the wall to ease himself upright, but dignity compelled it. He didn't splash beyond the bucket. A little blood tainted his urine. From adjoining cells, he heard Chinese voices and one British voice. His taps on the wall got no response. A Japanese guard brought him a mug of water but no food. The hours passed with the guards banging on his cell bars and shouting every ten minutes. Sleep deprivation: he called up his on-call skills and drifted off between the clanging.

Bleary and dirty, he faced Toshio in the same room at the compound the next morning. "Where is the blond man who told me there were other new access roads to artillery batteries? What is his name?"

Jake had a glimmer of what had got under Toshio's skin: the humiliation at the checkpoint to Praed Point last July. As per army regulations and the Geneva Convention, he stated his name, rank and serial number. "Where are the other men in your unit?" Same answer. "Where are the hidden American weapons?" Name, rank, birth date, serial number.

At Toshio's nod, two soldiers pushed him outside. After stripping him to his underwear, they tied him to a palm tree with a rope around his waist, his hands still tied behind him, ankles in irons. The sun glowered on him. They alternated face slapping and beating his chest, back and legs with planks of wood. He tried to keep his balance, angling his body to move with the blows. But he couldn't. *This is happening to someone else. I'm an observer. I'm in a bubble bath, gentle, soothing.* But the shock of each blow made a mockery of his mental efforts. A nice Jewish boy; nothing in his life had prepared him for this. His grunts turned to screams. Instinctively, he sniffed shallow breaths, as if less air meant less blows. Then, his doctor's mind kicked in. *Breathe deep.* He gulped huge breaths. More and more he stuffed his diaphragm and lungs until he was light-headed. A flash of pain-free trance...then mercifully, nothing more.

He came to, water dripping over his face. A kick to his groin had him doubling over uselessly against the rope. More kicks to his kidneys and knees. Urine trickled down his thigh. Toshio came out holding a knife and laid about his face. Most blows hit the skin with the flat of the blade, but occasionally Toshio tuned the sharp end on Jake's skin. Blood trickled down Jake's forehead, nose and cheeks. More questions, the same answer. Toshio stalked off.

To Jake's surprise, he was left alone, sagging against the tree. Shock floated him into unconsciousness again. Then he felt tickling along his abraded skin. He was puzzled. Then he knew. Flaming pain on a speck of his neck, sudden flames on his arms, moving methodically upward—biting ants. The intensity of the bite was far worse than the jungle sand flies. He scrunched his eyes closed and tried to return to the bubble bath.

Hours passed, day slinking into night. At some point, he was taken inside and carried downstairs, his dirty shirt, trousers and boots thrown after him. Lying on the dusty wooden floor of a vegetable cellar, he felt congealed blood on his sunburned skin, cuts welcoming bacteria. A few flaming bites continued. He tried to roll over to squash the ants but couldn't move more than an inch. His ribs and back felt like they were being pressed together by stone blocks. Wip's ring rubbed his chest as he sniffed in short, agonising breaths. He hadn't betrayed the men in the swamp, or the lifesaving cinchona trees.

He barely registered Toshio's driver standing over him.

Some superhuman reflex got him into a foetal cower. The man knelt beside him, growling ferociously. He pulled the remaining ants off and ground his boot on them. Jake watched him blearily, "Whaat?" he whispered.

The man washed him gently. "Chai Hoon," he murmured, touching his own chest. He pulled down his sock, his foot at Jake's nose. At his eye level, he recognised the gold-painted, wooden frog whose shattered pieces he'd slipped into the driver's hand after the car crash at Praed Point. It was glued whole.

The next morning, Jake was marched to the centre of the courtyard in his tattered uniform. His wrists were untied, his feet tied a few feet apart by rope. A long, heavy block was placed on his extended arms. Jake toppled onto the grass right away. The sky darkened into a downpour as Toshio laid about Jake's back, neck, and head with a bamboo stick. He was pulled up, and the block was placed on his arms again. An entirely new excruciating pain seared his arm muscles and thighs. He couldn't hold his arms out for more than a minute. Whenever his elbows sagged, the bamboo stick crashed on him. Forcing a faint failed; the bubble bath wouldn't come into focus. Toshio's stick infallibly knew the spot where Jake hurt most. All went neon red, phosphorescent white. He knew he'd break. He did. "Gold mine," he croaked, and fell over again on top of the block.

The beating stopped. Jake's mind raced to the little alluvial gold mine where the gold for the ring Wip made him came from. The mine was hundreds of miles from the swamp and cinchona trees.

"What is the name of the blond man who told me about other access roads to artillery batteries?"

Jake stayed silent.

After one more kick in his ribs, Toshio stepped back. To Jake's amazement, he changed the subject. "Many of you cowards surrendered yesterday. I'll get everyone we want soon. Nippon cannot be resisted. Where were you when we invaded?"

Another beating was unbearable. *Forgive me.* "Vulcan beach," Jake croaked. "Why do you hate me? I accept my fate."

The evil lump that was Toshio ordered a soldier to help Jake up. Jake detected a hint of respect on his torturer's face. Miraculously, he seemed to have lost interest in Wip. *Is it accepting my fate or being at Vulcan?*

Back in the cellar, they were alone, a guard at the stairs out of earshot. Jake's wrists and ankles were roped together. He slumped over, craning his neck to eye Toshio, who was grimy from his exertions. *Not easy, the torturer's lot,* Jake thought, with sardonic hatred.

"That blond barbarian caused me to lose face," Toshio began. "I reported four artillery batteries. On the night of the invasion, I was put ashore early with my company. The entire fleet, the men in barges and the air force, waited for my flare to signal that we'd taken all the coastal batteries. I saw the destroyed guns at Praed Point immediately. It took four hours before I realised that the blond man had fooled me. It delayed our landing. I was shamed in the eyes of the Admiral and Japan's armed forces."

Jake spat blood onto his trousers through a wobbling tooth. He was in agony, but he could still think. The delay Wip caused had allowed A Company to form at Vulcan under the superb leadership of Bill Owen and throw the attackers back for five hours. If Jake's mates ever reached safety, they could prove the Japanese weren't invincible.

Toshio hadn't finished. "A thousand of our heroes were wounded or died charging Vulcan. Hundreds won the honour of dying for the emperor. You defenders fought well. But they would be preparing to fight in your corrupt homeland if I hadn't spent hours looking for phantom cannon." He fingered the silk bag at his waist. "For a despicable Westerner, you're not a coward."

The compliment plunged Jake into despair. The price of Toshio's revelation would be his execution. Did he have a minute? A day? *Everyone I've wronged, forgive me; God forgive me.*

Toshio left but returned—Jake had no idea how much later—scrubbed glowingly clean and in a fresh uniform. "Southern Cross, oh fabled star, prostrate yourself to the Rising Sun," he declaimed. "My haiku. But it cannot compare with Songi: 'Does not China lie beneath this self-same sky, bound in misery'. What do you think?"

He dresses up to recite poetry? "Both...good," Jake mumbled through spit.

"'Obsequious frog, croaking flatteries', wrote the great Socho." With that, Toshio stalked out.

Three guards untied Jake's legs and dropped him at Malaguna Camp, now crammed with prisoners. Guards manhandled him to a cot and flung him down face-first. When they left, unknown hands untied his wrists, cleaned him, rubbed fat on his insect bites, and forced pills down his throat. He fell into a stuporous sleep. Banging and shouting woke him at an indeterminate time. He opened his eyes; his fingers felt a different shirt and trousers. Not clean, but better than his. His unknown mates had shared what they had with him, the painkillers most precious of all. He felt an immense love for them.

The electric light burned his pupils. He closed his eyes, not wanting to credit what his brain had just registered. Five guards were marching Kelly and Robinson in, their hands tied, a stick along the length of each back keeping their steps short.

"We crossed the Keravat River and surrendered. Better for Robinson," Kelly whispered.

Jake's every breath was agony, the pain worse despite the pills. He could barely move. His brain formed *we dispatched a thousand at Vulcan, tell the lads,* but all he spat out was 'ooof w...w t...' He rolled his head left then right, meaning, "I gave up nothing." His heavy eyes fell shut, his only comfort that Wip wasn't with them. He heard Kelly's sob as the orderly grasped his and Robinson's awful mistake.

*
**

At dawn, Jake was tied in a new way: one rope around his waist securing both arms to his torso, ankles tied a couple of feet apart. He was pushed up onto a truck bed. The truck stopped at Toshio's compound, where eight Chinese prisoners were loaded. The prisoners were then roped together. Jake half-dozed through the bumping ride through Rabaul, every bump against the metal side a gulp of pain. He tried to find some sensuous pleasure in what he believed were his final minutes, but he couldn't. He called up Wip's face, his family, and his mates; he felt overwhelming love for them.

The truck stopped at the foothills of Tavurvur, a barren field of toxic ash adjoining the town's dump at Rapindik. Three civilians and one soldier roped together were already standing near a long, shallow trench dug into the soft soil. Two civilian men were protesting volubly, while the third opened and shut his mouth, a beached fish in a new world. The soldier, whom Jake didn't know, stared ahead. Hearing arrivals, he turned his head and mouthed at Jake *Good luck, mate,* then turned back, stoic, in a state of grace. Five blindfolded Tolai men were already kneeling, similarly roped, singing hymns or invocations loudly. A guard kicked them into silence; they sang louder. More kicks. Finally, compliance.

Jake was shuffled to the end of the trench. He leant against the next man, who was trembling as he leaked urine. Jake twisted his nose away and vaguely noted they were near the dump's fence. He tried to copy the soldier and find grace, but his heart was pounding too hard. He had an impression of black amidst green. He turned his head slightly. A black man on his stomach was watching from low bushes.

A second truck pulled up and disgorged about thirty soldiers with guns and swords. A minute later, Toshio arrived in a Rolls Royce flying the Rising Sun flag. His driver, carrying a sword and bayonet, walked to the dump and placed a spare ammunition clip on the ground. He stood behind Jake and his roped neighbour. *Does the Korean know it's me?* He turned slightly to show his profile, and heard the Korean hiss.

Toshio shouted an order, and guards began blindfolding the prisoners. Jake, blindfolded, felt the rope tying him to the next man severed. He was pushed into a kneeling position.

The killing sounded like it was beginning at the other end of the trench. Shrieks filled the air. Jake heard quavering pleas between gunfire, guttural yells from the executioners, and terrible laughter. He smelled shit, volumes of it, fart gas and tangy-sweet blood. His every cell thudded with skin-splitting terror—he had no idea his battered body had any adrenalin. Terror engulfed him, then burned itself out, filling him with pallid nothingness.

Between screams, he heard a different sound. It was coming from the dump: a long guttural rattle and wire shaking. He sensed Chai, Toshio's driver, raise his weapon and stop. There was a rustle of stiff khaki as he presumably turned. A louder rattling cry, nearer. A male call, 'ToMuruk." A frightened howl from Chai at a clink of metal on metal, something hard cracking something hard, and the rustle of something being dragged over soil. Chai's yell turned to pleas. Rustling khaki again. Jake's heart began to thump again. He felt a shocking punch into his hip, sucking resistance as the bayonet blade was wrenched out, another punch into his shoulder, the blade slashing his hand ties, freeing his arms. A kick to his buttocks got him falling forward. The body of the man next to him crashed on him a second later. Frantically, Jake clawed at the air. Swallowing ashy soil and another man's gore were his last sensations.

CHAPTER 33

· · · · · · · ·

J AKE OPENED HIS EYES to a voice screeching. A louder scream. Feral. Whose voice? Water was coursing into his wounds. He opened his mouth, gulped, and heaved out sea water. It was running all over his frayed skin. Another scream of agony formed, but a hand clapped over his mouth.

"Shut up. You'll get us all killed."

He, Jake, was the screamer.

"It's Wip. I'll give you a morphine jab."

When Jake woke again, the air smelt close. It was dark. He touched a mat under him that felt like woven plant matter. Under that was hard earth. Was he on a floor? His fingers rubbed unfamiliar cloth covering his groin and rough bandages on his leg. He felt hot; everything was swollen and excruciating. "Huunh?"

Wip's voice seeped into his bloodstream. "Can you hear me?"

Jake felt his terror thin. *Wip.* "Talk," he rasped.

Wip held up Jake's head, dribbled liquid into his mouth, waited for Jake to swallow, and then eased him back. Jake ran the tip of his tongue over his lip. *Sweet. Grassy.* "Sugar cane juice, love. OK, we're in a native Men's House. Are you with me?"

Jake nodded.

"I put a tapa cloth lap-lap on you, but I can get shorts if you want. Some of the Tolai lads have them. IaKumu's tribe says we can live here until you recover, then they're willing to help us get off the island to mainland New Guinea. I can be here, or Lee and ToSaina when I'm away. Not Iakumu. No female can enter a Men's House. She can come to the perimeter fence, call, and I'll go to meet her. I have morphine and pills for the pain, but it's bush medicine for the rest. IaKumu brought aloe for the bayonet wounds and some concoction for fever."

"Second chance?" Searing pain shot through Jake's arms as he tried to sit up. Groaning, he fell back on the mat.

Wip kissed Jake's tangled hair and then carefully combed it. "Rest. Let me fill you in. ToSaina and his brother, with IaKumu's dwarf cassowary, were at the dump. The bird went after rotting food, but couldn't break the wire…"

"Heard something strange," Jake mumbled.

"I reckon that bird saved you. It took your executioner's spare ammunition clip and chewed the bullets. IaKumu calls it Mr Glutton because it won't stop eating or pilfering. Anyway, it distracted him. He stabbed you, but not deep. I was hiding not far away; ToSaina said that I, meaning noisy, clumsy white, shouldn't be close and give us all away. We got you as soon as the Japs left. You were out cold, choked on dirt. I did CPR. We took you to the ocean to wash your wounds before bringing you here. ToSaina watched a Jap execution a few days ago. He says they came back after they'd left, loaded the bodies in a boat and took them to sea…"

Jake felt his eyelids, as heavy as theatre curtains, droop. When he forced them open again, he waded through cotton wool balls of shock and muddle. "Wip?"

"Here."

A warm hand on his. "Others?"

"Shot or beheaded. You're the only survivor, love," came Wip's terse reply.

The cotton wool balls frayed. Chai Hoon's yowl hit the

inside of Jake's skull; he relived the hard punches into his hip and shoulder. His mind was clearing. "Guard...b...bayonet me. Toshio's driver? Wild cass'wary, Praed. Crashed car...avoid hitting it, thinks bird's a god..."

"Of course," Wip said excitedly. "You're remembering. Marvellous. That day back in July. I found cassowary feathers on the road. We decided the crash happened before Toshio meant it to. Toshio beat the driver when they went to piss in the kunai grass."

"Driver...slashed my wrist ties...free hands." Jake wanted to say he also pulled biting ants off him after his torture. It was more than he could manage. "Sleep?"

When he woke, he was bathed in sweat. "Hot. Cloth off?" He managed to sit up.

Wip put his arm around Jake to keep him steady. "Oh, look, you're stronger. If it's malaria, I've got lots of quinine. Lee's bark saved me."

"Dunno," Jake muttered. "See wounds."

Wip mopped Jake's face, and Jake tried not to wince as Wip unwrapped the bandages. Wip shone his torch on the hip wound. "Shoulder's similar," he said.

Jake inhaled quickly when he fingered painful pink swellings with their crusty scabs oozing fluid. He felt the scabs on the back of his shoulder. *Infected, but how bad?* "Not malaria."

He let Wip rub aloe on the scabs and change the bandages. Wip fed him chicken broth with thin strands of meat, then gave him a drink. Expecting more sugar cane juice, Jake scrunched up his lips at the sudden bitter taste. He wanted to spit, but his throat muscles had already swallowed. "It's bark, lime and betel nut juice, bush medicine's best," Wip explained. "For fever and to relax."

Feeling better, Jake leant against the wall. Safety and being with Wip felt so astonishingly renewing that the throbbing pain seemed trivial. *I won't mention infection yet.* He smiled as Wip shone his torch around the space, saying, "Our hotel room."

"Smell? Not…food." Jake pointed at small bags on the floor.

"Secret plants for the men's magic. I promised we wouldn't touch them."

"No sulphur stink?"

"We're a long day's hike from Tavurvur," Wip explained.

Jake's eyes took in the spacious round house with log walls covered with matting and a roof of thick thatched grass and leaves. Several sleeping mats were stacked at one wall. There was no window. A sneeze tickled his nose. Eyeing the low, small door, he rehearsed the effort it would take to crawl through it.

"I'll take you outside whenever you want," Wip instantly said. "There are coconut trees, a cooking pit and water. But IaKumu's bringing food. You won't have to suffer my efforts. The foliage is so lush from outside the bamboo fence that you can't see the hut's size. We're some distance from the village. Japs already took two of the village's trucks, some pigs and vegetables, the bastards. Drums or a runner will warn us if they come again. We're well protected. Look up."

Wip pointed to shelves under the roof, stood on a stone and pulled down a club, axe, spear and rifle. "More up there, but just one rifle with ammo." He showed Jake the gun.

"Old?" Jake rubbed the wooden butt.

"Yep. Kraut settlers traded guns and steel for land. Then Tolai chiefs woke up to the amount of land they'd lost and rebelled. Government killed a lot of them. Ordered all guns given up, forbade Tolai to own a gun, but didn't return any land. This tribe's clever chief kept his."

"Look in mirror, we whites nasty bunch," Jake said. "Sleep."

"Get your strength back," Wip urged, replacing the weapons on the shelf.

When Jake woke again, he was ravenously hungry. "Anything to eat?" he asked plaintively. He managed to sit up with just one groan.

Wip broke into a face-splitting grin and danced around the room. "Food's coming; the King's kitchen has nothing on it," he sang. He scuttled through the door and returned with a brown and white mush on a big green leaf. "Roast pig in coconut milk." Jake crammed pieces into his mouth with his fingers, savouring the juices. "Tasty."

While he ate, male singing started outside: noisy, joyous seeming and foreign. A chunk of pork halfway to his mouth, Jake looked wildly at Wip.

"Relax, love. Tolai lads have just finished building a good bamboo litter. There's an abandoned animal trap in the jungle nearby, in case the Japs return. We can get you there fast."

Jake finished the meat and motioned that he wanted to stand. Wip helped him up. "What progress! You're measurably stronger," he exulted. Arm around Jake's waist, Wip walked him back and forth several times, stopping at a bucket to let him urinate. Soon, Jake sagged, fingers on his forehead. "Hot. Pain. Blue pill?"

Wip fed him more bark, lime and betel nut juice, then gave him a narcotic blue pill from his first aid kit. While Jake slowly slid toward sleep, Wip continued. "The trap is deep. We removed the spikes. I'll climb in with you if the worst happens." He paused, uncertain, then added, "Japs have started killing Tolai who help us. It's stupid."

"Won't there be…signs of us…here?" was the last thing Jake asked before all went dark.

*
**

Drumming reverberating in the air: Jake had no idea how much time he'd been asleep. He was alone. Intimations of bright light filtered through fibres in the wall coverings. He sensed it was early morning. Outside, male voices chattered, fast and agitated. Panicked, he fought through pain and crawled to Wip's mat, looking for his pistol.

As he aimed it at the door, he heard Wip outside say, "No worries. I'll get him," then "Calm down," when he came inside. Laughing, Wip waved the pistol away. "I just need to get you outside so these men can get some stuff. I'll explain."

Wip helped Jake through the door and steadied him as he stood. The scents and brilliance of a hot day assaulted him. All was woody, fecund green. Wip brushed ants off a tree stump and covered it with a cloth. At Wip's "Your throne, Majesty," Jake managed a grin. *I want to clean my teeth* was his odd thought as he sat and moved right then left, seeking a comfortable position. He took in four young men, who immediately stopped talking. They gazed at him, then at a grey-haired, powerfully built man standing apart.

The older man looked familiar; he'd glimpsed him on the veranda of Hotel Pacifica. *Must be IaKumu's father. I still have a brain.* He bowed his head and steepled his hands in thanks. The grey-haired man smiled black teeth and pink gums, then offered his hand. Formally, they shook hands.

The other Tolai men went inside and returned with the weapons. A moment later, another Tolai man rolled two thigh-height wheels of shell money into the Men's House. Then, quickly, everyone but Lee left. All the while, the distant drums were banging some message.

"Sir," Lee said, sitting at Jake's feet. Jake got the impression of muscled bulk, sun-darkened skin and a toughened feral wariness. "There's no danger now, but we're preparing. The drumming is from a village two miles away. Japs took produce and paid with one Jap paper note. They made the villagers watch soldiers smash their shells. Everyone has to use notes."

"Disgusting!" Wip snorted. "They're stupider than I thought."

"So," Lee continued, "ToBalamat is hiding our shell money and issuing weapons to the men so we can hide in the jungle and hunt, if necessary."

"I don't understand. You just rolled two shell wheels in there," Wip said. He slapped a mosquito. Woozy, Jake fought the blue pill's lingering effects to follow the conversation.

Lee chuckled, white teeth splitting sweaty cheeks. "ToBalamat has a sense of humour. They're fake. Someone diddled his ancestor by paying for land with German machine-cut shells. Leaving worthless wheels here will distract the Japs from searching for signs that you're staying here, while you hide in the trap. Also, it will satisfy their orders to eliminate shell wealth. If they make our villagers watch a smashing ceremony, they'll hear laments like you've never imagined."

Jake looked at Wip, who was laughing. "Wip, m…must leave. Too much t…trouble."

"You stay until you recover, sir," Lee insisted. "There's a plan for when you're better." He and Wip walked away to study a map. Jake surrendered to the soporific humidity and dozed.

Wip woke him some time later—the sun's angle had shifted—and they went inside. "Some of our mates who were a day ahead of us at Mandres Sawmill hiked south." He showed Jake the map and traced what looked like a non-existent route. "About 120 miles from here, it's possible to get a native canoe off the island, or call for our boys on the mainland to send a boat. There are some hidden radios…"

He paced around, clenching his fists. Suddenly he shouted. "Twenty-four hours! You and Len Henry and the others waited a day for me to get over a malaria attack, and see what happened. I caused your torture and his death. It's my fault."

"No." Jake waved his hand. "Robinson's was worse, Egan shitting out his guts. I'm the doctor. We voted. No guilt."

Wip exhaled and sat. "How can I not hate myself for what happened? Anyway, the Japs have the coastal road. They come unpredictably to the harbours, plantations and missions. It means native tracks and rope bridges over rivers. The lads here will carry you; everyone loves you after IaLasliklik's recovered.

But ToBalanat's influence extends only about twenty miles. He'll send runners to negotiate with other big men. So, rest, eat and improve. I've got amphetamines for when we start."

Things were peaceful from then on. The Japs stayed away; at times, Jake imagined they were staying in an unoccupied land. But he didn't get stronger, he endured. His fever felt higher or lower, but rarely absent. He sensed his new-gained strength ebbing, along with his appetite, and he vomited more frequently. Outside, when he strained to urinate, little came out, even after he drank a lot of water. One afternoon, he slumped against the wall, shivering under the glowering sun. They both noticed blotched skin on his shoulder and hip. Wip raised his eyebrows; Jake bit his lips but said nothing.

That night, IaKumu and Lee brought new plants. "Lee says it's matmat plant to bathe the skin patches, and marmar leaf for chills," Wip explained. "IaKumu is anxious about you, nearly cried as she gave me the leaves. I'll go out and boil the plants."

When Jake emerged, he saw an empty aluminium boat and a cauldron of pungent steaming fluid whose stink flooded his nostrils. "No bath. Patches only." He unwrapped the lap-lap and sat, rolling his eyes as Wip daubed the fluid on a mottled pink rash under Jake's thigh and a broad purplish oval with small circles on his arm. "Humour… them," he rasped. "Mean well. Sorry… blood p..poisoning won't…wash away. Tell girl no white man medicine heals this…Sepsis…" He smiled at Wip.

"No! It can't be!" Wip yelled, his face feral with horror and fear. "You can't leave me. Ever. Let's talk options, like your Pa said: the Catholic hospital at Vunapope." He smashed his fist against the log wall and then stared at Jake, willing him to take back his diagnosis. Jake looked down. "Surely," Wip said desperately, drying the patches and bringing Jake inside.

"Ask n…nice Japs medicine?" Jake sneered. "Stay here…. with you."

Wip lay down, cradling him. "Your heart's racing," Wip said, uneasy.

"Yes," Jake said simply. He felt Wip's body trembling against him, felt the hot tears slither down his neck and dribble over his shoulders. The tears kept coming. When he'd caught his breath, he tried for humour. "You smell of wonderful you: no army soap or laundry starch."

Over the next week, Wip cleaned his wounds, bedpanned him, and washed his covers and mat. Most of what Wip fed him came back up, and daily, he felt Wip touching his ribs, estimating how much weight he'd lost.

One morning, Jake woke to find Lee sitting beside him. Terror jerked him up. *Wip captured? Killed?*

"He's fine, sir. He's bartering quinine. Back tomorrow."

Jake eased down, melting with relief.

"There's news, sir. The Americans bombed Rabaul yesterday, February 20."

"Heard rumble. Yanks. Our lot betrayed us."

"Yes, sir. They did. Japs took Vunapope the day after the invasion. The army nurses are prisoners, but the houseboys say they haven't been hurt. Are you in pain, sir?"

"Not much. Baby?"

"Soon. Sir, do you remember my wife was supposed to marry a man from another tribe?"

Jake didn't. What were the names of Wip's niece and nephew? He couldn't remember even that.

Lee pressed on. "She didn't want him; she had visions of them both dying. Apparently, he was a bragging hot-head. Well, he neck-cracked a Japanese soldier. The Japs beheaded him publicly and destroyed everything the tribe had. So, everyone now loves our marriage. And the baby to come."

Jake managed a smile.

"Sir, are you able to go outside and walk through the perimeter fence? IaKumu and ToSaina want to show you something wonderful and ask you a question."

Recognising Lee's urgency, Jake willed the strength to stoop through the door, stand, and, with Lee's arm around his waist, walk through the fence gate. Sitting on a mat Lee had placed under a palm tree, he blinked against the light. Tropical flowers were strewn around the tree roots. Their scents amplified warm air refracted through damp green foliage to caress his skin. Spectacular red or green parrots squabbling over perches, squawked, flew, and shat. IaKumu, her belly huge, and ToSaina stood, shy but intense.

"Whooeee!" IaKumu called. IaLasliklik emerged from the bush, walking with a slight limp. She knelt at Jake's feet and gave him a paw paw. At Iakumu's wave, she got up and walked back into the bush.

Jake gave them a slow smile. "Ahhh." He felt a laugh bubble in his chest. It emerged as a cough. He wanted to say "Marvellous" but couldn't form the word.

"Should Japan Big Man be our Big Man?" ToSaina suddenly asked in English.

"N…never," Jake replied.

"Should your Big Man be our Big Man again?" he followed up.

"Bombom bad," IaKumu cried. "Japan. You. Our earth, our trees, our mangroves."

The moment settled on Jake; he still had enough of a brain to understand them. *They practised this. Independence.* He wanted to get his answer right. The words *worker strike* floated above, then in front of him, eluded him again. He coughed spasmodically. Then he got it: Father Rowland's story at Cohen's ball. Rabaul's Tolai workers had all walked off their jobs together but had no idea what to do next. They won nothing but jail sentences.

From his depleted flesh, Jake dragged out his answer. "Yes, not…long. Visit my land. Learn all. G' luck… mates."

Lee helped him inside and settled him on the mat. "Thank you, sir. They had to hear it from you." He left.

I don't want to die, Jake's thought. Two tears snaked down his stubble and meandered through his moustache. He tasted their salt as he fell asleep.

*
**

When Wip returned, he found Jake noticeably weaker. His heart raced faster, and he was often short of breath. Despite frequent washing, his skin smelled un-alive, like old clothes. Jake murmured, "Tell me our lives."

For hours over several days, Wip would improvise their house in Rabaul, his coffee, their pets, and Jake's research. He threw himself into his creations as if each piece of furniture they bought, each trip they took, and each bush they planted would keep Jake with him. He saw Jake willing the fantasies into time-warp reality. "Nice life...so... happy," Jake would sigh, an expression of ineffable acceptance in his eyes.

Nights were full of Jake's babble, some in Latin but more in a language Wip assumed was Hebrew. Once, something repetitive about Wip delaying the Japanese invasion. When Jake woke, Wip grasped his wrist, kissing the veins below his palm. "You were ranting about me delaying the invasion. What do you mean?"

"Car crash...you...hinted... more... new roads." Jake struggled for breath. "Toshio thought...many cannons. Said so."

"No!" Wip jumped up. He picked up a stick leaning against the wall and beat his temple. "You suffered because I was arrogant and stupid."

"S...stop. They torture, no reason."

Wip stopped as he saw Jake's determination to explain. "Invasion night. Toshio land early, long... time look more guns... give us time...Vulcan. We threw them back...many times. You'll win this war."

"Thought I was helping at that time. Shit. Consequences."

Jake's eyes closed. "All…good."

Wip realised that Jake had known for a while, perhaps from his first look at his wounds, that he wouldn't recover. He needed Wip to catch up with him. *How selfish I am.* Wip kissed his hot, sweaty forehead and gave him a blue pill.

When Jake woke next, he kept down sugar cane juice. Knowing he shouldn't put this off, Wip cleared his throat. "Um, I hate these words, but IaKumu asked if you want to be buried in the village."

"All…OK." Jake licked his lips. It was nighttime, a kerosene lamp casting an eerie glow around his mat. "Better than Tavurvur's ash. Yarmulke and ring. See moon?" He dozed, then asked with a strange urgency, "What…you do? Get off… island?"

Wip paced. He hadn't accepted being without Jake; there was no 'after' in his mind. Finally, he sat. "Probably not leave the island. It's risky for the Tolai lads and their families. Different in your case. I mean, to get you to a hospital. All is nothing without you." He thought, then said, "I'll give the bark to allies, barter it for land or gold to anyone else. Join a resistance if it develops. Document atrocities. New Guinea natives will want independence after all this misery. I understand your Jewish homeland issue now. I really do. We colonists have lost all credibility. ToSaina has the making of a leader. If I make it through, I'll fund Tommy and Sally's studies and help people here prepare for self-government." He turned away but couldn't hide his tears.

When he turned back and sat, Jake touched his cheek and licked the salty moisture. "Bless you. Find new…love. Doctor… prescription." He clutched Wip's shirt. "Hug my sisters…tell them… happy, lucky, in love, work. Complete."

The moon was full a few days later. Wip, Lee and two village men carried a near-comatose Jake to a hillock overlooking Ataliklikun Bay. Far to their left, pinprick lights winked—a Japanese garrison. Patrols didn't venture inland because mysterious disappearances happened. The men strung a hammock made of a mat fastened to a fishing net between a bukubuk and a palm tree. The apple-like scent of bukubuk fruit intoxicated Wip, but he didn't know if Jake could still smell. After Wip and Lee eased Jake into the hammock, Lee and the others left to stand watch. When Wip climbed into the hammock, Jake stirred, "Ta… love."

Wip watched the moon light up the ghostly stillness of Ataliklikun Bay waters with a tunnel-like shaft of radiance. It made velvet blue the mud bank and pearl stings of driftwood; paint acrylic black the green leaves above them, and shimmering white the waving grass below. He described every flicker to Jake, along with the dancing swarms of fireflies. They lay entwined through a symphony of crickets, cicadas, bat-clicks, frog mating songs and the occasional thump of a coconut on grass. Wip slept.

He woke to a soft snuffle from Jake's chest. It got louder, rattly, uneven. Then nothing.

POSTSCRIPT
· · · · · · · · ·

Every Leaf That Falls Never Stops Falling.
Passage, by Victoria Chang

Melbourne, Australia.
Saturday, 18 August 1951

Hurrying through winter drizzle, Wip sprinted up the steps of the Victorian-era town hall. Standing between two faux Greek columns, he watched bumper-to-bumper cars wait at the traffic light, only to amble a block to the next red light. It felt odd being in a city in winter, even though Melbourne was his hometown. It had all begun on the balcony above him a decade ago, when the eager men of the 2/22 battalion had paraded and saluted their Governor General. He was already a veteran, but it had begun here for Jake. Jake had enlisted and changed Wip's life.

Frowning, Wip lit a Gauloise cigarette. Most of the men of the 2/22 battalion were dead. Of the approximately hundred and forty who'd escaped Rabaul after a harrowing, starving trek down the island, only three were fit to return to the island and fight the Japanese four years later. Egan, Kelly and Robinson had died in a tragic mischance. They were among eight hundred soldiers and two hundred civilians crammed into the hold of a Japanese cargo ship, transporting them to prison camps in Japan. The ship, *Montevideo Maru,* had no markings that it carried prisoners. An American submarine torpedoed it. There were no survivors. The six army nurses on a different ship *had* survived as prisoners in Japan, barely escaping starvation. Palmer, OC of A Company, 2/10 Field Ambulance Unit, had treated many soldiers on New Britain island and in subsequent campaigns. Scanlan had found his valour. Although he could have escaped, he'd surrendered, hoping to save his men. Surviving POW camp in Japan, Carr had found the grit to lead men off New Britain island. But those were the few; the government was intent on covering up the earlier bad decisions that had caused Jake's death, and the rest.

"Fuckin' betrayal," Wip would swear whenever names haunted his dreams or his guilt-suffused reveries. His anger hadn't abated over the years. Now, at Melbourne Town Hall, where Jake's journey had begun, he snorted, "Shithole fuckin' betrayal."

He startled people in their finery, jostling past him to enter the concert hall. In his artillery captain's mess dress of a long navy-blue tunic with brocaded gold and red epaulettes, Wip looked anything but a gutter-curser. Waving tickets, the attendees gave him a wide berth. The two-thousand-seat hall was sold out for Wip's nephew, Melbourne's own Thomas Whipple, piano soloist in two concertos for piano and orchestra. The Melbourne Symphony Orchestra would be conducted by Alceo Galliera.

Wip had survived the Japanese occupation and Allied bombing by living with Lee near the cinchona trees. They'd bartered quinine for land and gold but gave it free to Australia's allies. One Japanese patrol had nearly discovered them. But, as stealthy and skilled as the Japanese were at jungle fighting, they weren't silent enough for this sacred area; a map in a cave showed the location of seven graves. After that, the enemy stayed away despite their garrisons being stationed nearby. Life, Wip had concluded, was a mystery, often full of malice.

For years, every breath in a world without Jake was a misery, but he'd endured and found reasons to live. After Japan's surrender, he'd supervised Japanese prisoners in the rebuilding of Rabaul. Toshio had somehow got off the island, escaping accountability in the war crimes trials that followed capitulation. The corpse of his kind Korean driver had washed up on shore with a bullet in his head. Wip assumed Toshio had burrowed into the bureaucracy of new Japan, but he knew Toshio's face and would never stop looking.

On the positive side, IaKumu got her store, doggedly rebuilding after a fire in her first year and that year's earthquake. He revered the way she worked her dream. Lee was teaching at the new government school and sending money to his parents. Wip sometimes cautioned him, "Go easy on this science stuff with your wife, mate. Tolai have their ways of interpreting the world that sustained them for centuries." Lee and IaKumu had three children, and Wip had seen her push Lee away when her mind needed space. If not in the first bloom of love, they seemed happy. Wip envied them. He'd had this push of differences and pull of closeness with Jake. Now? No one.

After testifying at war crimes trials, he was given back the captain's pips he'd lost when he fought Bruiser for Lee on Zealandia. With the last trial done a few months ago, he'd sold his land, gold and equity in the coffee plantation. He was flush with ready money, looking to settle it on a cause better than himself.

Hard times had only marinated his good looks. His glistening white-blond hair and deep-set tanned skin intensified the blueness of his eyes and highlighted his perfect nose and chin dimple. Now, he stubbed out the cigarette in a foyer ashtray and found his seat. He'd booked in the front row left, with a view of the piano keyboard.

A reduced ensemble for the opening work was onstage, scraping a cacophony as they ran through passages in the night's scores. Wip balanced his cap on his lap, removed his gloves, and opened the programme. He feasted on his nephew's face. Tommy had his dead father's straight nose and thin lips, but Tommy's dark hair was clipped to surgical-glove closeness, where Ron's had been unkempt; Tommy's expression was non-committal, where Ron had been a life-of-the-party joker. Wip twisted his Rabaul ring. Grief desiccated him again; it came in unpredictable jabs. He was here because Jake had kept his malaria down and led him to Lee's cinchona trees. After brushing away a tear, he read Tommy's biography: now twenty-three, he'd won the Australian Broadcasting Commission's Concerto Competition in 1949, and many local contests. Tommy would perform Haydn's "Concerto on D Major for piano and orchestra" and Liszt's "Totentantz," variations on the medieval chant Dies Irae (Days of Wrath) for piano and orchestra. Jake's sister, Talia, was mentioned as Tommy's first teacher as a child. Tommy was now studying under renowned teacher John Templeton at the University of Melbourne.

Wip turned to scan people finding their seats, looking for a woman with features like Jake's. He'd written to Tommy and Sally from New Guinea after the war, saying that he was alive and well and would visit when his contracts ended, but he hadn't contacted Jake's family. With no idea what the army had told them about Jake's fate, it had felt horribly intrusive. Not finding anyone resembling Jake, he returned to the program. *Is Tommy as nervous about performing as I am about meeting my relatives and maybe Jake's sister?*

Excitement built when the principal oboist, then concertmaster sounded "A" to tune up. To applause, Galliera strode to the podium. Slim, with oiled grey hair, he looked patrician and broodingly sensual, Wip thought. Galliera raised his baton, and the orchestra thundered into "God

Save the King." The national anthem was muffled by four thousand feet suddenly standing, and then settling back down, rustling clothes, before the end, amplified by rolling winter coughs.

Tommy Whipple walked onstage, moving in an almost indifferent stroll. Here was Wip's blood, one half of his dream of supporting his talented kin. Tommy shook hands gravely with the concertmaster, then Galliera, and adjusted his seat's height. He looked up at Galliera and nodded.

Wip held his breath as a glittering passage emerged from his nephew's coiled posture. His ornamentation was wittily mannered, the melody in slow movement spun out tenderly, and the rambunctious last movement was dispatched at reckless speed. Wip sensed he was holding back, playing from a small piece of his sensibility, like breathing from his lung's upper lobe, rather than his diaphragm. After the thunderous applause, Tommy left the stage with the same indifferent stroll. Wip got the impression of self-containment.

Wip daydreamed through trumpeting and impassioned string playing until Tommy reappeared. Liszt's diabolical "Totentantz" opened with the soloist's full-throated chords hammering against winds blaring the medieval chant. Massed piano sound rose, like an organ vibrating the ceiling. Tommy was transformed as if he'd unknotted his tie. He swarmed the instrument, hands tossing out a blur of Liszt's maniacal complexities, spine-chilling glissandi, and staccato rat-tat-tat variations on the chant. It wasn't all fast and loud. In a melody with limpid embellishments, Tommy engaged in loving dialogues with clarinet, then xylophone, then flute.

The music demolished Wip. He felt his flesh dissolve as all human experience poured from the stage. He heard the bombs of war and swayed to the succulent melody that recreated Jake's tenderness, felt himself trip over jungle roots during pizzicato sections, sank lower in his seat at rat-tat-tat staccato variations that reminded him of Vickers machine guns, and stiffened with determination in the massed chord climaxes. Jake died to defend society's creativity like this. This was what lasted.

He remembered Jake saying one night at their cave of love that every baby was a miracle of possibility, that all the strangers around the exhausted mother shared the hope that *maybe we can make the world right for **this** one.* He, Wip, would make the world right for his gifted kin. Then what? Then something.

At a second of stunned collective silence, Wip sat up. Was it over? The hall erupted in a prolonged standing ovation. Tommy accepted his accolades with vague puzzlement.

People rushed for the exits. When Wip reached the backstage dressing rooms downstairs, he stared at Jake's look-alike: a woman with his bushy black eyebrows and hair, his nose, his thick bones, but a fuller mouth and black eyes, not hazel ones. *Jake's sister Talia.* His heart thumped a second time at the sight of a willowy young woman accompanying Jake's sister: Wip's mother's freckles, his blond hair and blue eyes. *Sally.* The two women were outside Tommy's room, apparently in no hurry to go in.

His pulse racing, Wip approached Sally. "Excuse me, would you be Miss Sally Whipple?" The young woman started and nodded. "I'm your uncle, Captain John Alexander Whipple." Ignoring her gasp, he pulled an envelope from his pocket, eased out a page, and held it out. "You painted this?"

Sally looked at cracked paint in the grimy middle, edges curled and rotted, but two faces separated by a swirl of upward striving dots were clear. "Noooo, can it be?"

"Oh, my brother!" Talia exclaimed. "How…"

Both women moved to the wall, allowing friends and autograph hunters to swarm into Galliera and Tommy's rooms. After a moment, Talia said, "Jake wrote us a censored letter. We only made out that some relative wanted to help Tommy and Sally. The name was blacked out. Was that you?"

"Yes, ma'am. You must be Talia. Captain Friedman told me about you."

"You knew him…" Talia's tone was flat, her face pale.

"I painted this years ago." Sally was uncertain of what to do next.

"Jake insisted I keep it. You and I are kin," Wip said shyly. He yearned to explain how they'd passed it back and forth as a talisman, but they wouldn't understand. Only someone who'd been there could.

Talia said, "Sally's work is even stronger now," patting the girl's arm.

Sally's eyes were pooling with tears, and she stood stiff, Wip assumed with anxiety. There was an awkward pause. Who owned the painting now?

"It belongs to you," Sally offered, wiping her face. "It's lived your journey, not mine."

"Miss Whipple," Wip answered. "I'd be honoured if you'd show me your work."

Sally gave him her card, nonplussed but curious. Wip's blue eyes held Sally's. Her eyes seemed to absorb whatever poured in from the world. Sensing fragility, he wanted to protect her, help her to have an easier life than his "How is your Mum?"

"She doesn't go out," Sally sighed. "She'll ask me to read her the reviews."

"Ah, I'm sorry." Wip felt useless. Monica had never got over the loss of her husband, and she still dumped the burden of coping on her children, as Jake had once told him.

Just then, the door of Tommy's room swung open. A middle-aged man strutted out, trailed by a phalanx of young people. *Master teacher with student acolytes,* Wip guessed. The great maestro boomed at Talia, "You did a decent little job getting him started. But aren't you astonished at how he's blossomed under my tutelage?"

"Oh, definitely," Talia loudly agreed. Wip sensed she was amused rather than resentful. Something political was going on, something beyond his frame of reference.

"I want to introduce myself to Tommy," Wip said to Talia,

"but may I walk with you after? I'd like to ask your advice." Talia agreed, curiosity and nervousness passing over her face.

Finally, they got into Tommy's room. To Wip's surprise, his nonchalant-seeming nephew gave Talia a wink, smile and hug. After pleasantries and Wip's request to visit him, they left Tommy to his other admirers. Sally stayed with him.

In a few minutes, he and Talia were walking along one of the wide footpaths on Princes Bridge. The rain had stopped. "May I smoke?" Wip asked.

"I don't, but go ahead," Talia answered. They leant against the railing. Wip lit up, turned and looked at the coursing Yarra River.

"I can't bear to talk about Jake," Talia burst out.

"Of course," Wip said. The grief she was trying to keep at bay washed over him. "Help me understand what I saw a few minutes ago. Why did Tommy wink at you after his teacher left?"

"Oh, that's music politics," Talia answered out of the darkness. "Templeton controls the competitions and music jobs here. If you want to get ahead, he must be your teacher. But he's not that good. Half of his students secretly study with other teachers. Tommy never stopped working with me."

"What will happen if Templeton learns he's coaching with you?"

"He'll blackball Tommy." She paused. "It wasn't always like that, but when salaries at the Conservatory of Music equalled other university pay, the men grabbed the jobs and pushed the women teachers out."

"I see. It's disgusting, but I suppose it happens in many places."

"I've heard that," Talia confirmed.

"The advice I want is, well, I have money. How can I help Tommy and Sally? I need a proposal when I visit them."

"How wonderful," Talia exclaimed. "It will make all the difference."

Wip saw wariness in her eyes. *Is he legitimate?* Behind them, trams rumbled in both directions. He saw Talia turn and glance at Flinders Street train station. "I'll ride you home in a taxi," he said. "Don't worry about the last train. I know I've appeared out of the blue, but you can trust me."

Talia relaxed. "Tommy has to leave Australia. He needs a recital debut in London, plus ten years of support. He knows how to navigate the politics."

"And Sally? She seems, well, sensitive."

"Well, aren't you perceptive?" She looked at him with interest. "She's strong, but she takes everything in, and things weigh on her. She needs a gallery in Melbourne or Sydney, and funds for a year abroad. Sally loves the light here; I don't think she wants to live elsewhere. But she'd want to see the main museums and galleries." She paused. "Why are you thinking of this?"

Wip sighed. "I wanted so desperately to be a dancer that I tattooed Nijinsky on my foot."

"Really? How…unusual. Can you show me?"

They moved under a lamp. Balancing against the stone base, Wip took off his shoe and sock. Talia looked at Nijinsky in his impossible airborne leap. "Ah, sad."

"A broken heart is on my other foot." He removed the other footwear. Both tattoos had survived Rabaul. She nodded. After wiping his freezing-wet feet with his gloves, Wip put his socks and shoes back on. He and Talia exchanged smiles.

After a moment, she asked, "Were you born in the wrong generation?"

"I suppose so. Nobody has quite put it that way. I was bullied at school because I danced in the street. I learned to fight the, um, rotters. Then, the first war came, where I served the last six months. I was too old to dance, then this war came, and suddenly, I'm middle-aged, a somewhat fixed arc of life. In Paris, I went to galleries, dance, and opera, but always as the outsider looking in. I want my resources to help these kids.

Tommy was born to play the piano, and Sally to draw or paint. I spoke about this to Jake."

Talia smiled sadly. "This spot," she patted the wall, "is where Jake and I watched the unit he joined parade. And there," she pointed down at the riverbank, "is where Jake told me he was enlisting. We miss him so, so much. Was he born at the wrong time?"

He watched her hands tightening on the railing; she'd broken her own taboo. "What does the army say?" he asked.

"Captured, then executed five days later. Place and method unknown, remains not found. No witnesses…My cousin Sylvia says he was probably beheaded."

"I'd like to put this Sylvia over my knee and spank her," Wip burst out. "He wasn't beheaded, and he didn't die on that day. Should I continue?"

He saw her chew her lip. Finally, "You'd better."

"Jake was bayoneted. He died a month later of blood poisoning. His wounds would have been survivable with penicillin, so yes, he was born a year too soon. He had some happy moments during his illness. I was with him."

"Oh, that's better than my nightmares. We read terrible stories of torture and beheadings. An officer in Jake's battalion was vivisected by a Japanese doctor. I've never got the worst visions out of my mind." She paused. "You're his lover." It was a statement, not a question. "I was sceptical about Esther, though she sounded wonderful."

"Yes." Wip showed her his ring. Now, she wanted to hear about their lives. An hour later, he concluded, "He insisted that our group of fleeing soldiers move at the speed of the sickest, which included me, I'm sorry to say. All the lads agreed. So, we were behind several others who got away the day before the Japs captured him. One night in a fisherman's hut, to let us sick men rest, made the difference. Before the Japs attacked Rabaul, Jake had treated a native girl for polio and got her mobile again. He was loved by the men, his patients, the girl's tribe, and me.

I'm going to fund a grant for research in tropical medicine in Rabaul, in his name…"

She turned and hunched over the rail. He touched her back; her chest was heaving. "Do you need a moment?" he asked.

"No." She turned back; she hadn't cried, but her face was tense. "Go on."

"There's one more thing. You could get his remains back for a Jewish burial. The tribe of the girl he cured buried him on their land. We spent his last month hiding with them. It accorded with his wishes."

Talia kneaded her hands. Finally, she asked, "Would there be paperwork?"

"Yes, and you'll have to go there. The army won't like it. They're busy scotching any investigation into their mistakes. With different decisions, almost all the blokes could have escaped. But I can get a reburial done."

"I'll talk to my husband. The army says they're making plaques there and here. Simon will probably say to let things be. We have two children; life goes on. You can't imagine the agony of waiting: no news, constant dread, floods of crying, wondering if we'll ever be cried out. The day after communications went out at Rabaul, a newspaper article reported that contact was lost, but no one should assume anything had happened to the garrison. Ha, right? Simon worked at the barracks; he tried every day for news, but only silence. Months later, a Japanese plane dropped letters from prisoners of war over Port Moresby. None from Jake, but maybe his was lost? Five years before clarity that he'd died, but with no details, no closure. I imagined him vivisected; no, he'd escaped and was alive, but lost his memory. To reopen it all… I'm so glad you were with him. What are you going to do? You're giving away your money."

"I'm keeping enough for my basic needs. I hadn't decided until tonight. I'm not suited to post-war Melbourne. My way of loving, well, creates difficulties. That was true in

Melbourne after the first war, and it's true today. I have one more conflict in me."

"But you've suffered so much. How can you endure more?"

Wip paused, unsure if he understood it himself. He felt his way. "I'm meant to make things safe for civvies like you, like Tommy and Sally, as Jake did. Military family, hereditary. I seem to have a knack for survival. Perhaps it's Sally's painting protecting me. I'm going to accept a two-year contract in your father's homeland…"

"What? You mean Israel?"

"It's the least I can do for Jake. I'll set up defences in vulnerable agricultural settlements near the armistice line. Training and equipping. Jake didn't live to see Auschwitz, but he sensed it. When we were, um, together, my nightmare was the atom bomb. Those camps? I never imagined *that*. Then I'll return to New Guinea. The indigenous tribes want independence. They've had German, Australian and Japanese rule. We colonialists have messed up too many things; it's time to step back. I want to help my tribal friends to prepare. Jake would approve.

"Ah, you're a good man. If you decide to give Melbourne another chance, please don't be a stranger." Talia's sigh signalled the end of their talk.

Wip added, "Jake said 'Hug my sisters, say I was happy in work and love'. He used the word *complete*."

"I can never accept 'complete'," Talia protested. "But I suppose he proved things to himself: war hero, medical hero, everything. He needed that. My sister's away, but I'm here."

They kissed on each cheek, then burst into tears and hugged hard and long. Wip saw Talia to a taxi and paid the driver. "Goodbye, then. For the time being."

Two weeks later, Wip left for Rabaul via Tel Aviv.

AUTHOR'S NOTE

I write fiction that rests on a foundation of historical facts. After my debut novel, *The Reversible Mask: An Elizabethan Spy Novel,* was published in 2018, I was drawn to a more personal story—a mystery of my maternal uncle Bertie, a doctor who volunteered to serve in World War II and was posted to the country that is now Papua New Guinea. Although I never met him, as a child I'd been moved to tears by a photograph of him. This graduation head shot hung on the wall over our dining room table, the wall's sole decoration. What made me cry was a troubled sadness in eyes that seemed to hold a question.

"You mustn't cry," my mother exclaimed. "It's not good to be sad. I'll put the photograph away."

"What was he like?" I persisted.

My mother's expression turned distant then taut. "The most wonderful brother anyone could ever have." Next day, the photograph was gone. My mother's reaction wasn't unusual. Cones of silence enclosed the suffering of those who served in World War II and those who waited for them. It didn't do to dwell on the past; people got on with life in the new world order.

I too went on with life, leaving Australia to settle in the USA. But I never forgot the photograph. I knew that Bertie stuttered as a child, which he conquered by winning elocution contests. I had the medals-- gold or silver, never bronze. When

I rubbed my thumb over his etched initials I'd wonder: *What happened?*

I plunged into five years of reading and exchanging emails with experts on the war where he served. I had to come to terms with the fact that he was in Lark Force, the lone battalion of volunteers sent to defend Rabaul, capital of Australia's Mandated Territory of New Guinea.

In 1941, the Australian Army's battle-hardened divisions were deployed to the Middle East, fighting Axis powers. The Government sent token garrisons with mostly World War I weapons and a few trainer planes to the South West Pacific territories. They were codenamed Lark Force (Rabaul); Sparrow Force (Timor); Gull Force (Ambon); Wren Force and Heron Force (Nauru); Robin Force (New Caledonia). Little birds.

When war with Japan began, there was no intention to reinforce, withdraw or extract the men. The government's indifference to its units is now regarded as a shameful episode. The Minister for External Affairs, Herbert Evatt, conveyed a secret cablegram to President Roosevelt via the Australian ambassador describing the units as too small to repel a Japanese assault but useful forward air observation lines. A second secret cablegram spelled out to Roosevelt that with U.S. Lend-Lease support delayed, no rescue was envisaged, that the units would be "hostages to fortune," left to their fate.

Some soldiers in Lark Force escaped into the jungle (with no jungle survival equipment), made a perilous trek down New Britain island and found boat or plane transport to Australia. But their health was broken. Most were executed after capture or sent to Japan as prisoners of war. The Australian War Memorial cites only 28 Australian fatalities during the invasion. The scale of subsequent losses was the scandal. Despite public pressure after the war for an investigation, the cablegrams were concealed for 50 years. This concealment compounded the anguish of families mourning the loss of their beloved volunteers and kept survivors' instinctive feeling that they'd been dealt a rotten hand vague, but raw. As for my uncle, Herbert Nathan Silverman, after being listed as "Missing" in 1942, his file noted "Believed deceased, date unknown," "one report beheading" later in 1942. After the war, the Army assigned him a date of death "for official purposes," at the hands of the Japanese, place and method of death unknown. With no witnesses, no remains or identity disks found, this was less than definitive.

The fate of many Lark Force soldiers remains unclear. In 2023, the wreck of an infamous Japanese transport ship, the Montevideo Maru, was discovered in the South China Sea. Crammed with more than 1,000 military and civilian prisoners, it left Rabaul in June 1942 for Hanan Island. The ship bore no markings that it carried prisoners; USS Sturgeon, a submarine, torpedoed it, sinking it with presumably no surviving prisoners. Or could there have been? 17 Japanese crew reached the Philippines. Names of the prisoners on board have never been confirmed.

The ten-month run-up to war unfolded in a colonial town of irresistible tropical beauty, periodically disrupted by volcanic eruptions. 'Pearl of the Pacific' was Rabaul's reputation. Being there must have been enchanting. The town hosted a diverse population of Australian administrators playing the part of colonizers, a Chinese business community, Tolai tribes who worked for the Australians and tended their own land as farmers, a few Japanese residents and spies, and missionaries, cultures that were interdependent but opaque to each other. An intriguing diversity. The question throbbing my mind was *What did Lark Force men feel when they grasped at their time of annihilating peril that their government was abandoning them?*

How people felt meant writing fiction. The fate of Lark Force was so dire that the idea of love relationships of personal growth grabbed me. I knew that homosexual liaisons happened in the Australian Army. In 1943, the year after Rabaul fell, the Army investigated many reported incidents of male-male intimacy in mainland New Guinea, leading in

1944 to a strengthening of Army rules against 'unnatural' practices.' Gay soldiers gave their all to their country like any other soldiers. Why not a relationship between two officers in Rabaul? Which brought me back to my uncle's troubled eyes in the photograph. Family anecdotes that he showed no interest in girls or women and his wanderings suggested that he was at odds with something in his circumstances. Unmarried at 30, a handsome Jewish doctor and only son of orthodox parents, he left home early according to voter rolls. He returned for my mother's wedding then again after his parents died, living with my parents before joining the Army. Army photographs show a happier man. I have no idea what troubled him; his silence requires reverence. But giving Jake a conflict between Jewish values and his natural inclinations was a rich theme to explore. What does being Jewish mean? The questions is as relevant today as it was then. Is it blood purity, beliefs, practices, Zionism, self-definition?

The car accident in Jake's dreams did happen to my uncle and was reported in local newspapers. But what the urgent care call was that got him and three nurses driving 80 miles is lost to history. I chose polio, which threads through the novel. Sister Elizabeth Kenny's methods were well known in Australia, the UK and USA, and in her book *The Treatment of Infantile Paralysis in the Acute Stage* (Bruge Publishing Company 1941), she recounts treating a child from Rabaul in her Queensland clinic. Jake is a Kenny advocate.

Beyond the Bukubuk Tree is mostly fiction. Readers often ask me what gaps in the historical record my imagination filled. Although Jake is fictional, Army dispatches mentioning my uncle pin the details of Jake's actions, while a photograph of a compelling Tolai woman he sent home generated the Tolai characters. Historical people include Colonel John J. Scanlan, Lieutenant Colonel Howard H. Carr, Major Edward C. Palmer, Major William T. Owen, Lieutenant Lennox Henry, Colonel F. N. Nurse, and Rabbi Jacob Danglow. I have done my best to accurately represent where they were and what they did, but what they said I have imagined. All of the other characters, including the obnoxious dwarf cassowary ToMuruk, are fictional. The transport ship Zealandia carried Lark Force soldiers to Rabaul in April 1941, but what happened after the soldiers embarked is fiction. Australian Prime Minister John Curtin's address to his nation upon the declaration of war against Japan is quoted verbatim, while Zero Hour broadcasts by Radio Tokyo I wrote in the broadcast's style of 1942. Canny Chinese entrepreneur Ah Kuan Ho and his cinchona trees are a product of my imagination. There's no evidence that a merchant with foreknowledge of the war grew a supply of quinine. But I was thrilled to discover, when I spoke to Albert Konie in the secret Tubuan Society in Rabaul, that such a scenario could have been plausible in the densely forested area I'd chosen for the medicinal trees. Tolai big men were known to permit non-indigenous notables to plant or hunt in the spirit-inhabited area, provided that they respected the norm of silence.

Dear Reader, I am humbled that you have walked this journey with me. If you have questions, my website is:

www.lorettagoldberg.com.

ACKNOWLEDGMENTS

An old African proverb holds that "It takes a community to raise a child." In that spirit, several communities helped me to birth this novel. There are so many people to whom I'm indebted that it's impossible to thank them all.

Special thanks to my childhood friend, Mary Clare Adam, for her encouragement and suggestions from the beginning. A resident of Papua New Guinea in the 1970s, she collected regional artifacts for the Village Arts store in Boroko, Port Moresby, and has deep knowledge of the country. Later, she was appointed Honorary Consul for Israel to Papua New Guinea in Jerusalem and is currently Honorary Consul for Israel for the Solomon Islands. Thanks to her also for permitting me to use Mary Adam's, her mother's, photographs of Rabaul on the cover.

Angelique Giranah, Tolai researcher and director of Niugini Sindauk Ltd, a consulting company headquartered in Kavieng, New Ireland, edited the draft as a Sensitivity Reader. During my substantial stay in Rabaul and Kokopo, East New Britain Province, where the action is set, Daniel Burua got me up and down the active volcano Tavurvur without tripping, and was indefatigable in taking me to settings in the novel beyond standard World War II tours. Albert Konie found little-known places to land a boat so I could see old Australian fortifications, now overgrown, that feature in the novel. Mr. Konie was an inspiration in helping me frame in local terms flora and places that I'd intuitively chosen for fictional scenes. Susan McGrade, owner of the iconic Rabaul Hotel, was a generous host who shared her friends with me. They were open about their enduring love of Rabaul, their frustrations at its current condition and hopes for its renewal. Regarded as 'the pearl of the Pacific' from its founding in 1905 until the volcanic eruption of 1994, Rabaul has been disinvested in since 1994 and is a shell of its former lushness. Part of my soul now lives in its forlorn roads and enchanting environment. Thanks also to garamut (slit drum) players Francis Toia and Francis Totu, and the owners of the garamuts, Edward Malana and Oscar Toma, who gave me a private session on tapping out traditional warnings for my book trailer.

Before a draft, award or book contract can materialize, there are years of rewriting. My two writers' groups are fundamental to my process. Thank you, author colleagues Jeri Hilderley, Janet Mayes, Sarah Relyea, Kate Gale, Sandy Macdonald, Ellen Rachlin and Susan Wands. Developmental Editor Leslie Wells did an excellent job shaping the draft, but I plead guilty to not adopting 100% of her recommendations; the novel's faults are mine, not hers. Most of all, thank you, my first reader and life partner, Jane Southern. Your patience and support are indispensable.

For advice from experts, Drs. Robert Likeman and William Southern, and retired nurse Harriet Stein, were helpful on medical issues, while Jack Knapp, a rebuilder of vintage cars, explained car technology of the 1930s to me. At that time, Rabaul boasted of having the highest per capita car ownership in the world, so understanding how cars crashed then matters. Captain Roger Crossland, retired US Navy Seal officer and award-winning author of war novels, has been a meticulous communicator of military information. While I was in Melbourne, Dr. Jean Douglas, who wrote a short article on each Australian doctor killed in World War I or II for the unveiling of a statue honouring them, gave me a fact about my protagonist not in other records.

To an abbreviated list of sources: thanks to the Australian War Memorial for permitting me to reproduce the map *Dispositions 2 a.m. 23 January* (Australia in the Wars 1939-1945 Series One—Army Volume IV The Japanese Thrust Page 401) which provided the model for the third map in this novel. And for their digitized first-person accounts by soldiers in Lark Force who survived longer than my protagonist. Thanks to Schindler Video Productions for the DVDs compiled from material from the Australian War Memorial and live interviews of Lark Force survivors. I used the factual foundation related in Bruce Gamble *Invasion of Rabaul,* Zenith Press 2006; Peter Stone *Hostages to Fortune,* Ocean Enterprises 1996; Lex Ashley *We Who are About to Die,* Bantam Books 2007, and a seminal article *Praed Point Battery, Rabaul* by Colonel F. N. Nurse, Australian Army Journal #195, August, 1965

Memoirs by Alice M. Bowman *Not Now Tomorrow,* Daisy Press 1996; David Selby *Hell and High Fever,* Currawong 1956; John Baptist Crasta *Eaten By the Japanese, The Memoir of an Unknown Indian Prisoner of War,* Richard Crasta 2012; and Eric Feldt *The Coastwatchers': How a Handful of Men Lived for Months on Japanese-held Islands and Radioed Warnings of Enemy Attacks,* Doubleday, 1979 were illuminating. For the racist attitudes common to Australians at the time, Jan Roberts *Voices From a Lost World,* E. J. Dwyer Pty. Ltd, 1996; and Ouyang Yu *Chinese in Australian Fiction 1888-1988,* Cambria Press 2008 were revelatory and often sickening. A. L. Epstein *In the Midst of Life: Affect and Ideation in the World of the Tolai,* University of California Press, 1992. was my first source on Tolai anthropology, supplemented by books on Tolai mythology, Sir Paulias Matane *My Childhood in New Guinea,* Oxford University Press 1974, and other memoirs, poems and short stories by Papuan New Guinean writers.

All of this communal wisdom contributed to my tale; I am deeply grateful.

ABOUT LORETTA GOLDBERG

Australian-American **Loretta Goldberg's debut novel,** *The Reversible Mask: An Elizabethan Spy Novel* (MadeGlobal Publishing, December 2018), won an International Firebird Book Award for Historical Fiction in 2023 and a Book Excellence Award Finalist in 2019.

Her second novel, *Beyond the Bukubuk Tree: A World War II Novel of Love and Loss* (MadeGlobal Publishing 2024), won an International Firebird Book Award for War Fiction in 2023. She came to the USA on a Fulbright Scholarship in Music after earning a BA (Hons.) in English Literature, Musicology and History at the University of Melbourne. Her first career was as a pianist and her CDs of new music are in over 700 libraries.

Her published non-fiction writing consists of arts reviews and mixed-media political satire. For the Historical Novel Society New York Chapter, she started the chapter's published writers' public reading series at the Jefferson Market Library, New York City, and is the chapter's current chair. She is a member of The Authors Guild and the National League of American PEN Women. She commutes between New York City and Chester, Connecticut, where she enjoys family and a broad community of friends and colleagues.

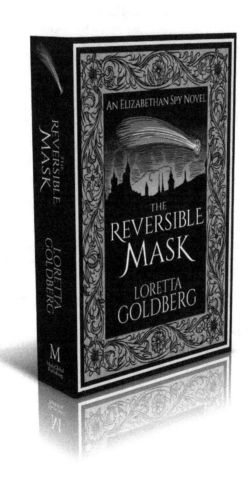

Historical Fiction

The Reversible Mask - **Loretta Goldberg**
The Sebastian Foxley Murder Mysteries
(currently 12 in the series in 2024) - **Toni Mount**
The Death Collector - **Toni Mount**
The Savernake Forest Series - **Susanna M. Newstead**

Non Fiction History

Captives to Freedom - **Douglas Thompson**
The Turbulent Crown - **Roland Hui**
Jasper Tudor - **Debra Bayani**
Tudor Places of Great Britain - **Claire Ridgway**
Illustrated Kings and Queens of England - **Claire Ridgway**
A History of the English Monarchy - **Gareth Russell**
The Fall of Anne Boleyn - **Claire Ridgway**
George Boleyn - **Ridgway & Cherry**
The Anne Boleyn Collection - **Claire Ridgway**
The Anne Boleyn Collection II - **Claire Ridgway**
Two Gentleman Poets at the Court of Henry VIII - **Edmond Bapst**

PLEASE LEAVE A REVIEW

If you enjoyed this book, *please* leave a review at the book
seller where you purchased it. There is no better way to thank
the author and it really does make a huge difference!
Thank you in advance.

Printed in the USA
CPSIA information can be obtained
at www.ICGtesting.com
LVHW090809120724
785283LV00004B/11